T0148367

Sparky and the Cowboy
And Other Stories

Tim Hulings

iUniverse, Inc.
New York   Bloomington

iUniverse books may be ordered through booksellers or by contacting:

iUniverse
1663 Liberty Drive
Bloomington, IN 47403
www.iuniverse.com
1-800-Authors (1-800-288-4677)

Because of the dynamic nature of the Internet, any Web addresses or
links contained in this book may have changed since publication and may
no longer be valid. The views expressed in this work are solely those of
the author and do not necessarily reflect the views of the publisher, and
the publisher hereby disclaims any responsibility for them.

978-1-4401-0985-0 (sc)
978-1-4401-0986-7 (ebook)
978-1-4401-0987-4 (dj)

Library of Congress Control Number: 2008911950

Printed in the United States of America

iUniverse rev. date: 12/19/2008

Give me such philosophic thoughts
that I can rejoice everywhere I go
in the lovable oddity of things.

Amen

Carmen Bernos De Gastold

(a portion of The Prayer of the Elephant
from The Prayers from the Ark)

Introduction

Here is a collection of thirteen short stories. These stories have been a labor of love and were not written with publication in mind, rather, they are an outlet for the characters and situations that danced in my imagination. As they are my characters, I have tended to treat them kindly. They are all fictional and any similarities to actual people are purely coincidental. I have been encouraged by many 'private readers' to publish these stories and give the characters a wider audience.

The phrase "Here's to Romance" was one my father used. I, like him, have the heart of a romantic and hopefully these thirteen pieces convey a little of that old fashioned type of romance. I write about people interacting with other people, or with dogs or mice or horses. I consider myself a philosopher of life (unpaid but not uncompensated). These short fictions are a way for me to set down a portion of my philosophy, but read them not for any motive, moral or philosophy, but for pleasure. As I treated my characters kindly, I believe that they'll do the same for the reader.

The stories are not published in chronological order but placed as they seemed to fit in the collection. The earliest date from about 1996, the latest was finished in early 2008. The two Cowboy selections can be read together as a novella, but they were written separately with years between them. They were intentionally separated in the publication.

*   *   *

The excerpt from The Prayer of the Elephant used on the title page and the three poems, The Prayer of the Little Ducks, The Prayer of the Cat and The Prayer of the Old Horse found in the story The Hermit of Lindos are from the PRAYERS FROM THE ARK by Carmen Bernos de Gastold, translated by Rumer Godden, copyright © 1962, renewed © 1990 by Rumer Godden. Original Copyright 1947, © 1955 by Editions du Cloitre. Used by permission of Viking Penguin, a division of Penguin Group (USA) Inc.

*   *   *

I offer a special thanks to the many friends and relations that have encouraged me to publish this collection. Particularly helpful, really indispensable, has been the editing help of Alecia Ball.

MAGIC BEANS

A fable

EVEN FROM THE BEGINNING, Ev had a most curious feeling about this character. The beginning was a Saturday afternoon in March. There was a knock at her door. Two Boy Scouts, dressed in blue uniforms, and their scoutmaster, attired in like manner, stood at the threshold. The boys did not look familiar, but, as her children had grown well beyond the scouting age, that was not surprising to her. The scoutmaster too was unfamiliar, and living in a small community, that seemed a little strange. The trio was about its annual troop fundraiser, a spring seed sale, and was asking the neighborhood to please look at their offerings and purchase a packet or two?

Most of Evelyn's garden had already been planned and material purchased, so she did not have much need for the seed; but, in the interest of helping out, she bought an envelope of lettuce and another of marigolds. To this point her dealings had been with the young lads. The scoutmaster had stayed in the background. After completing the transaction and exchanging the seeds for money, he stepped forward. As was mentioned before, she did not know him. Although his face was unfamiliar and unremarkable, there was a most peculiar aura about him.

"Ma'am," he said, "I would like to give you magic bean seeds."

Evelyn stood there puzzled at this remarkable statement, unsure of what kind of nut she was dealing with.

He commented, "I can tell you have a talent with plants and these are truly magic beans that need special attention."

Ev replied, "No, I am not interested, thank you."

"Ma'am, only three seeds," he insisted. "Plant them in a favored spot. You will be surprised at how they will grow. These seeds are a gift. They will only grow if given away. I give them to you."

The man was weird but not scary. How could anyone be scary, accompanied by two Boy Scouts and dressed like one himself? Ev really did not want the seeds, had no use for them, but the manner in which he presented himself and his offering made her, as I have said, very curious. She had never planted magic beans before. Perhaps she should have said "Good afternoon" and closed the door. Perhaps.

He gently reached for her hand, taking hold of it, and placed three unassuming beans on her palm. They were a light brown color with darker speckles, quite ordinary looking for magic beans. She was about to laugh at this character for pulling a joke when he said, "Sissy, take these and plant them in a favored spot after all danger of frost is gone. Plant them on the evening of the first crescent moon, as it sits in the western sky."

Very few people knew that Evelyn's childhood name had been Sissy. How did this man? She was dumbfounded. She stood with her hand open and the three beans lying there. After a moment of silence, and a second of hesitation on the stranger's part, he explained,

"No, you will not need this middle seed. It will be of no use to you." He took the bean back and returned it to the unmarked envelope.

This, of course, made Ev even more curious. *All three beans had looked the same, what was so important about that bean and why couldn't she have it?* She stood there not saying a word.

The man closed her fingers around the remaining beans with that same gentle touch with which he had put them into her hand. Evelyn held the two seeds securely. She could feel the beans move-not move exactly-but could sense that they were alive.

"Before you plant them," the man said, "hold them in your hand for ten minutes. Let them draw warmth and nourishment from you. You will not be disappointed. There are two beans. One is the bean of Luck. As you plant it make a wish and the wish will be fulfilled. One wish only, and be careful what you wish for. Make the wish while you are on your knees placing the seed in the soil. The second bean is the bean of Love, that is self-explanatory, no wish necessary."

Still puzzled by all this, she asked him, "How will I know which is which? They both look the same."

"You will know, for you are a natural gardener," he said.

"Mister, take back your seeds, I will not plant them," she said firmly. Now convinced that this was indeed some strange joke.

The stranger stood there still holding her fingers over the beans. It was an unremarkable touch, but still unusual in that a stranger would feel so free as to touch her like that. The strangest thing though, was the energy she could sense from the beans.

"Keep them," he said. His two companions, the young scouts stood one at either side of him, and lent him an air of credibility.

"May I ask what the third bean was for, the one you took back?"

He smiled and there was a mischievous glint in his face. "Fertility. I did not think you would have need for that one."

"Rolin put you up to this! This is a joke. It is not April Fool's Day yet!" Ev declared in a mocking tone, thinking that her husband was probably watching all this with much laughter. But the visitor still had that smile on his face. He was not laughing at her, but his merriment was clear.

"Mrs. Crenshaw," he said switching to a formal tone, "wait until all danger of frost is gone, and plant them on the evening of the new crescent moon."

With that he turned, put his hands upon the shoulders of his young friends and walked away.

Evelyn took the lettuce and marigold seed packs and put them with her gardening things. The two beans, though, she carried into the bathroom and placed amongst the toiletries and sundry items that resided there. She was not sure why she did this, but it was done.

Sissy was still certain that Rolin was responsible for this practical joke. That evening and all through the rest of the weekend she waited for him to say or do something that would tip his hand. He acted innocent, but she knew that her husband was up to something. Sunday night drew to a close and he still had not acknowledged his role in the charade. She began to consider that it might not be Rolin responsible for the beans, but rather someone at work. All that next week she was on guard for some sign from her workmates, but she could find no indication of their involvement.

Rolin, whose powers of observation his wife often underestimated, pointed to the beans on the bathroom counter one morning three weeks later. "What are these?" he asked.

He caught her unsuspecting. She looked at him with surprise, and then waited for him to start laughing, knowing the joke. He just stood there expectantly, and when she had no reply to his question, he asked again. "They look like beans. What are they doing in the bathroom?"

"Don't you know?" Evelyn replied with a question.

"I don't know anything about them. Why would I put beans in your stuff? How long have they been here?"

She was trapped. No way was she going to explain that they were Magic Beans. She still suspected her husband of instigating the trick. "None of your business," she answered curtly.

He looked at her, concluding his wife must be going through some woman type crisis, for that is how men explain everything unusual about their wives. He shook his head and walked out of the bathroom.

Eventually, the last danger of frost was gone. Spring was reaching its fulfillment. Much of the early garden had been tilled and planted. Tulips and Daffodils brightened the house and yard. Ev thought about the bean seeds. *Those silly things. What am I to do with them?* She even picked them up to toss them into the garbage, but as she held them in her hand, she could again feel their vibrancy. So instead of throwing them away, she consulted the calendar to see when the new moon was. Two days after the new moon, the crescent moon hung in the west, just above the horizon, as the daylight faded from the evening sky. Evelyn made sure that her husband was away from the house, and neither neighbor nor children were around.

She thought that she would place the bean seeds in a shaded corner where few things ever grew, but as she leaned down to plant them, trowel in hand, she recalled the stranger's words. "Plant them in a favored spot." So instead of putting them in the neglected corner, she walked over to the deck, and on each side of the centerpiece planter, she put in the seeds. As she knelt to place the first one in the loose soil, she held them in her hands the required ten minutes and thought about her wish. At first she was going to wish for money. Her second thought was to wish for health for her children, but she was reminded of the directions, "only one wish", and she had three children. Finally, she chickened out, and wished as she put the first bean in the soil, "I wish for a fruitful garden." She figured that that was a harmless wish.

The second bean she planted opposite the first, at the other end of the planter. This bean, she somehow knew, was the bean of love, and there was no wish involved with it. After planting the two seeds, Evelyn looked sheepishly around to be sure no one had watched.

As she headed out to work the next morning, her curiosity got the better of her again. She had to check to see if any activity had occurred with her beans. Normally it was much too soon for anything to have happened, but these were "Magic Beans", after all. Sure enough, the bean of Luck had miraculously broken through the soil overnight and was spreading its first leaves toward the early morning sunshine.

By evening, when she returned home, the Luck bean had grown a foot, with tendrils floating in the gentle breeze looking for some support. The Love bean did not show any sign of growth yet. Ev found a bamboo stake and placed it in the planter, thinking as she did so that Rolin was still playing some odd joke. She had never seen a bean grow this quickly, but there are no such things as Magic Beans.

At the end of the second day, the vine had grown three feet and nearly topped the stake that supported it. The growth was not spindly, as is common with something that grows so quickly, but full and luxuriant. The leaves were a dark green color and already little buds were developing. The bean of Love had not begun to grow, but the gardener in Evelyn noticed that everything in the garden, the flowers and the vegetables, the grass, even the trees seem to be fuller and richer than ever she had seen them at this time of year.

After a week, the Luck bean had begun to flower. The flower was the largest flower she had ever seen on a bean plant. It was an ephemeral blue color, pale and silvery, much more like a morning glory than a bean flower. The plant itself was now immense. It covered the tomato stake she had placed along side the bamboo. The entire yard and garden glowed with radiance.

So it continued for a month. The Luck bean flowered and brought forth its long, green pods. The neighbors began to grow envious of Evelyn's garden. Her flowers were larger, more fragrant, her produce earlier, tastier and many times more abundant than usual. There were no insects, except for fireflies and ladybugs.

Rolin, ever astute, noticed and said, "Ev, you have outdone yourself this year."

But she knew where the credit lay. Unfortunately, the bean itself produced inedible pods, and the inner beans were of no value, withered and hard.

The Love bean, on the opposite side of the planter, was much more the normal bean plant. Its first sign of growth was exactly a week after planting, as the shoot broke through the crust of the soil. After the incredible success of the Luck bean, the Love bean was almost a disappointment. The flowers were inconspicuous white blossoms hidden underneath the leaves. The plant's habits were much more of the bush bean variety, and seemingly unremarkable. Still, Ev was anxious to try the legume at the dinner table, for although it was a shy barer, the pods looked quite edible.

One evening in mid-summer, as she sat on her deck overlooking the magnificent garden and yard, it occurred to Ev, that perhaps she had made a mistake. *This Luck bean is so wonderful. If I had wished for something really important, just think what I would have gotten.* As soon as the thought formed in her mind, a dark cloud followed it. The bean plant seemed to shiver and lean toward her. Those iridescent blue flowers looked her in the eye with great sadness. And then they withered. Before her eyes, the plant shriveled. Evelyn ran for the watering can so to revive the thing, but she knew it was hopeless. She had killed it with her greed. As she surveyed the garden, the flowers and vegetables all seemed to lose their special spirit. They all turned rather ordinary. All but the Love bean.

Its first fruit was ready for picking. There was just a large enough mess of beans to use as a side dish for a meal with Rolin.

So the next evening, with the Luck bean dead, and the insects busily munching on the rest of the garden, she sat at the dinner table with her husband. The beans tasted like beans. She had steamed them string bean fashion; their tender goodness and pleasing texture were evident, although nothing about them seemed extraordinary. The taste held no hint of something special. Perhaps, after all, these beans were just beans. As Ev sat and shared the meal with the man of her life, however, an unusual atmosphere entered the room. I would write that they each took on a glow, but that seems so inadequate a term. Rolin looked at her and she at him. "Excellent dinner, Ev," he said, his eyes twinkling with a light that hadn't been there in years.

After wild, spontaneous love making on the kitchen floor (And she thought she was too old), Ev did the dishes, wondering how long it would be until she could harvest another mess of beans. The answer was quite regularly, once a week. While the rest of the yard and garden turned ordinary, the Love bean became her pride, and surely her joy. The love was not only a physical love, a sexual love, but her relationship with her husband was better that summer than it had ever been. It thrilled her to feel his touch, her body so vibrant and hungry for him, but also the manner and easy attitude that she shared with him was a blessing. The children were co-operative and pleasant, (I mentioned that this was a fable) although she did not fix any of the beans for them; she thought it unwise for they were all beyond puberty. Rolin never did associate the beans with the love. He thought he was just getting better with age. He could not understand why Ev kept fixing those same old beans once every week. She knew why.

She also knew that the plant would not produce forever. There was not enough fruit from the bean bush to can, barely enough for the once a week tryst. Toward the end of the summer she decided that she had better save the seed so that she could plant this Love bean again next year. She gave up one of her weekly dinners so as to save the seed. Twenty-four beans did she dry, ever so carefully, making sure that the birds did not rob her and the sun did not dry them too fast. After drying, she placed them in an unmarked envelope, just as she had seen them stored by the scoutmaster.

The summer was over and so also the season of the Love bean plant. As Ev's garden had turned ordinary after the death of the Luck bean, so her marriage turned ordinary after the passing of the Love bean. Ordinary is not bad, only ordinary. She, however, treasured the seeds that she kept in her special desk drawer. A place no one dared open. It occurred to her that perhaps she could grind a bean to powder and then sprinkle it over scrambled eggs. She was tempted to try, but the experience of wanting too much with the Luck bean made her hesitate.

Early December arrived and in the preparation for the Christmas season she barely noticed a plain envelope with the markings of a mass mailing that appeared in her mailbox. Mrs. Evelyn Crenshaw, it read, with one of those preprinted address tags. She almost threw it away, except that she noticed in the corner where the return address was, the letter and logo of the Boy Scouts of America. No other return address was listed. She thought *I need to send them a donation,* and so she opened the letter only to find, not a request for funds, but a handwritten list.

The list contained the names and address of twenty-four people. Some of the people she knew, a friend from along the Oregon coast, a few folks from Ohio and Toronto, her oldest son. Others were unknown to her. One name that she knew stood out. It was the last name on the list. It was her ex-husband in Michigan. Of all the things that Evelyn might wish for him, the love and happiness that she had felt with Rolin this past summer, was not one of them. On the reverse side of the list was this note:

Mrs. Crenshaw – Sissy,
Please include planting instructions. Not all of these
people have as green an eye as you (Oh, you thought it was the
thumb?).

That was it. No signature, no further directions. Twenty-four names for twenty-four seeds.

Evelyn waited until February, then sent the seed, along with instructions and explanation, to the first twenty-three people. That last name and that last seed was the most difficult thing to do. Once the envelope was in the mail, however, she did feel better. That night when Rolin got home from work, she said, "Take me on the kitchen floor again like you did last summer."

He looked at his wife strangely and wondered if she were going through another one of those woman crisis things. "Can we wait for after dinner and in bed?" he replied.

Bed, how ordinary, she thought.

All that spring Evelyn kept waiting for the Boy Scouts to appear at her door. By mid-April she were getting nervous, so she called the national chapter to find out the name of the local scoutmaster, and when someone would be around to sell seeds. The national office told her that the Boy Scouts of America had not sold seeds door to door as a fundraiser for eight years.

*   *   *

The fable ends here. If it were in the least true, I would have enclosed the seed you were hoping for. But I do not possess any; I was not on the list of twenty-four. Husbands, though, can be occasionally persuaded to make wild, spontaneous love on a floor, even without the help of beans.

SPARKY AND THE COWBOY

1
The Cowboy Gets His Name

BUDDY FELT LIKE BEACH scum. He thought of the debris, the dried sea foam, the bits of Styrofoam, cork and assorted garbage that collect along the high tide margin of the beach. He felt sandy and salty and sun burnt. It was five thirty on a Saturday morning. His body was wasted. His head banged with its usual hangover.

He did not walk from the cement dormitory to his job in Barn E; he shuffled, barely picking up his feet. The stink of his clothes, the stubble of his beard, the rasp of his breath and the sunken eye sockets were indications of what he was, an alcoholic. His life, his education, his family all ruined now, he found himself washed up as flotsam, washed ashore on this beach known as the backstretch. He was washed ashore with hundreds of men and a few women, all like him, all ready to be moved along the sands by the next high wave, none able to regain any of the usefulness they had once maintained.

Buddy was a hot walker. His job was to shovel horse shit out of the stalls of the racehorses that filled the long barns of the backside of the racing establishment and to cool down the racehorses when they came off the track sweaty from either morning workout or afternoon or evening racing. Buddy walked with the animal on a long rectangular stroll. Sixty yards along one side, cross to the opposite side and sixty yards back under the awning of the barn, past all the other horses, past all the stalls, past the hay bales and the empty cans of cheap beer. Buddy's job was to walk the horses one after another until they cooled their overheated bodies, put each horse into its designated stall and then gather up the next returning horse and do it again.

Most of the horses had learned the routine and could walk themselves. Others needed the guidance of the hot walker to make it around the rectangle. Some wanted to drink too much water, only so much was allowed during the cooling off process. Other animals wanted to display their studliness by bellowing and cajoling the horses they past in the walk about. Most though, knew the routine. It was not a job that took much intelligence. It was the lowest level of work, done by the lowest level of man. Buddy fit.

John, the groom, walked along at a quicker pace than Buddy that Saturday morning. The groom's job was to care for the horses, to brush them and bathe them. A groom had responsibility and was much valued by the racing community. They were much more stable than the hot walkers, often working with the same horses for years and the same trainers for decades. The grooms looked down on the hots. If a hot walker stayed a month, stayed two weeks with one outfit it was considered long term employment.

John walked past the shuffling Buddy as they entered into barn E. They both worked for a young trainer, a woman just starting out. John had come from a barn where he had been assistant head groom. He was a black man, strong in his younger days, but now he used his wisdom with the horses rather than his strength. He had come along with Mary when she formed her new team, gathered a few owners and a few horses. He was head groom now, something he might never had achieved at the old, larger stable where he and Mary had worked.

John looked at Buddy as he past him. It was a look of disgust. Buddy was a bum. Hot walkers were. Grooms had standing. John asked Buddy, "Another rough night?" It was not so much a question as an accusation.

"Hey, 5:30," Buddy replied, wiping off the crusted saliva from his lips. "I'm here to shovel shit." Buddy felt as if he needed a drink. Buddy always felt as if he needed a drink. He had found his way to the racetrack during his last attempt at coming clean. The AA program director had placed him here, found him a job, found him a room in the urine stinking, cement block building that was called a dormitory.

Buddy had stayed even after he resumed his nightly drunks, because he had nowhere else to go. There was regular food in the backstretch canteen, and the bed he shared with the lice was better than sleeping the winter on the street.

'God Damn,' he thought to himself, *'I need a drink.'*

He would have picked up a beer instead of the pitchfork, but the pitchfork was handy, a beer wasn't.

It was early March, and the pre-dawn glow was beginning to light the sky in the east, but the naked, incandescent light bulbs covered with eons of cobwebs and filth were what lit the barn and shed rows. Buddy had been with Mary for three weeks, about half the time she had been out on her own. In those three weeks he had missed four days, which for him wasn't bad. He hadn't formed an opinion of his boss yet, except to think that she was too young. He hadn't formed an opinion of the horses either. They were animals to him, things to walk around the barn with, things to clean up after. He used to love animals. Back when he had a family, there was always a dog. He could remember the joy he had shared with his daughter and a puppy one Christmas. *'Christ, how long ago was that?'* he wondered.

He usually did not care to think of family; the family that he had abandoned. He only did so during sober moments, and whenever he did, it made him want a drink.

John opened the first stall. "Old Dummy races tonight, so while I take him out and wash him down you muck out the stall," he directed Buddy.

Old Dummy was a seven-year-old gelding racing at the bottom level of the claiming ranks. He was a useful horse to have around, hardly ever winning anymore, but usually placing in contention and earning a paycheck. You never could tell about Dummy. Some days, when he took it upon himself to try he was pretty good, other times he would loaf. But he was a healthy horse, a professional. In a stable just starting out it was important to have a horse like him, if nothing else, to keep all the stable hands' interest aroused.

Mary had eleven horses under her care. For hired help she had John, the head groom, she had a morning exercise rider, a young lady named Carol, and she had two hot walkers, Raymond and Buddy. Ray and Carol were to come in at six this morning and take the first horses out for their exercise. Dummy, because he was racing tonight, would not go out, but stay in his stall. Miss Evangeline, the star of the young stable, was also racing tonight in the feature race, an allowance race for four-year-old fillies.

Miss Evangeline was new to Mary. Her owner was one of those dandies that thought he knew everything about horses and changed trainers with each disappointment. His horse was good, but no horse is going to win all the time, and after her last poor showing, she was yanked from her old trainer and given to Mary. Mary was her fourth trainer in three years.

Miss Evangeline's regimen for the day was to take a few turns around the shed row before being placed back in her stall to await her post time. As he cleaned up Dummy's stall, Buddy wondered what Mary could do with Miss Evangeline that other trainers hadn't done. He liked the old bay gelding they called Dummy better than the pretty and fast Miss Evangeline. Neither horse ever paid any attention to Buddy.

John led Dummy back into the stall as Buddy finished. "New horse coming in today, first of the two-year-olds," John stated. "Go clean up stall four, put down new bedding. Make it look presentable; this is a new owner for us, Mary's uncle."

Spring is the time when the first of the two-year-old horses show up at the track, young, edgy, full of hope and promise. Each one is a potential stakes winner, all undefeated because none of them have ever raced before.

It did not take Buddy long to prepare the empty stall, and he moved on to the next, made vacant as a horse was taken to the track for its morning exercise. He pitch forked the manure into a wheelbarrow, spread new straw, and replenished the water and hay net. He emptied the wheelbarrow into the large dumpster sitting outside the barn that the mushroom farm hauled away when it was full. Buddy concluded that he was just part of the chain of events that went into a thousand pizzas, pepperoni and mushrooms. Buddy didn't really mind shoveling horse shit. It reminded him of his mother's garden when, as a teenager, he would help her prepare the beds, clean the debris and do many of the heavy chores for her.

As the morning light turned to full dawn, the pace of the backstretch gathered steam. Horses traveled to and from the nearby racetrack for their morning workouts. Some were sent to gallop leisurely; others were set at a little harder pace. A few were asked to run fast and were timed by their trainers with stopwatches. The exercise riders hopped from horse to horse, pausing only to get directions from the trainers. Grooms prepared the horses, bathed them, and rubbed them down. Hot walkers mucked out stalls and walked endless rounds of the shed row. Buddy and Raymond were each walking their fourth horse of the morning. *At least I can keep my legs in shape with this job,'* thought Buddy.

By nine in the morning, the activity around the barns was winding down. The last horses were being rubbed down and cooled off. Although it was a typically breezy March day, Buddy had worked up a sweat, or maybe it was the alcohol evaporating from his system. He ran his tongue over his parched and cracked lips as he leaned the pitchfork against the back corner of the tool room.

"Buddy." He heard his name being called.

"Buddy." It was Mary. She was assembling all her staff to review the schedule for the rest of the day.

"We've got the new horse coming in probably in about an hour," she began when everyone had gathered around. "John, we'll need you here for the unloading. Miss Evangeline and Dummy are in the eighth and ninth races tonight, so Carol you'll act as pony girl to warm them up and Ray, you take Dummy over to the Lasix Barn, he needs to be there by five-thirty. John, you bring Miss Evangeline up to the paddock for the eighth and Ray will bring Dummy from the Lasix Barn for the ninth. I have to deal with Miss Evangeline's owner, the bastard, so I'll meet you in the paddock. After the new horse comes in, you all take the rest of the afternoon off.

"Buddy," she said as she turned to address him for the first time. "The new horse is a two-year-old and will probably be real nervous. I'd like you to just stick around the barn, keep an eye on her until the rest of us get back, and then you can have the evening off if you like."

Buddy was silent, thinking about the ordeal of waiting until evening for that much needed drink. Mary made the mistake of assuming his silence was sullenness.

"Do you have a problem with that?" she asked the old drunk.

"No," he lied.

"Good," she said to the whole crew. "Any questions?"

Ray headed off to spend his free time doing what ever he did with his free time. Carol and John were anxious to see the new arrival, so they stood and chatted with Mary, asking questions. Buddy found himself a bale of straw to sit upon and waited. What, besides the new horse he was waiting for, he didn't know. Maybe it was to die, he thought.

A short time later, a pick-up truck and horse trailer pulled up in front of the barn. Mary's uncle was in the passenger seat, and a family greeting between he and his niece ensued. It was a small, two-horse trailer. The rear ramp was let down, and John backed a sparkling chestnut filly out. Buddy turned on his straw bale and watched. She was a beautiful horse, small compared to many, but straight and lean. Her orangey red color was enhanced by a white blaze down her forehead and two white socks on her right side. John cooed to her as he led her around the railing and into her stall. Mary and Carol admired her as she followed John nervously. The other horses all stuck their necks out of their stalls to see the newcomer. Old Dummy, who had seen hundreds of horses come and go in his time, was unimpressed, but all the others greeted the newcomer with nays or whinnies, or by pawing the ground.

After a few minutes the welcoming party disbanded. Mary went off with her uncle to find some lunch. Carol left and as John was preparing to leave, he came by the bale where Buddy was sitting.

"Her name is Morning Thrill," he said, an edge of dislike to his voice. "But they call her Sparky, and she'll kick you in a minute, is what the van driver told me. She's awfully skittish so you watch her, understand? Make sure she settles in."

John looked hard at Buddy. "Watch her, you can go get your booze when we get back."

John did not like Buddy. Buddy was used to people not liking him. He didn't like himself.

John left when it became apparent that Buddy was neither going to move nor to say anything in reply.

After the groom had departed, Buddy got up and lifted the straw bale he had been sitting on into Sparky's stall. He placed it in the back corner, and standing inside, closed and latched the bottom door of the stall. He then went and sat on the bale, pulling his knees up against his chest, and started to shake. Just about all the free alcohol had left his blood stream. What was left was a crystallized accumulation of thirty years of abuse. The hangover was gone, replaced by a blinding need. He sat there, his chin resting on his knees; his arms wrapped around his legs and he shook.

At first the horse paid him no attention, for she was to busy taking in all the more interesting features of her new surroundings, but after about an hour of pawing and pacing her stall, she turned towards him and sniffed. After sampling his smell, (which was not at all pleasant to a human, although I cannot speak for a horse's preference) Sparky turned and went back to gazing out over her door, ignoring him.

Buddy didn't sleep. He didn't think. All he did was sit and shake.

Later in the afternoon Mary came back to the barn to prepare for the evening's races. At first she was convinced that Buddy had abandoned his post and had gone off drinking, but when she looked into Sparky's stall she saw him sitting crouched up on the straw bale.

"I asked you to watch her," she said. "I didn't mean you had to sleep with her."

"Wasn't sleeping," was all Buddy replied.

"I'm here now, you can go home," Mary suggested then walked away.

As Buddy was standing to lift his impromptu couch from the stall, he heard raised voices, angry voices coming from the barn entrance. As the anger didn't seem directed at him, he hesitated, not wanting to get caught in the middle of some fracas. Not until the noise had subsided did he venture out of Sparky's stall.

Mary and John were in obvious turmoil.

"Buddy, come here," she demanded.

When he had joined the others she began, "Raymond just showed up stinking of pot. You know we can't have pot and coke around here. Your alcohol is bad enough, but at least that doesn't taint the horses. Pot or cocaine on a groom's hands rubbing on a horse, show up as a positive in the drug tests. I lose my license. No way. I just fired Raymond. He knew better."

Buddy stood there listening, not sure what all this meant. He had just enough money for a bottle of Mad Dog from the convenience store right outside the backstretch gate, and that's all he cared about. He never had gotten into pot or the other drugs. Booze was his craving.

Mary continued, "I'll need you Buddy, to take Dummy over to the Lasix Barn, sit with him while the vet gives him the shot and then bring him up to the paddock for the ninth race. John will be busy with Miss Evangeline who runs the race before, Carol will have to be on the track to pony both horses, I have to deal with Miss E.'s owner, so that leaves you to handle Dummy."

Buddy didn't want to handle Dummy. Buddy had never been to the Lasix Barn. Buddy didn't care about any bastard owner. Buddy had done his duty and now he wanted to drink.

"Ma'am," he started, "I need a shower. Let me go back to the dorm and get cleaned up a little bit first. I haven't had any food all day."

John interrupted, saying to Mary, "You let him go, he ain't comin' back. Look at his eyes."

Mary considered a moment. "Take your windbreaker and shirt off and wash up with the hose outside the barn. John will take you over to the canteen and get you some lunch."

Buddy thought it was much too cold to be stripping down. He thought it was much too late in his life to be babysat by some old black dude. He wanted to tell Mary to leave him alone, and he wanted to walk away. He didn't. Instead he unzipped his badly stained jacket, unbuttoned his frayed flannel shirt, and stripped to the waist.

He cleansed himself with the warm water hose that they used to bathe the horses. Mary watched him, looking at his emaciated torso, starkly white. *'He must have been a good looking man once,'* she thought, *'tall and strong.'*

After rinsing himself off and drying with a barn towel, Buddy stood quietly replacing his shirt.

"John, take him over and find him something to eat," Mary commanded. "We don't have long. I'll get Dummy ready."

John placed a hand on Buddy's elbow. "Let's go Buddy," he said. "I ain't never had to watch over no wino before. Seems like a new low in my life." Together they walked toward the backstretch canteen.

Buddy had planned to head to the store, buy his bottle and find a place to drink it. He had not figured on being escorted to dinner. John had already eaten, but he selected a piece of apple pie from the pie safe. Buddy got a large bowl and filled it with vegetable beef soup from the tureen at the end of the cafeteria line. He also grabbed a great handful of saltine crackers.

They sat across from one another. Neither spoke. Buddy crumbled the crackers into his steamy soup. Then he took the pepper shaker and covered the top black. It was if he was trying to make up for the lack of alcohol with pepper. John looked at him again with disgust.

"Mary has the touch," John said to Buddy. "She's goin' places. And I ain't lettin' you screw it up. If you could stay sober, you'd be doin' good to hook on with her, but I don't believe you could stay sober."

Buddy just looked at him, slurping his soup and crackers. He'd had to break his last five-dollar bill to pay for it, and now he wasn't sure he had enough cash to buy the bottle he wanted so desperately.

When he had finished, John got up and said, "We need to be getting back."

"Give me a minute," Buddy replied, "I need to run to over to the store."

"No way," John retorted. "I told you I ain't lettin' you screw this up. After the race, you can drink all you want to, drink yourself to death for all I care, but nothing before. Understand?"

Buddy understood too well.

When they arrived back at Barn E, Dummy was haltered and ready to be led to the Lasix Barn. "Do you know what you're to do?" Mary asked Buddy.

"No," was his simple answer.

"Walk the horse over to the second barn from the track entrance, " she explained. "You've been assigned stall sixteen. You wait there for the vet to come by. He'll check the horse's tattoo and then give Dummy a shot of Lasix, to thin his blood. Most all the horses in his race will be somewhere in that barn, most all the horses racing tonight will probably be in the barn.

"After the vet comes by, you just wait. Wait all evening. You're in the ninth and last race. While the eighth race is being run, they will notify you to get your horse ready. Take Dummy up to the track entrance, where they'll check his tattoo again and then you walk him into the paddock. Just follow the other horses, should be no problem. Dummy has done this a hundred times; he'll show you what to do. Got it?"

Buddy was quiet a minute, thinking, then asked, "Why do you call the horse Dummy? I mean, if he knows what he's suppose to do, he can't be so dumb."

"Dummy? It's his name," John broke in. "Dromedary, Dummy for short."

"Dromedary, you mean like in camel?" Buddy asked.

"Yea, like a camel, like being in the desert and able to go a long time between drinks," John answered the pithiness of his tone making his meaning unmistakable.

Buddy turned to Mary, "Ninth race, right? Write down the stall number."

"Sixteen," Mary responded, searching for a scrap of paper. She found a copy of the Daily Racing Form, torn off a corner, wrote *16* on it and handed it to Buddy. "I'll be along to be sure everything's OK in about fifteen minutes, then you'll have to be on your own."

Buddy took hold of Dromedary's lead and began the walk to the Lasix Barn. He wished he had a flask in his pocket to make the wait until the ninth race bearable. He was becoming incurably thirsty.

Once in the medication barn, he led the horse into stall sixteen. It was at the end of a long aisle of stalls, many of them already containing a horse and with an attendant sitting outside. As Buddy closed the bottom half of the stall door, he noticed a jet-black horse being led into stall fifteen. The groom was a Latino looking fellow, short and middle aged. After the newcomer had settled his horse, Buddy leaned over and asked, "Hey, Poncho, you wouldn't have a little nip on you, would ya?"

The little man looked up at Buddy with glaring, dark eyes and said in accented English, "Fuck you, Cowboy! You old wino, stay away from me. We got too many drunks around this place already. You just sit there and dry out." He paused a moment then added with vengeance, "And keep away from my horse, understand, Cowboy?"

"Screw you, Poncho, I just asked for a friendly drink," Buddy replied meekly, finding a hay bale to rest on.

A short while later Mary came by, to check on the horse and Buddy. The vet made his rounds, injecting each horse with the prescribed amount of the legal medication. "It helps prevent bleeding into the lungs as they race," Mary explained to Buddy, who hadn't asked, and didn't really care.

Buddy was wondering if the vet had any alcohol in his bag.

The loudspeakers for the barn area soon started calling for the animals to be brought forward for each of the races. Beyond the backstretch, the public address system for the grandstand could be heard announcing the races, one by one. All the commotion didn't mean much to Buddy. He sat on his hay bale, and began to shake.

Poncho looked at him and said with no sympathy, "Cowboy, you dumb sucker, stop shaking."

Buddy turned and looked at his tormentor. Without saying anything, he got up and opened Dromedary's stall door, walked in, and leaned against the horse. He whispered to the Camel, "Tell that scrawny wetback to shut-up."

Poncho, not hearing what the Cowboy had said, but knowing that his needling had had an affect, called from the aisle, "What's the matter, Cowboy, asking the Dummy there if he has a bottle? You wino's make me sick. You and that beaten down old horse, you got no business here. That's the trouble with this place." Poncho's voice rose in intensity. "This whole place headed to Hell, 'cause of bums like you and your horse. They'll take the horse for dog food, but what the hell they goin' do with you, Cowboy?"

Buddy grabbed the horse's mane and held tightly as a series of shakes and shivers ran through his body. He could feel creatures crawl beneath his skin. *'He had been kicked at, spit at and peed upon before, so these insults meant little, but why did Poncho have to slander the horse?'* he thought. Dromedary's big stature absorbed all of Buddy's shakes without affect. Buddy was grateful for the ability to share his discomfort with a living being even if it was a horse.

He stayed in the stall through the rest of the evening. Finally, the horses for the last race were called. Race eight was about to start off and the participants in race nine should be in line to enter the track. Race eight was the highlight of the night's contests, an allowance race restricted to fillies and mares four years old and upward. The purse, although meager by industry standards, was a good one for this out-of-the-way track. Miss Evangeline was competing in this race, and while not the favorite, due to inconsistent recent performance, there was hope that a new trainer could bring out her obvious potential.

As Poncho led his black horse from stall fifteen to answer the call to be ready, Buddy did the same with Dromedary.

"See this black tail, Cowboy?" Poncho taunted as he wheeled his horse in front of Dromedary. "That's the only thing your bag of bones will see."

"Poncho," Buddy replied forcefully, "Camel here is going whip your ass."

As they brought their horses to the back track entrance, the eighth race was headed into the homestretch. Buddy heard the track announcer's excited call as Miss Evangeline charged up from the middle of the pack to challenge the leader. Apparently she missed winning the race by a head. Buddy wondered if that was a good outcome or not, but he could not dwell on that much, for it was his turn to walk the Camel into the paddock.

He had never done this before, so he was glad to be able to follow Poncho and his horse. As they entered the track to begin the hike past the grandstands to the paddock to be saddled, each horse had to stop and have their tattoo re-checked to be sure that each was identified correctly. Before stepping on to the track, an inspector lifted the front top lip of each horse to verify that the number found there was identical to the one on the horse's registration.

Poncho stopped his black horse for the check. "Number seven, Night Lightening," Poncho announced. After the check the employee waved him on, handing him a tag with the number seven on it.

Buddy pulled the Camel up to the inspector. "Number eight, Dromedary," he said.

"Who are you? Haven't seen you before," asked the man suspiciously.

Poncho, overhearing this as he walked away, answered in a loud voice, "He's Cowboy, a drunk with a flea-bit horse."

The inspector checked the tattoo, looked at Buddy, hesitated, then handed him the number eight tag and waved him on.

The saddling area was in the middle of the grandstand. Bettors that wished to could come and examine the horses at close range as they received final preparation for the upcoming race. This is the time when jockeys and owners and trainers all give last minute instructions to one another, while the grooms tend the animals. The horses sense the excitement and know that shortly they'll be asked to run as hard as they can. There is a routine, a standard mode of operations to the paddock and Dromedary had been through it so often he knew what his role was. He let Buddy walk him around the sawdust-covered arena a few times, before being taken into the number eight slot to have the tiny racing saddle and girth put on him. Then he was led around a few more times for the betting public to judge him against the other horses.

Poncho and Night Lightening were doing the same from slot number seven. The black horse was the even money favorite to win this last race of the night. Usually the eighth race on the program was a higher-class event with faster horses, while the last race was set for the bottom rung of the claiming horses. These were the professional horses, older and wiser, but now slower than their younger brethren. Night Lightening was the horse with the surest form, the best recent record, and the talents of the leading jockey to guide him.

Mary waited in slot eight as the Camel walked slowly around the ring. "OK, Buddy, bring him in," she said.

Buddy obliged as the line of jockeys entered the paddock for the last minute conference and the call for 'riders up'. Some of the horses had owners and trainers and jocks all going over race strategy, but for Dromedary it was only Mary and the jock. The jockey, dressed in a black shirt with a blue band on his sleeves, chatted with the trainer. "I think I've ridden Dummy a dozen times," he said, a thin little fellow dwarfed by the horse. "Anything new I should know?"

"He should be ready, although it can be hard to tell with him," Mary answered. "But the number seven looks head and shoulders above the rest of the field. We may be racing for second money tonight."

Buddy, who had been paying close attention to his duties, so as not to screw things up, overheard this. He also noticed Poncho's sneer as he prepared to lead the black horse out toward the racetrack.

"Rider's up!" Came the call, and one by one the jocks mounted their steeds and walked or trotted out to the track to begin a few minutes of warm-up. Number seven swung in front of number eight on their way to the track. As he did so, Buddy leaned into Dromedary and said, "Crush his balls."

Once the jock was given a leg up and secured in his seat, he leaned toward Buddy with a half-smile and asked, "Whose balls are we to crush?"

"That black horse," Buddy replied.

"Hah," laughed the rider. "He ain't got no balls to crush. He's a gelding."

Buddy nodded to Dromedary and said, "The Camel knows what I mean."

After handing over the horses to the pony riders as they entered the track, most of the grooms headed back to the betting booths to place their wagers. Buddy did not, but took a spot along the rail to watch the race and be ready should the horse have any need of him. Gambling had never been a vice of his. Usually one addiction leads to another, but Buddy had never had much use for gambling, drugs or even tobacco. His only addiction, his continual craving, was for booze.

Poncho noticed that Buddy was not headed to lay a bet. He announced in a loud voice, "Cowboy? What's the matter, you ain't bettin' on that dog you call a horse? Got no guts?"

Buddy motioned for Poncho to come closer. "If I place a bet, will the horse run any faster?"

"Cowboy, horse don't care if you bet nothin'."

"Thought so," was all Buddy said, and turned away from the conversation. He felt in his pocket for the few dollars he had there. He hoped that there was enough to buy that bottle from the store. It had been almost twenty-four hours since his last drink, and he was terribly thirsty.

Buddy stood by the rail in the chill of the March night. The track lights shone on the dirt oval. Most of the crowd had already departed after the eighth race, and all that were left were the diehards, those suckers hoping to make back all that they had lost on the previous races. The lights and figures on the tote board in the grass infield showed that Night Lightening, number seven, was considered the likely winner. Dromedary had some support, and was listed at seven to one; a two-dollar win ticket would gain fourteen dollars. Most of the other horses were ranked somewhere between the two, with a few tired nags being sent off at long shot odds.

This was a long race, a mile and one sixteenth, twice around the grandstand. The horses entered the starting gate on the far side of the track without incident. These were all hardened veterans, and they knew what was expected. As the gates banged open the horses charged out together, but quickly Night Lightening moved ahead of the field. In the grandstand there are television cameras placed to relay the action, but standing at track level, as Buddy was, it can be hard to judge the action when the horses are on the far side. It was easy to pick out the black horse though, as he glided away from the others, glided away from all but one of the others. There was a horse on his outside, stuck like glue against his hip, matching his strides three quarters of a length behind. Buddy did not need to see to know which horse it was.

As the beasts swung around the turn and down the home stretch for the first lap, the leader was going easily, smoothly. Dromedary came into view as the only other horse able to run with the pace. All the others had fallen back, their only hope was the front two would exhaust themselves.

Horses love to run. They can run for hours uncontested. Only the best though, and sometimes not even those, can sustain their stride if constantly under pressure. Night Lightening was only the best compared to this field of bottom dwellers. His jockey knew it. Dromedary's jockey knew it. Dromedary knew it.

A horse has its eyes set not to look forward, but to see nearly three hundred and sixty degrees. Dromedary was running just at the edge of the black horse's field of vision. Night Lightning knew he was there, could feel him, could hear him, and could barely see him out of the corner of his eye. As they went around the clubhouse turn, because the black horse had the inside position, Dromedary had to lengthen his stride to stay in place on the leaders hip, and lengthen he did. Down the backstretch they raced, Night Lightening unable to shake the Camel; past the starting point of the race and around the far turn for the second time. Again Dromedary had to lengthen stride to match the black, and again he did.

As the two horses headed down the home stretch, headed for the finish line, Night Lightning's rider knew they were in trouble. She started to use the whip, to encourage her mount, to urge her horse home, to put distance between themselves and the adversary. Racing under pressure the entire way though had taken its toll. Night Lightening wanted to win, but the gas tank was empty. He had tried to put daylight between himself and this other horse for an entire mile, but now the black horse was too tired. Two horses had raced around the oval. One had run hard; one had cruised from the start. It was as if two geese were flying in formation. The leader had broken the air while the other coasted in its drag. Now the leader was forced to give up the lead.

Dromedary had taken the measure of his rival. With half a furlong left to run, the Camel sailed on by the tired favorite, the jock never even threatened to use the whip. Buddy, standing motionless by the rail, was close enough to hear the crunch as his horse passed the winded leader. The race was over. Dromedary was clear two lengths ahead of Night Lightening at the finish, the rest of the field far up the track.

Buddy had never done this before, but he knew that he must go out and walk the Camel back to the winner's circle. There, assembled for the obligatory picture were Mary, an old lady, Buddy holding the horse, and the jockey, still mounted. After the picture was taken, and due fuss made over the victor, Mary said, "Now you have to lead him to the test barn, where they'll take a sample of his urine to test for drugs. Know where that is?"

"Not a clue," Buddy replied.

"It's the small barn just past the Lasix Barn. You go on. I'll be there in a minute."

Buddy was left alone to walk the hot horse to the area where urine samples would be collected to test for foreign and illegal substances. The track was empty, the grandstands empty. Buddy looked up at the Camel, and forever after swore the horse talked to him. The Camel said with an air of satisfaction, "Busted his balls."

2
Demons Explained

SUNDAY MORNING AT THE racetrack is usually a quiet time. The track is closed for training purposes, the horses and staff given a break from the regular routine. Racing is held in the afternoon but this Sunday Mary did not have any horses entered. Horses still needed to be fed and watered, but the level of activity along Barn E was much less intense than on a normal morning. Carol had been given the day off, and John and Buddy were not expected to be in until nearly 9 am, and then for only half a day.

Mary was surprised to find Buddy in Sparky's stall when she drove up as the sun was peeking over the ridgeline. "Thought I told you that you didn't have to come in until nine this morning?" she asked. She wondered if he had been drinking and had been up all night, but noticed instead that he had shaved and showered. He still looked ragged and worn, but again she was reminded as she looked at his sunken eye sockets and drawn cheeks, that he must have been a handsome man at some time in his life. "Always liked to get up early," he replied, as he groomed and curried the young horse.

"Seeing as you're here, would you mind walking Sparky around the barn a time or two, she probably wants some exercise, and we'll see how she moves," Mary suggested.

The horse was nervous and full of energy. "Watch her," Mary admonished. "She'll kick you in a minute."

Buddy looked at the skittish athlete. "Come on Sparks, let's go for a walk."

He snapped a lead to her halter and led her out of the stall. Together they strolled down the barn aisle. The horse cocked her head to and fro trying to take in all her strange new surroundings. The older, established horses stuck their heads out of their stalls to examine the newcomer. Some went so far as to threaten a bite her on the backside, but Sparky skipped away from them. Buddy began the slow schooling process of teaching the horse the method, manner and hierarchy of the barn.

Mary watched the animal carefully as they made the circuit around the barn. The trainer was looking for hints of smoothness in the gate, fluidity in the movements of the equine. After the third trip around Mary said, "Put her back in."

Buddy followed the directions. He unsnapped the lead rope, patted his charge on the shoulder and silently reassured her that she had been a good girl.

"We had a good night last night Buddy," Mary announced when he was done. "I'll grain all our gang, then we'll go over to the canteen and I'll buy you breakfast."

"That's alright, I'm fine here," Buddy politely refused.

Mary looked at him quietly a moment, then turned to the feed chores. Buddy passed out the buckets as she filled them and instructed him as to which horse got what amount of grain.

When the animals had completed their breakfast she turned again to Buddy, "I want to talk with you," she insisted. "I'm hungry, come on."

Reluctantly Buddy followed as she strode briskly across the yard toward the cafeteria. After they had traveled half way, Mary spoke. "I need to ask you this, Buddy. After the race last night the jockey swore that Dummy had been juiced up. Did you see anybody around his stall in the Lasix Barn?"

"Just you and the vet," he responded with a tinge of defensiveness.

"You stayed with him the whole time?" she returned.

"I was in the stall with him, nobody came, nobody bothered him." Buddy remembered hanging onto the horse for hours.

"In the afternoon," Mary continued, "was there anyone by the barn?"

"I was sitting inside with Sparky, didn't see anybody. I reckon I would have heard somebody had they been around."

"Dummy's never run that well for me before, can't figure it out," Mary concluded as they entered the track kitchen door.

Mary selected a high cholesterol breakfast, saying that Sunday breakfast was her one treat on a tight diet. Buddy chose a bowl of hot oatmeal and asked the attendant if there was any brown sugar to sprinkle over it. They gathered their utensils and found seats at the end of a long picnic table facing each other.

They sat and ate in silence.

"You drink coffee?" Mary asked after a few minutes. "I'll get myself one, you want one."

"No thank you," Buddy replied, putting his hand around his glass of water as if she might take it away.

When Mary returned with her steaming cup, she sat and again began devouring her vittles in quiet.

Buddy asked her, perhaps the first time he had spoken to her without having been spoken to first, "Who was that lady last night in the winner's circle?"

Mary looked up at him and smiled. "That was my Grandmother. Dummy is her horse. She claimed him so I would have something to train."

Mary was glad Buddy had inquired, for now she had a subject to talk about with him. "My parents think I'm crazy. They never encouraged me at all. They want me to go back to school and get a government job or something. Granny understands. She talked Uncle Joe into getting into thoroughbreds as a hobby too. Uncle Joe is Sparky's owner. Together they give me the support I need. They and a few other owners."

"Buddy?" Mary changed the subject with her question. "John's got plenty to do with grooming all the other horses, and there will be a few more two-years-olds coming soon. Would you be willing to be Sparky and Dummy's groom? I can't pay you much more an hour yet, but it would be a start for you."

"Groom? You mean like, be responsible?" Buddy hesitated.

"They'll nearly become your horses. You care and tend them, lead them to the track, watch out for them," she explained. "You've seen what John does."

"No, ma'am. Don't want responsibility."

"You like Sparky, I can tell, and you did real well with Dummy last night. I need you to be more than just a hot walker."

Buddy lowered his head to watch his spoon play with the last clumps of oatmeal left in the bowl.

Mary was insistent. "Tell me why not."

Buddy was quiet for a long time and then said, "I ain't nothing but an old drunk."

The young trainer looked across the table at the man, the defeated man. "I need a part time groom to help John. I can't afford another full time groom yet." Mary had an eye for horses, she had a touch, as John said, but she was inexperienced dealing with people. She was uncomfortable as she sat across from Buddy.

He was silent for a while longer. Then he said, softly, still looking at the leftover oatmeal in his bowl, "Everything I ever did, I screwed up. You put responsibility on me and you'll find me dead drunk one morning, or maybe not find me at all."

Mary wanted to help him now, not so much to turn him into a valued employee, but because she could see humanity in him that she hadn't noticed before. "Tell me how I can help?" she asked.

He looked at her with a strange, defiant gaze. "You don't know the demons," he began. "Maggots, they're like maggots crawling inside your head and your gut. They crawl up the inside of my cheekbones and fill my eyeballs. They crawl out my ears. They're maggots but they aren't. They're red demons, with stingers, like centipedes and each foot stings as it walks around your brain. They fill your mouth. You can't spit 'em out. They clog your throat. You can't breath. They pack into your stomach. You can't eat. They burn. They sting. Nothing makes 'em go away. Only one thing takes the sting away. Booze.

"The sea floated me up on this beach. I'm a drunk and that's all that I am." He said that with finality that he hoped would silence her, but it did not.

"Let me help," she implored.

"You?" He spoke with more authority than she had ever heard from him. "Listen, I've tried to quit fifty or sixty times. You think you can make a difference? You don't know the maggots. For maybe thirty or forty of those times, I had angels by my side, and I still couldn't quit. They finally got tired of trying. I don't blame them. I got tired of trying. I'm not trying anymore. I don't want to be a groom, understand?"

He looked across the table at her. She was innocent and uncomprehending. "Look," he continued, "yesterday I was clean 'cause it was an accident. Today I'm clean 'cause the demons must be sleeping. I won't stay clean. I ain't tryin' to stay clean. I like walking horses. If you want me to walk your horses I'll do it, but I will not take responsibility."

The conversation was over. She had no response. As they began to gather up their dishes, Poncho came up to them. He came to speak to Mary. "Hello," he started, then, realizing that she might think it impolite to ignore her companion he turned to Buddy and said, "Hello, Cowboy."

"Hello, Poncho," Buddy returned and before the Mexican could start his speech to Mary he continued, "Hey, Poncho, did you see anybody around the horses last night? I mean besides you and me?"

"You mean in the Lasix Barn?" he answered. "Nah, just you and me."

Poncho turned to start again with Mary, but before he could, she asked Buddy, "Cowboy? You two know each other?"

Poncho replied for both of them with a certain amount of sarcasm, "Yea, we're old friends, eh, Cowboy?"

Finally Poncho began his prepared statement to Mary, "John says you got the hands, the touch. You're goin' places. I want to go too. He says you may need another groom."

Mary cast a quick look at the Cowboy. "I lost a hot walker yesterday," she said, "but I don't need another groom right now. You work for McCoy don't you?"

"Yes," Poncho responded, "but he's not goin' anywhere. I'd like to start with a new, small outfit and grow. John says you're good. I take his word for it. I saw your horse run last night."

Mary paused, looking at him standing beside their table. "I can't pay what McCoy is giving you. Stay where you are until I get more horses and you'll have first call."

"OK ma'am. Don't forget me. John will vouch for me." Poncho looked at the Cowboy.

The Cowboy grabbed all the breakfast dishes and carried them off to the return counter, thus escaping. When he returned, Poncho had left and Mary was waiting for him. Wordlessly they exited the canteen and walked back across the yard toward Barn E.

The Cowboy cleared his throat and spoke. "Mary?"

This was the first time he had ever spoken her name. She was surprised to hear it from him. Without looking at him she said, "Yes?"

"Thanks for breakfast."

He fell silent, but they both knew he was trying to say something else. Finally, just before reaching the barn he spoke again. "Would you do me one other favor?"

"I'll try," she said.

"Quit calling him Dummy. His name's Dromedary, or maybe Camel."

She stopped, speechless, turned to look at the Cowboy. He looked down at her, for although stooped he still was a tall man. He returned her gaze, unaware that he was smiling. It was a wane, little smile, but it was a smile. Maybe it was the first smile he'd had in years. Mary didn't say anything although she thought that he was in need of dental work. She never called Dromedary, "Dummy" again.

3
Mary Finds Success

JOHN WAS RIGHT WHEN he said Mary had the touch. Not every horse she entered in the races won each time, not every horse stayed healthy. She won enough, she had horses in contention enough, and she had horses stay injury free enough that knowledgeable people began to take notice.

Dromedary was moved up one rung in the claiming ranks, and won at next asking, although without the same authority and verve as his last race. Miss Evangeline beat a good field as the favorite in her next allowance race. All the other horses in the stable improved their position. An air of confidence pervaded Mary's barn. The horses could feel it and so could the help.

Miss Evangeline's owner, ever the loud-mouthed buffoon, began spreading the word that he had discovered the next training genus. No one really believed him, but they did take note, and watched the young trainer. Gradually new horses and new owners filtered into Barn E. Three more new two-year-olds joined the band, as did several older horses, their owners dissatisfied with their former trainers. Mary knew that these animals, like Miss E. would probably last only as long as the next poor effort, but it was still good to be given a chance at improving a horse, and making a name for oneself.

The Cowboy stayed clean. He did not actually try to stay clean, but the demons and the maggots mainly left him alone. Those times when temptation began to lead him back to the bottle, some collision of circumstance would keep him dry. He still had the shakes and when they got bad, he'd throw that bale of straw into the back of Sparky's stall and go shiver for an hour or two. No further word was spoken of the Cowboy becoming a groom, but it was understood that the Camel and Sparky were his horses to look after and maintain. He was their groom, but neither he nor Mary would admit to it.

Poncho joined the crew, and he and the Cowboy developed a silent respect for one another. Each used the name the other had bestowed. It was Poncho's glare that quieted a stray maggot or stinging centipede from time to time. The Cowboy knew though, that despite Poncho, despite Mary, the demons were only playing with him. He knew that when they really came after him, he would not resist. Maybe today they would come for him, maybe tomorrow, but eventually he knew that they would come.

The track chaplain came by a week or so after Camel's first victory. He had watched Buddy as he had watched a thousand other lost souls. The chaplain was persistent. He was both the back stretch minister and drug rehab leader.

"Cowboy," the chaplain started, for everyone was now calling Buddy, Cowboy. "I hear you've been dry for a few days now?"

It was a question but it wasn't a question. Cowboy did not answer.

"Come to the AA meeting this evening, Cowboy. Maybe we can help," the chaplain persisted.

"Been to too many meetings, they never did help," the Cowboy replied and began doing some menial chore so he could turn his back on the minister.

"Cowboy, nobody ever stays dry without meetings and support."

The Cowboy turned back toward the preacher but did not say anything.

The chaplain waited a minute then said, "You're welcome anytime. Come when you want. You know where the meetings are held. Every night we're not racing."

Cowboy stood there looking at the man saying nothing.

"And three weeks from Sunday, Easter sunrise service. Right out on the track. Think about it."

As the Cowboy stood silently watching the chaplain, he was thinking of the countless days and nights he had spent on his knees preying to God and Jesus and anyone else that would listen to free him from the demons. He could remember his knees being raw from the preying. He could remember he and his wife, hand in hand, begging for temperance. He could remember each time the demons came upon him harder, the maggots more gross, and the centipedes more torturous than the last time. God, if there was one, had abandoned him to the Devil.

He went to the Easter service but stood a distance away from the small crowd gathered in the grassy area at the center of the racetrack. He could barely hear the words. He did not want to hear the words. He had been brought up a Christian, but there was none of that left inside him. He turned and walked away before the service ended.

Dromedary, because of his consecutive victories, had caught the eye of several trainers around the track. Mary choose to move him up again in competitive level and claiming price, but she was still afraid that someone would purchase him through the claiming box, as she herself had done when he raced at the bargain level. Claiming races are the great equalizer in everyday horse racing. Race a good horse against poor, and someone lays a claim, and the horse has a new owner. Place a horse in competition better than its talent in order to keep it safe from the claim, but then it does not win.

The Cowboy and the Camel were waiting in the stall of the Lasix Barn before the race. Each somehow knew that this was the last race for the partnership. The Cowboy leaned against the gelding as he had done on the night of that first race five weeks earlier. It was not an act of affection, but one of humility. He led the horse to the paddock, and to the race. Camel did not win, but he came in a respectable second. As the Cowboy was preparing to snap the lead on the sweaty horse, another groom, a stranger intervened and took Dromedary away. The Cowboy was left holding the rope without a horse to take back to the barn.

Mary motioned to him and said, trying to console him, "That's horse racing, Cowboy. The best ones get claimed away. Grandma more than tripled her money in three months. She wants me to start looking for another horse for her. Maybe a two-year-old at the sale coming up, one with a little more class than Dromedary."

The Cowboy did not need consoling. Throughout his life he had lost far more than a horse, but that last remark of Mary's made him turn and look at her. It was his habit that when disappointed with people he was silent.

Payday was every other Friday. It was toward the end of May, and the Cowboy had been over two months without a drink. Paychecks were handed out and a steady stream of backstretch workers headed to the convenience store situated directly outside the gate, where, for a small fee, the proprietor would cash the checks. Normally the Cowboy got his cashed in this manor, but on this day, one of John's friends pulled along side Barn E with his pickup.

The day was warm and the windows of the truck rolled down. "John, goin' downtown to the bank, want a lift?" the friend hollered.

"Yea, that'd be great. Can't stay long though, got a horse in tonight," John answered.

"What race?" the friend asked.

"Seventh," replied John.

"We'll be back in plenty of time," the friend assured him.

John swung himself into the truck and then noticed the Cowboy leaning against one of the awning support posts. "Cowboy, you want to go to the bank instead of that clip joint across the street?"

The Cowboy didn't think, but simply answered, "Sure," and climbed into the bed of the pickup, sitting back against the cab.

At the bank the three cashed their checks. The Cowboy was the last of the three, and he stood at the window counting his money. An idea came to him. An idea that he knew he must act upon immediately or it would slip away.

He leaned back in toward the teller and asked, "Can I buy a sheet of paper and an envelope from you? I need to mail a letter."

This was an unusual request, but the teller looked around her cubicle. "The only envelopes I have are with the bank's address on them," she said. "Wait, I've got these gift envelopes to send money in. Will that work?"

The Cowboy looked at the gift envelope. "That'll be alright, but I need a sheet of paper to write a note on."

"No problem," the teller replied with a smile. "Want me to cut the letterhead off the top?"

"Yes, please. What do I owe?"

"Nothing, sir, my pleasure."

The Cowboy returned her smile, and turned to find John and his friend waiting impatiently. "You all go ahead," he told them. "I'll walk back."

"Man, it's a long way. Sure you want to walk?" John questioned.

"I've got things to do, you go ahead back." The Cowboy motioned them on.

John shrugged his shoulders, thinking that the Cowboy wanted to stay in town and find a drink. John had never trusted him to stay sober. John gave the Cowboy a last look to make sure he hadn't changed his mind. The Cowboy again motioned with his hands for them to go.

When John and his friend finally drove off, the Cowboy went to the island in the center of the bank waiting area, the counter where the deposit slips and such were kept. He found a pen chained up there, and he began to write:

Mrs. Steadman,
> *You never liked me. Well, you never thought I was good enough for your daughter. You were right.*

The Cowboy hadn't written in such a long time. He was halfway surprised to see that he still could. His handwriting was not a good as it used to be, but it was still legible. He was writing to his former mother-in-law, whom he had not seen in many years. He wondered if she still lived at the address he remembered, the house on the tree-lined street where he used to pick up his date during those college years. Perhaps she had moved. Perhaps she was dead. Perhaps it did not make any difference.

> *I have ruined people's lives. My own life is ruined. I am not looking for sympathy. And I know there is no way this meager little bit could ever repay or repair the damage the demons that possess me have caused.*

He stopped and thought a moment. Then he went back and crossed through the last phrase so the sentence read:

And I know there is no way this meager little bit could ever repay or repair the damage I have caused. Give this money to my daughter or my

He hesitated again. So long ago, yet still he could not bear to call her his ex. He again crossed out and completed the sentence thusly:

Give it to my daughter or your daughter as you see fit. Do not tell them where it comes from, or even that I am alive. I know that you will not say anything for you, of all people, know the damage that I can do.

I would like to promise that I shall send more as it becomes available, but I have broken a thousand promises before.

He decided that he need not sign his name. She would know who sent the letter. He counted out his money. He worked for minimum wage and there really was not much altogether. He folded the letter around five twenty-dollar bills, put it in the money gift envelope and licked the back. On the front he put his former mother-in-law's name and address but no return address. All he needed was a stamp and a mailbox.

When he inquired of a bank guard where he might find a stamp, he was directed to the post office, two blocks down the street. As he walked through town toward the post office he past by a liquor store. He did not even notice. He found the post office, found the stamps, plopped the stamp on the envelope and sent it on its way. He walked back out to the street, looked up and down, and had to ask the way back to the racetrack.

4
Sparky's Story

MARY TRIED TO INTEREST the Cowboy in grooming one of the new arrivals to make up for the loss of the Camel, but he would not be persuaded. He walked the hot horses until they cooled, did assorted jobs as asked, but the only horse he tended to, the only one that he paid more than passing attention to was Sparky. Whenever she was on the track being schooled and he had a break in his morning duties, he would go to the rail and watch her. At times he was joined there in wordless company by Sparky's owner, Uncle Joe.

When the horse got sick, as almost all the two-year-olds do, as their immune systems are confronted with the array of germs from the other horses confined in the barns of the track, the Cowboy groomed and curried her. He petted and coaxed her. Stayed with her almost around the clock.

"It's just a cold," Mary told him. "She'll get over it. All the two-year-olds get 'em."

The Cowboy found comfort in trying to give comfort to this filly. He remembered sitting and holding his young daughter in his arms those times when she wasn't feeling well. He would sway with her, sitting in the rocking chair. He remembered that no matter how deeply inebriated he was, he never raised his voice to his daughter. Now, as he cared for this mildly sick animal, he wondered why he could not remember how old his daughter should be. He could not recall the year of her birth. She must be near college age, he thought, or beyond. He wondered what she looked like. He hoped that she had recovered from whatever mental or social scars he had inflicted on her. A horse can't wipe its own nose, doesn't really care too, but the Cowboy wiped away the mucus from Sparky's nostrils, smiling, recalling the times he had done the same for his toddler child.

The illness was mild, as Mary had said. The horse was soon back to galloping with the other horses every morning. It is common practice to work the youngsters together, to gallop around the track, to school them in the ways of racing. Steps are taken slowly, and by training them together, it is easier to see which horses are ready to proceed to the next lesson, and which need more time. Even to the Cowboy's untrained eyes, Sparky was falling behind her companions.

It was not that her stride or effort was at fault, but the pieces, the building blocks weren't shaping into a cohesive mold. Mary usually had the mount during the morning workouts, and the Cowboy could see her urging Sparky time and again to keep her mind on business. On mornings that Uncle Joe was at the rail, Mary would always speak encouraging words to him.

"She's moving forward." she'd say, or "Taking one step at a time. She's getting there." She said it though, with more hope in her voice than enthusiasm. Uncle Joe was not a horseman, but he too noticed that of all the two-year-olds under Mary's care, Sparky was the laggard.

Spring moved into summer. Every other Friday, the Cowboy would hitch a ride down to the bank and post office. He'd place the cash, without a note, in a plain envelope. He would stamp and seal and mail it. He never knew if it got to where he intended. He hoped it did, but he knew that it was the giving that was important. No amount of money would ever make up for what he had done, but by sending it, he felt just a little better about himself.

After Poncho came to work for Mary, he and the Cowboy found common interest on paydays. The Cowboy had held it a private matter, his sending the money, but Poncho soon noticed the mutual meetings at the post office after the paychecks had been disbursed.

"Sending money back to the family in Mexico," Poncho announced to Cowboy as they stood in line together. The Cowboy wasn't sure if Poncho was seeking out the destination of the Cowboy's money, or simply announcing his worthiness.

It was Poncho that eventually taught the Cowboy to purchase money orders instead of simply putting cash in an envelope.

It became a routine, Poncho and the Cowboy sitting in the back of someone's pickup on the way to or from town. They never said much to one another. They were not unfriendly, but there was no string of chatter, no reason to talk. Finally, one August afternoon on the way back to the racetrack, Poncho suggested, "Cowboy, what you need is a woman."

This statement surprised the Cowboy enough that he had to confirm what he thought he had heard. "What?"

"Not an all the time woman, just a woman for some love," Poncho said slyly. "A Mexican woman."

The Cowboy turned back to his silence, not thinking it worthwhile to even respond. The conversation did cause him to think though. He tried to remember the last time he had had sex. He could not remember the last time when he was sober, or when the woman had been sober. He did not want to remember the last time he wasn't sober. Alcohol had robbed him of half his brain cells, he thought, and all of his sex-drive.

That particular Friday night, the two-year-old that Mary had purchased for her Grandmother with Dromedary's earnings was racing for the first time. Two of the other youngsters had already started with moderate success. Sparky was still working towards her first race, but most of the stable's hopes were placed on Granny's young colt. John paraded him to the paddock; Mary saddled him. The track's best jockey had been persuaded to ride him, and the crowd, thinking they saw a winner made him the favorite. He won going away, giving a lift of excitement to all of Barn E.

The Cowboy had watched from the shadows of the backstretch. After the race he carried his straw bale into its place in the back corner of Sparky's stall. He gave his friend a pat on the rump, then crouched on the straw and started to shake. The horse had long ago gotten use to this strange behavior, and thought nothing of it.

Two Friday's later Mary entered Sparky to race. That afternoon, after the paychecks had been handed out, Poncho looked to see if The Cowboy planned to ride into town.

"Can't go today," He answered the inquiry. "Sparky runs tonight."

"Ah, Cowboy, you'll be back in plenty of time," Poncho responded.

"Might be. Too nervous to go," was the truthful reply.

"What about the person you send the money too, they'll miss it. You'll be too busy to go tomorrow, and once you get out of the habit, too easy to forget."

The Cowboy knew that Poncho was right. Perhaps one of the reasons the demons had stayed quiet for so long was the bi-monthly offerings he sent to his former mother-in-law.

"Wait," the Cowboy said, determined not to abandon his filly now. He signed the back of his check and got an envelope that he had already prepared with the scribbled name and address. "Buy me a stamp and a money order for a hundred bucks, please."

Poncho took the check and envelope. "You got time."

"Go on, I'll stay here, and thanks, gracias." The Cowboy waved the Mexican to the waiting truck.

Poncho started toward the vehicle but stopped. "Man, you ain't got no return address on this, suppose something happens to it?"

The Cowboy just looked at him. Poncho shrugged and climbed into the bed of the truck.

Uncle Joe came by the barn to see his horse before the race. The Cowboy overheard owner and trainer discussing the chances of victory.

"Don't know Uncle, we'll give it a shot," Mary said. "She's got all the tools, smooth stride, but something is missing. Maybe she just needs some competition to get her juices flowing."

Uncle Joe patted the horse's forehead and then scratched her under her long chin. It was obvious that the owner and the horse were affectionate with one another. The Cowboy liked Uncle Joe. The owner had always shown a quiet respect for him. Most owners simply ignored the hired help. While Uncle Joe had never said more than 'Good Morning,' he had a lilt in his manner and they shared hope for their mutual friend, Sparky

No need for Lasix on this first time starter, Sparky would go to her first call to the post drug free. The Cowboy would take her there, drug free. He smiled at the thought of it. It had been several months since his last drink. All those half-a-hundred other efforts to stay away from the booze, all the counseling and the crying and the bitterness and the will power, all had failed. The Cowboy knew that this period of abstinence would fail also. He knew that the demons would come back. He had gained a little confidence though, for he knew they wouldn't be back tonight, at least not until after his girl had raced.

Thoroughbreds love to run. They love to run, but not necessarily to race. It is our idea, not theirs, to run for some part of a mile or more and then declare a winner. Horses are social animals and most are content to run with the pack. It is the rare animal, the exception, which displays the grit to struggle to put their nose out in front at the finish line. No owner, no trainer, no groom knows for sure if a horse is that exception until the gates open on the first race.

Two-years-olds, as they prepare for that first race are all nervous. The saddling paddock is unfamiliar territory, so different then the accepted routine of their home barn. Nervousness spreads from one horse to another. The handlers are nervous; the jocks try not to be. Even the Cowboy, as he prepared Sparky for the race in front of the crowd was nervous. The betting public leaned over the wall separating them from the horses, and tried to analyze the chances of these unaccustomed racers. The Cowboy felt the need to take a leak, although he had done so only twenty minutes ago. He clung to his horse, she responded to him as the only familiar anchor in this vast unfamiliar kaleidoscope of color and noise and smell. Together, wordless, he led her through the saddling, the mount-up and the walk from the paddock to the track. When he let go of her lead and she entered back onto the main track, she pranced sideways but Carol, sitting atop her pony, was there to escort Sparky during the warm-up. The Cowboy had no time to wish his horse luck, no word of encouragement. They were gone, the jockey, the exercise rider, the escort pony, and the horse. They went trotting off in the post parade, and then warmed up on the far side of the track.

The Cowboy walked up to the nearest betting window. In all the time he had been working for Mary, he had not laid a bet. Tonight, for Sparky's first race, he had set aside six dollars to play two dollars across the board. There was a small line in front of the window. He stood there, rope and halter in his hand, ready for his friend's return. When it got to be his turn, the teller asked him what he wanted to bet.

He had practiced this, "Two dollars across the board, Win, Place and Show on Morning Thrill." The teller automatically punched the buttons, and a little ticket emerged at the window. The Cowboy handed over his six bucks. As he took the ticket, he realized this was a mistake. The horse did not care whether he bet on her or not. He was not supporting his animal. He took two steps away from the window, looked down at his ticket, and turned to an old lady that was waiting her turn in line.

"Here Lady," he said, handing the surprised patron his betting stub. "Hope this is a winner. I don't bet."

He walked down to the rail separating the fan apron from the dirt track, and waited out the few minutes to post time. He could barely see his horse beyond the inner circle of track. He stood there alone, amongst the crowd of Friday night race goers. Sparky was too far away to give him any comfort and he began to sense the demons. They started in his toes; crawling up the inside of his skin from his toes to his ankles. "Lord, not now," he begged. He moved his tongue over his lips and to the roof of his mouth. He could taste the dried saliva; taste the beads of sweat that dotted his upper lip. With both hands he grasped the top rung of the chain link fence. He felt the devil cockroaches ascending the insides of his legs between skin and muscle, and the centipedes stinging his flesh. If it were any other time, he would not have fought the call of the devils, but would have departed to find a drink. This, however, was his girl, her first date, and her prom. He had missed that once before with his own daughter. The Cowboy moaned aloud, and the nearby patrons looked at him and edged away.

The track loud speaker announced that it was "Now, Post Time." The horses had made their way to the rear of the starting gate and began to load, one by one. This is usually a difficult and anxious time, especially so with the young two-year-olds, but everything went smoothly enough, no major distractions or incidents.

The Cowboy loved that horse, but the agony he felt was not the agony that a mortal could endure. His eyes were shut. One hand clung to the railing, one to the rope and halter. He was about to break and run, to hide, to find his drink, when the gates sprung open, bells rang and the announcer hollered "They're off." Even that was not enough to completely still the vermin within his body, but as the announcer ticked off the horses and their positions, the name Morning Thrill called.

Sparky was mid-pack moving along the backstretch of the racetrack. This was a short race, just over a half-mile long, but the Cowboy could not see her well. He had no field glasses, and was nowhere near the television sets showing the race. All he could see were occasional glimpses of her chestnut coat, and the blue and white colors of the jockey's silks.

He cursed his demons, demanding that they leave him alone, for he was not about to abandon his horse to feed their need. As he said this, the horse on the lead entered the turn followed by three or four others. Sparky held her ground but could not gain on those ahead of her. The animals swung around the turn and headed down the home stretch. The Cowboy leaned over the rail and could see her racing towards the finish. She had moved toward the outside of the racetrack and had a clear shot but still could not make up any distance. The fans cheered for their choices as they thundered toward the finish. The Cowboy thought his horse was marvelous, although the spectators that had wagered upon her abilities crumpled their tickets and threw them to the ground in disappointment.

Sparky finished mid-pack, a non-threatening fifth. As the last horse crossed the finish line, The Cowboy hurried out onto the track to welcome his tired, sweaty girl and walk with her back to the barn to cool down. She had not won. She had shown not great talent, but not a lack of talent either. The Cowboy, though, was as proud as a father could be. He did not notice that the cockroaches and maggots and centipedes had receded. The jockey directed Sparky toward the Cowboy, jumped down and unbuckled the small saddle. He gave her a pat on the shoulder as he started to walk away, and said to her, "You'll do better next time."

The Cowboy put the normal halter on her, removing the racing bit and bridle. He wondered briefly why the jock would say what he did. Sparky had been splendid, why would she need to do better next time? He shrugged his shoulders and together, horse and partner walked back to their barn.

5
Disappointment

THROUGH THE REMAINDER OF the summer and fall and into early winter the running line was similar. Sparky was sent off to the races with much hope and high expectations, but she continued to place mid-pack. Mary tried different situations. She entered the horse in longer races, she put the hood blinders on her, she altered the training regimen but nothing seemed to improve the final results. Gradually the horse's time got better, but so did the competition's. Her best finish was a fourth; her worst was a seventh.

What made Sparky's tribulations worse in a way, was the success that Mary was having with all her other horses. The two-year-old she had purchased to replace the Camel was sleek and muscular, and had the look of a stakes winner. He had won easily the first time out. All the other horses in the barn were performing up to, if not beyond, their owners' expectations.

Mary was attracting new owners, and more horses. The feeling around the stable was upbeat, positive, and lighthearted. The one frustration was Sparky. Cowboy never lost faith in his charge, but also, never gained from the accomplishments of the other members of the stable. Every time Morning Thrill raced, he was pleased with her effort. Every time she needed a bath, he bathed and polished her coat. He was her groom, and she was his salvation. When she was close-by, the demons did not bother him. More than one night, he snuck back to the barn to sleep propped on a hay bale in her stall, so that the parasitic maggots would leave him be. Poncho and John were busy handling all the other horses, maintaining order. They left Sparky to the Cowboy.

He would cool off and would wash the other horses. He would muck out stalls. He would listen to the banter of the conversation around him, but he had only one attachment. He had his Sparky, and he had the routine of his trip to the post office every payday.

Mary sent him to the dentist to have his teeth worked on. She sat down once a week with him at the breakfast table in the canteen. While she still wondered about the man, she had come to appreciate his quietness. She never asked him personal questions and he never volunteered any information.

Mary's uncle used the same restraint whenever he and the Cowboy met. He was a kind and understanding owner and respectful of his niece but the Cowboy could see the hurt within him every time his horse failed to make progress. Together they shared Sparky. Both would talk with her when they were alone, but they did not speak much either to each other or to the animal when the three were present together. Owner and groom together hoped only for success for the horse. Success, however, seemed beyond her grasp.

What motivates a horse? Mary was frustrated that of all the horses in the barn, the one she could not figure out was her uncle's.

Mid-winter racing is a mostly spiritless exercise. Morning Thrill was slated for a mid-level maiden-claiming race in early January. Before the race Mary called the Cowboy aside.

"We've tried everything with this horse," she began. "I don't know; it probably won't make a difference, but I think I'll tell Poncho to be her handler in the paddock tonight. Maybe, somehow the change will make her run faster."

As she said this, Mary knew that she had made a grievous mistake. Mary had anticipated that the Cowboy would be disappointed, but she had not expected to see maggots crawl out of his eyes, centipedes from his mouth, or cockroaches from his ears. She had suggested the switch thinking that the horse needed variation, a different atmosphere. She was grasping at straws, hoping for a good showing in an insignificant race at a down-and-out track, but her words had stung the Cowboy, and there was no way she could un-sting.

"I'm sorry, Cowboy." She leaned forward, wanting to put a hand on his arm. "I'm sorry, but we've tried everything that I know of, maybe she's just too attached to you." She realized now, that if by some chance alternating handlers would make a difference to the horse, the winning of a race was not worth the ruining of a man. The Cowboy was lost. All the effort over the past nine months evaporated during that short conversation.

The Cowboy had a pitchfork in his hand. He leaned it against the barn, turned and walked away. He said nothing.

John and Poncho were working at the far end of the stable, out of hearing, but they noticed him walk away. They both could tell that he was through, that he was going to drink. He walked the way he had when he first he came to work at the barn, slouched and shuffling. He did not answer when they called to him.

Mary came down to where the two were standing.

"Where would he go to get a drink?" she asked.

"I doubt that he has any in his room, so probably over to the Quik Stop," John replied, nodding in the direction of the convenience store outside the gate.

"Poncho, you get Morning Thrill ready for tonight," Mary stated. "John, I might need you to act as trainer. Tell my uncle that I made a big mistake and I'm trying to fix it." After she said this, she walked hurriedly in the direction that the Cowboy had taken.

She arrived at the store just as the Cowboy was placing a bottle of the cheapest liquor on the counter. She grabbed it from him and said, "If we're going to drink, I got to have something better than this cheap crap."

He was taken completely by surprise; otherwise he would have resisted. She had the booze and he apparently wasn't going to get it back. She looked around the store, and then headed toward the wine and spirits department.

"Come on," she told the Cowboy. "They got to have something better than this." She walked back to the shelves; he followed.

After a quick examination, she replaced the rotgut and picked out two bottles of cheap California Chardonnay.

"Two bottles enough?" she asked. "Not much of a selection here, but at least this won't ruin my stomach."

Mary bent down and picked up a bottle of Riesling. "Hope this mates with the others, but I guess it doesn't make much difference."

"Ain't worried about my stomach," the Cowboy finally said.

Mary looked at him. "I ain't worried about your stomach either," she said. "I'm worried about mine."

She took the three bottles to the counter, paid for them and headed out the door. As an afterthought, she turned and motioned to the Cowboy, "Almost forgot, get two cups from the drink dispenser."

"I don't use a cup," he replied.

"Tonight you will," she countered.

After he had followed her instructions, she asked him as they exited the store, "Where do you go to drink?"

"Don't need to go anywhere," he said.

"Cowboy, it's the middle of January. We can't drink outside. We can't go back to the barn. Let's go to your room."

The Cowboy did not care where he drank. He did not want to drink out of a cup; he only wanted to satisfy the devils within himself. He did consider knocking her down to get to the alcohol, but he sensed that she was stronger than he was. He realized the easiest way to relieve his thirst was to play along and take her back to his room.

Mary had played this scene spontaneously. She had not given any fore thought to her actions, but now, carrying three bottles of inexpensive wine to the dormitory, she understood the great risk she was accepting. She was setting aside her responsibilities as a horse trainer, her obligation to her uncle, to his horse and to her stable, to preside at the inebriation of an old drunk. He was a quiet old drunk, so that if there was to be any conversation she would be the one talking. Thinking about it this way, she almost lost her nerve and handed the brown bag to the Cowboy who was following a few steps behind. She did turn, but as she did, she thought about the envelope that he mailed every other Friday. She thought of the slow progress he had made since last spring. She thought of his devotion toward two horses, Dromedary and Morning Thrill. She swore softly to herself and continued on toward the dorm.

As they neared the building, she slowed so that he could lead the way to his home. They had climbed the stairs to his second floor room, and he unlocked the door. The place was bare - sullen and bare. A bed with exposed springs was placed in the middle of the room; a single chair was the only other furniture. No wall hangings, no curtains on the dingy window, only two small piles of clothes, one clean, one dirty filled two corners of the abode. The bed was made, but the dust and grime and stench inherent in such quarters assaulted the nostrils. Perhaps it showed that there was some small possibility of his redemption that the Cowboy felt embarrassed to have a guest in his room.

"You wanted to see my room," the Cowboy said. After a pause he continued, "One habit stayed with me since childhood, my mother taught me to make my bed. You sit on the bed, I'll take the chair."

That was the most talk that Mary had ever heard the man say at a stretch. She smiled and wondered if perhaps he wasn't a talkative drunk after all. Gingerly she sat upon the bed, hoping that alcohol in the blood would deter lice and placed the bag with the three bottles on the floor at her feet. Pulling out a bottle of the Chardonnay first, she said, "Damn."

"I usually buy the stuff with the screw top," the Cowboy said, understanding her dilemma.

Mary reached for the slim pocketknife that she carried in her jeans. It was not one of those fancy gadgets with twelve different tools, so she had to dig out the cork with the knife blade.

"Better open all three now," she laughed. "Might not be able to finish the job when the time comes."

Cowboy smiled at her and held out two cups as she dug out the last pieces of cork from the bottle. "A sip first," he suggested.

Mary held the bottle and rationed the wine. The Cowboy thought that she was miserly in her portioning out the stuff, but in truth, he was glad for the company. The two began drinking with a silent toast. Mary began talking, and talked of many things. She talked of her life with horses, her dreams as a young girl. She spoke kindly of her grandmother, not so kindly of her parents. She talked of her uncle, and how, although not a rich man, he had followed her grandmother's suggestion and supported her with the purchase of a young racehorse. He was no longer married, had no children of his own, had always looked upon Mary as his special niece. He had fallen in love with Sparky, then a yearling filly of questionable lineage, at an auction sale a year ago last fall.

Mary talked; the Cowboy held out his cup waiting for her to get to a place in her talking where she would pause and refill their glasses.

The more that she drank, the angrier she got. She got angry with the owner of Miss Evangeline. She got angry with her old boy friends. She got angry with men in general.

The Cowboy listened to it all, drank his wine and held out his cup for more. At first the demons could not be satisfied so he drank his cupfuls quickly, but gradually they loosen their grip. He was still aware of the flow of Mary's conversation. Mary, though, unused to imbibing, was not. She began to babble, to feel sorry for herself, her lifestyle, her loneliness. Somewhere toward the middle of the third bottle she turned to the Cowboy.

"Do you wanna screw?"

Long-term abuse of alcohol demolishes the neurons of the brain. The Cowboy had lost many of his, but there must have been a few left, for this question of Mary's made him curious, a state of mind he was not used to. He wondered again how long it had been since he had been with a woman. He remembered rejecting Poncho's suggestion of a Mexican woman. Perhaps it had been a decade he conjectured since a woman had wanted him for more than fulfilling some bodily function. Longer than that, he was sure, since he'd had a woman while he was sober, or while she was sober. The current proposal would not change that track record.

He looked at his employer. She was not unattractive, although she never displayed her femininity. She was dressed in her customary winter outfit of jeans and flannel, with a down vest lying beside the bed. It had never occurred to him to consider her a sex object. He looked into her face, really for the first time. He smiled, his new dental work showing through.

Somewhere in his brain, via those few working neurons came a conclusion. He took the least damaged cork and stuck it back in the half empty bottle. "Sparky was in the seventh race, right?"

Mary was surprised by this question in return for her offer of sex, but she nodded in the affirmative.

"What time is it?" The Cowboy looked over to the alarm clock sitting on the floor by the bed. "Quarter to ten. Let's go see how she did."

"Don't you want to make love to me?" Mary asked both dismayed and relieved.

"Mary, I have a daughter somewhere, maybe only a few years younger than you. You don't want an old, smelly bastard like me."

6
A New Woman

THE EVENING THAT MARY and the Cowboy had drunk together, Morning Thrill had finished third, her best showing so far. It was enough to keep Uncle Joe from taking the horse out of training, but her earnings did little to pay her room and board tab. In her next start with the Cowboy back at her side in the paddock, she came in third again, and then a fourth. She was racing a notch better, but still not competitive enough to win.

At the beginning of March, Mary's uncle said it was time. The Cowboy noticed the two in conversation in Mary's office just off the main stable area of the barn. He could not hear the exchange but he could sense that Sparky would be going away. She would not be going home, this was home, she knew no other now, after a year in the same stall. She would be going away; maybe to become someone's pet, a trail horse or a show horse.

The Cowboy went up to the open office door and knocked on the jam. "Excuse me," he interrupted. "None of my business, but I have faith in that horse. Your niece did me a big favor last January, and your horse does me a favor every day. I don't have any money, and I don't make much, but if it helps to keep her here for a little while longer, I'll give up half my pay toward the expenses."

Uncle Joe and Mary looked at each other a minute, then he said, "Cowboy, you and I haven't talked much, but we know each other. We love that horse. I haven't figured out why we do, but I'm sorry, I can't accept your offer. We've done our best. Time to give up on her. Mary doesn't need my help; she's on the move. I'm sorry, but it's time."

The Cowboy had anticipated this response. "Two months. Give me, give her, two more months."

The three of them were silent for some time.

Finally, the Cowboy said, "I'm not begging. It's your horse, you can do what you want, but she just needs time to grow up. She's almost there."

"Cowboy," Uncle Joe said. "I never have had a family of my own. Mary has been as close to a daughter as I could get. But Sparky, well, in a strange way, she became my daughter. Every time she races and doesn't win it tears me up inside. Do you know what it feels like to lose?"

Cowboy glanced at Mary then returned his gaze to Uncle Joe. "Two months," he said, and walked out of the doorway and back to the horse's stall.

Mary said to her uncle after he had left, "No charge for two months."

Her uncle smiled resignedly. "Such a deal, how can I refuse? She has to win a race in two months."

Shortly thereafter, Mary's grandmother's horse, the horse that had replaced Dromedary, was entered in a minor stakes race at Keeneland in Kentucky. A minor stakes race at Keeneland is a major deal anywhere else and a tremendous milestone for a small backwater stable such as Mary's. The entire barn was excited, was both nervous and hopeful. Keeneland in April is where the stars of the sport race, where the Kentucky Derby horses sort themselves out in preliminary matches. To achieve success here means something.

Mary was already setting plans to move her base of operations to one of the larger mid-Atlantic area tracks. If the horse could do well in Kentucky, that would be one more ladder step, one more selling point to new owners. Everyone's attention was tuned to preparation of horse, trainer and staff for this opportunity. New two-years-olds were also arriving daily, full of promise. Little attention was paid to Morning Thrill. She was not forgotten exactly, but why dwell on the one animal that is the exception to the rule, the failure when all around her is success?

The stable hands were pressed into extra service. John and Poncho were riding high, directing new hires and supervising the grooming and handling of every horse. Other trainers came by to consult with Mary, to ask her opinion on all sorts of matters and to wish her well.

On the Thursday morning prior to the departure of horse, trainer and groom for Kentucky, the Cowboy was cooling out an animal just returned from his workout on the track. He walked, as he had walked a hundred other horses. Four turns around the barn, check to see if the horse had cooled down, then turn it over to the grooms to wash and return the horse back to its stall. The Cowboy was almost always silent in his walking. This morning was no exception. As he walked the rectangle he heard a vaguely familiar voice say, "Nobody ever told me you liked horses."

There was venom in the tone.

The Cowboy pulled up his charge and looked over to the outside railing. There, under the lip of the awning covering the walkway he saw a young woman. For a moment he was amazed and stunned.

"Lisa?" he said under his breath, seeing a vision of the woman he had married so long ago. It couldn't, of course, be Lisa, but it looked so like her, he thought.

"Granny died last November," the woman said, bitterness still in her voice, as if untouched by hearing herself called her mother's name.

The Cowboy heard and understood the tone of voice. Behind him, other horses and their handlers had begun to back up and were getting impatient.

"Walk with me, up to the end of the barn."

Together they walked toward the spot where John was waiting to take the horse for its bath and brush. The Cowboy walked on the inside, then the horse, then the porch railing and then Lauren. Neither said anything during the short trip; each was caught up in strange and unexpected thoughts.

John took the horse from the Cowboy without saying anything. He nodded toward the woman and excused himself to begin his work. The morning's last string of horses was coming from the track, just as this exchange was occurring. Carol, not noticing that the Cowboy had a visitor, hollered at him, "She's looking good this morning Cowboy. She had a fine workout, full of power."

The Cowboy turned to his daughter. "Would you mind walking with me round the barn a few times while I tend to the horse?"

Lauren hesitated.

"Horse won't bother you. She's a good horse," he said, giving his favorite a pat on her sweat stained chestnut shoulder. What he meant to add was, 'I won't bother you either.' But he didn't.

So together they began the slow walk around the rectangle of the barn, the horse striding between them. This time the daughter was on the inside of the railing. The barn was alive with the sights, sounds and especially the smells of the horses and their handlers. For the first stretch neither father nor daughter spoke. Finally, as they turned the corner at the opposite end of the walkway for the first time, Lauren repeated, with a little less anger, "Never knew you liked horses? And where did you get the name Cowboy?"

"Just a stupid name," he replied. "How did you find me?"

"Granny's dead. I was helping Mom go through Granny's stuff, and I found this pile of cash and money orders. It didn't make sense, the money I mean, in an unmarked envelope every two weeks. I decided not to show Mom until I could figure it out. All I had was a postmark. I dug around some more and found the note you sent her last summer.

"Couldn't find your name in the phone book for this area," she continued. "Had to trace you through your social security number. They wouldn't have given me that except that Mom had tried to get you for lack of child support years ago."

Lauren reached into the pocket of her windbreaker and pulled out an over-stuffed envelope. "Here," she tried to hand it underneath Sparky's chin to Cowboy.

He did not acknowledge her action except to say, "That was for you."

"I don't need your money!" Her anger returned full force. "Mom thinks you're dead. I never told her what I found out. Take this and don't send any more!" She tossed the envelope at her father. Sparky, sensing the friction in the air, and seeing the rapid motion so close to her chest, pulled up and whinnied. The Cowboy moved to calm his horse. When she had settled, he bent and picked up the packet.

"I needed to send it," he said, as he began walking forward again.

"Look, you old bastard," she spat. "We don't need your money, we don't need you. Keep your lousy dollars and leave us alone."

The horse again reacted instinctively and pulled away from the verbal conflict.

"Whoa, girl," the Cowboy made to calm her. "It's alright girl." He tried to keep the pain from showing in his voice.

"Lauren, I was the worst father in the world. Nothing I could ever do will make up for that. I hoped that this little bit of cash could someway help in your education."

Lauren laughed quietly, humorlessly. "My education was paid for by scholarships. I graduated from City College and have an MBA from Hofstra. I make more money in a year than you probably have all your life."

Together they walked around the far corner of the long barn and headed back toward their starting point. He was proud of her. He knew that he deserved all the disgust and bitterness directed against him, but he was unprepared for the words she said next.

"Listen to me carefully old man. Don't you ever try to contact Mom or me again." She turned and disappeared in the direction of the shed row parking lot.

The Cowboy was left holding the horse. The horse needed to be walked. He hesitated a moment to watch his daughter as she left then he resumed the slow stride of the hot walker.

7
The Wager

WORDLESSLY THE COWBOY FINISHED walking the horse. Wordlessly he sprayed her with water, brushed her, and groomed her. Wordlessly he delivered her to her clean stall. He filled her hay net and filled her water bowl. When he had done all this, he looked at his equine companion and said, "She was a good looker, wasn't she? Looked just like her Momma did."

Many times in his struggle with alcoholism he had wished himself dead. This morning was one such time. He bowed his head and closed his eyes as he stood before the horse. If despair and anguish were terminal, he would have died standing there.

"When you're done, Mary would like to see you." Carol had come down the aisle to stand beside the old man.

The Cowboy straightened up and looked at her. For over a year now they had worked together, never exchanging more than a nod or a short sentence. Carol knew how much Morning Thrill meant to the derelict, that the horse was probably the only thing keeping him from destruction.

"Carol, you ever thought about an education? Study to be a vet or something?" the Cowboy asked, turning to walk to the trainer's office.

"Nah, Cowboy, I'm happy were I'm at," she answered truthfully.

The Cowboy patted the stuffed envelope that stuck out of the back of his jeans. 'Can't give my money away,' he thought ruefully.

He stood in the doorway to the trainer's office. Pictures of horses in the winner's circle papered the walls. Mary leaned against the front edge of her cluttered desk. "Cowboy, I need you to ride with Granny's horse tonight when the van comes to pick him up. It's a big van, high class, not like the old horse trailers we're used to. You ride in the back and keep the horse company. You'll get into Lexington early in the morning. John and I will drive ahead in my truck so we can be there when you arrive."

"Don't know that you need me," the man responded. "Take Poncho or one of the new fellas."

Mary looked at him silently. She could see that he was still shaken by the argument she'd witnessed with the young woman.

"Would you rather John rode with the horse and you ride with me?" she asked.

"I don't mind being with the horse, just I'm not real keen on going," he answered.

She smiled, noting the inadvertent pun he had made. "Keeneland, name of the track in Lexington. You might not be keen on going, but you're going to Keeneland. Got any clean clothes? The van will be here at four. I've already talked with the driver, so he knows you're going."

"No smokers. I ain't having smoking in the van." The driver of the horse trailer was a big man, a determined man. "Don't know why we need passengers anyway. Horses travel fine at night. Sleep most of the way, and be ready to jog in the morning when we get there."

The driver turned to Mary, "Are you sure he don't smoke?"

"And no drinking either, partner," he said turning his gaze on the Cowboy. "Understand? You been to the toilet? Once we get rolling, I ain't stopping for probably five hours. Ashland, Kentucky. You got a problem with that?"

The Cowboy shook his head; he had no problem with that. His second pair of jeans, his clean shirt and clean underwear were in a brown paper bag in Mary's truck. Good thing he'd done laundry yesterday.

John and the Cowboy led Granny's horse onto the van ramp and into its appointed stall. There were three other horses already aboard, watching the new arrival.

"See, ain't nobody traveling with these other horses," the driver explained. "I ought to charge for the passenger. Maybe I should be a Greyhound bus driver." As he closed the ramp, he hollered back at the Cowboy who had remained by his animal, "No smoking!"

In the dim light that entered through the skylight of the van, the Cowboy pulled a hay bale along side the entrance to Granny's horse's stall and sat down. Outside he could hear Mary say to the driver, "Don't forget him when you stop." And then he heard her truck's engine start and roll away. Shortly thereafter the horse van got underway.

He looked up at the horse. After an hour or so, the motion of the trailer had become a sedative for all the horses. They slept standing, swaying to the pitch of the floor. For that hour, the Cowboy had done nothing but look at the horse. No thought had entered his mind. No dream, no remembrance, his mind was blank. The demons were quiet, as they had been since the night of drinking with his boss. Then, he spoke to the animal.

"Why do they call you Granny's horse? I mean you are Granny's horse, but her first horse was called Dummy. Least that's what everyone called him until I told them otherwise. Dromedary. The Camel. Nobody ever calls you anything except Granny's horse. I don't even know your name. You seem to be doing alright being called Granny's horse. Going to, what's the name of this place? Keeneland. In Kentucky. Stakes race. What's the track announcer goin' say? 'Here comes Granny's horse around the bend'?"

The horse did not respond. The Cowboy quit talking. For the next several hours, he sat on the hay bale, his mind blank. His mind was blank except for the image of his ex-wife that floated in front of his eyes from time to time. The image, like the horse, said nothing.

After a long time, the day gone and faded into night, the driver pulled the rig off the road and opened the side door. He poked his head in. "Hey, Buddy, you awake? Pee break."

The Cowboy smiled to think that this fellow knew his name, when everyone else seemed to have forgotten it.

"Come on, Buddy, let's get a burger at the lunch counter. This is one of my favorite truck stops."

The Cowboy had not eaten since early morning, and the burger and fries helped ease his hunger. The driver flirted with the waitress, whom he seemed to know. Toward the end of their dinner, the driver asked Cowboy, "You sure don't talk much, do ya' Bud?"

"Mister," the Cowboy answered with a question, "you got a daughter?"

"Yea, I do. What's it to ya?" he retorted.

"Nothin', 'sept mine is smarter than yours."

The Cowboy reached into his pocket for the twenty-dollar bill Mary had given him for meal money, but he tried the wrong pocket at first and felt the wad of money that his daughter had thrown at him. He had forgotten about it. He reached in his other pocket and pulled out the twenty. "Will this cover both yours and mine?" he wondered.

"Yea, a twenty should, not counting the pie I'm about to order. Maybe even with the pie."

"Good," the Cowboy said placing the cash on the table. "If there's any left over, leave it for your lady friend. I'll wait for you with the horses."

The Cowboy left the diner, climbed into the van with the beasts, sat himself upon the hay bale in front of Granny's horse and felt satisfied with himself. He was glad to know that indeed his daughter probably was a good deal smarter than the driver's daughter, probably a good deal smarter than many people's daughters. With a little smile on his face, he leaned back and fell asleep.

Early in the pre-dawn of the next morning the horse van arrived in Lexington. The Cowboy led Granny's horse down the ramp of the van. Mary and John were there to meet them, having arrived an hour before.

"Horse didn't say a thing all night, loved the ride. Your man there did nothing but snore," the driver explained to Mary.

"Will you be driving for the return trip on Sunday?" Mary asked, patting the animal.

"Unless the schedule changes, I'll be driving," he said.

Mary nodded, "Good, same arrangement then. You take my man in the back to watch the horse."

"Lady," the driver protested, "I ain't a cab service. I got a video camera in the cab. I can watch and hear all that goes on in the back. What if everybody that wanted to ship a horse had a man to go along?"

Mary simply looked at the burly fellow.

"All right, Lady. I got nearly a full load headed east on Sunday. Maybe the old guy can be sure that all the horses got water and hay."

Later that morning Granny's horse was taken for a slow gallop around the oval of the main racetrack at Keeneland. He was an easy traveler and had no problem adjusting to the well-maintained surface of the Lexington track. The horse seemed to sense that this was to his shot at the big time. After the work out he was returned to a stall in the receiving barn. Mary was out taking a nap in her truck. John sat in a chair on one side of the top half-open stall door; Cowboy sat in a similar chair on the other side.

John had given up his disgust for the Cowboy, but not his dislike. They were part of a team, however, a three person, one animal team. John was the ultimate team player, so he set aside his own feelings, and sat reading over a series of papers in his hands.

"Cowboy," John asked after a while, "you go to school?"

The Cowboy, pulled himself from his blank void, and answered, "You mean college?"

"Mary gave me these papers to study. She wants me to become her assistant trainer, but you got to pass a written test. I ain't no account on this book learnin'"

"Yea, I went to college. Long time ago."

John looked over at him. "What you study?"

The Cowboy pondered the question then replied, "I forgot everything. Only thing I remember was how to party. Seems like I learned that too well."

"Ever thought about trying again?" John asked, learning more about his companion this day, than he had in the last year.

"Hah, you mean trying school, again?"

"No, tryin' anything," John said. "Do you care about anything?"

The Cowboy was quiet.

John continued, "Mary treats you like family. All you care about is that damn Morning Thrill. Man, there are a whole string of other horses. I don't think that you even care if they win or lose. See that horse, sticking his head out between us? That's

Mary's ticket. That horse wins tomorrow, or even comes close, she's on her way. I don't care for you. Man, I don't give a shit about you, but you should want him to win for Mary."

The Cowboy sat there.

John continued after a pause. "The lady's got class. Listen, she could have had a big time rider, a name jock ride this horse tomorrow. Pat Day or Jerry Bailey or somebody like that. No, she brought Rollins from home. Who ever heard of Christie Rollins? Mary's taking her shot, but she's bringing all of us along for a shot of our own. We don't need you here. Mary was afraid you'd go out and get plastered and never come back. My feelin' was that ain't no big loss, but she cares about you. I can't see why, but she does."

"John," the Cowboy asked when he had finished. "You got any kids, a daughter?"

John was pretty sure his sermon had been wasted, but he was surprised by the question. "Two boys. Their mother moved out to California with them, long time ago. Why?"

The Cowboy was quiet again for a while then asked, "Granny's horse, how come nobody calls it by its real name? What's its name?"

"Smeltzer," John answered. "Stupid name."

"Where'd it get a name like that?"

"Came with it. Maybe that's why Mary could afford it. Nobody else wanted to buy it with a name like that. We were goin' call it Smelly, but you showed us not to call a horse Dummy."

The Cowboy fell silent again, and John went back to studying his trainer manual.

Presently Mary appeared looking a little refreshed. After a brief examination of the horse she turned to the two sentinels and said, "Come on fellas, this is Keeneland. Let's go over to the grandstand and watch the afternoon races."

It was Keeneland in early April. The dogwood trees and the redbuds where just beginning to show color. The grass was sparkling. The place reeked of money and status. The three watched the races from a side corner, not wishing to mingle with the patrons dressed in their finery.

As the afternoon wound down, Mary began thinking out loud, "Cowboy, I want you to lead Granny's horse into the paddock tomorrow. John and I will be waiting there, but we need to get you some new clothes. This is, after all, Keeneland, in Lexington, Kentucky. Granny and Uncle Joe and even my mother and father are coming in tonight. I'll have dinner with them, but before that let's go by that mall down the road and find you some decent trousers."

The Cowboy had gotten used to taking orders from her, so offered no protest except to say, "Hang on a minute, please, I need to see if I can make a bet on tomorrow's race."

John and Mary looked at each other in surprise for they had never known the Cowboy to gamble. He went up to the nearest mutual window.

"May I place a bet on tomorrow's race," he inquired of the clerk.

"You mean a race here at Keeneland?" she responded.

"Oh, yes, Smeltzer is the name of the horse."

"What number is the race? And what is the horse's number?" she asked.

"Fifth race I think. Don't know the horse's number, but his name is Smeltzer."

The clerk scanned the starter's list for Saturday's races, "Here he is. Fifth race, number 6. What do you want to bet?"

The Cowboy did not hesitate. "Does not have to win, just has to be close, John said."

The clerk looked a little perplexed. "Come in second then? You want to lay a place bet?"

"Right," said the Cowboy, pulling out the envelope that contained the wad of cash and money orders. He started counting it out on the shelf in front of the iron grating separating him from the clerk. He had been sending money every two weeks, every payday, for the past ten months. When he finished counting, excruciatingly slow for the clerk, he pushed $1,050 in cash towards her, retaining the money orders and fifty dollars in cash to pay for his new clothes.

"You want this all for a place bet on number 6 in the fifth race tomorrow?" She wanted to be sure he was aware of what he was doing.

"Smeltzer. All he's got to do is be close. Yea, all of it." He motioned at the pile of money.

She counted out the bills again, pushed some buttons on her auto tote keypad and out popped a ticket from a slot beneath the iron grate.

The Cowboy wasn't sure if he was supposed to grab the ticket or wait until she gave it to him.

"There it is," she said. "Read it to make sure that it's right and good luck."

The Cowboy picked up the ticket and smiled back and left to rejoin Mary and John.

An hour later, as Mary and the Cowboy were picking out slacks at the Belk's store she asked him, "I don't remember you betting before. Why'd you place a wager this time?"

The Cowboy thought deliberately and said, "Horses don't know, don't care whether you bet on them or not. Maybe people do."

Mary looked at him and raised her eyebrows in wonder then returned to her task of selecting an appropriate outfit for him to wear at the races the next day.

8
Racing at Keeneland

THE NEXT MORNING GRANNY'S horse was taken to the track to jog an easy couple of laps. Mary said it was to have him a little more familiar, more comfortable with the place. Mostly though the reason was to keep everyone active, rather than just sitting and waiting. While the horse was out on the track, the Cowboy walked by himself to the paddock to practice his afternoon tasks. When Smeltzer returned to the barn, and after the Cowboy had walked him around the shed a few turns, Mary and John looked over the day's program and newspaper reports.

The fifth race was a minor stakes race for three-year-old colts and geldings run at an even mile on the dirt with a purse of $200,000. It wasn't the draw of the day, merely support to the main feature of the afternoon, a graded stakes for older fillies and mares contested on the grass with total purse money of $500,000. This other race had attracted some of the best female horses from around the country and with them the best jockeys and the best trainers. The trainers had brought their second or third string runners to contest the fifth race.

According to the morning line program in which the track handicapper tries to judge the merits of the horses, Granny's horse, while no where near the favorite was given a chance at 8 to 1 in a field of ten. His past performances showed ability and improvement. But Mary was an unknown trainer, never seen in these parts before, and Christie Rollins, the jockey Mary had brought from home, was even more of an uncertainty. Mary could have chosen a name familiar with the crowd, one familiar with the racecourse, but she picked instead a jockey familiar with guiding her horse.

The afternoon of racing began and it was not long before the call for horses for the fifth race. Mary gave Smeltzer a pat on the ass and the Cowboy a smile and said, "I'll see you both in the paddock." She then motioned to John and they took the short cut to meet Granny and the rest of the family in the saddling enclosure. The Cowboy got in line behind the other horses. Neither he nor Smeltzer seemed impressed by the more than ten million dollars worth of horseflesh parading in front of them.

"Made me put on these damn new clothes," the Cowboy told the horse as they headed down the dirt track in front of the grandstand.

The horse did not reply, but looked around at the good-spirited crowd.

"Most people I ever seen at a horse race," The Cowboy commented again.

Again, the horse did not reply.

When he led Granny's horse to his appointed spot for saddling, Mary and Christie Rollins were standing there talking.

"Nervous as hell," Christie was saying. She looked nervous, dressed in the black and blue silks that were Granny's colors. "Not too late, maybe I should call off and you could get another jock."

"Don't be stupid," Mary replied.

"Look at 'em," Christie responded. "The best jocks in the country and who am I but some hick."

Mary replied strongly, "Look at the trainers, the best in the country, half of 'em already in the hall of fame. Don't you think I'm nervous? But listen. Only one isn't nervous is Granny's horse. He'll feel your nervousness though. He don't know anything about those trainers or those jockeys. All you got to do is let him run his race. Give him confidence and let him go."

The Cowboy didn't know anything about who was famous and who was not. He held the horse while John and Mary cinched the saddle and then walked him out of the ring and onto the track with Christie on his back. As he was unlatching the lead he told the horse, "Be close for Dromedary."

Mary and most of the rest of the family found seats in the owner's box, but her uncle came to watch the race from the rail, standing next to the Cowboy. As the horses warmed up, he glanced at the tote board indicating current odds. He said, "Not getting much respect from the crowd. Granny's horse looks like he'll be 16 or 17 to one by post time."

The Cowboy turned to look at him. "Hmm?"

Mary's uncle tried to explain, "No one else thinks he can win. A two dollar bet will bring you back more than thirty dollars if he does."

The Cowboy replied, "Don't need to win, just to be close."

Uncle Joe looked at him wonderingly, but the Cowboy's eyes had returned to the starting gate where the horses were beginning to line up.

Many horses considered long shots to win will try to steal a race by grabbing the lead and running out ahead of the pack then slowing down, hoping that the horses behind will be fooled into slowing down as well. Usually that tactic results in the speedster simply tiring itself out and finishing last, totally exhausted. It works just enough though, to make it a viable option for those animals without much chance anyway. Mary's instructions to Christie expressly forbade that strategy. Instead, Mary told her to place Granny's horse in mid pack, let the leaders tire and then look for an opening to bring the animal to the lead through the stretch. This is the kind of plan that works when you have the best horse and a clean or uninhibited circuit. Sometimes a horse will fall or slow in front and there is nowhere to run. Sometimes the track is heavier and slower either on the inside or perimeter. Sometimes luck plays as much of a role in success as skill.

Today, it was all skill. Smeltzer broke from the starting gate well and raced in fourth position for the first two thirds of the mile. The horses in front of him began to weaken and he moved outside and easily overtook the leaders as they headed down the stretch toward the finish line. But even as he was making his move he was shadowed by a second horse. Gradually the other, a beautiful gray with a flowing mane and flaring nostrils gained on Smeltzer until they were even with 200 yards to go. Gallantly Christie and her horse fought back the challenger, but with about 50 yards left, the gray moved in front to stay. The final margin was half a length, which is to say about 1/10 of a second. There was clear daylight back to the third place horse.

Uncle Joe had been bouncing up and down, cheering, begging, pleading his Mother's horse home. The Cowboy had been quiet, but at the end he had a smile. As the horses flashed by the finish line, he gathered up his lead and halter preparing to walk Granny's horse back to the barn. Before he entered the track, he turned to look at Uncle Joe, who was both dejected and elated at the same time. All Uncle Joe could say was "Wow."

The Cowboy reached into his new windbreaker pocket and handed Uncle Joe the betting ticket. "Not sure that I'll have time, would you cash this for me?"

Uncle Joe said, "Sure. You had him to place?"

"Only needed to be close. John said so."

As he walked out onto the dirt to collect his charge, Mary was waiting there too. They could hear Christie swearing to herself as she walked the sweaty combatant toward them.

"Mary, I'm sorry. Damn it. My fault," Christie was saying.

Mary responded, "It was a great race, Christie."

"No, Mary. We could have won. We should have won. I got nervous." Christie jumped down off the horse, removed the saddle and walked beside the trainer toward the track scales to be sure that all was in order. The Cowboy walked a short ways behind, leading the horse, listening to the conversation.

"There, at the top of the stretch," Christie continued, her goggles sitting on the top of her cap, making her dirt covered face look strange with two clean circles around her eyes. "I should have been steady. I asked Granny's horse too soon. I knew I had those in front of me anytime I wanted them. I knew Pat Day was right behind me just waiting for my move. If I'd waited, just waited another furlong, another sixteenth, even, we'd of had enough to hold off the gray. He tried, Lord that horse tried, but I screwed it up for him."

Mary said nothing, but put her hand on the shoulder of her jockey. Cowboy walked the horse by the celebration that was beginning in the winner's circle. As he got away from the crowd a little, he turned toward Smeltzer and said, "Looked damn good to me."

Granny's horse, sweaty, tired, but undaunted, lifted his head and neighed in agreement.

After the Cowboy had completed the slow walk to cool off the horse, and John had finished the bath and the grooming, and after Mary had carefully examined every bone and muscle to be sure that no damage or injury had occurred, the rest of the party showed up at the barn. It was a party. Everyone had gotten over the narrow loss, and had come to realize how successful they were. They were pleased to be associated with the horse, with the owner, and with the trainer.

Granny stood, dapper and elegant, resting her weight on her cane. She said little, however the pride in her granddaughter was evident. Mary's parents were there, smiling, feeling uneasy, but also feeling the success of the moment. Christie came up to rub Smeltzer's forehead. She was beginning to understand that maybe the loss wasn't all her fault, maybe the day was a way of gaining experience, and maybe she was part of the success.

John stood a little away from the crowd, but he had a look of pleasure on his face. He had been the first to see that Mary had the talent and the luck to succeed. He had been right when he said all Granny's horse had to do today was be close. Mary was pleased that her parents had come to the race. She knew, though, that this race was not an end, but a step, a necessary step. She would have to decide where to race this horse next. Should she lessen the opposition by seeking an easier target, or should she continue to test the horse and herself by setting high sights? Mary pondered this while she enjoyed the good will of her family.

Uncle Joe was there, too. He felt good for his mother and his niece. He felt good for his brother, to see him reunited with the family, with Mary. He also felt a little left out. His horse was back home, had not yet won a single race, and he was upset with the Cowboy.

The Cowboy had left the party and sought quieter company at the far end of the barn where he sat watching two kittens play with a strand of yarn. Uncle Joe walked down to join him.

"I don't understand," he said to the Cowboy. "I don't understand. You gave me a ticket to cash. I thought it would be for two dollars or something. I went to the window and cashed my own ticket, then gave the teller yours. She runs it through the machine, then tells me I got to go around the corner to get my money. I try to tell her it's not my money, but a friend. She says for me to go round the corner."

The Cowboy sat watching the kittens.

Uncle Joe continued with the story. "'Congratulations', they say when I go round the corner. 'Before we give you your cash, though, you got to fill out these forms for the IRS.' 'It's not my money,' I tell them, 'I was only cashing the ticket for a friend.' 'Well, where's your friend?' I say 'he's back at the barn hot walking a horse.' They say, 'what's his name?' I say, 'Cowboy.' 'Cowboy what?' they want to know. 'Never heard anything but Cowboy,' I say. 'Social Security number?' I say 'if I don't even no his name, how could I know his Social Security number?'

"How much is the pay out for anyway?' I ask. Seems like a lot of trouble for a place bet. 'Five Thousand nine hundred and sixty-eight dollars,' they say. 'Plus the original thousand and fifty bucks.' No wonder they didn't believe my story about some character named Cowboy."

Uncle Joe handed the Cowboy an envelope printed with the logo of Keeneland racetrack on it. "I had to put the damn thing on my income taxes. I had them with hold 28 %. Here's you money. Counting your bet money, there's $5,346 there."

The Cowboy looked up and accepted the envelope; the only thank you was in his body language.

"Only thing I can't figure out," Uncle Joe continued. "I can't figure out where the hell you'd get that kind of money to lay the bet in the first place."

The Cowboy looked at Uncle in that quiet way of his. "You don't have a daughter," he said.

"You know I don't," Uncle Joe replied. "What's that got to do with anything?"

The Cowboy thought for a moment. "Nothin', Everything."

9
The Cowboy Meets Polly

As scheduled, the horse van arrived the next morning. "Full load this time, twelve critters," the driver called out cheerily. "Your man goin' ride in the back?"

When Mary answered in the affirmative, the driver said, "Good, usually with this many horses I have an assistant along, just in case, but as this is Easter, we gave him the holiday. If our Buddy here could just keep an eye on the water and hay for all twelve, that would be a help."

The Cowboy answered the question with a question; "Easter?" then shrugged his shoulders, and climbed on board, positioning his hay bale directly in front Smeltzer's stall.

"We'll stop for lunch at the same truck stop," the driver yelled as he shut the van door. "You buying again?" He laughed as the ramp closed with a bang.

The Cowboy spent the morning quietly. He was glad to be out of the new clothes and into his old jeans and holey shirt. Once, when the two horses in the way back got into a nagging contest and splashed the water out of their buckets, he moved to fill them back up. Otherwise the day was quiet.

It must have been 1 p.m. when the van stopped and the side door opened.

"Lunch time!"

As the driver and the Cowboy walked to the restaurant door, the Cowboy asked, "Why do you work on Easter? Why aren't you home with your family?"

"Double time and a half, partner. Besides my ex has custody this holiday. We swap every other holiday."

They took seats opposite each other in a booth. Again the driver seemed to know the waitress, although it was a different lady this time. He called her Sugar and Angel put his arm playfully around her waist. She was either naturally friendly, or perhaps used her charm to entice larger tips. She called the driver by name, "Billy, who's your friend here?" she smiled at the Cowboy.

"This dude, Sugar? He rides in the back with the animals. He's buying my dinner, right guy?" Billy smiled at him. "He don't talk much, but I think they call him Cowboy."

"Welcome then, Cowboy," she said as she handed them the menus. "This ain't nothin' but an old truck stop, but the food's good and the toilets clean. Right, Billy?"

Billy retorted, "And the help is mouthy." He laughed at his own joke.

"Look these over and I'll be back shortly." With that the waitress was off to the next table to assist the diners.

Billy read the menu. "Man, look at this. Easter and they got lamb! You like lamb, partner? You don't often see lamb, especially along the road like this, that's why I love this place; all sorts of variety, that and the good lookin' ladies that will let you pinch their ass from time to time."

The Cowboy was looking for oatmeal on the menu, but the mention of lamb brought back memories of Easter dinner at home when he was a very young boy. He had thought that nearly all his memory cells had been demolished by the alcohol, but now he could see clearly that annual spring feast cooked by his mother and grandmother, complete down to the mint jelly.

"Does it come with mint jelly?" he asked Billy.

"Doesn't say anything about no mint jelly," he answered looking carefully at the handwritten paper clipped to the regular menu. "Wait! Yea, here it is. Mint jelly, I'll be damned."

When the waitress came back, they both ordered the lamb special complete with mint jelly, and iced tea. The Cowboy was glad that the driver did not order a beer. The demons had been quiet but they weren't dead.

When the woman brought the dinners she made friendly small talk. The Cowboy was more serious, and asked her, "Do you have a daughter?"

The waitress was a little surprised by the question, but more surprised by the tone in which it was asked. "I've a daughter, eleven and a son, eight."

"Easter Sunday, why aren't you home with them?" the Cowboy probed.

"Oh, I'd love to be Cowboy, I'd love to be."

Billy sat quietly watching and listening.

"Well, then?" the Cowboy continued, not letting that last comment suffice.

"Somebody's got to pay the bills, and they need me here today."

Billy broke in, knife and fork already at work on his lunch, "Hell, Angel, your old man probably pays enough in child support to take care of them kids."

The waitress straightened up, and her eyes glinted down at Billy, "That asshole left six years ago and I ain't seen two pennies from him since. He usually forgets to even send Christmas gifts to his kids."

She turned and left the table abruptly.

The Cowboy began eating his dinner slowly, thinking about long, long ago. Halfway through, the waitress came back to the table with a pitcher of tea. Billy smiled his best smile hoping for forgiveness, but did not say anything. Cowboy stretched his neck to try and read the nametag she was wearing, but none of the three said anything. The waitress did not return Billy's smile directly, but reflected it with one of her one toward the Cowboy.

During the feed, Billy occasionally tried to start a conversation with the Cowboy. The only time he succeeded was when he asked how the horse had done.

"Came close," the Cowboy responded.

"Close? As in close but no cigar?"

The Cowboy thought a minute. "Don't need no cigar."

Billy thought this a strange answer, but could think of nothing to say to it.

The Cowboy continued after a long pause. "Can't smoke, anyway."

Billy laughed. Billy liked to laugh. "Not in my van anyway, eh Ringo?"

When dinner was finished, Billy pushed back his plate. "Fella, that was good! Now what's for dessert?"

Cowboy had eaten more in this meal then he had in any one meal in years. There was no possible room for dessert.

The waitress came by to collect the dirty dishes. The Cowboy again tried to read her nametag.

"Dessert?" she asked. "We got deep dish apple pie, unbelievable."

"Mark me down, Babe," Billy said. "How about you, Slick?"

"Molly," the Cowboy began, "if I left you a large tip would you go home to your children?"

"Polly, not Molly," the waitress laughed pleasantly.

"Damn, Bud," Billy laughed. "You were trying to read her name tag. I thought you were staring at her tits."

Polly laughed at this minor vulgarity, and put her hand on the Cowboy's shoulder. "Cowboy, don't worry about my kids. They're spending the afternoon with my Mom. We got up this morning and went to sunrise service down along the river. My kids will be alright."

The Cowboy looked up at her, feeling her fingers through the thin, worn out flannel. "Cherish your children," he said.

She smiled at him, "Do you want some of the pie?"

He replied with a question, "You make it?"

Billy doubled over with a sudden burst of laughter. "Christ, Polly, you got this old dude believing you're a church goin', pie bakin', home-body!"

She turned with a flare of anger toward the driver. "Shut up Billy! I ain't much of a Christian, and I sure ain't much of a cook, but there's a whole side of me you ain't never seen."

Polly turned back to the Cowboy and said much more tenderly, "Mabel, the cook, bakes the pies. They are delicious."

The Cowboy got up out of his seat. "Tell who ever made the dinner that it was as good as my mother used to make. Give Billy an extra piece of pie for me."

He turned to Billy, "How much is this going to come to?"

"Stay right there," Polly said, "I'll do the bill while I get Billy's two pieces of pie."

The Cowboy, impatient to get back to his seat in the horse van, followed her up to the counter by the cash register. She wrote out the bill, and rang up the charge on the machine. The Cowboy ignored the pocket with the cash Mary had given him, instead reaching into the pocket with the Keeneland envelope. He brought out enough bills to cover both dinners and leave a substantial tip. When she made an offer to return his change, he just waved her away. She thanked him and wished him a safe trip home. On her way back to the table with the pie, she had to pass him. Cowboy was not agile, but he had managed to roll up five one hundred-dollar bills from his stash and as she went past, he reached and slipped them in the pouch of her apron.

She deposited the pie at the booth where Billy sat, then reached into her pocket to see exactly what the Cowboy had put there. When she counted it, she yelled to him. He was nearly out the door, but he stopped when he heard his name.

"Cowboy?" Polly walked towards him. "This is way too much. I can't take your money." She tried to hand the cash back to him.

"Polly, I was an asshole. Just like the man that left you. I can't do anything about what I was, ever. Go home and spend the rest of Easter with your daughter and your son."

The Cowboy walked out the door and let it swing shut behind him.

A few minutes later Billy opened the rear of the horse trailer and handed the Cowboy a warm take-out container and a fork. "Polly sends this to you. You'll be hungry by the time we get you home."

Billy exited, closed and latched the door. A minute later, he opened it again and stuck his head inside. "Buddy, where in Hell did you get that money?" Then he laughed and closed the door again.

The Cowboy shouted, "Billy, wait!"

Billy opened the door a third time.

The Cowboy asked after the door had been cracked, "You think she'll go home?"

"Nah."

Wordlessly the Cowboy asked why not.

All Billy said was "Duty." He closed the trailer up one final time, and soon the van was speeding down the highway.

10
The Cowboy Gets Mail

AFTER A COUPLE OF detours to unload some of the equine passengers, Billy drove into the lot beside Mary's barn as the last of the evening twilight was fading. Mary and John had not yet arrived, but Carol was there to greet Granny's horse and offer congratulations.

"Watched it on the simulcast," she told the Cowboy. "We were all rooting and cheering louder than if we'd been there."

The Cowboy stretched his stiff knees and his sore bones, glad to be finished traveling for a little while. Billy, anxious to be home, closed up the van and jumped back into the driver's seat. "Hey, Cowboy dude," he called from the cab. "Thanks for dinner, and you can ride with me anytime."

Carol turned to the Cowboy. "You bought him dinner? Never bought me dinner."

The Cowboy smiled at Carol. "How's Sparky?"

"She's fine. Go talk to her. I'll bed down Granny's horse."

The Cowboy walked down the aisle to Sparky's stall. She heard him coming and stuck her head out over the lower half of the Dutch door. He stood there, scratching her chin and telling her all about Keeneland through his fingers and his thoughts.

He stood there for some time, under the naked barn lights, dangling on their cords from the ceiling. Mary walked up to him as he stroked the horse. He had not noticed her arrival, or the conversation she and John had held with Carol.

"It's been a long day; a long weekend," she said. "Sparky's entered in for a race Wednesday. So we'll see if she really has improved. Go on back to your room and rest. I want to talk tomorrow about some important things."

The Cowboy shrugged his shoulders in the affirmative and gave Sparky a last pat before heading to his bed.

"Cowboy!" Mary called to him as he was about to leave the barn, "Cowboy, thanks."

Late Monday morning, after all the horses had been worked and groomed, the Cowboy sat on the ratty old chair in Mary's office. The walls were still covered with winner's circle pictures, but now only the most important of victories made it on display. Most of the other photos were piled into a folder, waiting to be sorted. The Camel's picture was still there though, on the wall behind Mary's desk.

"Cowboy, do you have a bank account?" Mary asked, beginning their conference. "Someplace safe to put your money?"

The Cowboy was silent, but as he did not shrug Mary believed that the answer was no.

"You know that money will get ripped-off. People know you got some cash and they'll look everywhere 'til they find it. After lunch I'll drive you into town and we'll get you set up with an account. Maybe you should use some of that money to get yourself an apartment or rent a trailer somewhere, away from that stinking dorm."

The Cowboy just sat there, unresponsive.

"Least knowing that you got some money, I don't feel so bad about docking your pay to cover part of Sparky's tab."

The Cowboy did respond to that statement. "You're not suppose to feel bad. That was a business deal."

"Oh yea, I know," she replied, "But I also know how little I pay you all in the first place."

The trainer changed the subject. "Cowboy, I want your opinion. You never say much, but John says you've been to college. After Saturday's race, two different buyers came asking if I wanted to sell Granny's horse. I wasn't worried about selling him, hadn't even thought about it. They offered large sums of money, so I thought about it real quick. I told them to give me a couple of days to make up my mind.

"I could take the money and search for a few more horses, buy some two-year-olds, buy some yearlings, or claim some good horses. Or we can hold on to the horse, and hope he does even better.

"But it's not that simple. See, I was planning to move us all down to the Maryland tracks or maybe Delaware. Better purses, better facilities. Sunday after you left, some of the people from Keeneland came by. Said they wanted me to move out to the Kentucky circuit, Churchill Downs, Turfway, and Keeneland. I told them I was thinking about moving my stable, but that I didn't have any clients in Kentucky. They said that there wouldn't be much trouble building up owners. They might be able to direct some clients my way, and that if I could get established I'd be a whole lot better off than what I am now.

"So what do you think? If I sell Granny's horse I'd have enough money to buy some young ones, but if I do sell him, then not much use to move to Kentuck', 'cause I wouldn't have a horse good enough to compete. Remember Miss Evangeline? Remember what a prick her owner was? Might have a lot of owners like him in Kentucky. The state might be full of pricks. The good owners already got trainers."

The Cowboy sat in the chair listening.

After a pause, she continued, "John wants me to sell. He says, 'Sell horses, hold on to humans.' Then he says to move to Kentucky. He says that if you want to be the best, you got to run with the best. Poncho says Granny's horse hasn't reached his full potential yet and we should wait 'til we win a big race then sell him. He wants to move to Maryland and gradually build up a high-class stable. What do you think?"

The Cowboy sat there thinking.

Mary wondered at herself. John knew so much about horses. Poncho had a touch and a feel for the creatures, but of all the staff, she wanted to hear the Cowboy's opinion the most. Why was she so attached to this man, old before his time?

The Cowboy finally spoke, "That's a picture of Dromedary behind you, there, isn't it?"

Mary turned to see, "Yea, so?"

"You sold him didn't you?" Mary, thinking she saw the connection, said, "Sort of, in a claiming race. That's a lot like being sold."

The Camel had been claimed and Mary had used the money to buy Smeltzer. "So you think I should sell the horse? And where do you want to move to, Kentucky or Maryland?"

"I should stay here," he answered.

This took her by surprise. She was not expecting this answer, for of all the people she knew, the Cowboy had the fewest reasons to stay.

"Why do you want to stay here?" she asked.

"She might not be able to find me if I was somewhere else."

Mary thought about the reply for some moments before the light of understanding dawned. "We'll send her a note telling her about your change of address."

The Cowboy shook his head. "No, she said never to contact her. Wouldn't know where to send it even if I could. Her grandmother's dead and that was the only address I had."

Mary thought of her horses and her staff as family. She could understand someone bettering themselves, or being fired for abuse of privileges, but of all of her help, why was she so attached to the Cowboy? She had once proposed sex to him! She had endured his silence. Now the thought of him staying here while she moved on was troublesome.

"You would just sit and wait here, in case she came back looking for you?" she pondered.

"Somebody always needs a hot walker."

"Cowboy, you're much more than a hot walker. We need you. Hell, I need you."

A second thought crossed Mary's mind, a second reason why the Cowboy wanted to stay. "You want to stay with Sparky don't you? You know she's not good enough to go to either Maryland or Kentucky?"

The Cowboy spoke very softly, "Even if she wins." It was not a question. It was a statement.

Mary had known little girls to love a particular animal this much. She had known grown-ups who would over look any fault in certain of their horses. She had known love and devotion but never between an old man like the Cowboy and a horse like Sparky. She could think of nothing to say.

So she said, "Let's go to the bank and deposit that money of yours."

On Wednesday afternoon, Sparky ran her best race yet. She finished third, only a nose away from second and a body length away from first. Uncle Joe was working and was not there. Afterwards Mary informed the Cowboy that the deal remained in effect. Sparky must win within the two months, and this meant she only had time one more race. The race was two and a half weeks away, on a Friday night, a contest for maiden three-year-old fillies.

Granny's horse was sold to a syndicate that paid an outrageous amount of money for him. Mary banked most of it, and also sold off a few of her less promising animals. She made several trips to Maryland in preparation for securing stable areas, to meet clients and to scope the competition.

Mary had offered to send a letter to the Cowboy's mother-in-law's address expecting it to be forwarded to his daughter. "You wouldn't be contacting her, I would," she argued. The Cowboy refused to give her the address.

The day of Sparky's definitive race finally came. It was the end of April, a wonderful spring day. It was early afternoon and everyone and everything was relaxing in the warmth. Carol came down the barn runway to find the Cowboy leaning against the outer railing, dozing in the sunshine. "Mary wants to see you," she said.

The Cowboy walked into the trainer's office.

"Got mail, Cowboy," she offered him a clean white business envelope.

The man's heart leapt. Maybe Lauren had had second thoughts. Maybe she wanted to see him, or know what he was doing. He was almost afraid to take the letter, afraid of the disappointment.

Mary, sensing the reluctance, turned the letter in her hand so that she could read the handwritten address to him. "Cowboy, In Care of Mary Engler, and then the address of the track. Post marked from Ashland, Kentucky."

The Cowboy's tentative joy faded. He didn't know where his daughter lived, but he felt sure it wasn't Ashland, Kentucky. He could not recall knowing anyone from Ashland, wasn't sure exactly where the place was, so the mystery was still there, but the hope was not.

Mary could see the disappointment in his face. "Take it and read it," she urged when he continued to hesitate.

He took the envelope and opened it. It was a handwritten letter, scratched in pen on stationary with the letterhead of D & S Truck Stop, Interstate 64, Exit 4, Ashland, KY. He moved some of the condition books and Daily Racing Forms from the sofa chair in the office and sat down to read it.

Cowboy,

I hope this note finds you. The next time Billy came through, I asked him about you, if he had an address or something. He said that he did not know your last name, but that he did remember who you worked for. So I hope you get this.

I was thinking about the money you gave me. At first I didn't want it. Maybe you were a drug dealer or something. I don't want to take any drug money. I asked Billy and he said, no, he didn't think you were a dealer, but one of those 'crazy bastards' he called them, got more money then they know what to do with, and pretend that they're poor and can't even afford new socks. Eccentrics I think they're called.

I was still uneasy about that tip. I mean, that is the biggest tip I ever got, except from one or two guys that wanted sex in the worst way. I gave it back to them, but you didn't seem like you were after sex, even if you were staring at my tits (laugh).

What I don't want is sympathy. Maybe you thought I was poor and my kids hungry like some African country. My kids and I are alright. I like my work (most days) and I get OK pay and good tips. I bet there are ten million single mothers, and I don't need any more sympathy than any of the others. All of them were married to assholes. It seems so was your wife. Least that's what you made it sound like.

So I didn't want sympathy money, and I didn't want drug money. But I had this money, what was I to do with it? We had been saving up for a computer for Emily and Buster to use. With your $500 bucks we had enough, so now all my kids do is play computer games and ride on the internet.

They say not to give out your e-mail address, but I trusted you enough to take your money so I guess, what's the worst you could do? Send me more money? Here's my address.

Oh, and one more thing. I do cherish my children.

Polly

The Cowboy read the letter twice. He turned to Mary, "Your computer, do you know how to send to this kind of address?" He handed Mary the letter.

She looked at it, glancing at the name at the bottom, "Oh, sure. You want to send Polly a reply?"

The Cowboy thought while Mary turned on her computer and cleared the clutter from the keyboard. She connected to the Internet and to her mail server. "See, I get and can send messages across the country, around the world. What do you want to say? Wait, let me type in the address first, there, O.K."

The Cowboy pondered, "Type in, *Billy's right. Eccentric. I'll send more money. You send more pie. Also socks. Cowboy.*"

As Mary typed she said, "That doesn't make any sense."

The Cowboy answered, "When you're done typing, read the letter."

When she was finished, the message sent, Mary quickly read through the rest of the letter then handed it back to the Cowboy with a smile.

11
No Extraordinary Measures

JUDGING FROM HER IMPROVING form and past performances, the Friday night crowd made Morning Thrill the favorite of the third race, a maiden-claiming event for three-year-old fillies going six and a half furlongs. The best jockey, Christie Rollins was riding. The hottest trainer, Mary Engler was saddling.

Granny watched the activity in the paddock from the railing above, while the Cowboy circled the horse prior to saddling. No one spoke a word. They had all been through this enough times to need no instruction. It was almost as if they were afraid to jinx the outcome if they spoke. Uncle Joe was there, looking nervous, as he always did.

"Riders Up" was called. Mary gave Christie a leg up and Cowboy led horse and rider down the runway, all without saying a word, not even a "good luck". Just before releasing the horse and rider to Carol, who was waiting at the track on the pony horse, the Cowboy made the unusual move of saying "Hold back!' as a signal to the horses behind to stop. He leaned into Sparky's neck and whispered in her ear. "You don't need to win, girl. I know you're the best." Then he let her go and she bounded out on the track. As she did, he gave her a slap on the rump, hand meeting hide perfectly, causing a loud whack that echoed along the track.

He gathered his lead and halter, and walked along the grandstand apron in the direction of the starting gate. On a short track like this, the six and a half-furlong position of the starting gate is just to the left of the grandstand. The horses leave the gate, pass the finish line in short order, and then make a full circuit to cross the line a second and final time. The Cowboy always liked to go down as far as he could toward the starting gate to watch and listen as the doors clanged open and the horses broke out. Uncle Joe liked to stand in the same spot. They missed the angle at the finish, but they both figured that if it was close, someone would tell them who had won.

As they both leaned against the railing watching the horses warm up, Uncle Joe asked, "You put a big bet down?"

The Cowboy smiled a little, "Horse doesn't care if you bet or not, horse doesn't know."

They leaned silently for a while, counting the minutes to post time. Uncle Joe turned to the Cowboy again, "Mary doesn't need me, doesn't need my horse anymore, Cowboy."

The Cowboy said, "I know."

From up on the trainer's stand Mary watched her uncle and her hot walker through her binoculars. 'Two men,' she thought, 'not so far apart in age, but with so little in common, except the love for that dumb horse.' She smiled to think of her own affection for the two of them.

All the barn staff had come to see this race. They all knew that this was the deadline. Sparky had to win. Poncho and John and all the newcomers stood away from Uncle Joe and the Cowboy. They were there to be in the winner's circle, in the celebration, but the pre-race pressure belonged to the two principals. Carol, out on her pony, trotting besides Morning Thrill, warming her up, could feel the tension. Christie, attached only in a remote way to the owner and groom, could also feel it. "What is this, some kind of stakes race? Nobody said anything in the paddock."

Carol leaned toward her as she let go the reins, "Ride her like it is a stakes race. It means a lot."

The call came to the post, "It's Now Post Time!" One by one the horses were walked or shoved into the proper gate position. Sparky had done this so many times by now, that she was no trouble. Uncle Joe, standing only a hundred yards down the track could see her, feel her. He had to pee. The Cowboy felt like he had to pee, too. All in line, "And They're Off!"

Sparky wasn't off! She stumbled badly stepping out of the gate. She had gotten her feet tangled at the instant the doors opened. She bobbled, her head falling to her knees, Christie nearly coming right over the top of the horse. The jock hung on and the horse straightened, but she had given up so much ground and so much momentum to the field, it seemed hopeless. Christie gathered her up, set her in rhythm and began chasing the stampede. Six and half furlongs is a short race, a sprint. To fall behind such an amount, going for such a short distance does indeed seem hopeless. You don't quit. You don't give up hope. Not the Cowboy, not Uncle Joe, not Christie, not Sparky, especially not Sparky, because what does a horse know about hope?

What does a horse know about winning? A horse knows about running. A horse loves to run. Sparky started running. She started running like she had never run before. Passing the finish line the for first time, she was badly last. By the first turn she had overtaken the next to last horse. By the time the race was half over, she was fifth and continuing to move up. Her motion was smooth; her stride was long. Across the infield of the track the Cowboy and Uncle Joe watched her dark chestnut body pass one horse after another, until, going into the far turn, there were but two ahead of her.

Neither owner nor groom spoke or whistled or cheered. Uncle Joe had his program tightly bound in his hand and he beat out a tattoo against the railing, every beat equaling a stride of his horse. The Cowboy stood beside him, fists clenched.

Round the turn the horses came. The number two horse got tired and fell back. Morning Thrill was right there astern of the leading horse, in position to run past, but the leader was not about to give way. The two spectators could keep silent no longer. Uncle Joe bellowed, "Com'on Girl," not realizing that both horses would think that equal encouragement. Christie was going to the whip as her mount pulled nearly even. Sparky was nearly out of gas. She had used up so much energy catching up with the others, now all that was left was determination.

"Not the whip! Don't use the whip!" the Cowboy began to yell. It was Christie's instinct to use the whip. It was the way to encourage the horse, get the last ounce of effort. Both animals were nearing exhaustion, the finish a half-furlong away. Christie couldn't hear Cowboy, but feeling that Sparky was giving her best, she tucked the whip under her armpit and used her hands and arm motions and her voice to urge her horse forward. Neck and neck, stride for stride the two horses raced past Uncle Joe and the Cowboy. Then, only yards from the finish, the other horse slowed. Sparky managed a few more lunges at full tilt and the race was hers.

As the Cowboy turned to Uncle Joe and Uncle Joe turned to the Cowboy, they saw it together. One out of the corner of his left eye, the other the corner of his right. The handshake stopped in mid air. They both started running to the entry gate. It was only a hitch, a momentary fault, but these are thousand pound creatures racing on toothpicks.

By the time the Cowboy and Uncle Joe had reached the track, the crowd saw it. A silence, a hush of horror and fear hung over the crowd. Christie was off the horse, trying to give her comfort. Sparky must have known something was wrong but she kept trying to walk forward. She couldn't put any weight on her right front. The Cowboy arrived to place himself as her leg, to support her. Uncle Joe was there to hold her reins and bit and so to immobilize her head. Mary, Poncho, John and Carol all were soon standing there to offer the filly whatever help they could.

The track veterinarian drove up in his station wagon. It seemed like hours; it seemed like seconds to the Cowboy as he stood there trying to support his horse. He could feel her leg dangling useless beside his two. He could sense her going into shock. He could see the vet, working over the leg, doing a quick examination. He saw him give her needles. He noticed when the horse ambulance arrived, the back door open into a ramp. He was aware that they had put an air cast on Sparky's leg. He felt the hands at his shoulder, indicating that he wasn't needed anymore, that they were going to try and walk the horse into the ambulance. He heard the vet ask Mary if she was the owner. He saw Mary point out Uncle Joe. He watched as Morning

Thrill hobbled up the ramp and they drove her away. He did not hear what the vet asked Uncle Joe but he did hear what was said in return, heaviness in his voice, "No extraordinary measures."

The Cowboy fell to his knees there at the spot where Sparky had been standing. Uncle Joe stood by him and placed a hand on his shoulder. The Cowboy looked up, "You could have used my money."

Uncle Joe answered, "I know. I thought of it, but it's not about money is it? Sometimes you use extraordinary measures for people, but not for horses. She didn't win because you and I wanted her too, she learned to race. She was backwards, you know. Most thoroughbreds are born to run and then get bored with it. This spring Sparky learned the pleasure of running. I'm sure she won that race for her own satisfaction, not for you or I or Mary."

The Cowboy got off his knees. Mary came and slipped between them putting her arms around both men. The Cowboy looked through his tears at Mary, and thought, 'Thank you for extraordinary measures.' He thought it but he didn't say it; he didn't need to.

LOKANTA

THE THREE OF US were quite amazed. We were sitting around a small table in a small café or lokanta, in a small village in west-central Turkey. The Englishman was amazed for he was sipping a delightful cup of English tea. The American, a fellow from the state of Georgia, was amazed by the crackers and biscuits he was served along with his Coca-Cola. I, also an American, was amazed to find myself in this little bistro with these two companions, drinking a delicious glass of lemonade.

Lemonade is, in my opinion, the finest of summer coolers; sweet and tart , cool and refreshing. The proprietor of this place, a middle aged man with the standard Turkish mustache and dark eyebrows, stood behind the counter serving the local walk-in customers. Each one greeted him with a laugh and he returned the laugh as he handed them their purchases. The eating section of the lokanta had no more than five tables. We sat at the first of the five, closest to the door and the counter. The other four tables were unoccupied. But as the hour was five o'clock, and many of the townspeople were winding up their daily errands, a steady stream of clientele stopped in for a sandwich or a wrapper of cooked meat.

This small lokanta had a little of everything it seemed. The finest item on the shelf or menu though, appeared to be the good-will that greeted everyone that entered.

The Englishman was in this region to study antiquity. The man from Georgia, a religious man, he called himself, was searching for evidence of early Christian Churches. I was here not to study antiquity or God, but to study people, for I call myself a writer, a writer of stories. None of my stories have ever been published, for I write for my own pleasure, and the pleasure of those I write about.

We were well away from the region of tourists, this town being far from the seaside. We had seen no other foreigners in our first three days at the small hotel located across the street of this cafe. I think the three of us shared a feeling that this was the old Turkey, as far from modern life as possible, thus our amazement at our finding such agreeable refreshments. We sat engaged in conversation, the religious man boasting of his accomplishments. I had placed my chair intentionally so that I had full view of the door and counter. As we sat, my attention was drawn to a mother and her two children. All three were neatly attired, a cut above the everyday dress of the normal customers. They entered the lokanta and greeted the owner as a friend. The mother ordered ice cream cones for her children. One child, a girl, appeared to be around nine, the other, the boy, looked to be five. Each was excited and pleased to be offered the treat.

While the children were choosing their flavors, and the proprietor scooping the ice cream, our religious friend was making the boast that American culture would soon dominate the world - and none too soon. He then made disparaging remarks about the Turkish population and of Muslims in general, saying how much better this part of the world would have been had the early Christian Church been able to maintain its presence.

"Friend," I said, "does not Christ say, 'Love One Another?' He does not say to love only those that think like you or look like you."

He replied, lifting up his glass, "Sir, I use this drink, Coke, as an example. It is found throughout the world, and created by a fellow from Atlanta, I would add. Why is it found everywhere? Marketing. If we could package the Christian message like we package Coke, we could convert everyone, from the Muslims in Turkey to the heathens in China, to follow Christ."

"To my taste," I countered, more interested in which flavor of ice cream the children had chosen, "lemonade is a finer drink than your cola, and as far as I know, it may have been invented by a Muslim or a heathen, much as the heathen in China perfected the tea our Englishman is drinking."

"Indeed, invented, not perfected. Modified and perfected by us English," said the Englishman.

As he was saying this, the ice cream transaction was completed. The children headed out the door with their tongues lapping the drips of cream. The mother, having paid for the treat, turned to follow her children, and as she did, she glanced towards us. She caught my eye, as I caught hers, and we exchanged brief smiles. Then she was gone.

The next day, I was alone in the lokanta. I sat at the same table and waited for my family. Why I considered them 'my' family, I cannot say. There had been only a glance and a smile to reach across cultures. I sat there sipping my lemonade, but the threesome did not come. The next day was the same. When the time for the ice cream had passed, I approached the owner and with my Turkish phrasebook in my hand, tried my best to inquire about the young family. The proprietor was good natured and I was determined, but the limitations of his English and the non-existence of my Turkish made it impossible for me to communicate with him.

The following day though, as I sat scribbling notes on a pad of paper, the mother and children entered the lokanta. By the time I realized they were there, the business that brought them into the place was almost complete. The children were not having ice cream this time, but rather the mother had stopped to pick up some kebabs for dinner. I rose from the table and approached the group with my phrase book in hand, although I had been practicing my lines. "Merhaba," I said, surprising the children. I looked at the woman. There was something in her appearance that made me stop. "What makes me think that you know English?" I asked.

"Oui, monsieur, I know a little English," she replied with more trace of a smile than an accent.

"Bonjour, Madame, I think you know much more English than I know either French or Turkish. Would you allow me the pleasure of buying your children ice cream?"

From the reaction of the children, they must already have learned some English, for they turned to their mother with a pleading look in their eyes.

She seemed to hesitate. "Monsieur, I do not wish to spoil my children, too much ice cream cannot be good for them."

"Nonsense, Madame. There is no such thing as too much ice cream. Let me spoil the children and they can practice their English, for you all shall join me at the table while they eat."

"Very well, Monsieur," she said, and the children were forced again to think which flavor they would like. After the youngsters had selected, I inquired of their mother which flavor she would like. "Oh, none for me Monsieur. For my children, but not for me."

I ordered myself a chocolate cone and an extra vanilla one for the lady,

The four of us sat around the table licking our ice cream. The mother at first refused her cone, but when she saw that I was going to let it melt and drip all over my hand, she took it with another smile. I was becoming quite enchanted with her smiles.

We made introductions around the table, the children telling me their names and ages. The mother, however, remained quiet except to ask what I was doing in such an out of the way town as this.

"Madame, that first afternoon you saw me with two other men. The Englishman wishes to cross a bridge to the past so that he may learn from it. The religious man wishes to cross a bridge to his God so that he may be closer to Him. I wish to cross a bridge to people, so that I may touch and be touched by them. I am a writer of stories."

Hearing this, and understanding the English completely, the oldest child said, "Tell us a story."

"Oh, little one, it would be a pleasure to tell you a story. And I shall, but remember I am a writer of stories, not a teller, so my telling may not be as pleasing as you might think."

"Do you have a very short story, Monsieur?" asked the mother. "We have need to be home for our aunt is waiting on us."

"I would tell you a quick story of fireflies, my friends," I said to the children, "but I have not seen those insects around here, so you may not know of them."

"We know them from home," the boy replied, quite happy to contribute to the conversation.

"Home? I thought this was home?" I asked confused.

"No, Monsieur, we are here on holiday with our Great Aunt. She often comes to this, the village of her ancestors, to escape the troubles of our homeland," the mother answered.

"And where is your home, that has both fireflies and trouble?" I wondered.

"We live close to the sea in Montenegro," the girl volunteered.

I then began my story. "There was a little girl whose father loved her so much that he would catch fireflies on a summer evening, borrow their fire and place it upon her forehead."

"Momma has told us this story," interrupted the boy excitedly.

I looked at the mother again completely surprised.

"Finish your ice cream children," she said, "we need to be going. Tell cousin Georgio 'Thank you', and tell Monsieur, 'Merci'."

"Cousin Georgio," I inquired as we all rose from the table. "He is your cousin?"

"Only as God is our father, so we are all related," she returned, with that confounding smile. "He had told me that you were asking of us yesterday." She could see that I was dumbfounded. "He knows more English than he lets on," she said as explanation.

"Madame, would you bring your family again tomorrow, and I shall read them a proper story. The story of the dog that bit-off a man's leg."

"Non, Monsieur, not tomorrow, maybe Thursday."

As the children had made their proper good byes to 'cousin' Georgio, they came and said to me, one at a time, "Merci, Monsieur."

I replied, "Multimesc si cu plecere. Ciao bambinos".

After the family had left, I thought to myself that this had been a special afternoon, and that I had exhausted just about all of my limited knowledge of French, Romanian, Italian and Turkish.

Perhaps it is some flaw in my character, but I often am haunted. A pretty girl's smile, an unexpected welcome, or an engaging comment will set my mind down strange and curving avenues. Through the days that I had to wait until Thursday, my thoughts traveled down such a street. The young mother's smile, the brilliance of the reflection of the light in her dark eyes, the correctness in the way she approached me, and her underlying sense of humor all worked to distract and unsettle me. I could not write, or read or even sit contentedly, for the thought of her invaded everything I tried to do.

A thousand times I went over what I would say to the family when we would finally meet again. I selected an old story, *Harry*

Pitts the Protector, a dog story, a true story that I had put into words a long time ago. I thought that the children would enjoy hearing of the dog that bit off a man's leg. And I wondered how I could reach across the gap, how I could travel the bridge to touch the mother. I did not even know her name. Why I should want to reach her, I cannot say, except that I hoped that I could affect her a half as strongly as she had affected me.

Thursday afternoon found me sitting in the lokanta watching villagers come and go. Many of the regular customers had gotten used to me, some exchanging a nod or wave. Cousin Georgio did not say much to me, but from the glances that we exchanged, he was both leery and curious about me. I sat at my regular table, a plate of cookies before me, along with a copy of my dog story.

Presently the family came in, led by the youngest child. He turned to me upon entering. I could tell that he was glad that I was there, but I also could tell that he was under restraint. His mother had silent control of his actions. After greeting the proprietor, they came to my table. "No treats today, Monsieur, but the children would like to hear your story," the mother said.

"Did the dog really bite off a man's leg?" wondered the girl.

"He surely did," I replied. "Madame, I would not offer without your permission but, as you see, I have this full plate of cookies that I could not possibly eat alone. Perhaps the children and yourself would help me to finish them while I read my tale?"

The lady had a slightly exasperated look upon her face, but before she could make further objections Cousin Georgio appeared with four glasses of cold milk. "Ah, Sophie's homemade cookies and milk, nothing better," he proclaimed as he set the glasses around the table.

So we all took our seats, each with a glass and a cookie. "Before I begin, children, I need to compliment your mother on the fine family that she has. You are the best-behaved, the most charming children that I have had the pleasure to meet in a long time. I believe that your parents should take much pride in you."

"Monsieur," the mother said, "you offer way too much flattery as you offer too many sweets."

I could tell from her smile that although she meant what she said, she also was glad that I had complimented her on her children.

I read them the story of Harry Pitts. It is a fun story with simple meanings and universal humor. The children enjoyed it, understanding nearly all the English. At the end they asked me if Harry really did bite the man's leg off in real life, and again I assured them he had.

"Very well, children," the mother said. "Tell Monsieur, merci for the cookies and milk and the story."

"Must you go already?" I asked, hoping to prolong our chat.

"Yes we need to finish packing, for we leave for our country tomorrow."

I realized that I would not see this threesome again. "Oh, I wish you would stay and have dinner with me." I knew this suggestion would be rejected, but I thought there was no harm in trying.

"Monsieur, we are already the talk of the village. You would not wish to bring further shame upon us."

I asked the oldest child, "What is your mother's name? I do not know what to call her." I think the girl would have remained quiet, as obviously her mother wished her too, but the boy, feeling a certain kinship with the plight of men, spoke, "Diana, Monsieur."

"Diana," I said, turning to face the woman directly, "I have no wish to bring shame upon you or your family. You all have touched me, and I thank you for that. And as we are all children of the same God, then we are all brothers and sisters." I pressed my forefinger to my lips, and then to hers.

"Children, tell your mother that she is as the shooting star that blazes but a moment in the night, its brilliance dimming all the other celestial bodies in comparison. Then it is gone, and the observer is left to wonder if the marvel that he saw was only in his imagination."

DRIVEN

Driven. Many of Wendell's colleagues were driven, but not Wendell. Washington, D.C. is full of intense men and women. He was not one of them. However, it would be improper to say Wendell was a slacker, unmotivated or unconcerned. It would be more accurate to call him accepting.

He worked as a junior staff member in the Congressional Office of Rep. Holcomb of North Carolina. Driven people gravitated to Congressional Offices. Wendell was unusual for his laid back nature and easygoing smile. He would not have secured a job there, would not have ever applied, if but for his father.

Wendell made it through University with moderately good grades by applying himself sufficiently enough, and by distancing himself from both the good-timers and the over studious. When job prospects did not immediately materialize after graduation, his father, through political connections, landed him a position with Congressman Holcomb. Wendell's father, a dentist, was not considered a man of moderation, but a fellow who stood by his convictions, and he had given a fairly large sum to the re-election campaign of the Congressman.

Make no mistake; Wendell was good at what he did. He wasn't, however, overtly enthusiastic about his work, while other junior staff members lived and breathed the stuff. He took no real pleasure in his proximity to the movers and shakers of this country. He was not awed by seeing in person the names in the news, nor did he feel self-important because of his access to the halls of power. Wendell was a rarity in Washington, D.C. He was a young person in his mid-twenties that was a nice guy.

When he first moved to D.C. he roomed in the district with a couple of other staffers from the Congressman's office. He got along fine with roommates and his workmates, but there was a gulf between them. He wasn't interested in Rugby for it seemed a silly way to break one's nose, and he didn't care for all night political debates with the television. After a few months he moved across the Potomac to live with a Great Aunt in Arlington.

Wendell's current assignment for the Congressman was compiling raw statistics in an attempt to influence the drafting of an arcane piece of legislation concerning hog exports. The task suited Wendell well. He had always liked bacon. He could also set his own hours and separate himself from the public pressures of the office. He took to coming in to the Congressional Office building very early in the day.

Wendell was not a loner. He enjoyed the company of others, but all his associates were so damn driven to task, so conscious of appearances, so taken with their own self-importance that he found himself isolated. He came to enjoy his Great Aunt and her stories of the old time capitol. He enjoyed their meals together. She enjoyed him also, and considered that if he had not moved into the old house with her, she would have been forced into a retirement community. She was worried about him, though. An old Aunt was no good for company, and Wendell never talked about any of his friends. He never brought a girl by, nor did he go out much. She was afraid that he was lonely.

Wendell wasn't lonely, well, perhaps slightly so, but aren't we all? Wendell found satisfaction within himself. He had been with women. He rejoiced in their company, as he rejoiced in listening to the banter in the cafeteria at work. He listened but rarely took part. Wendell was a nice guy and a quiet guy and his Aunt worried about him.

In appearance he was unremarkable. He had brown hair trimmed to the collar. He did not wear glasses, did not smoke. He did his own laundry although his Aunt volunteered to do it for him. His clothes were always clean, but always needed an extra lap of the iron. The others in the Congressman's office all used the dry cleaners, but Wendell never saw the need for that. The ties he wore had all been gifts. His teeth were good, but there were two that lay a little crooked. His eyes were hazel. His nose was average. His height was a little less than six feet. He was not the type of person that would catch one's eye in the Metro, except that it was clear viewing him, that he was a nice guy.

Ethel was cursed. Ethel's best friend was Charlene. Charlene was a knockout, a whistle stopper. Charlene was tall and blonde and stacked and knew it. In the crowded Metro, Charlene would be noticed two stations away. Ethel's plainness was made more evident by her position next to Charlene.

Ethel's eyes were set a little too close together, giving her a cross-eyed appearance. She tried wearing glasses and contacts. Either seemed to help her vision, neither helped her looks. Her nose was thin and pinched. Her dark hair was dull. She was altogether too slim. She was cursed with an old lady name, who names their child Ethel in these days?

Every weekday morning at 6:40, before the real commuter rush began, Ethel and Charlene boarded the Metro blue line bound for the heart of the Nation's capitol. All the men and not a few women turned to watch Charlene. The regulars had come to expect her; they looked forward to her. Those that were close enough often said "Good Morning," or "Hello," or nodded a friendly greeting. Charlene always responded in a likewise friendly manner but she never encouraged further conversation. Charlene liked to sit and talk with Ethel. Side by side they would ride the swaying underground to Federal Station, talking of the mundane. They were best friends. Their paths did not often cross in the evenings, so it was the morning that was theirs.

The men, the regulars, in their business suits and with their briefcases would sit and speculate about the two, Charlene, dapper and charming, full of youth and vivacity; Ethel, drab. The men would wonder why a lady like Charlene would attach herself to a lady like Ethel. They would wonder and they would say "Good Morning," but mostly they would leave the two friends alone. Occasionally a young man would try to gain Charlene's favor by speaking with Ethel. Ethel enjoyed this, but she did not fool herself. She understood that Charlene was the magnet.

Wendell normally rode the 6:55 train into the Capitol Hill station. That put him into the office before most of the others, and let him start on his pig project in the quiet. One morning he was a little early and as he strolled out onto the loading platform for the 6:40, he was surprised how many fewer people there were. On his normal train he often had to stand, as passengers embarking at the earlier stations took all the seats. He did not mind the jostling of the crowd, but still it would be nice to have a seat each morning. So it was that he considered altering his schedule to take this unit every day.

Then he saw Charlene and Ethel. They stood several yards ahead of him waiting on the track apron. They did not notice him. The train came. He got in one car, they into the one ahead of him. He did not see them leave the train, although he tried to see which stop they got off. He definitely resolved to take the 6:40 again tomorrow.

The next day as he walked the platform waiting, it occurred to him that perhaps these ladies where not regular riders. Perhaps they normally took the Metro at a different time or from a different stop. He wondered why he cared. Then he noticed the pair stepping down the long escalator into the underground. He wondered again why he cared.

Charlene was not his type. She was a trophy, and he was not concerned with trophies. It would take a proud man, a driven, ambitious man to display such a beauty on his arm, to escort her around the mall, down to the Lincoln Memorial and out amongst the cherry blossoms. Wendell was not a proud man. He wondered why he had altered his schedule to catch the 6:40.

Charlene and Ethel greeted many of the others that had assembled awaiting the train. Wendell noticed their smiles as they did so. Too often in big cities, no one smiles, he thought. It was comforting to see these ladies smile. Charlene reminded him of a girl from High School. He did not remember her name, only her nickname, Sparkle, after the toothpaste. When Charlene smiled Wendell could almost see the gleam, the sparkles reflect off her teeth.

The train came. They all hopped aboard, this time same car, different opening. He was too far away to observe them in detail as they sat, and although a few seats were open close to them, he chose to sit a distance away. He did notice at what station they left the train, and he did notice that upon leaving the train, they went opposite directions.

On the third morning he exchanged "Hellos" and sat close enough so that he could see the backs of their heads as they rode into the city together. After the twosome had departed, the matronly woman sitting across the aisle from Wendell caught him off guard by saying, "It's impolite to stare."

Wendell turned to look at her. He understood that it was not said with mean intent for she was smiling now at his surprised look. He returned the smile and turned back to his inner reflections. The lady came to the conclusion from the returned smile that Wendell was a nice young man. She wouldn't have spoken to him if she hadn't thought so to begin with.

The fourth morning was Saturday. Wendell did go into the office for a few hours to wrap up his pork report. He would present it to the Chief of Staff on Monday. He did not mind working on Saturday; he did not have anything better to do. After work he walked through the sculpture gardens at the National Art Museum. Alone.

On Sunday he and his Aunt wandered through Old Towne Alexandria. They had a good time, the lady in her seventies, the man in his twenties. He was kind and patient with her. She was appreciative of him.

Monday morning Wendell said his "Hello", and sat a distance away from the two young ladies. His friend, Mrs. Thompson we shall call her, purposely sat across the aisle from him. After Ethel and Charlene had left the train, Mrs. Thompson turned to Wendell and asked, "Why don't you say something to her? Why don't you sit closer?"

Wendell replied, "I don't even know them. Don't know anything about them."

Mrs. Thompson clucked, as only matronly ladies can cluck, "Don't you want to find out?"

Wendell looked at her and smiled, ending the conversation for the morning.

His pig project was well accepted by the Chief of Staff. Later that afternoon, he sat in the office as the Congressman himself, listened to the Chief of Staff give the details and the game plan. After five minutes Congressman Holcomb interrupted and said, "Sounds good. We got the facts to back it up?"

The Chief of Staff did not hesitate. "Yes, Sir, Wendell here has done well."

"O.K.," directed the Congressman. "Take it over to the Ag. Sub-Committee staff for a look see. Hold off sending any more press releases until we see how it plays at the Committee level."

On Tuesday, Wendell was headed toward an isolated seat in the Metro. Charlene and Ethel were sitting by the door, as usual. They had accepted Wendell as one of the regulars, and paid him no more nor less attention than any of the other regulars. Mrs. Thompson caught Wendell's eye as he was preparing to sit. She motioned for him to come and join her. He wondered why. He also wondered why she was sitting almost directly across from Charlene and Ethel instead of in her usual seat, but he was a southerner and an obedient young man, so he came and sat next to Mrs. Thompson.

"I understand that you made a report to the Congressman yesterday," Mrs. Thompson started. "And it went very well."

"Yes, Ma'am. I suppose it went well, but it was no big deal," Wendell replied.

"Maybe no big deal to you, but some people might be impressed," Mrs. Thompson commented.

Wendell wanted very much to ask Mrs. Thompson who she was, and how she knew so much about him, but that would have been impolite. It was also impolite to stare at Charlene and Ethel, with them being so close and nearly facing him. It was easier to examine the backs of their heads from a distance. Wendell was not sure that he liked sitting so close. He and Mrs. Thompson fell silent as the Metro rushed under the Potomac separating Virginia from the District.

After the Federal Station stop and the two young ladies had departed, Mrs. Thompson turned again toward Wendell and asked, "What do you think?"

"About what?" Wendell asked in return.

"About your lady friends," Mrs. Thompson explained.

"How did you know that I worked for a Congressman and presented a report yesterday?"

Mrs. Thompson patted him on the arm. "Wendell, if you want me to butt out and not interfere, I will ride a different coach."

"No," Wendell said thoughtfully. "Your company makes the commute go faster. Do you know their names?"

"I thought that I was doing well just finding out your name."

The young man smiled that engaging smile of his. "How did you know?"

The older woman wondered if she should keep her secret, but then said, "I work on the floor below you. I followed you yesterday into Rep. Holcomb's suite. I know his Chief of Staff."

The train pulled into the Capitol Hill station. As the two of them got up to leave, Mrs. Thompson mentioned to Wendell, "I hope that you don't mind."

"No, Ma'am, just was a little spooky was all."

When the Chief of Staff came into the office later that morning he found e-mail from Wendell inquiring about the name of the lady who had asked about him yesterday.

Wednesday morning was rainy. Ethel looked damp; Charlene looked chic in her rain gear. Wendell had an out of date trench coat and Mrs. Thompson was sensibly attired with a raincoat and umbrella. Wendell nodded greetings to the two younger ladies, and welcomed Mrs. Thompson by name to a chair directly across from Ethel.

"Wendell, I see you have been doing your research," she said responding to her name.

Wendell was beginning to like her very much. She was a dapper lady barely turning gray. He guessed that she was about his mother's age, not old but experienced. They rode quietly that day, listening to Ethel and Charlene.

Ethel was beginning to notice Wendell, to single him out from the other regular riders. He never said much, never tried to make a move on Charlene. Ethel also noticed that he seemed to smile as much at her as he did at her sexy companion. Wendell, especially when accompanied by Mrs. Thompson, gave the impression of being safe.

Thursday morning the Capitol was abuzz with the latest broo haa haa between President and Congress. Wendell was only mildly interested. Ethel and Charlene talked about the color eye shadow of a mutual acquaintance. Mrs. Thompson, ignoring all the side conversations, asked Wendell of the progress of the report in front of the Agriculture Sub-committee.

"I was asked to tighten up some of the statistics," he answered, "but generally it is the same figures that I presented to the Congressman. I am sort of looking forward to my next assignment."

"Which will be?" Mrs. Thompson inquired.

"Don't know," was the truthful reply. "Others in the office are better at the political stuff. I'll just have to see what comes along."

After Ethel and Charlene got off the train, Mrs. Thompson changed her tone. "Are you ever going to say anything to those women?"

Wendell simply looked at her with his winning smile.

Friday Wendell came prepared. He handed Ethel and Charlene and Mrs. Thompson each a red carnation in a green plastic bud vase. Charlene and Ethel said thank you for theirs. Mrs. Thompson asked, "Wendell, what is this for?"

"Friendship," he said loud enough for all three to hear. And that was all he said that entire trip.

Ethel held her flower in her lap. She was beginning to think that Wendell was the nicest man she had ever known. On her way out the door she turned to him and said, "Thank you for the thought. Have a wonderful weekend." Charlene used the Sparkle smile on him. Mrs. Thompson and Wendell had developed the habit of traveling together as far as their separate stops on the Rayburn Building elevator. Without saying a word, they walked and rode together. As she left the elevator one floor before Wendell, she turned and gave him the thumbs-up sign.

On Monday morning Wendell was delayed at home and missed the 6:40. In its absence, he realized that the twenty-minute travel time was the highlight of his day.

The Tuesday morning traffic on the Metro was much heavier than normal. Most of the seats were taken and Charlene and Ethel were forced to sit across the aisle form each other and next to strangers. Mrs. Thompson found a seat further up the car and Wendell stood half way between them, hanging onto the grab bar. As was normal a third of the passengers got off at the stop with Charlene and Ethel. In the press of people, some staying, some going, Ethel managed to reach Wendell.

"Here," she said, handing him a brown paper bag. "They were fresh yesterday, but I didn't see you. They are probably not any good, but try them."

Wendell took hold of the bag, a few grease stains had soaked through to the outside. He opened it quickly and saw at least a dozen cookies. By the time he had recovered Ethel was nearly out the door. "Thank you," he shouted and she was gone.

He and Mrs. Thompson found each other to walk together to their offices. Wendell offered her a cookie. She accepted.

"Wendell," she said as she munched. "You don't need me anymore."

"She seems to be a pretty good cook. Now all I have to do is figure out her name," he suggested, spilling a few crumbs as he spoke.

"Ask her," Mrs. Thompson advised.

On Wednesday morning Mrs. Thompson was not there. Wendell sat in the row across from Ethel and Charlene. Ethel was on the outside, Charlene next to the window.

Wendell started the conversation, "Thanks for the cookies."

"I bet they were stale. I carried them around all day Monday," Ethel responded, looking at him.

"No, they were great. I saved a couple to have with my lunch today," Wendell said.

Then he was quiet. Ethel was quiet. Charlene looked out the window. Wendell missed Mrs. Thompson.

After too long a pause, he volunteered, "My name is Wendell."

Charlene began before Ethel could speak, "Yes, we know."

It was her way of preventing the passengers from getting to close to her. It was not said in an unfriendly way, but it made Wendell understand that the two ladies did not wish to become intimate with him.

Ethel looked at him and saw the disappointment in his face. She said softly, "My name is Ethel," then thinking it was Charlene's name that he really wanted to know, added, "and this is Charlene."

He thanked her with his smile. It was a good thing that he smiled a lot. People would have thought him very dull, otherwise.

Thursday morning Mrs. Thompson rejoined the group. Wendell greeted her with a good morning. "I missed you yesterday. May I introduce you to Ethel and Charlene? Ladies, this is Mrs. Thompson."

"I see Wendell that you made progress while I was gone," she replied, shaking hands with the younger women. "Congressional recess begins this afternoon. I'll be gone all next week, back in the home district. No telling what you'll know by then, my friend."

Wendell was slightly embarrassed.

On Friday Mrs. Thompson was absent again.

"Wendell, your friend Mrs. Thompson seems to be a very nice person," Ethel said. Charlene looked out the window at the curved walls of the underground tube.

"Yes," he responded. "She and I work in the same building. I gave her one of your cookies the other day." That was all Wendell knew of Mrs. Thompson.

"Would you like me to bake more?" Ethel asked.

Charlene gave her a sideways look.

Wendell noticed the look. "Pride of Iowa," he said. "Pride of Iowa cookies, ever have those?"

Ethel shook her head. Charlene did not respond at all.

"I'll make a batch myself and bring some in on Monday," he volunteered.

Ethel looked amazed. "You cook?"

"Not very well, but I can bake Pride of Iowa cookies. I'll show you on Monday."

Monday Wendell commuted alone. Mrs. Thompson was back in her Congressman's home district. Charlene and Ethel did not show. The Tupperware of cookies lay on his lap, during the commute.

On Tuesday when his friends were missing from the platform for the 6:40, he waited for the 6:55 train and then the 7:05 but there was still no sign of the women. Tuesday at lunch he passed around the cookies to the office mates. That afternoon, the Chief of Staff, arrived back in Washington a few days early and sent for Wendell.

"Congressman Brenner of Nebraska, head of the Ag. Sub-Committee wants to go over your hog export report."

Wendell was sitting in the cramped office along with a young, black woman. He listened as his boss set out the situation.

"Carol, you take Wendell over to see Paige, head liaison for the Ag. boys. Set out the report, answer their questions, wouldn't be surprised if Brenner himself didn't stop in. I hear he's back early from recess, too."

Wendell looked over to Carol. Carol was driven. She was on the fast track, the elevator. She was no more than a year older than Wendell, but she had mastered the talk and the walk. There must be something to this hog stuff, Wendell thought, if Carol's been assigned to it.

"Wendell, you let Carol do the presentation. You answer any questions. You seem to know this hog bull pretty good, and it is important to the Congressman. Two-thirty this afternoon, at the Capitol, HR 110."

"Do you know how many hogs are in Nebraska?" Congressman Brenner asked Wendell.

"It says right there on page six, sir," Wendell replied, beginning to find the page with the appropriate statistics.

"There's a whole shit pile, pardon my French," Brenner said, not needing the actual number. "If we can get another nickel a pound for our pork, if we can pry open those markets over in Asia. You know how many pounds of hog bellies, you know how much money that is?"

Wendell rightly guessed that this was another rhetorical question.

Congressman Brenner looked a little like hog jowls himself. Old as the Nebraska sand hills that he called home, overweight and callused, he was the consummate politician, and he knew how many votes an extra nickel a pound for bacon would bring.

"Paige here has already been in contact with Commerce," the Congressman continued. "We can't do anything without the Administration. Department of Agriculture folks are all for it, but we need to deal gently with the foreign desk at Commerce. Holcomb says he has full confidence in you two. Do you want Paige to go over with you?"

"Only if you feel she needs to be there, Congressman," Carol diplomatically replied.

Brenner looked across the table at Carol and then at Wendell. He was afraid of their youth, but he also could sense that this young, black lady was sharp. He sat stroking his chin a moment, letting his political instincts decide. "Go for it," he said.

Paige knew her key, "10:30 tomorrow morning, room 5114, fifth floor, Department of Commerce, meet with aides to the Undersecretary for Southeast Asia, Clammerty and Dubois. Perhaps the Undersecretary will be there herself." As Paige was saying this she was also writing it on a note card. "Good luck," she said, handing Carol the note. "Call me with a briefing tomorrow afternoon."

Wendell was lonely on the metro ride in to work. After a quick go over the presentation with Carol for the umpteenth time, he sat at his little desk in his little cubicle waiting until it was time to leave for the appointment. He had not felt this lonely in Washington before. He wondered why he should feel lonely now.

Carol hollered at him from across the room, and together they walked to the Metro. He liked Carol, everyone did. She was bright, articulate, with an easy laugh, and she knew the rules of the game. Carol liked Wendell, everyone did. He was steady, not bright, quiet, not articulate, with an easy smile, but no laugh and he did not seem to care about the rules of the game. They made a good team, he carried the briefcase with copies of the report; she carried the responsibility of making a serious presentation on a subject she could care less about.

It was only a few stops on the Metro to Federal Station and the Department of Commerce. Carol and Wendell chatted the entire way. One had to chat with Carol, she insisted upon it. From the underground to the street to the Department of Commerce took only a few minutes walk. It was a sunny Washington day, the kind of day one would wish to sneak off to Rock Creek Park or to the zoo, but Carol and Wendell had business to attend to.

They paused a moment after exiting the elevator on the fifth floor. "Room 5114," Carol said reading her note.

"Must be this way," Wendell nodded, figuring it was to their left.

Room 5114 was not really a room at all, but a foyer guarded by a receptionist. To her left sheltered from the foyer by a Plexiglas sheet was the typing pool, the administrative assistants. In years past they would have been slamming and banging their IBM Selectrics but now they were busy at their computer keyboards. Wendell glanced in their direction as Carol explained their appointment with the aides to the Undersecretary. He saw a familiar form at one of the desks closest to the Plexiglas. There was a clear glass bud vase with the remains of a faded carnation sticking out. The flower was past its prime and should have been thrown away, but Wendell was glad that it hadn't been. He tapped on the glass to get Ethel's attention. Simultaneously Ethel and Carol looked at him, the one with surprise and joy, the other with a scolding look. The boy gave a quick wave of his hand in Ethel's direction and then turned back to business.

After the interview and briefing ended, Carol and Wendell walked back through the foyer. Ethel's space was empty and the flower had been removed from the desk.

On Thursday and Friday Wendell rode into the city alone. Monday Mrs. Thompson had returned from recess and shared a bench with him.

"So how has it been going," she asked, noticing the absence of Ethel and Charlene.

"Gave the hog export report to Congressman Brenner, then to the Undersecretary of Commerce," he answered, knowing that was not what she meant.

"And how did that go?" she continued, knowing that he knew she meant something else entirely.

"I know her first name and I know where she works, but I don't know what I should do about it. They have been avoiding me."

Mrs. Thompson hesitated then began, "Wendell, every other man in this city hungers after Charlene, but you're interest is in Ethel. Why?"

Wendell did not answer. He remained silent for the rest of the commute. On the elevator he impetuously leaned to Mrs. Thompson and said, "I like you better than either of them. If you weren't married I'd ask you to dinner."

The effect was immediate. Mrs. Thompson, who had been the cool professional, burst out laughing. And as the door to her floor opened she stepped into the hall and turned back to Wendell before the door shut, "I'm not."

Carol checked in with Wendell when she arrived at the office. "What's the agenda today? Who do we talk pig with?"

Wendell interrupted his whistling, "Don't you remember? Paige from Brenner's office is coming to go over the proposed legislation before we run it back through Commerce."

Carol smiled at him. "Oh, I remember. And you seem in a good mood for a Monday."

"I've decided I like older women," he chuckled to her.

"Hah! How old?"

He scratched his chin, then, remembered a line from a song, "The older but wiser girl for me," he sang.

Carol laughed. "And is she white or black?"

"I am color blind."

Carol laughed again, "And is she rich?"

Wendell hesitated again. "Let's hope so."

Mrs. Thompson and Wendell sat side by side from Tuesday morning on as the metro daily slid into the District. They appreciated each other's company because neither tried to talk much. "Good mornings" were followed by long silences and then they began a curious game. Neither knew how it got started, and there never were written rules, but the game was this: each could ask the other one question and only one question each day, the other would answer in as few words as possible. For example, one-day Wendell's question was "Divorced or Widowed?" Mrs. Thompson's reply was "Both".

After a few days they stopped looking for Ethel and Charlene. One morning though, Mrs. Thompson queried Wendell, "I asked you once, you never answered. Why Ethel?"

"I thought her more interesting," he returned, which was only partly true.

Mrs. Thompson looked into his face, searching for traces of the lie. "Not true," she said.

The rules of the game required truth.

"Less intimidating," he answered the second time.

They enjoyed their mornings together, Mrs. Thompson and Wendell. They liked the question game they played. One question each per day, one answer. It gave them plenty of time to think of the question and plenty of time to analyze its answer. Wendell never threatened to take his companion to dinner again, and no mention was ever made of their meeting under any circumstance other than the commute. One day though, Wendell could not resist twisting the question game a little.

"Renoir?" he said with a question in his voice.

"National Gallery of Art, exhibit opens tomorrow, tickets are free, but I bet very difficult to get," was the answer.

Wendell reached into his shirt pocket and pulled out two tickets for 1 p.m. the next day. He handed Mrs. Thompson one.

She examined the ticket then asked her one question of the morning. "Why do you want to ruin our friendship?" She was not smiling, but serious in her tone.

Wendell, sensing her mood reached into his pocket and pulled out the second ticket and handed it to her. "I would not disturb our mornings. Go with whomever you like."

Mrs. Thompson held the tickets in her hand a moment, then handed one back to the young man. The smile had returned to her face, but she said not a word.

As they stood in front of the magnificence of the French Impressionist the lady asked in her cryptic way, "Want me to find Ethel for you? You should be with someone your own age."

Wendell answered without taking his eyes off the painting. "I could find her myself if I wanted. Besides, I find you more interesting."

"Or less intimidating?" came the retort.

"Hardly less, much more, but also more interesting." Wendell turned and looked at her. "Are you embarrassed to be seen with me?"

Mrs. Thompson laughed out loud in the austere gallery amidst the large opening day crowd. She put her arm inside his arm. "Boy," she said, "they think us mother and son. Why would I be embarrassed to be with you?"

"Well, Mom," he patted her hand as it lay on his arm, "let's keep moving or we'll never finish on our lunch hour."

The next Monday after the exhibit outing, Wendell and his mentor as he had come to think of Mrs. Thompson, were taken by surprise when Ethel sat across the Metro aisle from them. They had given up looking for the pair of women, and now, finding only one, greeted her with gusto. Ethel was pleased that she would be remembered and greeted so fondly. Wendell, though, was too polite to ask where she had been all these weeks. Instead he inquired about Charlene.

"Her Grandmother in Baltimore has become ill, and she has taken leave to care for her."

"Is it serious," Mrs. Thompson asked seeing that the subject caused Ethel distress.

"I am not sure, but I think so."

"If you see her, then," Mrs. Thompson went on, "give her our best, tell her that her Metro friends asked about her and wish her Grandmother well."

Wendell had known all along that it was Charlene that had kept Ethel away from the 6:40 train. Now that she was off to Baltimore, Ethel was free to ride whichever train she wished.

After the stop at the Federal Station, where Ethel departed, Mrs. Thompson asked her question, "Can you get two more tickets to the Renoir?"

Wendell in his slow, deliberate way said, "Don't want to, that was our afternoon." Then he asked his question, "What's your first name?"

Mrs. Thompson looked at the boy. She thought of him as a boy, the age that a son of hers would be. She had sensed them drawing closer together each day, but there was an edge, a difference. This was not mother to son, not mentor to student.

This was man to woman. She did not invite it; he did not instigate it, but there it was: sex.

"Mrs.," she said in answer to his question.

The news in Congressman Holcomb's office that day was that Carol had accepted a job in the Department of Commerce. She had impressed someone in that bureaucracy and had been offered a position. She hated to leave her place near the power center of Capitol Hill, but the chance for advancement in money and prestige was too great to turn down.

The Chief of Staff called Wendell into his office. "Can you handle the Pork Legislation without Carol?" He was thinking that perhaps the process had advanced far enough that he would not have to have two valuable staff people tied up.

Wendell responded, "I'll miss Carol. She made an excellent presentation, as was obvious from the job offer. But I know the statistics, I know the legislation."

The Chief of Staff considered. Wendell had earned respect with his knowledge of this arcane information. The Ag. Sub-Committee staff would be able to do the PR work that he might not be suited for. "The Congressman wants this thing done. You're the man."

"Thank you, I will miss Carol," Wendell stated. "Another matter, sir. Mrs. Thompson, the woman that asked about me some months ago from down stairs, what is her first name?"

"Mrs. Thompson? What do you want to know her first name for? Strange bird that one. Runs Congressman Blackwell's office. Don't know that she has a first name and I've known her for years. Strictly business. I've heard that she can be Hell on her staff."

"Congressman Blackwell?" Wendell pondered aloud, knowing that he could look her up in the building directory.

"She's been around for years, worked her way up, quite a good administrator from what I hear, but she keeps to herself. Doesn't do the cocktail party thing. You're not thinking of moving over to Blackwell are you?"

"No sir, I run into her on the Metro from time to time, and wanted to know her first name is all," Wendell answered.

"Good luck," the Chief-of-Staff replied. "I don't know anybody that calls her by her first name."

Later that afternoon Wendell searched the Congressional Directory and found, under Congressman Blackwell from Illinois, the Chief-of-Staff listed as Mrs. B. Thompson.

Wendell's question the next day after Ethel had disembarked at the Federal Station was "What does the B. stand for?"

Mrs. Thompson hesitated. Finally she said sternly, "Nobody calls me by my first name."

Wendell looked at her. "Would you rather I called you 'Mom'?"

Mrs. Thompson could not keep from laughing. "Wendell, use those boyish charms on Ethel and leave this old lady alone. Isn't it enough that we are friends?"

"Never had a friend that wouldn't tell me her Christian name before," he replied.

Mrs. Thompson did not reply. The train entered the Capitol Hill station and nearly all the remaining passengers departed along with our twosome. Wordlessly they rode the elevator to their separate floors, as Mrs. Thompson stepped off the lift, she turned back to Wendell and almost told him her name.

That morning Wendell looked over the hog export statistics again, searching and updating the information, but his mind was elsewhere. He considered his position. Should he pursue the ordinary Ethel and seek a spark of excitement there, or should he pursue Mrs. Thompson, more than twenty years his senior, and seek there for the spark of youth. He had the feeling that he couldn't do both.

The next morning, Thursday, Mrs. Thompson was not at the train station. Ethel and Wendell took their seats side by side. "I wonder where Mrs. Thompson is," Ethel said.

"I'm not sure, she didn't say she wouldn't be here today," Wendell responded.

"Do you work with her? She seems such a nice lady."

The young man answered, "We work in the same building but different offices."

Ethel asked another question. "I think I saw that woman that was with you that day at the Commerce Department."

"That was Carol, somebody over in Commerce liked her and offered her a job there. Why did you leave that day? When I came back to say 'Hello', you were gone."

Ethel reddened from embarrassment, but before she could come up with an answer, a gentleman, a stranger, approached them.

"Are you Wendell?" he inquired.

Wendell nodded, "Yes?"

The stranger handed Wendell an envelope. "I was told to give this to you."

Wendell took the envelope and could feel a pair of tickets sliding back and forth in the paper. "Thank you, who is this from?"

"Can't say. I was told to tell you to have a good time." Wendell opened the envelope and inside were two tickets to the Sunday matinee performance of the National Symphony at the Kennedy Center.

He smiled to himself then turned to Ethel. "Ethel, are you busy Sunday afternoon?"

"I usually stay home with my parents on Sundays, why?"

"Want to go to the Symphony? I've got two tickets courtesy of Blanche."

"Symphony? Blanche who?"

"Yes or No," Wendell said thinking that he might be a long pursuit to find that spark of excitement in Ethel.

The train pulled into the Federal station and Ethel got up to leave. "Yes, I think, but who's Blanche?"

"Here's my e-mail," he said handing her his business card. "Send me a message and I'll reply with the details. And Blanche is Mrs. Thompson."

Wendell smiled at the thought of his detective work. He figured that if he could find out all that there is to know about pigs, then he surely could locate Mrs. Thompson's first name.

At mid-morning, Wendell stood down the hallway from Congressman Blackwell's office suite. He spied a young staffer headed back that way.

"Excuse me, but would you do me a favor?"

"Sure, what?"

"Take this down and give it to Mrs. Thompson. She's in Blackwell's office."

"Why can't you take it?" the staffer replied.

"Would rather not have to hand this to her in person," he said truthfully. "It's not anything bad, but it would be better if she didn't see me."

The staffer shrugged his shoulders and held out his hand for the letter Wendell was holding.

Mrs. Thompson was a professional. She did not show any emotion, not anger or humor, as she opened and silently read Wendell's note in front of the messenger.

The envelope was blank on the outside, except for the Mrs. Thompson. Inside was a very short handwritten note:

Blanche,
    Wish you had gotten three tickets.

        Thanks,

        Wendell

On Friday Blanche was again absent from the 6:40 commuter train. Wendell and Ethel sat and chatted. Ethel was full of questions about the symphony. She had never been before and wondered what it was like, how long it took and what she should wear. Wendell, who had been only a few times himself, tried to answer the questions, and promised to take her out afterward to somewhere much less formal for dinner, Carolina style Bar-B-Que at the Pork Barrel. He was pleased to see her excited and anxious about the date; he was pleased that she had agreed to go. He wrote down the address and directions to her parent's apartment. As she got up to depart the train at her stop, she reached back and grabbed Wendell's hand and exclaimed, "Don't be late," and gave him the fairest smile. He could see the shine in her slightly crossed eyes. He smiled back.

For the short ride from the Federal Station past the Smithsonian Station to the Capitol Hill Station Wendell speculated about his situation. He viewed Ethel in a new and more charming light, but he also missed the wit and experience of Blanche. He thought to himself that if he had to pick one, which would he select? It appeared, he believed, that Blanche had chosen for him.

It took Charlene several weeks after her return to accept Wendell as the object of Ethel's attention. It took Blanche several weeks to feel comfortable enough to join them back on the 6:40. But Charlene was the maid of honor at their wedding and Blanche sat next to Wendell's Great Aunt in the front row of the groom's side. At the reception afterwards, in a quiet moment Wendell leaned toward his friend and asked softly, in the same tone that they had used on the Metro, "Weren't you ever tempted?"

Mrs. Thompson, Blanche, was caught off-guard. She thought a moment, knowing the rules of the game. "Mildly tempted though not driven to act on it," she said.

Wendell smiled at her with that winning smile of his.

WORK HORSE

A Simile

ALICE LOVED JAMES. SHE did.
James loved Alice. There were moments of exasperation, every marriage has them, but Alice and James shared memories from over a quarter of a century. They shared a life. In this age of revolving romances, they were an example of success. They were a team. They worked together, which, of course, was the problem.

They could be likened to a pair of workhorses side by side in the daily routine of their lives, each pulling their own weight. James was the muscle and determination; Alice was the insight and thoughtfulness. James knew the destination. He'd march with his head down, eyes peering forward, concentrating upon the ground, examining the terrain for safe footing. Alice would hum to herself sometimes. Occasionally she would lift her head and look around. She would see the fields and the clouds. She could feel the rain coming. She had a sense of wonder. James was content. They worked in harness together. He concentrated. She dreamed.

Henri needed Carol. He knew that he did. Carol was the string that kept Henri's balloon from drifting away. Sometimes the balloon resented the string. On quiet days the balloon wanted to fly above the trees to see what there was to see. On such days Henri often found the string tied uncomfortably short. On windy days though, the balloon was appreciative of the string, and being anchored firmly to reality.

When Henri was a little boy, while others dreamed of being policemen or doctors, he wished to grow up to be an artist. He had tried. Henri had the sensitivity and the imagination, but he lacked a necessary ingredient. He lacked talent. Now, after forty years of half-hearted starts and twenty-five years of Carol's restraint, he had come to a good place. He painted for fun. And only on his days off, and only watercolors, for they were less demanding than oils, and less expensive.

Henri loved to go a field and spread his easel, and splash the colors across the paper. He painted the far horizon. He painted clouds.

On Henri's first day of vacation (a vacation that he had allotted himself two hours each morning to sit and paint) he had only begun when he looked up to see a pair of workhorses pulling an old wagon along the road. Henri usually liked to work in the quiet, absorbing the sounds of the scenery, but every so often, he would lug his old boom box out and play classical pieces to get his blood flowing. At these times he wished for the clouds to hear the music so they could smile as he did. This morning was one such morning.

Alice, in her customary position alongside James, trudged down the road. It was a fine spring morning; the pastures bordering the lane were green and succulent with grass. "James, don't you ever want to go dancing?" she asked rhetorically, for she knew his answer.

"Alice," he said with the slightest tone of annoyance, which was the answer that she had expected.

"James, look at the fields around us. Can't you feel the springtime? We're not too old to go dancing around those fields," she said hopelessly. She was too old, and he, he had been too old since before he was born.

"Hmmp," was all he said.

She turned her thoughts back to the business at hand, but in the back of her mind lingered the dream of the dance. She walked on.

A horse with no imagination can shut out external stimuli, but a horse born with curiosity cannot, and horses have very large ears. From a long way away Alice heard the music. With each step it got a little more distinctive, a little louder, and with each step she became a little more curious. James, meanwhile, watched the road for unexpected bumps. He felt his partner digress, shifting more of the load upon him, but he loved Alice in spite of her fancies so he continued along without complaint.

Before long they came within sight of a man, sitting on a folding stool, an easel standing before him. Alice looked directly at him. She could tell that somehow he was responsible for the music.

Henri watched the pair plod down the road. He saw the pretty one lift her head and look directly at him. Henri could not speak with horses, but he was attuned to the ebb and flow of nature, for he was an artist. He could tell that the horse had wonder in her eyes. He had never seen a green-eyed horse before, and he thought her quite a character. Both ears were pricked in his direction, both eyes glued upon him.

"What is that delicious music," Alice thought.

"Beethoven, sixth symphony, the pastoral," Henri said aloud. "Makes you want to throw off your troubles and run around the pasture."

Alice glanced at James. He didn't hear a thing. He just kept walking. She wanted to stop and listen. If she couldn't dance, she should be able to listen, but when you are harnessed as a team, and the team says walk, you walk. It was a long time though, (for a horse's ears can swivel nearly backward) before they were out of earshot.

Henri painted the trees and the sky. It was one of the best paintings he had ever done. Perhaps even Carol would think it was not a complete waste of a morning. Perhaps. And tomorrow, perhaps, he would come here to this same spot and paint the team of horses. He had never succeeded with horses before, couldn't quite get the dimensions right, but perhaps tomorrow he would try.

The next morning Alice was eager to begin the journey. James noticed a lightness in her step that hadn't been there in a long time. He smiled to himself thinking his workmate was happy.

"James," Alice began as they shouldered the weight of their wagon. "Don't you think we need a little romance?"

He was surprised at the question, taken aback. "Alice?" He turned his head to look directly at her.

"Not love romance," she tried to explain. "Romance like in gallantry, and standing tall, and giving me roses, and forgetting work for a day. Romance like in doing things together."

"Alice, we work together. You and I, we work. What more together can you want?"

Alice became exasperated with James. James felt likewise toward Alice.

The first tinkling of the music came to her ears soon after they had begun the day's work. She somehow had known that the man would be back today. She smiled and forgot about James. Let him pull for a while, she was going to concentrate upon the music.

This music was different than yesterday's. Different but similar. Complex but with a melody. A melancholy melody. She could hear the tension beneath the melodic phrases. She could feel the rumble beneath her feet. Horses have sensitive feet. As the team came within sight of the man, she noticed that he was looking directly at her. The music arched and swooned and Alice stopped and stared back at the man.

"Alice!" James declared, "I'm trying to work here."

The wagon had banged to a halt and James, not hearing the music could think of no reason his mate would come to a standstill in the middle of the road.

Alice stood examining the painter.

Henri worked his brush and his washes.

"Alice! Let's go," James insisted.

Alice began a slow walk all the time watching Henri.

When she had gotten directly abreast of him, he said, "Dvorak, ninth symphony, slow movement. Stick around and hear the rest. It's very inspiring."

She wanted to stick around very much. Sadly she knew that she couldn't. She listened to the conclusion of the second and most of the third movement as she plodded on, James pulling all the weight. Gradually the sound evaporated. She wondered if she would ever get to hear the entire piece.

Henri was not satisfied with his portrait of the horses. It bothered him that he could not draw the scene as it actually unfolded. Maybe he should go back to sky and clouds. Maybe he would try horses again tomorrow. Maybe he should stay home and cut the grass tomorrow.

On the third morning Alice said nothing to James. She had an air of quiet resignation. Maybe the artist would be by the roadside again and maybe he would be playing music, but maybe listening only made things worse. Maybe, today, she would shut her ears and keep walking.

It was James' turn to talk.

"Stability. There is something to be said for stability, Alice. Watching for safe landings for all four feet. You can't do that running around in a strange field Alice. Stability and safety."

Alice said nothing.

They came to the point in the road where on the previous two days the music had first reached Alice's ears. Today there was nothing. In spite of herself, Alice was disappointed. Together she and James walked along. Rounding the bend she was surprised to see the artist sitting in the quiet. She studied him with a puzzled look.

"I couldn't decide today," he said. "I couldn't decide if I should even come. And if I came, what music I would play. You do appear to enjoy it, but your friend over there, he doesn't. He thinks we're silly. Maybe I should have stayed home, but I have a piece of music that I wanted him to hear. First I thought of Von Suppe, Light Calvary Overture, but then this came to mind. I had to play it for him. Can you help him hear?"

Alice stopped, bringing James to a halt.

"Alice, again?"

Alice pushed shoulder to shoulder with her mate and then nodded at Henri.

Henri had the music ready to go. It was unmistakable. The volume was turned to its highest. Even James could hear as the trumpet fanfare began from the William Tell Overture, better known to all horses as the theme from The Lone Ranger.......Hi Ho Silver, Away!

In the pantheon of horse myth there is no horse than can stir the blood like Silver. Every young horse is told the stories. Whenever the colts and fillies play cowboys and Indians, one horse will play the part of the brave Silver, rearing on his hind feet, pawing the air, and rushing off to the beat of drums and the blare of brass. All young horses mimicked Silver, even James. Now the music of the entrance of the Swiss guards worked its magic again. Jimbo threw off his harness, stepped out of the braces and ran as gracefully as an old workhorse can manage. By his side was beautiful Alice, laughing. In the glorious springtime two friends, two lovers romped the open meadow as they had done a hundred years before.

Henri watched as the two tore circles around him. Alice was the more nimble, but James showed hints of the dash and panache that must have won her heart those many years ago. It is a good thing though, that the finale to the overture is not very long; when the music ended, both horses were winded.

Henri turned the player off, knowing that he had done well. James gathered his composure and walked back to the wagon. Alice made her way to where Henri was sitting, and looked over his shoulder to the paper on the easel. It was blank. She was disappointed.

"Such invigorating music deserves broad brush strokes," she thought. Quite by accident she flopped her tail into Henri's open color box, tipping over the water jar in the process. With a deft swish of her tail the page was no longer blank but splashed with the most interesting array of colors.

Horses normally don't smile, but Alice smiled.

Henri laughed and stood up.

"I have been told," he said, "that of all the places horses enjoy being scratched, they enjoy being scratched on the belly most. Is that true?"

Alice closed her eyes in pleasure as Henri rubbed her underside.

"Alice, we need to be getting along," James called with reawakened appreciation in his voice.

The next morning James was too stiff to move from his stall.

"All that running around yesterday was too much. I knew I shouldn't have done it."

Alice said nothing, but closed her eyes and wished that someone would rub her belly.

Henri did not show Carol the painting by the horse. He did not know how to explain it. Carol insisted that Henri not waste away every morning of his vacation for she had chores for him to attend to, so on Thursday Henri stayed home.

Friday was the last day of Henri's vacation. For the week he had managed one good wash, one failure, and one horsetail. He was getting a little discouraged. A thought occurred to him that he should put away his paints and take up his fishing rod; that there might be better luck in the stream than at the easel. After some consideration, he chose his paints again, and he chose the same spot in the field.

James, still sore, stepped into the braces and shouldered his harness. Alice joined him. They had missed a day of work, so now they were behind. It didn't matter to Alice, but James hated to be behind.

It took a while to shake the kinks out of their muscles, but together they made good progress once they warmed to the job. Alice looked at her companion and said, "I'm glad that we danced. We don't have to do it again, but I'm glad that we did it once."

James wanted to complain about still being sore, and complain about being behind, but he exchanged glances with his mate and replied, "I'm glad that you enjoyed yourself."

Alice knew that his answer was as close as he would get to admitting he also enjoyed the run.

The team pulled close to Henri's field, but there was no music. James had closed his ears and would not have noticed anyway, but Alice was disappointed. As they rounded the bend, the two horses could see that though there was no music, there was Henri standing close by the road. In his hands he held two apples and two carrots.

"I want to thank you for being my friends for the past week," he said as they approached. "I've a carrot and an apple for each of you."

"Oh, no thank you," said James in horse talk.

Henri, not knowing horse, offered him a bite of apple, anyway.

Alice nudged James, "Take it, he's just being friendly."

James munched and Alice munched and Henri rubbed underneath of Alice's chin. It wasn't as satisfying for either of them as rubbing the belly, but her belly was difficult to reach due to the harness.

Alice wanted to ask about the lack of music, but she couldn't put it into human terms, so she said nothing, but Henri understood.

"I had the hardest time picking the music today. It's my last day and I wanted something that you would enjoy and something that summed up our week. I did find a piece. It's not classical and it is short, so I won't start it until after you finish your apples."

Alice liked the way the man talked and the way the man scratched. James finished his vegetables and was ready to move along.

Henri continued, "It's a song from the farthest memories of my youth."

He gave a final, friendly pat to the old mare. "Happy trails, my friend."

He went over to his stool and turned on the music as James started the wagon moving down the road.

Alice looked back at Henri as Judy Garland sang Over the Rainbow.

Henri sat and watched the team pull off down the lane and around the next bend. He said aloud to himself, "I suppose that there is something to be said for dreams and balloons and wizards and horses of a different color, but I suppose there is something to be said for home and stability and family, too."

He packed his paints without wetting a brush, and went home to see what chores Carol had left on the chore list for him.

THE HERMIT OF LINDOS

THE ISLAND OF RHODES (Rodos) is the southernmost and largest of the string of Greek islands that abut the Turkish Coast of the Aegean Sea. There are 16 major islands in the chain plus numerous smaller islets, rocks and bars, but only 12 are inhabited, thus the name for the islands: Dodekanese, Greek for twelve.

Rhodes is also the name of the largest city on Rhodes. Total inhabitants of the island number 120,000 with about half of them residing in the city. The major industries of the island are tourism, more tourism and olives. The climate is fine, never touching freezing in the winter and cooled by the northern breeze blowing off the sea in the summer. Flowers seem to thrive everywhere on the island, scenting the air and brightening its walkways.

There is much antiquity, with ruins dating back 400 and more years before Christ. One of the most interesting landmarks is the ancient acropolis at Lindos. Once a thriving center of civilization, Lindos now is a still quaint village of whitewashed houses at the foot of a hill overlooking the sea. Atop the hill are the remains of a temple to the Goddess of Wisdom, Athena. The town lies between temple and sea facing a picture perfect cove where the Greek tourist board usually anchors a yacht to complete the scene.

Tourists from the hotels and the cruise ships that stop at the port of Rhodes city are driven to Lindos by chartered bus, from there they trek the 300 steps to the hilltop temple. On their way back down the crowds disperse through the narrow streets of the village. These streets are hand paved with the beach pebbles. The stones have been carefully arranged to create mosaics from their dark and light hues. The narrowest alleyways are no more than a meter and half wide. It is along one of narrowest of these streets, in a small building, that the Hermit of Lindos has set up his shop.

Credo considers himself the hermit; others have not applied that name to him. He thinks of himself as the hermit with a small bit of pride. Credo Constantin is not Greek. His direct male-line forefather was, but his more recent ancestors have complicated his genetic profile with genes from various and sundry places. One of the few traceable remnants of Greek heritage remaining is his name.

Credo is a contemplative man, which is also perhaps representative of his Great, Great Grandfather's birthplace. It is an unusual trait though, for a man of his former profession, financier. Credo comes from Boston, and he stumbles through his Greek with a Boston accent. He left the city at the height of his career. The company was considered his, even though he owned only a small portion of it, for it was his name most identified with its success. He also left behind the remains of two unfulfilling marriages.

When his first wife left him, he had felt a cautious relief. When his second wife departed, he worried that it was either his choice in women that was flawed, or worse, there was something fundamentally wrong with him. Most men wouldn't have analyzed so severely, but Credo was a contemplative and introspective man. So when the daughter from his second marriage followed her two stepbrothers in taking up alternative life styles, he began also to question his ability as a father.

He questioned thusly, "If a man can be considered a success at work, but the people who know him best can not tolerate him, what has he gained by his labor?" He tried reconciliation but the more he acquiesced, the more his families took advantage of his wealth, and simultaneously showed their disgusted for his appeasements. He was disgusted with them, himself. His next reaction was to hammer himself to his work. At first he found some solace there, but he soon began to sense shallowness in his compatriots. He felt that they were as hollow as the words in the company's annual report. The words read well, and the intent was noble, but they were useless for they lacked truth. He wondered if he, too, was as empty as the people that surrounded him.

At the age of fifty-six, Credo gave his main house to his second wife, set aside a sum for each child, including his stepsons, who had done nothing to deserve such a legacy. He placed his investments and securities in mutual funds, sold off his boat, his cars and the condo in Montana. He kept only his lake house in Maine -that was too dear to his heart to sell – and he became the Hermit of Lindos.

Mariana was a moderate. She couldn't decide whether she was a conservative Democrat or a moderate Republican, but she knew that she adhered to the philosopher that proclaimed, "Moderation in all things." She was unaware that it was the Roman playwright Publius Terentius Afer, echoing the adage of the early Greeks of the Lyceum of Rhodos, where he studied a hundred and fifty years before Christ, who first penned those words. She was so moderate that she routinely scored smack in the middle of the physiologic tests that corporations occasionally give their employees. Sometimes it is said that moderates are so middle of the road that they are without passion. Mariana certainly had passion, if only in moderation.

Joining the Peace Corps is not normally an act of moderation, but if becoming a hermit is an extreme response to a life seemingly without purpose, signing up for two years of service in an underdeveloped country with the support of the United States government behind you might be viewed as a moderate option.

Mariana did not consider her life to be completely without meaning, only that it lacked 'something'. She was an accountant by training and occupation. She and her husband had drifted apart over the years, he disappointed in her moderation and she in his infidelity. Eventually they divorced. The children were grown and led lives of independence, as she had taught them. She was unencumbered by grandchildren and she had reached an age when there had been one tax filing season too many.

An acquaintance from church had recently had a son return from serving with the Peace Corps in Guatemala. For Mariana, watching the progress of this young man's adventure brought back memories of old dreams. She had been ten years old when John Kennedy proposed as an alternative to sending young men with guns around the world, sending them with shovels. That was more than forty years ago. When one is ten, one can dream such dreams. When one is over fifty, the time to accomplish any dream is rapidly slipping away, or so it seemed to her. It was not an act of desperation that she completed her application, but an act of reason and logic, for she knew it would be desperate to live the remainder of her life lonely and unfulfilled.

Romania is a country of unbelievable beauty and one of contrasting ugliness, often in the same frame. Optimists avert their eyes from the trash littering the roadsides, and see the natural beauty and the winds of change stirring the country. Pessimists notice the corruption, the garbage, and the insecurity of the people. Pragmatists see both sides. Mariana had been nearly a year at her Peace Corps assignment as a teacher in Satu Mare. The infinite wisdom of government bureaucracies had placed her, with her valuable skills in accounting and financial planning, as a middle school English teacher. She was a good teacher, though, and on good days her classes responded positively to all that she had to offer. On bad days, and there were some, the scoundrels couldn't be reached at all.

Mariana was approaching the halfway point of her service and she had begun to consider what would come next for her. Rarely in life does one start fresh without the baggage of accumulated past history. Most often we slide into new postures gradually, only realizing in hindsight that we'd changed direction so completely. Living simply, as she was now used to, learning to be thankful for the two hours of hot water, causes one to reduce excess baggage. In those quiet moments before sleep, she began to ponder her restart after Peace Corps. She would have to do something, but that something hadn't formed in her mind yet.

It was a winter that had stayed around too long, and after a week of being unable to reach her students Mariana decided it was time for a vacation. Many of her Peace Corps colleagues had already been to delicious places and related stories of sights to see. Most of the people that she had gone through initial training with were much younger than she was, and there was a gulf, a difference of attitude, between twenty something and fifty something. Heading off to some foreign country with them would be like going on vacation with one's children, satisfying for their company, but disastrous in the opposing choices of places to see and things to do. She often felt uncomfortable in their presence because of the difference in attitude and outlook. The younger volunteers were all given to extremes.

Mariana was as single and alone in Romania as she would have been at home, but here, she also struggled with the language. In Satu Mare, in the far northern portion of the country, she felt a sense of mission, at least. She understood that she was doing her part to present an attractive and tempered face of America to people that knew of her home only from the headlines and movies. But her state of mind was ready when her counterpart teacher, host country national, in Peace Corps lingo, asked her is she wished to tag along on holiday to Rhodes over Easter break. Mariana happily accepted.

So it was that Mariana wandered the pebbled alleys of Lindos on a sunny morning in late April. And so it was that when she turned a corner on her way back down from visiting the ancient temple, she was taken by surprise by a most unusual shop. From a distance, if one ignored the solar hot water heaters on the rooftops, Lindos could be mistaken for a village from the Greek Isles of memory. Up close, it was filled with shops that catered to the thousands of visitors who required trinkets and artifacts to signify their pilgrimage to ancient Greece. Houses selling baubles, plastic artifacts and some semi traditional crafts lined the narrow walks, and one store most often sold the same wares as the next. Mariana was thus caught by surprise by a shop of a different sort.

Lending Library the small sign atop the door said. Old paperback books sat on small bookshelves in front of the store, and inside more books lined the walls. The books were in English, which was also a surprise. Further down the storefront, on a small rack were some interesting note cards, watercolors of assorted Greek wildflowers.

Mariana stood outside, examining the note cards. She had many postcard views of Rhodos, some already posted home, of both city and Island, but these cards were of a different caliber, more art than picture record. As she looked over the assortment, she observed the transaction going on inside the shop. Some American tourists from one of the cruise ships were chatting with the proprietor. He was explaining that he was from Boston, and while all the books on his shelves were available for lend, he required that they be returned in three weeks or less. If you found a book you liked, you paid half the cover price. When you returned it, your next book was free. So long as you returned the books, you were entitled to more books.

"But I'm on the Mystery of the Isles, we leave port this evening," the visitor replied. She was a middle-aged matron, comfortable in her position as a tourist. Under her and her husband's arms were packets of previously purchased souvenirs of a more traditional nature, particularly lace and ceramics. "I've finished the book I brought along on the cruise, and I see a few titles that I want to read. Unfortunately I will not be back to return them."

The proprietor smiled. "Pick what you like, pay half the cover price, and if you, by chance, get stranded on Rhodes, come back within three weeks and get more. If you don't get stranded, what have you lost? You have good books at half price. See, you can't loose."

The husband, well trained, already has his wallet out. "Pick a couple," he said to his wife.

Mariana decided to buy the note card assortment so she went inside to pay for her purchase. The interior was filled with books, all in English, all paperbacks. Bookcases reached almost to the ceiling. Above the top row of books more art was displayed. In one corner the books gave way to more note cards and pencil drawings. She found the shop intriguing and the owner likewise. She wondered how he had ended up in Lindos selling or lending old books.

"Only the note cards, then?" he asked when she brought them to him.

"I'd love to look around some more, and I see you have different ones in the corner, but I'm afraid that I must hurry to catch my bus."

"You are on vacation. You should not need to hurry when you are on vacation."

Mariana returned the smile with which the admonition had been delivered.

He put her purchase in a small bag, slipped in a business card and exchanged the packet for a few Euros. Doing this, he watched her, waiting to hear what reply she would make.

As she accepted her purchase, she said quietly before walking out the door, "I believe that you are a wise man, but still, I must hurry. Good bye."

A few minutes later Mariana was seated on a bus half full of Romanian vacationers headed back to their hotel.

Her friend Olivia greeted her when she reached the adjoining seat. "Mariana, you stayed at the temple a long time. Did you get to shop in any of the stores?" Olivia was Mariana's co-teacher and counterpart. They were friends, though not close friends, separated by age, culture and temperament. It had been Olivia's suggestion that they book the Rhodos vacation over Easter break, and they were good enough friends to be roommates, if not confidents. Truthfully, Mariana felt more comfortable with Olivia than with most of the Peace Corps volunteers Olivia's age.

Olivia was much more confident in her English than Mariana was in her Romanian, so English was the language of their conversation.

"Just one," Mariana replied. "I found a most unusual store and I picked up a set of note cards. How about you?"

Olivia gathered up her bags and began to show her American friend the day's purchases. Appropriate ohhs and ahhs were shared, and Mariana put on her mental list another reason why she and Olivia would not be best friends, taste.

"It was a nice place, wasn't it, Lindos," she asked Olivia after they had examined the gewgaws.

"It was, but I wonder what they do in the winter when there are no tourists. Please let me see what you bought," she replied, pointing to Mariana's small package.

"Only a box of note cards. I think they're done by a local artist." As she reached in to show the cards to Olivia, Mariana found the business card that the salesman had deposited. *The Hermit of Lindos, Lending Library and Local Art Cards*. There was no telephone number, no address, and no hours of operation printed on the card. Mariana thought about the name, and wondered again what sort of man would open up such a curious store.

Olivia was not particularly impressed by the cards and her appraisal was apparent in her small praise, but Mariana was not concerned by the tepid reception; she was back again at Lindos replaying the morning in her mind.

She replayed her musings that afternoon sunning and reading by the hotel pool. Yesterday she had remarked to herself, that the human body could be one of the most beautiful things and likewise, one of the most ugly. Both examples were on display around the pool again today, fully exposed to the late April sun. Always the moderate, Mariana was not fully exposed, and she had a floppy hat to shield her face from the sun. Her book was in her hands, but her thoughts kept returning to Lindos. 'If I were to finish my book,' she thought, 'would it be worth the trip to buy another at half price? Certainly the taxi fare would far exceed the savings of even a dozen books. I wonder if another tour is headed there from the hotel tomorrow.'

Her train of thought was interrupted by the discovery that her glass was empty. As this was an all-inclusive package, including drinks, that seemed a waste of money, so she got up and walked over to the bar.

The barman greeted her with a friendly nod. "Another rum and orange juice?"

"No, let me try an Ouzo. Is that right? Ouzo?"

"The famous Greek drink inherited from the Turks, but don't tell anyone that," he answered. "One Ouzo."

"If I wished to get to Lindos tomorrow morning but didn't want to pay a taxi, what is the best way for me to go?"

The bartender looked at Mariana a moment before responding. "You mind traveling on the local buses?"

Mariana laughed aloud. "I've been traveling the buses in Romania. I doubt that the Greek version could be as bad."

"Well then, in front of the hotel, take the local bus in to downtown Rhodes. There you'll have to get a bus that goes down the southeast coast. It's cheap and there won't be many people headed out that time of the morning. Buy your ticket on the bus. Then check what time they return. Usually there's about 45 minutes between buses on the way back."

Credo believed that one reason for his success in business was his easy manner of making acquaintances. He also considered that his main failure in his personal life was his inability to change those acquaintances into lasting bonds of affection. He was as good in his store as he had been in finance, putting people at ease, especially in the spring before the full crush of tourists had asked the same questions too many times. From a distance, he could be charming and appear intelligent. Up close his imperfections were too exposed, or so he believed.

He watched the lady browsing the corner section of note cards. He couldn't remember for sure, but he thought that he had seen her yesterday. The shop did not receive many repeat customers. Pilgrims make one stop at Lindos in a lifetime, few people, except a couple of British and American ex-patriots, ever returned one book for another, so it would be unlikely if she were the same lady, but she still seemed familiar. She was taking her time, unrushed and apparently unaccompanied, which also was unusual for his customers. He hadn't spoken to her yet, except for a nod of greeting when she walked in, but he had watched her out of the corner of his eye as he waited on the few other patrons that had wondered in this morning.

She picked up individual cards and examined the artwork on them. Most were blank inside, but a few had greetings. A pen and ink drawing of a pair of ducks caught her eye. They were not cartoon ducks or a ducks flying wild, but more ducklings with an attitude. She opened to the inside and found the following poem:

The Prayer of the Little Ducks

Dear God,
give us a flood of water.
Let it rain tomorrow and always.
Give us plenty of little slugs
and other luscious things to eat.
Protect all folk who quack
and everyone who knows how to swim.
Amen

Carmen Bernos de Gasztold

Credo watched her read, watched her laugh. They almost always did, those people that took the time to search out his card corner and find these poems. He wondered which she would pick up next, either the cat or the butterfly. It was the butterfly.

He watched her look at the poem a long time. She turned the card back to its cover drawing of the insect resting on a flower. It was a more thoughtful poem than the ducks' prayer and it took people longer to get hold of, but he thought it a more worthwhile effort. He had made a study of how his customers reacted to these poems and cards. Some gave up now, turning to other thoughts, others were hooked and would examine the next two of the series.

Mariana choose the cat next:

Lord,
I am the cat.
It is not, exactly, that I have something to ask of You!
No-
I ask nothing of anyone-
but,
if You have by some chance, in some celestial barn,
a little white mouse,

or a saucer of milk,
I know someone who would relish them.
Wouldn't You like someday
To put a curse on the whole race of dogs?
If so I should say,
Amen

Carmen Bernos de Gasztold

He watched her laugh again, out loud and wondered if she was a cat person or a dog person. She looked like a dog person and he hoped that she was because he was. She picked up the mouse card next, examined the cover drawing and flipped it over to see if the back held any important information about either artist or poet before reading this one. Only then did she open the card to read the poem. She nodded as she read, apparently pleased with juxtaposition of cat and mouse.

Her smile was more reflective this time he noticed and he wondered if she'd pick up the card last in line. On its cover was penned an unattractive old horse, hanging its head. Often, those who had made it this far choose not to peruse the final card. He saw the woman hesitate when she saw the picture, but he was pleased to see her complete the set.

The Prayer of the Old Horse

See, Lord,
my coat hangs in tatters,
like homespun, old, threadbare.
All that I had of zest,
all my strength,
I have given in hard work
and kept nothing back for myself.
Now
my poor head swings

to offer up all the loneliness of my heart.
Dear God,
stiff on my thickened legs
I stand before You:
Your unprofitable servant.
Oh! Of Your goodness,
give me a gentle death.
Amen

Carmen Bernos de Gasztold

"If poetry is meant to touch you deeply, than I believe that is one of the best poems of all. Especially for us of a certain age," Credo said to her in a soft voice after she had held the card open a long time. "But I must admit, I sell many less of the horse than I do of the others."

"The drawing reminds me of some of the horses of I've seen, worn, tired and abused," Mariana said putting the card back in its holder. She turned to him and exclaimed with new enthusiasm, "These are wonderful. Who is the poet? Who is the artist? Are you?"

"No, not me, dear Lady. The art I commissioned from a talented fellow that lives near the village of Gennadi, down the coast a ways, the poems are from a French Abbyess, written during the Second World War. There are, I think, 28 of the prayers. I used the five you see. Perhaps, I'll get Arnos to do the others some time."

At this point in the conversation, more visitors came into the store and Credo's attention was diverted. Mariana stepped back into the corner to get a full view of her surroundings. Credo used his best charm on the newcomers, inquiring as to their origins and their destinations. He was using his charm not so much to impress the newcomers but to impress his lady of the note cards. He had liked the way she reacted to the horse poem, and he was now sure that it was she that had been in yesterday.

When the more recent arrivals had found a few books to purchase and departed, he turned back to her. "Not many people come two days in a row. I hope that you find something that you like. Do you mind if I ask where you are from?"

Mariana made a mental list of the shopkeeper. He was a little too short, a little too round, a little too bald and probably a little too old, but for what she was not sure. He made a perfect shopkeeper of a perfect shop. "I am from Satu Mare, Romania, and you are from Boston."

Credo showed his surprise. "Satu Mare, I would have said that your accent indicated a childhood in Michigan."

"Are you the Hermit of Lindos, stranded on the Isle of Rhodos?"

"Not stranded, here by design."

"And not a hermit, either, judging from your charm and conversation."

Credo bowed his head slightly, "just praying for a gentle death, dear Lady."

Mariana looked around the store again, admiringly.

"Do you commission all of the artwork?" she pointed to the paintings above the top level of books.

"Most are on consignment," he said. "The cards I have various artists do. I don't sell too much art, I don't display it properly. But I don't want to be an art dealer, just a used book seller."

"I think it is all wonderful," Mariana said with a little too much feeling. "I mean, it really is a quaint shop," she recovered to say in a more refined manor. "What brought you from Boston to Lindos?"

He replied with a question, "What brought you from Michigan to Satu Mare?"

"It is a long story, more boring than anything, I'm afraid."

At this point more tourists came into the store to interrupt their conversation. These were louder than the last bunch and

Credo showed them less patience. After a few minutes they left without a purchase.

"Sorry for the intruders," he said. "The morning tours all depart by one. Perhaps if you have time to wait, you would join me for lunch at the café?" His offer was unexpected, both to himself and to Mariana.

"Oh, no. Thank you though, but I'll be taking the local bus back to the city."

Rebuffed, Credo shrugged, ready to end the conversation.

Seeing his change of character, she wondered if it had been a mistake to refuse the impromptu suggestion of sharing lunch. To accept would have seemed too anxious, but to decline, as she had done, too unadventurous.

"I would like you to do me a favor, if you might," she said. "I would like to buy all five of the animal cards but I want you to sign the one of the horse."

"Do I so remind you of an old horse?" he asked with a half-smile.

"No, not that. Sign it because it is my favorite."

He looked at her, glanced to be sure that there was no ring on her finger and thought that he would like to have taken her on the ferry to see Symi, his favorite island. It was too bad that she had turned down lunch. He was not going to ask again, for he was the hermit, after all.

She looked at him and revised her mental list. He was not too short, too round, too bald or too old. She also realized that he had surprised himself with the offer to share lunch, and that he would not offer again. It was up to her. She was a moderate. Moderates can do impulsive, impetuous things, but only on occasion. Today she had already made this return trip to Lindos on impulse, but she had no reason to hurry back to her hotel and sit by the pool. She picked up one of each of the five cards, placing the one with the horse on the counter. He dutifully signed beneath the Poem of the Old Horse, "To my Lady from Satu Mare, Credo, the Hermit of Lindos."

He was tempted not to accept her money for the cards, but that might offend her, so he deposited her cash and returned her change.

"Thank you for appreciating the poems," he said. "Have a nice vacation and enjoy your stay."

Mariana thanked him in return, gathered her cards and walked out the door. She walked slowly along the narrow pathway, feeling the water rounded shore stones beneath her sneakers. She opened up the card with the horse again as she walked. She stopped. She smiled. She turned around and went back.

"Credo is not a name normally found in Boston. I wonder how it came to be both in Massachusetts and in Lindos?"

Credo looked to the door to see her.

"It's a long story, more boring than anything I'm afraid."

Mariana asked, "Is your offer to share lunch still open?"

GORGEOUS

HE WAS GORGEOUS. DROP dead gorgeous. Movie star quality gorgeous. He seemed to be about 29 or 30, which was much too young for Red. The age difference between them made him appear safe, at least at first. She could look at him and just admire. Admire his shoulder length hair, full and blonde, brushed away from his face. Admire that clear open face, blue eyes and burnished good health. Admire his cleanliness and good teeth. Admire his torso, athletic and upright. He had the Pacific look, as if he had recently walked out of the surf at Rincon.

Where he actually came from, Red didn't care. What brought him to this corner of Maine, she didn't care either. It was pleasure enough simply to admire him. He was Kyle's, her youngest son's, Junior High baseball coach. The lad adored him. Adored him not for his good looks, although even Kyle could tell he was a hunk, but for his affable nature and caring attitude.

Coach had replaced a stricken teacher at mid-year and had been asked to guide the baseball team in addition to his duties as Phys. Ed. instructor. Red had heard her son's glowing reports of the new man and on the first day of practice had come early to pick him up and see Coach for herself.

Coach stood tall, easily over six feet, in his electric blue nylon sweat suit and Nikes, directing the workout in the gym.

It was difficult to hold a baseball tryout in the confines of the gym but it was early spring, really before spring even started at this northern latitude and it was impossible to hold the tryout outside in three inches of snow. Red found a seat on the bleachers a few rows from the floor and silently watched the action. This was Kyle's first year in Junior High. She wanted to view her son, and judge his progress from last year's Little League. Her eyes instead kept finding Coach. He paid no attention to her, but concentrated on his young charges. To wrap up the session he told the boys to hit the boards and take five laps around the gym.

As the kids were running enthusiastically, all hoping to impress, Coach walked over to Red. Up close he was even more gorgeous than he had been from a distance, the pale softness of his eyes twinkling. "You must be Kyle's mother," he said.

It was not a Maine accent. It was southern, not heavily southern, but pleasantly so.

"How did you know I was Kyle's Mom?" Red asked.

"Excuse me Ma'am, but you both have the same good looks."

Red melted. She knew he must be a big phony and that his charm was all a put on. He must have women lined up a half mile, and she would be the end of the line, if in the line at all. Still, she melted anyway. *'God,'* she thought *'he is good looking.'*

What she said was, "You're not from around here." It was a statement, but it was a question, too.

"From a little town in East Tennessee, Ma'am."

The first of the boys had finished their five laps and surrounded Coach, taking him away from Red. Other mothers had gathered at the gym door awaiting their sons. Practice was dismissed and Kyle joined Red and together they walked out toward the car. Joey and his mother Darlene were parked nearby. Darlene turned to Red and said, "What a stud. I'm coming to watch practice every day."

Red laughed and wondered how she could manage to do so herself. Darlene was a tramp and for Coach's sake, someone needed to keep an eye on her.

So it was for that first week. Darlene and Red arranged their schedules to have the late afternoons free to watch ball practice. Tryouts are not normally of much interest to spectators. Occasionally a Dad or two would take part and try to help; sometimes a Mom would bring her reading or her younger children to sit and wait for the conclusion of practice, but Red and Darlene came to watch.

The second day of practice Red noticed that Darlene was wearing very tight jeans and a blouse open one button too far. While Red herself had taken care with her appearance, she thought her friend had gone overboard. They sat together on the bleachers.

"You ever had a man that well built?" Darlene asked as they analyzed Coach.

"Darlene!" Red exclaimed in mock amazement.

"No, I mean really, when you were young? You've got flair and good looks. Have you ever had a piece like that?" Darlene asked again.

Red looked at her companion and then back at Coach. "Hon, there's not another man in Maine looks as good as that."

Darlene answered, "Me neither. I wonder how big his pecker is."

"Woman, you are way too crude!" Red replied, laughing, and wondering the same thing.

After a moment of quiet, Red returned to the thought, "It's not his tool that gives me the heebie-jeebies, it's those light blue eyes."

It was Darlene's turn to laugh, "Red, it's the whole package. That's what makes Coach such an attraction. He's got it all."

Red contemplated a moment. "Wouldn't it be something, though, if his penis were only about two inches long, fully extended?"

Darlene shook her head, "Make you a deal. First one of us to find out, let the other know."

Red laughed. "Darlene, you're married."

"I ain't talkin' love here, sweetie; I'm talkin' lust."

The next day at practice Coach had the youngsters out on the ball field. The ladies sat on the top row of the bleachers wrapped in their windbreakers, the spring sun warming their backs, the breeze cooling their faces. Coach must have thought it warm though, for he had stripped off the top of his sweat suit, revealing a guinea shirt, thin straps over the shoulders and deeply scooped neckline. The lack of jacket revealed it all. Hard body. Chiseled biceps and triceps. Pectorals. Muscles. Tight, shiny, bulging muscles. He must spend hours in the weight room, Red figured.

Darlene gazed for twenty minutes before she said anything. "Doesn't he make you wet just looking at him?"

"Darlene!"

"Come on Red! You know that you want him as much as me. Maybe just for one night, so that when you get to heaven, when you get to the end of your life, you can say, 'I been screwed by the best lookin' fucker in Maine.'"

"Darlene! Don't talk that way."

"It ain't only me, Red. Look at the trio of teachers come out to spy on Coach. I bet he could have any women in this town."

"In New England," Red retorted.

"Hollywood, right here in Bridgeforth," Darlene announced.

On the last day of tryouts, before the final cut was announced, Red and Darlene sat in their usual place on the warped wooden boards. Kyle had a natural talent and Red had never considered his not making the squad. He had been an all-star at the lower youth league level and it only seemed natural for him to move up, even though he was one of the youngest players. Kyle was not so sure, but his mother had reassured him all week. It was Friday now and a creeping doubt had come into Red's mind. Kyle was hit a ground ball that he fielded and threw wildly to home plate. Seeing the miscue, Coach knocked a second ball his way, and again the boy muffed the chance. Kyle was anxious, pressing too hard to please.

Hollywood, as Darlene and Red had begun to call Coach, walked over to the lad and placed a hand on his shoulder. The two women could not hear the conversation. Red had gotten nervous. Perhaps he was telling her son that he was not ready to play for the Junior High team.

Darlene commented, "I sure wish Hollywood would put a hand on my shoulder like that. Maybe I ought to go on the field and make an error to attract his attention. Nothing else I do seems to work."

"Didn't wear your bra again today?" Red quipped, trying to hide her anxiety for her son.

"Yeah, but no way he notices these little tits from way down on the field," Darlene laughed.

"I don't know, seems like yesterday after practice you managed to rub 'em right up against him. I doubt that he couldn't notice."

"Oh, Red, I just happened to brush up against his arm, minor contact, but seems to me it's you that he pays more attention to."

"Darlene!" Red protested. "He doesn't pay me any mind. Why would he care about me?"

"Hey, he knows you're available. Plus he probably likes older women, experienced. I bet he gets tired of all the young bimbos."

Red was quiet as she watched practice continue. Coach had finished his conversation with Kyle and seemed to be wrapping up the day's activities.

"How long has it been since you threw out McPherson?" Darlene asked. "Two years, now?"

"Yep, a little over two years," Red replied.

"Had any men since then?"

Red turned toward her companion with a look of disgust. "There's been men, none very important, but I've had men. As hard as I worked to get rid of that one sucker, why would I go and invite another one in?"

Darlene chuckled, "Oh, Red, you know what they say, 'you don't use it, you lose it'."

"Darlene," Red retorted, "people would think you blonde the way you talk."

The two shared a laugh together, and then went down to the field to gather their children. On the way out to the car, Red put a hand on her youngest son's shoulder. Kyle was at the age when contact between Coach and player was fine, but public show of affection from a mother was another matter. He was a good boy though, and endured her attention.

"What did Coach say to wrap up the week?" Red asked, curious as to the state of her son's emotions.

"Says he's goin' go over the list and will make the cuts this weekend and post the team Monday morning," Kyle answered.

"You mean you have to endure the suspense until Monday?"

Kyle looked up at his mother, not as far up as he used to, but she was still a little taller than he. "That's what I thought, too, but Coach says a little anxiety, a little tension is good, keeps the juices flowing." The boy broke away from his mother and ran to the car with a smile. It was Friday, and he loved the weekends. "Come on, Ma, let's get going."

Red turned and noticed her hussy friend Darlene just now finishing up a conversation with Hollywood. Red smiled too, and jumped into the car, feeling the juices flowing.

That night Red lay sleeping alone in her bed. She often slept alone now and had almost gotten used to it. Hollywood came and sat beside her. She opened her eyes and looked into that gorgeous, youthful face and into the romantically pale eyes. He smiled at her and reached down, putting his large hand upon her shoulder, exactly as he had done to Kyle earlier in the day. As he did so, her nightgown began to evaporate from his touch. Starting at the point of contact and working down and around her body, the cloth turned into nothingness, leaving her white and naked against the sheet. His touch felt so good, wonderfully comforting. With his other hand, Coach smoothed a few wild hairs from Red's forehead. She rejoiced at the tenderness of the gesture, and wanted to close her eyes, but how could she, why would she, take her sight from this beautiful man? His blonde hair framed his face as he leaned over her. His face was soft and rounded in contrast to the tight masculinity of the rest of his body.

He had taken his hand from her shoulder and rested his weight on both arms straddling her. He leaned very close over her. Red ran her hands up his bare arms, feeling his strength and fitness. She felt the tautness of his upper arms and the power of his shoulders. Her hands met at the back of his neck and she pulled him towards her. They kissed a long, deep kiss, communicating more without words than they had done all week with them.

Coach flexed his arms to get closer to her, displaying his taunt muscles. Red pulled him even closer so that she could feel his weight upon her nakedness. Lying prone, her breasts were flattened against her body, but her nipples were hard and excited, and she could feel them brush his chest. Her body ached with desire for this man. He ended the kiss and began to taste her body, beginning with her neck and working down. He had, at some point moved from sitting beside her to spreading himself upon her, covering her with a seductive blanket of love. His hands caressed her sides and arms; his mouth moistened her neck and shoulders. He allowed his weight to press gently against her, wanting her to feel him.

Red could not keep her eyes open now. Her hands framed his face and caressed his head while he worked lower down her frame. She made moaning sounds, pleasure sounds when he reached her breasts. With one hand he cupped her left breast making it full and large so that his mouth could not inhale it all, although he tried. From left tit to right, he tongued her nipple and sucked forcefully enough that Red believed her soul might be sucked right into him if he continued. She could feel his chest between her legs. She began rocking her pelvis and driving her pubic hair up and down against his midsection.

Red wanted him to take her. She needed to feel the rush. She could no longer stand it. She grabbed his sides and tugged at him as a signal that she wanted him to move up to her again. He did so and kissed her on the mouth. She reached as far down as her hands would go and grabbed the cheeks of his ass. She pulled him towards her, to signal that she was ready for him to enter her, but he did not. She could feel his penis hard against her mound, but he did not enter her. Thinking that he had not gotten the signal right, and wanting desperately to have him thrust himself into her, she let loose one side of his butt and placed her hand between them to grab his throbbing sex. She was amazed at how large it felt, long and wide and full of excitement and energy. With her hand she began to work it with the rhythm of the rocking motion that they had both established. All this time they remained locked in a kiss, Red with her eyes shut.

Coach pulled out of the kiss, and lifted his body off of her, except for the pivot point where they soon would be joined as one body. Red directed the head of his penis to run down her pubic hair and over the lip of her mound. When the tip of his tool met her clitoris, she gasped aloud and in so doing, woke herself.

She was drenched in sweat and drenched with passion. Another sixty seconds, another thirty seconds, she knew she would have reached climax. She lay there in the darkness, in her nightgown, letting the pleasure ebb. It was a bittersweet feeling;

sweet to realize the fullness of her body and to think how close she had come to making love to the handsomest man in Maine. It was sweet also, she smiled, knowing that there was no sticky, wet puddle to avoid the rest of the night. Bitter, though, not having him cuddle beside her after the sex, which was always her most favorite part.

The next day was a glorious spring afternoon. Kyle had peddled off with Joey and another friend. Meg, the middle daughter, a junior in High School had borrowed the car to take to a function at school. Charlie, the oldest boy, had stayed the weekend at college, so Red was alone. She spent her time working in her vegetable garden, preparing the seedbed for the spring planting. As she bent over with a rake in her hand she heard a familiar voice calling.

"Dorothy!"

It was her neighbor Jane. Jane was a good-hearted soul, but a busybody by nature. She had true concern for her neighbors and would often advise them in what she believed was the proper action. She was older than Red and seemed to think that made her by degree wiser. Jane never called Red by any than her Christian name.

"Dorothy, I have someone for you to meet."

Red stood and brushed the largest portion of mud from her jeans and removed her garden gloves.

"Isn't it a little early in the season to make a garden?" Jane asked, before beginning an introduction of her companion.

"Only planting a few onion sets, some lettuce and radishes," Red explained. "They all can take the cold. I don't know why I plant radishes, nobody eats 'em, but they are so easy."

"Dorothy, this is my cousin Harold. He's a newspaper editor in Philadelphia and he's writing a book about New England. Come to stay with me while he does his research."

To Red, Harold appeared to be about as many years older than she, as she was to Hollywood.

Harold said, "Hello. Pleased to meet you."

"Pardon my appearance," Red said as she shook his hand.

He seemed a pleasant enough man, although about as different from Coach as could be. Not that he was obese; rather he was pudgy and soft. He was sedentary. What little hair he had was gray. He wore bifocals and was dressed like a newspaper editor would on an off day.

"I've never met a newspaper editor before. What sort of book are you writing?" Red asked.

"I'm afraid my cousin exaggerates. I am only editor of the food section. Philadelphia Inquirer. A rather non-stressful job," Harold replied courteously.

"Sounds interesting to me," Red responded politely.

"Tell her about your book, Harold," Jane prompted. "Oh, and Dorothy my cousin is a widower, quite available." This of course embarrassed both Red and Harold.

"Cousin! I am sure Mrs. McPherson could care less about both my book and my marital status," Harold countered. "Now that you have sufficiently embarrassed both of us, let's be going."

Jane would not leave without commenting, "I was just stating facts, Harold. Dorothy, Harold is a wonderful cook, as you might imagine. Join us for dinner one night."

Harold had begun to walk away, so his cousin was obliged to follow.

Red called after the duo, "Harold, call me Red, everyone does. And I am interested in the book."

Harold turned, smiled and waved. "A pleasure, Red. Come along, Jane."

Shortly after the neighbors left, just as Red was preparing the seedbed for her black-seeded Simpson lettuce, Meg pulled into the driveway.

"Mom," she said in an aggravated voice. "Mom, we need to talk."

"What's the matter, Hon?" Red asked, turning away from her garden to see what was troubling her daughter.

"Mom, I am mortified. Completely embarrassed. How could you?"

"How could I what?" Red asked, bewildered.

"How could you go around like some teenage groupie?" Meg responded. When she saw that her mother still needed further explanation she continued, "Every afternoon you and Mrs. Henson, acting like tramps around Kyle's baseball coach."

"Meg!" Red answered. "You know that I've always liked to watch Kyle play and practice."

"Mother, you were heard speculating how long the man's ding dong was!"

"Meg! Don't talk that way," was what Red said; what she thought was *'Damn, who overheard that!'*

Seeing that her daughter was still upset and rightly so, Red tried compromise. "Listen, Meg, if it makes you feel any better, should Kyle make the team, I won't go to any more practices. When the games start, though, you know I intend to watch your brother."

Meg correctly took this as an admission of guilt. It satisfied her a little bit to know that she had gotten her mother, as her mother had often gotten her. She turned without further comment back toward the house.

As she was headed away, Red got the almost irresistible urge to call to her, "But he IS a hunk." She wisely resisted that urge.

Kyle did make the team. For the next three weeks he rode home from practice with Mrs. Henson, Joey's mom, or found some other way. The first game was on a Tuesday, and Red could not make it to the park until the third inning. She purposely sat a distance away from Darlene and tried to concentrate only on her son's play. She would never admit that Kyle was her favorite of the three children, but there is something about the youngest, something about the undeniable fact she would never bear another child again; that this was her last chance at child rearing.

Kyle played well. He was the starting first baseman and handled every ball thrown his way. He fielded two routine ground balls without incident. At the plate he only had a walk to show for four at bats, but the team won the game, six to two. It was a successful beginning to the season.

Red never looked in the Coach's direction.

At home that night the phone rang. Meg answered as she was expecting a call, but turned the receiver to her mother.

"Hello, Mrs. McPherson? This is Kyle's baseball coach"

Red nearly dropped the phone.

"I was glad to see you at the game this afternoon. I have missed you at practice and I think Kyle missed you, too."

Red stammered, thinking she had to say something, "It was a good game."

"Yes, Ma'am it was and Kyle did splendidly. But that's not the reason I called. I need a favor."

"Sure," Red replied. "What can I do?"

It was Coach's turn to stammer, "Well, you see, I wanted to ask you because, well, all the other teachers and women that I know, well, they seem just to be interested, well, how do I say this? Sometimes it's really bothersome, the way women look at me. I think you're different, and I wonder if you'd go out to dinner on Saturday night?"

Red's heart was in her throat.

"You see," Coach continued, "my fiancée is coming for a visit and,"

Red's heart returned to were it belonged.

"I think she gets tired of talking only to me. I thought it would be good if you and Mr. McPherson would join us for dinner."

"Oh, I'm sorry. There is no Mr. McPherson. Actually, there is one, but he doesn't live here anymore."

"I didn't know." Coach sounded genuinely surprised. "Is there another, umm, a boy friend that you'd like to bring along?"

Red thought for a moment and then realized that any male friends of hers would be disappointing in comparison to Hollywood. "I'd truly love to go, but I can't think of anyone to ask as my companion. Wait."

A thought had entered Red's mind. Two weeks ago Jane had asked her if she would care to come to dinner with Harold. Harold was such a good cook, after all. Red had politely refused, but now she wondered if Harold would be interested in going out to dinner as a safe substitute for the absent Mr. McPherson.

"There is someone, visiting my neighbor. Perhaps I should ask him and the four of us could go out to Chantilly's for seafood. Your fiancée likes seafood?"

"That would be great," Coach replied. "She loves seafood, being from the hills of Tennessee."

Red cautioned a minute. "This is Tuesday. I will have to try and get a hold of this individual and see if he's available. Can I give you a call back tomorrow?"

Coach agreed and gave her his telephone number.

Red phoned down to Jane's asking to speak to her cousin. He was out of town, over in New Hampshire doing research for his book, but she expected him back the next evening, and no, Jane did not believe that Harold had any particular plans for the coming weekend.

It is a strange and a welcome thing when strangers communicate. It took only moments for each participant at the dinner table to realize that this was going to be an enjoyable evening.

Mandy, Coach's finance, possessed all the softness and refined taste of a southern lady, but also bright intelligence and a quick and happy wit. She was not particularly beautiful. Red thought that Coach would have attracted a real dazzler to go along with his own good looks. She was not unpretty, only plain. Red soon forgot all about Mandy's looks, for her friendly manner and warm personality would win over anyone.

Mandy and Coach seemed a perfect match. They had met in college, at Vanderbilt University. Together they had come to the sensible conclusion that a little time apart before marriage would be beneficial. Now that time was almost over, and their genuine affection for each other was evident. They were to be married in the summer however it was still to be decided whether she would give up her job and move to Maine, or he his and move back to Tennessee.

All this came out through the dinner conversation interspersed with much laughter and good will over lobster, oysters and clams. Red was on her best behavior. Meg was their waitress, after all. The restaurant was very comfortable and congenial; the summer crowds were not yet here. This was the time of year when the locals preferred to eat out, and the place was nearly full of people who knew each other well.

It wasn't until mid-way through the main course that Red understood she was sitting next to a professional. Not only was Harold an editor, a reporter on food, and an expert on taste and presentation, but he was also the penultimate dinner companion. It was his quiet prompting, his genial questions that elicited all the information about the individuals at the table. He had known that three out of the four were strangers to each other, and so steered the talk away from the mundane to find common interests. Red and the others told stories on themselves at his suggestion. He was the master of the table without anyone knowing it.

During a brief pause in the chatter, as Mandy finished explaining a story of her cultural shock in Maine, and before Harold could lead the path of conversation in whatever direction he intended, Red said, "We have heard much about the three of us, but Harold has said nothing of himself."

"Nothing to tell, my dear. Just an old newspaper man taking a vacation," Harold answered modestly, but sincerely.

"Writing a book," Red prodded. "What sort of book. Tell us about the book."

Harold wiped his chin with his napkin and took a sip of beer. "I am afraid that I would bore you all with the details."

Mandy laughed, "If you think the book would bore us, your friends, what makes you think anyone else would want to read it?"

"Touché, my Tennessee belle," the editor responded. "You have a wit about you, but there is truth in what you say. Are you sure you'd like to hear about my book?"

After everyone had answered in the affirmative he continued. "The working title is *The Search for the Perfect Éclair.* I was the youngest of three boys, coming along late in my mother's life. Being her youngest son, I believe she thought me special. I must have been around four or so, my brothers were in school. My mother and I would go shopping together and as a treat, she would take me into the local bakery. While sometimes we sampled other goodies, it was the chocolate éclairs that were our favorite. We always ate them in the store or out on the sidewalk. We never took any home for the rest of the family. It was our secret.

"Although this meal has been excellent, and I will compliment the chef; in my mind, there is nothing so good as the memory of those chocolate éclairs. The book I am beginning to compile is anecdotes, recipes and reviews of family-owned bakeries throughout the United States. One might call it sort of a travelogue with calories."

Red looked at Harold and thought of her own son, her youngest son, and wondered what he would remember of his mother when he got to be gray.

Meg came by and asked if the foursome wished to see the dessert menu. In unison they groaned from the completeness of the meal, but coffee was ordered all around.

Mandy leaned toward Coach, "Should we tell them what's back at your apartment?"

He smiled at her lovingly, "Are you sure? We do have an expert here, after all.

Red looked at the conspiring couple, completely baffled.

"It's Granny's recipe," Mandy stated. "The pecans were harvested from her front yard. I've been practicing. Yep, I'm ready." Hollywood turned to the others to explain. "I told Mandy I had hoped to take her out with some friends for a real Downeast seafood dinner. She wanted to impress you locals here with a southern dish in return, so she's baked a pecan pie. Ice cream is in the freezer. After coffee, let's walk around the dock for a while, and then back to my apartment for a taste of heaven. It may not be as good as Harold's chocolate éclairs, but it'll be close."

"Before we do that, though," Mandy said, "I need to find the ladies room."

"I'll go with you," Red volunteered.

As they stood side by side washing their hands, Red said, "Mandy, Hon, you are a lucky woman."

Mandy smiled at her knowing what she was thinking. "Red, it's funny. I mean an hour and a half ago, we were strangers. Now, I think, we are more than friends. I want to tell you something. I have never, ever told anyone this before, not even my closest friends. I would make you promise not to spread this around, but that's silly. If I didn't trust you, I wouldn't tell you, and I have to tell someone."

Red felt privileged to hear the secret, although she had no idea what the secret was about. "I would promise to keep quiet, but who would I tell anyway?"

"Coach says you're different."

"How does he mean different?" Red replied, not sure if this was a compliment or not.

"You've seen how gorgeous the man is. You've seen the women drool over him. He says that you don't care about any of that; that you like him because of what's inside."

Red did not say anything, because she did not know what to say.

"Women think of me as the luckiest woman in the world," Mandy continued. "And I am, but not for the reason they think. I love Coach for himself, his body means nothing to me."

Red responded quietly, "Yep, but you will admit, his body ain't bad."

Mandy turned to Red. "This is what I need to tell somebody, just one person. Red, it's not but two inches long, fully extended."

Red looked back at Mandy in shock and disbelief. Slowly her visage changed from surprise to amusement. Finally with a burst of laughter Red embraced the younger woman. "Always something wrong with the suckers, darling. Never been a perfect man made yet. For awhile there I thought you had one."

Mandy returned the laugh. "No not perfect, but almost."

Red batted back, "Almost perfect, just comes up a little short."

The two returned to the table better friends than when they left. Red put her hand on Coach's shoulder as she passed his chair, just as he had done to Kyle. She leaned down and whispered. "Coach, you got a good one, don't ever let her get away."

She straightened and looked at Harold. Harold returned the look. He knew a lot about food and entertaining. He had never, though, figured out the mysteries of women.

They left the table and the restaurant to walk along the pier before heading toward Granny's pecan pie. Mandy snuggled against Coach. Harold and Red walked side by side. Red looked up to Harold and asked, "Tell me about éclairs."

"Oh," he responded. "Let's see, they are a not-so-simple, elongated French dough with vanilla cream extruded into their center. Often times they are then topped with chocolate or another flavor."

"I know all that," Red said as she grabbed his hand playfully. "Tell me how long they are," she whispered so that Mandy would not hear.

"Six inches or so," Harold guessed, using his free hand as a ruler.

Red laughed to herself and squeezed his hand, *"fully extended,"* she thought.

THE MISFIT

RENAE FELT THAT SHE was a misfit. She was fourteen and her childhood peers seemed so adolescent. Those adults she associated with seemed so remote. She belonged to neither the world of grown people, nor of growing people. She was lost, or at least that is how she felt. When she was a child she used to smile often. Now as a teenager, she rarely smiled. In her attempts to find her place, she tried everything, but in all her acquaintances, there were no friends, in all her loves, no romance, and in all her trials, no success. Her attitude was made worse by each failure to find satisfaction.

Renae was a turtle. She carried her shell around everywhere she went and often retracted herself from unwanted attention. Few people tried to reach her, and those that did try were rebuffed. She was intelligent, but refused to use that intelligence. Over time her teachers ceased to ask her to learn, only requiring that she not be disruptive. Her cronies were useless to her.

Chad was the opposite. He was a friendly boy, not bright, but determined. He was not overly popular, nor did he excel at sports, but he had his circle of friends and at home he was exposed to various ideas, experiences and challenges; for fourteen he was a well-rounded fellow. Teachers liked Chad and thought that if he continued to apply himself, he would turn out all right.

It was a Monday, lunchtime. Chad sat with two of his buddies, Mort and Ken. Mort was a loud mouth, not really Chad's good friend, but they often shared lunch together as they had the same fourth period class. Ken was Mort's sidekick, and as such, he normally said very little, except to agree with his partner. On this particular Monday Renae sat alone, ignored by and ignoring everyone, at the table next to the three boys. She was facing Chad while Ken and Mort had their backs to her. She sat quietly eating her banana.

Mort was in exceedingly high spirits and was louder than normal. "Chad, man, your father is crazy!" he declared.

Chad, who had often been embarrassed by his father's actions cautiously agreed, "Yeah, I know," but was unsure of which particular instance Mort was speaking of.

"No, I mean real wacko," laughed Mort.

"Space cadet," volunteered Ken.

Chad could sense that this was not going to be pleasant, and swore under his breath at this father for setting him up like this.

"Ken and I were riding our bikes down your street yesterday afternoon, and we see your Old Man out riding his lawn mower, singing as loud as he can," Mort began.

"Yeah, I know. He likes to sing whenever he mows," Chad responded hoping that this was all there was to the story. He could guess, though, judging from Mort's glee that there was more to come.

"The deal was," Mort continued, "the grass didn't need to be cut. He was just riding around singing!"

"Something about some prison or something," chimed in Ken.

"Ken and I pulled our bikes over at the corner and watched. It was hilarious to see the dude, singing and mowing, his arms a swayin'. He was having a grand time."

Chad could picture his father doing this; he had done it before but never in full view of the neighborhood and never in front of Chad's friends. Chad had only recently come to the realization that his father was not the worst father around. Certainly not the best father, but still not the worst. Mort's father was a drunk and Ken did not ever see his father. But now Chad was deeply embarrassed, and his face showed it.

Still, Mort was not done. Encouraged by Chad's discomfort, he continued the story with a sinister glee. "And then he goes riding his mower over to where your Mom is working in her flowers. He must have been attracted by something, 'cause he turns off the engine, jumps off the mower and runs over to your Old Lady and grabs her on the ass!"

"He was hot, you could tell," added Ken.

"Hot, nothing, he was ablaze," returned Mort. "He started hugging your Mom, kissing on her neck and sliding his hands up her shirt." At this Chad's face turned a deeper crimson. He wanted to run from the table, he wanted to punch both his father and this loud mouth in the face. Chad felt sure he was about to die, but knowing that he wasn't, made the embarrassment worse.

"Your Mom puts up a little argument, like women do," Mort continued, "but he persuades her to go into the house with him. I think she went because she was afraid he would strip her down and take her right there on the front lawn if she didn't."

"So, we thought the show was over," Ken interrupted.

"Yeah, we were getting ready to ride away, when we notice that they had not made it into the bedroom. Your Old Man was ripping the clothes off your Mom in the front room!" This was Mort talking and laughing again. "We were getting an eye full, before your Mom breaks away and pulls down the blinds."

"Your Mom's got pretty big knockers," added Ken.

If it were possible to die of embarrassment, we would be reading Chad's obituary now. He had no escape, not even death. He simply sat at the lunch table and turned twenty-five shades of red.

"I wish my father would sing," Renae offered softly from the next table. It was a simple statement, spoken only loud enough that few could hear, and said as if to herself, but Chad heard it, although Ken and Mort seemed not to, for they continued their laughter.

Chad looked across to Renae. He had grown up with this girl, had been in the same classes in the early grades, but he had never really looked at her until now. Why had he not noticed her? He forgot about his friends and their silly teasing. Their eyes met. Hers were full of sympathy for this boy so tormented by his comrades and full of sincerity as well, for she did wish that her father would sing. His eyes were filled with thankfulness for being rescued by someone he had known forever, but until now had never known as a friend.

As they gazed into each other's faces across lunch tables, Renae smiled a wane little smile. Chad returned the smile. The bell rang announcing the end of lunch break. Time to move to the next class. Renae had gathered her books together, disposed of her trash and was headed down the hall well ahead of Chad. Chad's next classroom was down the right hand hallway, while Renae was traveling down the left.

Chad pushed left through the class change crowd and managed to catch up with Renae and touched her shyly on the arm. Surprised, she turned to see who wanted her attention. She regarded him with a puzzled look for she thought their conversation had ended in the lunchroom.

"Harry Bellefonte and Johnny Cash," Chad said.

"What?" she asked, quite bewildered.

"Harry Bellefonte and Johnny Cash. Songs by those old timers is what my father likes to sing." As Chad said this he realized how crazy he sounded. He smiled, for it reminded him that his old man was crazy. But his old man sure seemed to get pleasure out of life.

Renae smiled back, a broad and genuine smile. A smile unlike any she had chanced to use in years. Subconsciously, she swept back her disheveled hair from her face, pleased that this boy would care enough about what she thought to catch up with her and then tell her 'Harry Bellefonte and Johnny Cash'.

They exchanged smiles a moment longer, then, without saying another word, Chad hurried back toward his next class and Renae resumed her walk to hers. Warmed by the exchange Renae thought that she felt better than she had in weeks. Chad, as he sped along in the opposite direction, thought that he felt better than he ever had in his whole life.

THE MOUSE QUEEN
A Fairy Tale

I AM SURE THAT you have seen pictures of the Fairy Queen, standing tall amongst the dew drops, her subjects in poses of submission at her feet. The Fairy Queen has her wand, her blonde locks, her gossamer wings and her smile. But now imagine if you will, a Mouse Queen. Not a mouse at all, but the Queen of Mice. She is human, without wings, but with as pretty a smile, as bountiful a head of hair, and as impressive a wand as any Fairy Queen. Instead of in buttercups, this Queen reigns in the subterranean tunnels and passageways beneath the houses of the village of Kamloops, Canada.

She is tall, this Queen, and barely fits in the tunnels. The mice have had to enlarge many of the smaller ones so their monarch can get through. Instead of the crepe and crinoline of the Fairy Queen, the Queen of the Mice wears a most luxurious fur coat, made from the pelts of hundreds of the finest mice. These mice were honorably sacrificed so that the Queen could have a regal cloak, a queenly cloak to wear for warmth and appearance.

The mice love their Queen; they adore her. She is the charm that gives their kingdom class. They are proud of her and often brag to mice from the neighboring fiefdoms of their good fortune in having such a benevolent and beautiful ruler. They are her loyal subjects and would do anything for her, as evidenced by those that gave their lives to provide her coat. She accepts their devotion with gracious good will, but often she wonders if she was meant for Queendom. *'How many girls,'* she muses *'dream of growing up to be Mouse Queen?'* She can think of none.

Truth be told, she was coerced into the job. It had been her plan to be a country music singer, famous, with a band standing behind her. How strange it is that fate brought our lady to stand before a band of mice instead of musicians.

I recall a story I read in High School, *The Man Who Shot Snapping Turtles* by Edmund Wilson. The man in the story enjoyed seeing mallard ducks swim on his pond. In the springtime, when the ducklings would first venture upon the water, the snapping turtles that lived in the pond would catch and devour the slowest ones. This infuriated the man. He began a vendetta against the turtles, shooting them on sight. Gradually, though, he learned to respect his enemy, and before long he was offering solace to the creatures instead of killing them.

So also it was with our Queen. Her house had been invaded for the winter. Mice were scrambling everywhere. Her dogs were driven batty by the rodents, and called to their mistress to destroy the invaders. Destroy them she tried, but like the man with the snapping turtles, gradually, grudgingly, she came to admire the mice as worthy adversaries. She began to see individual mice, to name them, to talk to them. She still tried to kill them, but it was much more in sport now than in anger. As time went by, even the thrill of the sport was gone. One evening on the first of December, which coincidentally was her birthday, she lay upon the sofa in the den considering her miserable situation and talking to herself. She could hear the scampering of the tiny feet. "Why am I the one?" she asked aloud. "What have I done to deserve this?"

A wee, high-pitched voice answered her, "Judi, we love you. We are devoted to you. As long as we live, we will never go away. And we are so many; you will never destroy us all. Accept us for what we are."

Our Queen thought she had been drinking too much. While she had talked to the mice before, none had ever answered her. Thinking herself either drunk, or delirious, or senile she replied to the voice, "Go away."

This was followed by an eerie silence. No scurrying, no nibbling, all was quiet. Our lady could hear the ticking of the old mantle clock. Curious, how such ticking fades into forgottenness except at times when the quiet is most unnerving. After several minutes of this silence, the soon to be Queen said, "I know that you're still here."

"Judith, Queen of Mice," a squeaky but still stately voice said from the end of the couch where her feet lay, "we adore you."

Our lady looked between her bedroom slippers, and there standing on two feet at the end of the sofa was a mouse of official bearing and considerable age. Amazed to see this mouse standing on two feet, dressed in a morning coat and speaking to her, she could say nothing, and so remained silent.

"Worthy Madame, accept our adulation," the mouse continued. "Let me introduce myself as the Lord Chamberlain of our band. Be our Queen and we shall look after you all your days. We humbly beseech you to reign over us, to guide us. We are a great nation, and though each of us is small in stature, we make up for our diminutive size by our numbers, our devotion and our breeding capacity."

'This has got to be a bad dream,' Judi thought. 'This can not be happening.'

"I know that this must seem preposterous, oh regal monarch," the wise old mouse continued. "We mice have great virtues and value. All we lack is leadership. We are prepared to hand you undeniable power and riches beyond belief."

"Power and riches?" Queen Judith asked mockingly. "You are but mice, rodents. What riches do you have?"

A smile appeared upon the Lord Chamberlain's face. "Bring our Majesty her royal necklace," he shouted and spread his arms wide to accentuate his words.

Around the couch, a multitude of mice appeared, singing. Across the floor, a train of mice shouldered a necklace of exquisite pearls. Each mouse bore the weight of two pearls and there were twenty mice in all. The Queen looked astonished. "Madame," said the Chamberlain at her feet, "we may seem poor, but we find the missing and hidden treasures in all of Kamloops. Accept this ribbon of pearls, each pearl a discard until we pieced them together, as a token, a small token of our high esteem for you."

With this said, our Queen sat up, being careful where she placed her feet so as not to crush any of her new subjects. The line of mice carrying the string of pearls climbed up the couch and along the back. They were all very reverent and solemn and soon they had the necklace strung around the Queen's neck. Beautiful they were too, the pearls, made more beautiful by the beauty of the woman that wore them. "My Lady," declared the mouse spokesman with a deep bow, "the radiance of the pearls are increased ten-fold by the radiance that emanates from you. Pardon me for being so bold, but my dear you are stunning."

Stunning or not, our Queen was a sucker for compliments. The necklace did indeed compliment her natural good looks, and she knew it. As she sat there feeling the pearls on her chest, she wondered what other treasures these mice might have. When she thought of all the valuables that she or others she knew had lost, it dawned on her that these mice must surely have hordes of treasure. She turned to look at the Lord Chamberlain and asked, "And what about power? You mentioned power and riches. I can see and feel the riches, but what power would the Mouse Queen have?"

"Madame, we mice, ten times ten thousand strong, would befriend any friend of yours. Likewise, would we be enemies to any enemy. We have in the recent past caused you grief. Imagine what we could do to others should you command. We know that you are not a vengeful lady, but certainly there is mischief that we could do on your behalf. Someone that irritates you, we could irritate. Someone that ignores you, we would not ignore, if you understand my drift. We stand by to do your biding."

"And what am I to do then, as your Queen? What are my duties?"

"You will be high judge in mouse disputes. You will represent the kingdom at the annual convention of Western Canadian Mousedom. You will, in all things, be supreme ruler."

As Queen Judi sat in her bathrobe, warm-up pants, bedroom slippers and her pearls she happened to glance to the kitchen. There were her two dogs, miserable that their mistress would allow such goings on as a coronation by the horde of mice. "What, friend?" she asked of the Chamberlain, "am I to abandon my job and my dogs for you mice?"

"Your two dogs shall be your guides and your pillars. One will sit at your right hand, the other at your left hand. Each will offer the comfort and security that only a dog can offer. We shall obey them as we do you. We take no offense with dogs, for we have a common adversary. As for your current employ, my Lady, that would be up to you. We can provide you with funds for whatever purpose you need, but it may be that you would wish to keep your current position for now, at least."

As an after thought, the old mouse said, "Queen Judith, you can also sing to us whenever you wish. While none of us have the talent to play an instrument, we can all hum along. We have heard you singing in the shower, and your voice is divine."

The Queen looked again to the kitchen and with a nod invited her two canines to join her amongst the rodents. "Dogs, what do you think?" she inquired when they had carefully come and sat beside their mistress. "Shall we bond with this motley crew? Didn't you always want to be in charge?"

The dogs, being dogs, loyal and trusting forever, simply wagged their tales and were glad that at least this vermin surrounding them were not rats.

These were mice, a much nobler breed than rats; nobler than squirrels who are but rats with furry tails. Judi accepted the monarchy although she did not give up her day job; content to be Mouse Queen only in her off-hours. The mice seemed to appreciate this arrangement as well, for it preserved many hours of freedom to which they had become accustomed during the years without a Queen.

Queen Judith took over the finances with the advice of the chief mouse of the exchequer. Soon the country was prosperous from all the dimes and quarters the mice collected. Industrious creatures by nature, they were made even more so by the encouragement of their ruler. Judith stressed education for all mice, strengthening the public education system. Health care was another of her priorities. Soon the entire area around Kamloops was home to prosperous, industrious, educated mice.

Other communities of mice came under the sway of the success of Queen Judith's minions. One after another of these bands asked for merger with the Kamloops clan. It was not long before all the mice of the Province pledged by allegiance to this handsome Queen. There were setbacks and misfortunes along the trail, but eventually the mice of the principality entered into a true age of enlightenment. There was one thing amiss, however. Each new success brought our Queen a new feeling of emptiness.

She could easily have given up her regular employment, but she thought that perhaps, for her sanity, real work, honest work might be needed. After a hard day on the job, however, she would wonder if it weren't the employment that made her crazy and the mice that kept her sane. She had her coat and her pearls, but she could not show them off, for fear of the questions people would ask. She used the mice for her own ends very little, but took great satisfaction in helping the mouse community to grow and prosper. These were however, mice. Every once in a while, she would exchange glances with one or the other of her dogs and in the silent communication the mutual thought would be *'What in the world is going on? Why are we doing this?'*

Judi did become attached to individual mice. In particular Lord Chamberlain, whose guidance and authority she could not have governed without, was a favorite. It was a great shock and sadness when the old fellow died in his bed one night. All mousedom attended the funeral and Queen Judith herself gave the eulogy. The Chamberlain's absence created a void in the society of mice. A search committee was formed to find a replacement. The Queen appointed a panel to interview all worthy candidates. Eventually a new mouse was named to the post, but the bond of trust and affection was never the same.

So our Queen was taken with a certain disaffection, an emptiness. She was still a superb ruler, a kind Queen, a most benevolent and fair Monarch, a true philosopher Queen; yet she and the mice knew that something was amiss.

In the Province of humans for this portion of Canada, there is a lottery. For a dollar, one can purchase a chance to win millions of dollars. Of course, in order to win millions, millions of people must participate with their dollars, and thus the actual chance of winning is very small. But it happened that someone from the village of Kamloops won the biggest prize ever in this lottery. It was assumed that it was someone from Kamloops, for that was the location of the store that sold the ticket.

But no winner came forward to claim the prize. No winning ticket was produced. Weeks went by and the unclaimed money sat in the Provincial vault waiting. Soon the entirety of the human community was awash in curiosity. Who won? Why did they not claim the fortune? The mouse community did not normally pay much attention to the news and gossip of their human co-habitants, but even they wondered about this. The new mouse Chamberlain wondered, too. He knew that he would never be accepted as the old fellow had been, but he thought, *'If I could do something spectacular, even Queen Judith would appreciate me. If I could produce that winning ticket....'*

Quietly he spread the word, *'Find that lottery ticket'*. All the mice were soon inspecting every likely hiding place, everywhere that a scrap of paper might end up, every crack and every cranny. Every wastebasket was checked. Every drawer in every desk examined. Even wallets were opened in the dark of night to see if it might be there. Who better to find a missing treasure than a horde of mice? And, sure enough, after a long search in every likely and unlikely hiding place, the winning ticket was found. It was found in the shirt pocket of a man who had then deposited the shirt in the laundry basket. Apparently, before the shirt was washed, the man's wife had run away with the regional beer distributor's head salesman. The husband, being distraught and not much of a housekeeper forgot all about the shirt at the bottom of the laundry basket. In forgetting about the shirt, he also forgot about the lottery ticket that he had purchased hoping to share the winnings with his wife.

It was a determined mouse that braved the horde of neighborhood cats to find that ticket. The new Lord Chamberlain was ecstatic. He called a convention of the mice together so that he could present the ticket to Queen Judith with proper pomp and circumstance. "Dearest Queen," he said while handing the slip to his surprised Monarch, "Here is a fortune offered to you on behalf of all the subjects of your kingdom. This small, determined mouse by my side located the forgotten and misplaced lottery ticket. After consultation with the mouse Duma, we have decided to turn it over to you to use in whatever way you see fit." As the ticket was handed over to Judi, the mouse chorus began to sing, *For She's a Jolly Good Fellow,* and the entire assemblage of mice roared their approval.

The Queen was shocked. She looked down upon her loyal subjects and smiled a wane smile as she tried to think of a proper response. Her first words were, "Excuse me please." She left the room and went to the telephone stand. She thumbed through the phone book for the number, then dialed up the local lottery office. As the clerk read off the numbers of the winning ticket, and as those numbers matched the ticket she held in her hand, Judi was even more astonished than before. Here was a real fortune. Of all the creatures to find this misplaced ticket, doesn't it make sense that the mice would be the ones? What other creature frequents the hidden corners, the cracks and crevices of life, the abandoned laundry? Judi was resolved in her mind though; she knew what was right.

Upon returning to the gathered mouse horde, she called them all to attention. "Dear Friends," she began, "I know now why there has been a recent increase in the loss of mice to traps and by cat attack. You were searching for this ticket. My congratulations to the one that found it." The Lord Chamberlain spoke up, "My Lady, it was Henry here, that located the prize." Henry stood back, shyly bowing his head but glowing all the same.

"Excellent job Henry. You will be given a medal for your bravery and success," the Queen said. "Listen, all you mice. I realize the sacrifices that all have made to secure this paper, but unlike the pennies and nickels we find in the dirt, this we must return to the proper owner."

All the mice were shocked. Their dream of buying and then exterminating all the cats in the Province was dashed. The Lord Chamberlain, recovering his composure dared to interrupt, "But Queen, the ticket was fairly lost, would never have been turned in, was forgotten. It is ours by right of the finder, for it was lost, not stolen. My Lady, we are not thieves!" This little mouse potentate was becoming more upset as he spoke. First, the thought of losing the many millions of dollars, and then the idea that his mice were somehow being accused of stealing, made the blood run to his face, and the temper to his head.

"No, my friends," spoke the Queen. "In all honor and justice we must return this ticket surreptitiously, as it was removed. I know that you did no intentional wrong in bringing it here, but we will do much right to return it to the person to whom it belongs."

The mice were silent.

"Henry," asked the Queen after a pause. "Henry, would you like the honor of placing this ticket in the path of the human?"

Henry, obedient but also aware of the great danger in entering the house which stood next door to the home of a hundred cats, bowed his head and said nothing.

"Your Majesty," spoke the Lord Chamberlain, "We mice have risked much in finding this ticket, and Henry in particular, for there is a house of stray cats that live next door to the house of the ticket. We will do what you ask, but please be alert to the danger to any mouse that would return the slip of paper."

The Queen thought for a while. "What is the address? We can mail it."

The Lord Chamberlain was forming an idea of his own. If the mice could not have the fortune for themselves, perhaps a share of the prize would still be possible. Surely the owner, in his gratitude for discovering the ticket would propose a finder's fee. Ten per cent of such a trove would still be ample to buy and deport all the felines of the valley.

"Madame," the Chamberlain suggested, "would you risk such a valuable token in the mail of this country? And what would the owner think, upon opening such a letter? Would he not be suspicious? I think it needs to be hand delivered to the winner, and Majesty, if I should be so bold, you are the one to deliver it."

Queen Judith responded, "You know the owner and it is a 'he'? Lord Chamberlain, you were promoted to your position for your wisdom and good council. I see the logic of your thought, and furthermore, I have no desire to risk another mouse's life returning this lottery. When I was a child there was a weekly story of a man that delivered a million dollars to people to see what they would do with it. It was everyone's dream to be the recipient, but I always wondered what it would be like to be the deliverer.

New Lord Chamberlain smiled. Queen Judith smiled. The whole of mousedom smiled.

"Tell me more of this winner," asked the Queen. "I have no reason to know, but my curiosity is now aroused. I shall while away an hour here listening to your stories."

So the Queen was informed of the man that had misplaced the ticket. There were certain embellishments to be sure, in particular the matter of the hundred or so cats that roamed loose over that neighborhood, and the matter of the attractive looks of the gentleman. All in all, though, the truth was spoken.

The end of our tale is here. And what of the Queen meeting the man? What of the plan to buy all the cats? This is a fairy tale, and as fairy tales end happily ever after, you already know the answers.

PUPPY LOVE

Blonde Jokes

NANCY DELMINOSKI'S HAIR WAS dark, brunette, nearly black except for those few independent strands that had turned gray. She wore it cut short to accent her gracefully long neck. It is important to know that although her hair was dark, she never looked upon blondes as in any way inferior. She was proud of her hair, and would not change it even if she could. Some days though, some mornings on the fourth floor of the Tompkins County Mental Health Center, Nancy felt the need to smile. She felt the need to be brightened, to let a little lightness into her heart. For this she had come to rely upon one of her cubicle mates, Doris. Doris was blonde, naturally blonde.

Doris was always up spirited. It was to Doris that all the workers on the fourth floor looked when they needed a laugh. Doris' energy and enthusiasm for life made the workday go by so much quicker. She always had a story or joke to tell, and being blonde, she loved to tell blonde jokes and laugh at herself.

Reserved Nancy had taken longer than most to warm to Doris' charms, but she too came to rely upon the good humor and camaraderie that the blonde spread around the office. Nancy did not normally care for ethnic jokes. Although sometimes seeing the humor, she always felt demeaned along with which ever group or class of people the joke humiliated. She often wondered if generalizing about blondes was not also demeaning. How could you not laugh though, when it was blonde Doris making the joke about herself?

It was a Monday morning and Nancy had had a difficult weekend at home. On days like this, work seemed a refuge and a curse all at the same time. It was a refuge from her domestic trials but also a curse, to be here, in this office, with these clients, instead of on the farm that she loved. Days like this made Doris seem especially valuable.

"Heard a new joke over the weekend, Nana," Doris began as soon as Nancy had removed her coat and sat down at her desk. "Are you ready for it?"

"Doris, I need a lift right now, tell me your joke," Nancy replied.

"Three blondes, walking along a beach. As they walk, one of them kicks an old oil lamp in the sand. She reaches down and lifts up the lamp and as she brushes the sand from it, a puff of smoke comes out and *poof* there is a Genie."

Doris said all this while standing along side Nancy's desk and with all the proper pantomime and voice inflection. She was excellent at telling jokes and Nancy could picture the situation clearly through her words.

"Anyway, this Genie pops out and says, 'All right ladies, three wishes, you each get one.'

"The first blonde thinks a minute and says 'I wish to be twice as smart as I am now.' Genie says 'No problem.' And POW, she turns into a brunette.

"Second blonde sees how her friend has changed and considers a minute then says, 'I don't need to be twice as smart, just half again smarter than I am now.' Genie says, 'No problem.' And ZAP she is a red head.

"Third blonde looks at both her friends, then says 'I like being blonde. Better make me half as stupid as I am now.' Genie says, 'No problem.' And WOP, she becomes a man."

Nancy, caught off guard by the ending, laughed out loud. "Doris," she said, "I've had a terrible weekend, and you are always so upbeat, I am glad that you are around to cheer me up."

Doris paused a moment, the twinkle diminished in her eyes. "Nana, I use these jokes to hide a lot of things. It pains me to think about my troubles sometimes, so I tell these jokes and when I see other people laugh, it makes me feel better."

Nancy had never seen this side of Doris. She looked at her friend standing by the desk and together they shared a wordless moment of understanding. Then the first crisis of the week began.

"I have to see Nancy Delminoski!" shouted a female voice from the alcove of the elevator.

"Where is she? I need to see her right away," the lady demanded.

Nancy took another glance at Doris, who was back to herself, and retreating toward her own office space. A smile of acceptance passed between them as she left.

Nancy was aggressively approached by a short, indeterminately aged lady with the lightest blonde hair imaginable. The hair was not white, but true blonde, the hair color sometimes observed in young boys. The lady wore heavy rimmed glasses and carried a large purse, which she plopped upon Nancy's desk.

"Nancy Delminoski, I need to talk with you," the woman said as she deposited herself in the chair across the desk from Nancy.

"We normally have appointments to see clients. I am sure that the intake officer made that clear downstairs," Nancy replied.

"Oh, no time for that, this won't take but a few minutes," the woman said, decreasing her tone of voice, and becoming a little less haughty.

"Do you have the necessary intake form for me?" Nancy asked.

The woman pulled out an empty form and handed it to Nancy.

"This needs to be completed downstairs before you can come up here," Nancy explained, seeing the empty form.

"Listen Honey," the woman asserted herself. "You start filling out the form; you and I will reach an understanding, and then I'll be gone and you can get on with the rest of your day. You and I are both too busy to worry about all this other crap."

Nancy was beginning to wonder if she needed to make an immediate referral to the detox unit for this lady. There was, however, something completely different about her that intrigued Nancy. This was obviously not the ordinary client.

Nancy took the form and began by asking, "Last name?"

"O'Peers," answered the woman, spelling out the double e.

Nancy had never run across anyone with that particular name and she asked, as a way of building the bond between client and provider, not that the question was on the form, "Irish descent?"

"Part Leprechaun on my mother's side," came the unexpected response.

"Hah!" chuckled Nancy and then to herself, 'Might have to send this one to the wacko ward.' "First and Middle names?" she continued.

"Jean Ellen."

"Address?"

"Look, Honey, you got all the information you need to know. Don't be wasting my time or yours." As she spoke Jean pointed to her name on the form.

Nancy looked at the finger in amazement. There was an extra joint in it, and in all the fingers of her hand. Nancy could not recall ever having seen such a deformity before, and was taken aback. Even more unusual, though, was that somehow the information on the form had changed. No longer was the name *O'Peers, Jean Ellen*, but it had become switched around and modified to read *Jean E. O'Peers.*

Nancy was speechless as she looked from form to face.

"Why do you make fun of blondes, Nana?" Jean E. asked.

Nancy's jaw dropped. 'How did this woman know her familiar name? What was going on here?' she wondered.

Nancy gathered herself and said in a firm voice, "This must be a joke. I wish you would tell me what this is all about."

"Sure, but that's one," countered Jean E.

As she said this Jean E. opened her purse and put a cigarette to her lips, lit it and began to puff.

"You can't smoke in here!" admonished Nancy. "This is a public building. No smoking allowed!"

"Sorry," said Jean E., crushing the fire of the cigarette out with her fingers and putting it back in her purse. "I do better with a little smoke."

It occurred to Nancy that Doris must have something to do with this practical joke. "Doris!" she called, but Doris had left the floor on an errand so there was no answer.

Nancy looked at the lady again and said, "This is some kind of joke. You can't come in here without filling out an intake form. You have to have an appointment. You can't smoke. Ms. O'Peers, I am not stupid, someone put you up to this and I wish I knew who it was."

"I'll tell you in a minute, but that is two. You only have one more left." Jean E. said in a resigned manner. "Look, Nana, you asked me to explain what this is all about. Sit there a minute and let me before you waste your last wish."

Nancy sat back in her chair, shaking her head, saying under her breath, "This is unbelievable."

"I know you don't believe me," began Jean E. "Most people don't. But what do you have to loose? You think your friends put me up for this? I don't come so cheap as what they could afford. You were expecting some dude in baggy pants and arms folded across his chest? Listen, it ain't like that. Me and you. And you've already wasted two of your wishes. You thought blondes were dumb, at least they made three real wishes."

Nancy was astounded by the acting ability of this woman. She seemed so naturally aggressive and confident. Nancy wondered if somewhere a video camera was running, recording all this for playback at some future County office picnic. She decided to go along with the gag, but for good measure and to show that she knew it was a joke, she crossed the fingers of her right hand.

"My first wish was for you to explain what this is all about," Nancy said. "That means I should be able to ask questions without jeopardizing my final wish?"

"Right, so long as the questions refer to the process," replied Jean E.

"How does it work? How do you expect me to believe that you really can make wishes come true?"

Jean E. gathered herself to explain, "Nana, it's not belief, it's not trust. You think your friends have sent me here to set you up. Screw your friends, pardon my English. Think to yourself, what is the one thing in all this world that you want? Most people, first desire is money, which is stupid. Besides we don't do money any more, to much hassle with the IRS, withholding and all that. You want me to explain so I am telling you, you don't want money.

"Some people want love," she continued, warming to the subject. "You know what I give 'em, those idiots that want love? I get a puppy. Even a puppy pees on the rug, but that is better than most things that offer love. Nana, you don't want love.

"Other people waste a wish on world peace or some grand thing like that. What do they think I am? Hell, God hasn't even been able to deliver much on that world peace dream. A sunny day I can do. I've already brightened your day."

Nancy had to admit that she was now enjoying this conversation, not that she had uncrossed her fingers.

"Well, Jean, what kind of thing can you deliver, if not money or love or world peace?"

"Nana," Jean E. said as she leaned forward toward her. "Look into yourself and see what it is you really want."

"I would like a friend to talk to," Nana replied.

"I like you, Nana, so I won't let you use that wish," Jean E. said. "You've got good friends already, especially Doris. She understands you, you don't need another friend, just value the ones you already have."

"Jean, you said you don't recommend love. All I want is a little romance, is that too hard?"

"Romance?" exclaimed Jean E. "I can do romance."

"Huh?" questioned Nancy.

"I know what you mean. Real romance, consider it done. So those are your three wishes. Been a pleasure talking to you, I'll take back the intake form and you can get on with your day." As she was saying this Jean E. was pulling herself together, gathering up the purse and form. She stood and left the office without further comment, leaving behind an envelope.

Nancy looked at the envelope and opened it cautiously with her left hand, holding the crossed fingers of her right hand in a conspicuous pose should there actually be a camera filming. Inside the envelope she found a ticket for a four-day cruise to the Caribbean. Also included was a handwritten note that said, *Have a good time, I promise you romance, and I will eventually answer your second question as to who sent me.*

Nancy was as puzzled at this last written comment as by any thing else that had happened on this most unusual Monday morning. She felt the first tinges of anger as she dialed the 800 number listed on the bottom of the ticket. Of all the people to play a joke on her, who had it been?

After successively pressing the appropriate numbers at the successive prompts, Nancy finally got to speak to a live voice.

"Carnival Cruise Lines," the voice said.

"Yes," Nancy began, "I have been presented with a gift, and I need to know more about this. My ticket number is 7097 66651 1476. Could you give me more information please?"

"Oh, yes ma'am," the voice returned. "Mrs. Delminoski, we have been expecting your call. You are booked aboard the Ecstasy on a four-day, four-night cruise to Cozumel and return. You will depart Feb 26th from Miami at 4:00 in the afternoon. You need to be on board no later than 3 o'clock that day. I show you confirmed in an outer cabin on the Rivera deck. The Rivera deck is our lowest deck, the cabins are very nice, but you may wish to upgrade for a small charge if you like. We also show a confirmed airline ticket for you from Newark to Ft. Lauderdale then ground transfer to the ship. You may use the same confirmation number when you contact the airline to secure your seat assignment. Any other questions?"

Nancy was quite astounded by this response. If this had been a fairy tale she would have been in the princess suite and not on the bottom deck, but it was an outward facing cabin, which meant it did have a window overlooking the waves.

"Yes, one question," she said. "Will I be sharing the cabin with anyone?"

"No ma'am, the cabin does have two single beds that can be joined to make a double, and it also has a bunk bed which can be lowered into place, but we show the cabin as booked to you only. For a charge we can allow a guest to accompany you."

"No, that won't be necessary," Nancy replied. "And thank you very much, the Rivera deck will be suitable, I am sure."

"Very good, Mrs. Delminoski. Carnival will be sending you your coupon book for gratuity and bus fare from airport to ship approximately ten days prior to sailing. We know that you will have a grand time on board."

As she hung up the phone, Nancy very slowly began to uncross her fingers.

The Raffle

ANDY TUCKER WAS A miserable creature. He had not always been so, but he was now. His wife had died four years earlier after a battle with breast cancer. Andy carried around a wagonload of guilt along with his loneliness. While his wife was incapacitated, he had, once, only once, sought relief with another woman. Since that time, he had felt dirtied and unworthy of what-ever happiness might come his way, so he made sure to avoid any chance that something good could happen to him.

He was a mortician, an undertaker. He knew all about death, about grieving, about consoling. He was successful at his work. Way back in high school, he had found a job at the neighborhood funeral home, and had stayed there ever since. The family that had run the place for generations sold out to a national chain, and Andy had been moved to manager. That was several years ago now. The community depended upon him. He was a pillar, but after his wife's death, that pillar had withdrawn himself.

The only respite Andy took from his work and from his empty house was to attend Church, St Timothy Episcopal every Sunday. His wife had been raised Episcopalian and at first he had attended to please her. Gradually he had become indoctrinated. He found that he enjoyed the ceremony, enjoyed the music and enjoyed the gentle hand of the reverend's sermons. He had had to drag himself away from his home on Sunday's after his wife's passing, but now, it was natural for him to be there, and if he should miss because of the press of business, he felt badly for a week.

He seldom talked with anyone at church, and outside church, talked only with the families that he served at work. He had become quiet and withdrawn. This man, who had seen so much grieving, could not see the community grieving for him. He sensed himself slipping into a hole, a dark place, but he felt as comfortable there as anywhere. He felt as if that was what he deserved.

One Sunday noon, directly after the Church service, before Andy could slip away, Rev. Olbert clamped a friendly hand upon his shoulder. The Reverend had set himself a mission, and that mission was to save Andy, not his soul so much as his spirit.

"Andy," the reverend began in his usual cheerful voice. "I know that you've heard about the ladies auxiliary raffle we'll be holding. We need to sell tickets, and I thought you could sell a few books for us down at the funeral home."

"Pastor, what's the raffle for, I've forgotten?" Andy asked skeptically.

"Four day cruise for two down to Mexico, I'm sure you remember."

Andy thought a minute. It seemed that there had been some mention of this in a newsletter or Sunday bulletin he had read. "Reverend, I don't like to sell things at the home, you know that. Not right to be hawking raffle tickets at a time of sadness."

"I know Andy, but we've got to sell these tickets," Pastor Olbert replied, hoping that he had presented the baited hook with just the right finesse.

"How many tickets in a book, Pastor?"

Olbert smiled. "Twenty coupons in each book, a dollar a coupon."

Andy reached into his wallet and withdrew two twenty-dollar bills. "Here. Let me pay for two books, you fill them out for some needy people in the neighborhood."

"I'll put your name on them Andy. Maybe you'll win."

"Don't bother, never win anything, wouldn't go even if I did win. Use your name, or put some poor person's name on them."

Olbert reeled in the forty bucks.

Three weeks later, right after Church and prior to the Church Council's annual congregational meeting, Mrs. Downey, a little old lady that had recently lost her husband, her lifelong companion, leaned upon Andy's arm. "Mr. Tucker, would you please walk me downstairs to the meeting. I want so badly to see who wins the cruise."

"Perhaps you'll win Mrs. Downey. The sun would do you good, an escape from this miserable weather," Andy said, letting Mrs. Downey lean against him.

It had always been Andy's job to offer old ladies his arm, so naturally he accompanied Mrs. Downey downstairs. Otherwise he would have gone directly home and not bothered to attend the meeting, not caring whose name was drawn for the trip.

When everyone had assembled in the community room below the Church proper, a volunteer was chosen to lift a ticket from the fishbowl. Maggie, aged 8, was chosen to do the honors. She reached into the container and pulled out a stub, handing it to Reverend Olbert.

"The winner is," Olbert announced, hesitating for proper suspense, "Andy Tucker!"

The congregation erupted in cheers and applause. Mrs. Downey, holding tightly to Andy's arm, pulled him up toward the front to receive his prize.

"Andy," the reverend was all smiles. "A four day cruise to Mexico for you and a guest," he said as he handed Andy the envelope containing the ticket and information. "Congratulations!"

Andy was shocked and surprised and embarrassed. He was also a little miffed that someone he considered a friend would disobey his wishes, and fill the tickets out with his name.

"Pastor, I can't accept this, I have no one to go with. Let me turn this back in and draw someone else's name."

But the assembly would hear none of that. With one voice they hollered for him to go, with several women suggesting in jest, "Take me, Andy."

What Andy did not realize but everyone else knew, was that all 4,207 tickets in the fishbowl had Andy Tucker's name written on them.

The Toast

NEITHER NANA NOR ANDY expected to go on the cruise. Nancy had quizzed every possible friend or relation searching for clues to the source of the ticket. All of them pleaded innocent or appeared clueless. She had checked to see if it was possible to cash it in, but was told that it was non-refundable. Had the winter not been so dull, cold, wet and disappointing, she would not have gone. But one day in early-February, she got fed up with it all, went out and bought a new bathing suit and six days reading material, arranged for childcare and husband care, put in for leave at work, and made up her mind to go. 'Forget Romance,' she thought, ' Just give me a little tan to lighten my winter.'

Nearly everyone at St. Timothy's had hoped Andy would take along a lady friend when he went on the cruise. Rev. Olbert was simply praying that he would go at all. He was also praying that no one would die and need Andy's services in the days immediately preceding the trip, giving Andy an excuse to back out.

Andy did not want to go. He did admit that it had been nice to hear the genuine encouragement from his fellow church members and the community at large. If it had been left up to him though, he would have been content to sit in his quiet house forever, but he decided to go so as to please them, and as it seemed such a waste to turn the tickets back in now. He went to the public library and checked out enough books to fill six days worth of lounging.

So it came to be, dinner the first night of the cruise. The ship had disembarked a few hours earlier, and now Nana and Andy where being seated for the early dinner, the 6 o'clock sitting. The Windstar Dinning Room was filled with circular tables, with ten place settings each. It was, of course, by chance that Nana and Andy were assigned to the same table. He got to the dining room first, promptly at the opening. She was not far behind and was aided in finding the table and selecting a seat by the staff. They sat, not directly opposite, where they would have had to gaze at each other all through the meal, nor close enough that they could hold conversation without shouting, but cattycorner.

Soon their other dining companions appeared and were seated. There was a young couple slobberingly in love, two couples in their sixties traveling together, and a middle-aged pair completed the table. Introductions were made all around and Andy immediately forgot everyone's name. He was on vacation, and while he did not plan to be impolite, he felt no need to be congenial either. Nancy was more curious; alert to whatever strange destiny awaited her, suspecting that something interesting might happen.

The middle-aged fellow asked if he could order wine for the table, which arrived, was opened and poured for all, while the menu selections were being taken. When the waiter had finished explaining and collecting everyone's orders, the man stood and proposed a toast.

"This is our first cruise, my wife and I," he began. " And I would like to make a toast to begin our vacation, but bear with me for a true story before the actual honors.

"1938, my mother had just spent a year caring for her mother, who died of breast cancer." Andy, who had been expecting some humorous monologue, immediately felt a pang of remembrance.

"Mother had taken a leave of absence from her teaching job," the fellow continued. "Her mother died in the spring and the family, in appreciation of the care Mother had given her, all chipped in and bought her a ticket on the cruise ship Mexico, bound for ten days to Havana and Vera Cruz. Mother was 30 at the time, with no regular beau, and quickly slipping beyond the marrying age.

"From her pictures, she must have been quite a good looker, and unaccompanied, she was invited to the Captain's table for dinner. The third mate, also 30, was assigned to keep her company. He must have been a dashing sight in his uniform with his cap tilted at a jaunty angle. He had a whistle and a laugh and a self-confident air about him. Six months after the cruise they were married, the schoolteacher and the third mate, and they remained married for over 50 years.

"He was sailor, a seaman all his life, and, like most seamen, he loved to bend the elbow, and he loved to offer the toast. To you, my friends," the man pointed toward the young couple with his glass. "And to all of you," he extended his arm to include the whole of the table, "the toast my father always offered and may it be true for you as it was for him and his bride; *Here's to Romance.*"

There were smiles all around as the glasses clinked. Nancy was warmed by the good wine as she sipped, and she was warmed by the man's story. Andy, whose first inclination had been to decline the wine, was glad that he had relented. He had no need for romance, but it was a fine story to begin a cruise.

After supper, most of the passengers attended the evening cabaret show, but Andy decided to walk the deck and explore the ship. It had become breezy and the ocean swell of the Florida current made the ship sway gently. Along the port side of the promenade deck, Andy stopped and leaned against the rail. Couples were walking by together; other travelers were leaning against the railing at regular intervals and taking in the sea air.

Nancy noticed the single man who had shared her table at dinner come and stand eight feet from her. He did not seem to notice her. She had come out to watch the moon rise. Both Nancy and Andy had remained very reserved at dinner, neither one was impolite, but neither had had much to say. Andy had wondered whether his New Zealand lamb had really come from New Zealand, and Nancy had wondered what the difference was between shrimp and prawns.

As she watched the glow of the recently full moon ascend from the waves, she smiled and thought what a miserable night it must be back home. "It is prettier than I had imagined," she said of the moonrise.

Andy, realizing for the first time that he was standing a short distance from the lady at the table, turned towards her and wished he had remembered her name. Feeling that he needed to reply to her statement or seem rude, he asked, "I wonder if that story was really true."

"You mean Mr. Cooke's story about how his mother and father met?" Nancy asked. "Perhaps we should ask him to tell us more about it?"

They fell silent again, leaning on the railing, looking out over the sea.

After a while, Nancy said, "It has been a long day, what with the airplanes and connections. Goodnight Mr. Tucker, is that right?"

"Yes, that's right, but Andy will be fine," he responded. "Good night."

Nancy went below to her cabin, opened the shades so that she could see the ocean waves reflected in the ship's lights, and was asleep within five minutes. Andy stayed on deck a while longer, then he too made his way to his cabin, which, coincidentally, was but three doors away from Nancy's. He too opened the shades to watch the waves, and fell asleep within five minutes.

Number 45 Protection

ANDY WAS, BY NATURE, an early riser. He watched the sun come boiling out of the ocean as he had watched the moon rise the night before. After a few minutes viewing, he went into main dinning area to sample the breakfast buffet. He was one of the first through the line and noticed empty tables outside in the sunshine. He gathered his food and made his way to a table so he could feel the gradually warming sun upon his face.

Nancy, by nature, was an early riser. She had gotten on deck just after the sun had come up. She stood by the railing, watching the scene, and then she too went in to sample breakfast. She made her selections, and noticed that there was still an open table outside in the sunshine. As she walked to the table with her tray of food, she realized that Andy was sitting by himself a few tables before the vacant one that she was headed for. . Nancy wondered if she was being impolite by not inviting herself to sit at his table. As she passed him, they exchanged smiles, but no spoken word. Then she thought, *'I suppose I did ask for romance, but I only came on this trip for the sunshine. Who needs romance?'*

Andy noticed the woman. He wondered why, on a ship with two thousand occupants, he kept running into her? He also wondered if he was being impolite by not offering her a seat at his table. Then he thought, *'I didn't come on this trip to pick up women, besides I can't even remember her name.'*

They sat and ate breakfast alone, back-to-back three tables away from each other. She ate her melon. He sucked on his pineapple slice. Each enjoyed the sunshine. It felt good on Nancy's winter weary bones. It felt good on Andy's demeanor.

Nancy decided to avoid contact with the man so she waited until he had finished and was gone before she signaled to the steward to clear her place. *'What a marvelous day at sea,'* she thought. *'I'll go get my book, find a lounge chair on the upper deck and waste the day away.'*

Andy had found himself a lounge chair on the upper deck in a patch of shade cast by the smokestack. It was an altogether pleasant place to be. As he had been one of the first to have breakfast, he also was one of the first sunbathers of the morning. Andy was not exactly sunbathing, lounging in the shade and not taking off his shirt, but he had his book and he had all day with nothing else to do.

After finishing the first four chapters of the biography that he was reading, he noticed that the turning sun had caused his shade to move. He stood up to adjust the placement of his chair. As he stood, he noticed the great sea of bodies around him. The cruise was filled with mostly young people in their twenties, party animals, with clean, robust figures. He was amazed at the various stages of dress, or rather undress he found sunning themselves around him. He was a mortician. He knew the human anatomy, better perhaps then some doctors. He looked around, particularly at the women in their skimpy bikinis and wondered how they would look dead, on his prep table. He was not turned on by the sight or by the thought.

The cruise business is, he understood, a celebration of sunshine and mammary glands. He, however, preferred shade and backs. There was something about a woman's back, the smoothness of the transition from neck to shoulders, the curve of the shoulder to the arm, the form of the shoulder blade, the freckles showing through the soft short hair. A number of the ladies around him were lying on their stomachs. Andy's eye went from one to another of these, and settled on a particular lady. She had a one-piece bathing suit on, modestly cut. Her back was white from a long winter of being covered, yet her form was exquisite, her grace clearly visible. She lay sleeping upon her lounge chair, her book face down on the deck, twenty feet from where Andy stood. He was drawn towards her. He noticed the crispness of her short dark hair, with only the occasion independent strand of gray to enhance her appearance.

He found an unoccupied chair a few feet from her, and sat and looked. As he looked a hundred haunting memories came back to him. Memories of his wife. Memories of the great sin he had committed. A sin, he believed, that reserved a place in Hell for him. His wife had been dying of cancer, yet he had to be satisfied. The infidelity had given him thirty minutes of release and a lifetime of guilt. It had taken his laugh away. It had taken his smile away. All these things ran through his mind as he gazed at this woman's back. She was sleeping so she would not notice him staring at her.

Only after several minutes sitting there beside the sleeping form, did he realize that this was his woman. The lady that kept being placed in his path. *'Why can't I remember her name?'* he thought. As he looked at her back, tanning in the tropical sun, a great urge came upon him. He wanted badly to say to her, "You have missed a few spots on your back. May I apply some more sunscreen? Otherwise you will burn." And he would have said it too, except, he couldn't think of her name.

Nancy laid there, her eyes shut, her faced turned the opposite direction, and wondered how long he was going to sit and stare. She thought, *'I asked for romance and this is what I get? A dope that doesn't say anything.'* Finally she said, her eyes still closed, "Mr. Tucker, are you going to sit there all day or are you going to say something."

"Me?" was all Andy could say, caught completely off his guard.

Nancy opened her eyes, Pushing up on one elbow and twisting her head towards him. She observed his face closely for the first time. She marked his cleanliness, his openness and his natural good looks. What she said though was, "I did not come on this cruise to be picked up by some man."

She said it with just the right firmness. Too softly or too loudly, he would have been stung, and wilted away, but her tone was just the right one.

He examined her face before replying. The sharp features struck him, the symmetry of the cheekbones and the set of the eyes. *'Top shelf,'* he thought, but he thought it too loudly and the thought turned into a spoken phrase. He recovered himself and said, as he stood up, "Lady, I did not come on this cruise to pick up women."

Before he could depart, she asked, "Mr. Tucker before you go, would you do me a favor?"

"Andy," he said with a hint of aggravation in his voice. "What can I do for you?"

Nancy countered, "Would you be so kind as to spread some sunscreen on my back? Do you know how difficult that is too do by yourself?" As she was asking him this, she picked up the tube of lotion and held it towards him with her free arm.

He took it and leaned down beside her chair. She turned again onto her stomach and closed her eyes as he applied the solar block. He noticed that she was using the maximum, 45-degree block, and he smiled. As he rubbed the lotion into her skin he said, "Even using 45 you need to move the straps of your bathing suit, otherwise you'll have white marks."

She responded by shrugging her shoulders a tad, which slipped the straps a few inches down her arms. He applied the sunscreen to the portion of her back that had been hidden by the suit.

He snapped the lid back on the lotion and set the tube down beside her chair.

"Thank you, Mr. Tucker," she said.

"My pleasure," Andy replied truthfully as he rose and left to find some shade to sit in.

Andy went back to his cabin and stayed there most of the afternoon, reading. As the ship approached the harbor at Cozumel, he ventured again on deck, toward the bow and the shuffleboard court to watch the pilot boat and the sights of the shoreline. He hoped that he would not run into the lady again. He even considered not attending dinner, thinking that it would be better if he had no further contact with her. Reason, though, suggested to him that denying himself the opportunity to sample the ship's menu because of some woman was silly, so he returned to his cabin to get cleaned up.

Nancy lay in the sun awhile longer, and then she too went to her cabin, where she took a marvelous nap. When she awoke, she decided to skip dinner for she did not want to be troubled by Mr. Tucker. She had skipped lunch, though, and her stomach suggested it was silly to deny herself the pleasure of eating because of some stranger. She dressed simply and informally.

Chance would have it, -- if you really believe it was chance maybe you should be reading some other story – Nancy and Andy exited their cabins simultaneously. After closing and checking the locks on their respective doors they turned toward one another.

"Lady," Andy began, "I am an idiot." He was preparing the ground to ask her name, but she interrupted him in mid-stream.

"I've come to that same conclusion," she said, and in her saying it, she smiled.

He responded to the smile with one of his own….

Together they went up the elevator to the dining room. Together they sat side by side. Together they spent the dinner listening to and enjoying the stories of the other couples around the table. Together they walked the promenade deck afterwards. Together they stood overlooking the main swimming pool and swayed to the beat of a calypso band; watching the younger couples dance and party. Together they avoided any question or statement that might indicate something of the other's past, which meant that often there were long silences in their togetherness. Together they refrained from touching one another.

Others at dinner had made plans for the next day's sightseeing excursions on the mainland, or snorkeling along the coral reef, but Nancy said that all she cared to do was to find a few trinkets and souvenirs to take back home. Andy wondered whom he should buy something for. At first, sadly, he could think of no one, but then he remembered that Mrs. Downey had asked him to bring her back a memento.

Cookies and Cream

THE NEXT DAY SAW Nancy and Andy walking the shops together. He had asked her name, and she had stopped calling him Mr. Tucker. Nancy found the things she needed and Andy picked out a stone ornament for Mrs. Downey. Andy remarked to himself the number of gifts that Nancy was purchasing for those back home. He did not wish to seem too intrusive, and she volunteered little information. They were not expensive items. Obviously some were meant for work mates others where child-sized. Andy was too polite to inquire so he did not learn more than his eyes could tell him.

Nancy noted that Andy bought only one thing, a pretty thing. He said it was for a friend from Church. Although it was nice, yet it seemed rather a stingy thing to bring back for a girl friend or a wife. Nancy was as curious as Andy was, but also as polite.

While they were strolling through the business district on their way to stand in the sand of the beach, Andy noticed an ice cream shop. As the day had become very warm, and it was getting toward lunchtime, Andy offered to buy Nancy a cone.

"What would you like," Andy asked as she walked along the glass counter looking at the possibilities.

"That one," she pointed out. "Cookies and Cream in a saucer not a cone please."

"That's the one with the Oreo cookies crumbled into the ice cream?" Andy inquired.

"Yep, in honor of a friend from St. Louis," Nancy replied. "What kind are you going to have?"

"Coffee with chocolate sauce. My favorite," he responded.

"I hadn't noticed that you had coffee at dinner or breakfast," she stated, "yet you like coffee ice cream."

Andy was dying to ask about her friend from St. Louis, but that would have broken their unspoken rule concerning personal questions.

They placed the order, then took their desserts and sat at a little round table by the window. They looked at their ice cream. They looked out the window. They were quiet. Eventually their eyes met and they smiled. Andy hadn't felt so fine in a long time. Nancy hadn't felt so relaxed in a long time.

After the ice cream, they found their way to the beach and walked along it barefoot, Andy carrying half of Nancy's packages.

The periods of silence between them seemed to be getting longer. The awkwardness of not touching, not holding hands was becoming greater. For this romance to continue, to grow, one of them was going to have to **do** something.

Neither one did. They walked along the beach, and then returned, put on their shoes and hiked back to the ship. As they made their way back to their cabins to refresh themselves and deposit their packages, Nancy turned to Andy and said, "It was a wonderful day. Thank you for the ice cream and the company."

Andy looked at tall Nancy, her eyes shining behind her wire rim glasses and replied again with honesty, "It was my pleasure."

This was scheduled to be the 'formal night' dinner in the dinning room. Nancy asked, "Would you accompany me to dinner tonight?" It was kind of a silly question, for they had accompanied each other last night, and to breakfast this morning and around town most of the day. It was kind of a silly question, but it was the perfect question.

Andy smiled the broadest smile, and said, "It's a date. Shall I pick you up at five minutes before six?"

Nancy smiled back at him, "Until then."

Incorrigible

THEY MET BEFORE DINNER in the hallway outside their cabins. Nancy was radiant in her simple blouse and skirt, gold chain and small earrings. She was radiant, not because of her outfit, but because the outfit let her glow, let her smile show through. Andy was dressed in his work suit, his business suit. He had not planned to bring along a suit for he had planned to skip the formal dinner, but here he was, dark suit, dark tie, black shoes.

When she first saw him, Nancy stifled a laugh. He noticed and asked, "What? Is there something wrong?"

She replied only with a wave of her hand to signal that nothing was wrong, but Andy had learned when a woman laughs like that, she means something.

"Tell me," he said.

"Andy, don't worry about it," she countered.

"No. Tell me what is so funny."

She thought a moment then said, "You tell me what you meant the other morning when you whispered "Top shelf" and I'll tell you why I looked at you funny."

As this conversation was occurring they began walking through the ship toward their dinner.

"Top shelf," Andy started. "Let's see, how should I explain? In fancy restaurants, when a waiter takes a drink order, often times they will ask if you want the drink made with the most expensive liquor. He refers to this by asking if you want 'top shelf' meaning the best stuff is kept there.

"Does that make sense?"

Nancy asked laughing, "So when you looked at me and said 'top shelf' you thought I was liquor?"

Andy laughed in return, "From the top shelf."

They were both silent for a moment while the elevator took them from cabin deck to the dining room deck.

Andy said eventually, "Why did you laugh at me, back there?"

Nancy tucked her arm inside his and leaned against him affectionately. "Couldn't help but think that you looked like an undertaker all dressed in black."

Andy felt her pressure against him, felt her affection. He turned and looked at her face. She was looking at his. He decided not to tell her that he was an undertaker.

At dinner they asked Mr. Cooke to explain a little more about his parents. "Joe, call me Joe, goodness we've been on this cruise for three days and you still are calling me Mr. Cooke?" The fellow laughed.

"Haven't you figured out by now, I love to tell stories? Be glad to tell you about my parents," he began. "My father was incorrigible. My mother tried for over fifty years to control his bad habits, but she never did. She put up with a lot. My dad was loud, flamboyant, and drank too much, but in fifty-three years of marriage he never lost his laugh, he never lost his whistle, and he always wore his cap at a jaunty angle."

"You seem too young to have parents that were thirty back in 1938?" Andy asked.

"My mother was 42 when I was born, the youngest of three boys," he answered. "I was a pretty baby, you can't tell it now, what with all this gray, but I had golden curly locks and a sweet smile." As Joe Cooke was saying this he was looking at Nancy with a knowing look.

Nancy had seen that look before. She had seen it on a client, a strange client who wouldn't fill out an intake form. Nancy glanced quickly at Joe Cooke's fingers but they all seemed normal.

The moment passed and the dinner was served. Everyone around the table was having a marvelous cruise and was in high spirits, all dressed up and spiffy. Both Andy and Nancy became more talkative, revealing to each other, in their conversations with their tablemates, more than they had in their own private exchanges.

After dinner, after listening to piano music in one of the many bars on the ship, after watching the ship disembark from Mexico and begin the voyage back to Miami, after all that, Andy and Nancy leaned tightly against each other by the railing of the upper deck. They had become inseparable. They each knew that they had but one more day and then the vacation would be over. Each would return home. Each would return home refreshed, changed.

Andy softly said to her as they stood against each other, "Nana." He used her familiar name for the first time, although she had given him permission to use it hours ago. "Nana, I should tell you something."

'Oh, no. Here it comes,' she thought.

"Nana, I am an undertaker."

She pushed herself away from him, so she could look into his face, an amazed look upon her own face.

He mistook her reaction and said in a downcast manner, "I'm sorry, that is what I am."

She laughed a loud, relieved laugh, for she had expected much worse news than this. Then she put her arms around him and gave him a hug. It was an embrace to make up many years of neglect. He returned the hug as poignantly as she offered it. There was no way to make up for the sin he had committed, or of the years of guilt, but this embrace was a release for him.

She could feel a burden lifted from him. He could feel one lifted from her. Gradually the emotion subsided and they stood there, arms entangled, Nancy's head resting against his shoulder.

"Andy," she asked, ending a long period of silence. "Do you pee on the rug?"

PARCUL CENTRU

I

IT WAS POSTED FOR the world to see. The listings were taped to the outer door of the courtyard. Any passer-by needed only to take three steps from the strada and they could read the results.

She had hoped for so much. She had tried so hard. It wasn't a surprise to her, she had feared it coming, but still in the back of her mind she'd held a faint hope that a miracle might happen, that God might smile upon her. Here, though, pasted on the school's front door was proof that there had been no miracle.

Zona found herself at the bottom of the list and that made it worse. The professor had taken the trouble to arrange the tabulation from top grade to lowest. Had the list been left alphabetical by last name, she would have been in the middle somewhere so hers would not have been so easily spotted as the poorest grade.

She was ashamed. She had given it her best effort. She had studied, asked help from classmates; even had special assistance from the professor. The grade was not as much a failure of Zona's intelligence or her work ethic, as a rupture in the communication from the texts and instructor to her brain. Whatever reasons for the failure, as she stood there seeing her final grade she felt naked to the world.

Her husband was a lout and would never make anything of his life. He preferred beer and football above all else. They lived with her mother-in-law who chained smoked her way through the day watching Latin soap operas. Zona had a child but lost it to an accident, and now refused thought of another. The class had represented a way up for her, a hope, and now that way was removed, the hope withdrawn.

She would have made a fine young, urban professional. Although she was nearing the end of her youth, she had the looks for it, the wit and the drive. Her manner was a little too friendly, but that could be overcome. She dressed well; though if you saw her often, you'd realize that she didn't have many options for changes of outfits. She had stood tall, unbowed by the troubles of life until, seeing the posted results, her name at the bottom, she slumped.

Gheorghe lifted his long, tubular fishing rod and the line picked up from the water. He checked his bait and tossed it out again, the float landing almost exactly where he had aimed. Gheorghe was an old man, but not an elderly one. He was retired and one of his favorite pass times was meeting Florin and walking together down to the lake in the park to fish. They hardly ever caught enough to make it worthwhile, but that was a side issue. It was their friendship, the sunshine and the act of fishing that were more important than any catch.

In Romania everyone under a certain age is slim. Nearly every one over a certain age is not. It is not a gradual change. The older folks are overweight, with extended bellies and stodgy walks. Not every one of course, but Gheorghe and Florin were. They'd lived in the same block of apartments for the last forty years. You would think that they had talked over every idea there was to talk about in that time, but still they gained knowledge from one another in an easy sort of way.

It was a quiet morning in the early fall. The water weeds had grown in around the lake and the challenge in finding open spaces to lay down the hook made the fishing more difficult. The weather, though, was ideal. The pond was still as there was no breeze and the paddle boaters had not taken to the water yet. There had been no sign of a fish, but that was only a secondary consideration.

"Window shopping, Adriana always said I could window shop," Gheorghe stated.

Florin looked around to see what window it was that Gheorghe would have been shopping in. Often times pretty women strolled the path along the lake, and something must have jogged his thought. Florin didn't see anything worth looking at, so brought his eyes back to his bobber.

"As long as I didn't touch the merchandise," Gheorghe finished after a pause.

He was a man and had all the conceit of a man, but at his age and in his condition he knew that the only way he could touch merchandise was to pay for it. He hadn't ever stooped that low and wasn't about to now. He looked over to Florin, sitting on his cushion on the bank of the lake. He wondered why he liked Florin. Florin was not a philosophical man, Gheorghe was. Florin was a doer, always wanting to get things done. He had taken awhile to adjust into retirement. Gheorghe was a natural pensioner, not that he was lazy, but he was content with his thoughts.

Gheorghe rubbed his chin and asked tentatively, "Ever touch any merchandise, Florin?".

That was not the kind of question that old friends ask each other. They respect each other's privacy. Besides, if Gheorghe could remember, he probably had a pretty good idea if Florin had ever strayed from his wife.

"Not in the last two weeks," came the diplomatic answer.

"Hah, not in the last twenty years."

"I guess we're too old and ugly to fool around now," Florin added as a point of fact.

"Look at us Florin. What woman would want an old, flabby bull like us anyway?"

"Some old cow might," Florin commented then added, "but why would we want another old cow, we each got one now."

Gheorghe looked out across the lake. It isn't a large lake and the benches on the opposite side can be easily seen. There was a lady sitting on a bench across the water. He hadn't noticed her there a moment ago, but she was there now. She was not a regular in the park, Gheorghe knew by sight, if not by name, all the regulars. He hadn't seen her before.

It was not so much her looks that caught his attention as her attitude. She would have been a fine looking woman, certainly worth window shopping, but even across the lake he could see that she was despondent. He thought to himself 'There may be few things as unappealing as a woman depressed.'

He had seen all sorts of drama in the park. That's one reason fishing here was such an interesting past time, because it gave the fishermen time to look around. He and Florin could have taken up chess down at the tables, but you become too busy with the game to see things. Fishing was better.

Gheorghe's mind began to roam. 'Why is it that one day a fish is drawn to my bait and one day not interested? Is it only hunger, or is there some communication beyond what we know?' He watched the lady. She did not notice him watching.

He stood up with an effort and a grunt. He wiped his hands on his towel and said to Florin, "Watch my rod. I'll be back in a minute." He climbed the short bank to the path and headed toward the far end of the lake and the restaurant without further explanation.

Zona sat on the bench trying to piece her future back together. The immediate future would be explaining to her husband and her mother-in-law that she would be taking no more classes.

She doubted that they would care much, except that he had welcomed the idea of her having a better job to bring home more money. There would be no extra money now.

The future that bothered her the most was the rest of her life. It seemed to stretch forward through the smelly fumes of old cigarette smoke. She was a failure. Everything she had touched was a failure.

She cried silently.

Gheorghe was not a hero. He was not a man to do heroic things. Between the two, Florin would be the better hero, but sitting on the bank on the other side of the lake, he had felt a connection with this woman on the bench. He didn't know what to do or what to say to her. He had gotten up, and walked the long way around the lake so that he could buy a bag of popcorn from the popcorn vender. He walked towards her unsure if he should follow through and invade her privacy. A coward would have kept walking past her and he was tempted, but he was drawn to her for some reason he couldn't define.

He sat down on the other end of the bench from her. As he sat, she made as if to leave.

"No, please don't, I have something for you."

She hesitated, looking at him. "Do I know you?"

He pulled out the hanky from his back pocket. It had recently been washed, so he knew it was clean. He handed it to her. "No, I'm only a stranger with a clean hanky and a bag of hot popcorn."

Parcul Centru
II

THE LAKE IS IN the southwest corner of the park. Separate from the lake the main pedestrian walk runs from west end to east, broad and gravelly. It is flat and a perfect surface for joggers. On weekends a fellow guides a pony wagon and sells rides to children. On each side of the walkway chestnut trees grow.

I wonder at these trees. In America the chestnut has disappeared from our forests, felled by the blight. When I was young there was a mighty horse chestnut that grew outside the north porch of our house. Scientists used to come and poke around the tree, wondering why it hadn't succumbed to the disease. We moved, and I'm not sure what became of the tree, if it died from natural causes or destroyed in building an office park. Perhaps it is a different variety, but here in Romania, the chestnuts flourish. During the first days of school the nuts burst from their protective, spiky husks and fall to the ground, bright pebbles for school children to collect and examine.

A British gentleman comes often to the park on sunny days. He takes a spot on one of the benches flanking the walking path. I say he is British, but that is an assumption. He strolls from the British library at the consulate office, located across the street from the park. He has the air of an Englishman, the way he carries his umbrella, his suit of clothes and his book. He prefers the mysteries. If it is a warm day he sits in the shade and reads, if it is cool, he finds a bench in the sunlight. He reads for roughly half an hour, then marks his page with a bookmark and heads, I presume, home.

I have heard him say "Buna Ziua" on occasion, but I have not noticed that he has ever engaged in conversation with passers-by. He is content to read his book and enjoy the weather.

No one ever gave the dog a name. He was a stray, living on the edge of society. Romania has a million stray dogs, and though the city of Cluj has done a fair job in clearing the streets, there remain a few. This dog without a name was one. He had bright eyes and an easy manner. He was a medium sized animal, and slim, like all the strays. He was black and had inherited no sign of breed or distinction except for his intelligence. He liked the park. He had lived here all summer, alone, finding sustenance from the ice cream wrappers and other debris. Because he had the wisdom to stay out of people's way, keeping just beyond their circle of rejection, they left him alone, sometimes tossing him their unwanted tidbits.

What it was that attracted the dog to the Englishman, I cannot say. The man never had food, so had nothing to offer him. I never saw the man coax the dog, or speak to it either in Romanian or in English. As the end of summer approached, the dog perhaps sensed that he'd need to find other arraignments for surviving the Transylvanian winter. Perhaps the Englishman had a particular scent that attracted the dog, I cannot say, but I do know that the dog adopted the man.

It was a slow adoption. On the days the gentleman came for his read, the dog would appear and either sit or lie close by the bench the man chose for his leisure. On each succeeding day the dog moved closer to the man. At first the gentleman paid little heed, only to interrupt his reading to be sure that the dog was no threat. He had never been attacked by a stray but he had heard stories.

It wasn't until the third or fourth afternoon that he took full account of the dog. I suspect he wondered why the same dog seemed to hang around. I saw him put aside his novel and sit and contemplate the animal for some minutes. He said nothing. The dog said nothing. The man picked up his book again, read to the appointed time, and got up to leave. In doing so, he looked back at the dog. I could see the dog return the gaze. I've known enough dogs to imagine the mournful look the beast gave the man. Finally, the man retreated from the park. The dog stayed put for some time as if waiting for the man's return.

The gentleman did not have a pattern of reading every day. Often there were gaps of two or three days. I never saw him at all on the weekends. I saw the dog but I did not see the man.

It was a day following the night rains when the Englishman next showed. The earth smelled clean and new. The rain had brought down more of the chestnuts and dried leaves. The man had picked an all-together splendid day to enjoy the last sparse shade of the trees. He pulled out a napkin to wipe the droplets of water from the bench before sitting. I watched him and I watched the dog.

The dog moved closer than it had in previous days. It sat directly next to the bench in such a manner that its head made a near perfect arm rest. He looked straight ahead, almost as if he too were reading some imaginary book.

The man tried reading but found that the quality of his concentration was affected by his guest. He put the book in his lap. He turned to look down at the dog. The dog turned to look up at him.

"I used to have a dog, you know."

Dogs can't answer directly, their conversation takes a more roundabout form, but it was clear that the animal was listening.

"When I was a lad I had a dog."

I wondered if the dog had ever had such a discussion with a non-dog before. He seemed perfectly at ease, all rapt attention. The conversation was in English. Perhaps the dog would have preferred either Romanian or Hungarian but it seemed content enough to listen.

The gentleman must have found his audience agreeable as well for he continued.

"We shared many fond times, Kanga and I. I named him after my favorite character in Winnie-the-Pooh."

The man said everything slowly to the dog. I doubt that it was because he felt the dog slow to understand; rather it was the way the memories awakened in his mind, slowly.

"He was a good dog and the day that he was hit by a neighbor's auto was one of the saddest of my childhood."

The man paused for a long time. The dog sat waiting for the rest of the story. It did not come, at least, not that day. The man picked up his reading, lasted only a few more lines, closed his book and departed.

I looked over at the dog sitting still after the man had left. I wondered if the canine thought that he was making progress or if he was wasting his time with this gent that spoke a foreign language that the dog didn't understand at all.

The next day the Englishman came back, but not with a book in his hands, but rather a paper bag. He looked around as he walked, searching for his dog. It was his dog now, that's what the bag signified. He sat upon the same bench as he had the day before, but there was no sign of the dog. I could see from the slightest slump in an otherwise straight shoulder that the man was disappointed not to find his dog. He sat there for a while, considering whether to walk the park searching or not.

I'm sure the dog was testing him. After all these days of gradually gaining the trust of the man, he wanted to test that trust. I imagine the dog had a motto, "Easily adopted, as easily dismissed." I don't know how to say that in Romanian. I believe that the dog did though.

The man sat a full fifteen minutes with no dog. He had given up the idea of strolling through the park, I believe because it would have seemed undignified to be searching for a stray. As I watched him I saw his countenance brighten. He had seen his dog, and his dog, as if to make up for his tardy arrival, came bounding towards the man.

As he got closer to the bench, the dog slowed, then stopped and stood. The gentleman patted his black head.

"I shall have a name for you. You are not a Kanga, there was only one, besides you don't look anything like a Kanga."

He leaned and scratched behind the dog's ears. The dog closed his eyes and I imagine he said to himself, "So this is how it feels."

The man continued, "My favorite character from the mysteries is Constable Perkins. He is a wily and intelligent fellow. I shall call you Perkins, if you don't mind."

The dog hadn't ever been called a name before. He'd been yelled at and called unpleasant things, but those aren't names. "Perkins," the dog said to himself.

The gentleman reached into his bag, produced a dog biscuit and held it for Perkins. The dog hesitated. He'd never been offered anything like this before and wasn't sure what he was suppose to do with it.

"Go ahead. It's good. You'll like it."

Perkins looked up at the man, then took a deeper smell of the treat. He opened his mouth and grabbed the bone but made no attempt to eat it. He simply held it in his mouth. His saliva must have dripped the taste of it onto his tongue, yet still he held it.

Reaching again into the bag the man pulled out an aerosol can.

"This is for the fleas. We mustn't bring any of the fleas home with us. Once we get there we'll have a proper bath in the tub, but now we'll use this so that none of the buggers will follow us."

This was all foreign to the dog. Even if it had all been spoken in Romanian or even in dog talk, the meaning would have been lost for lack of experience. The dog stood there, his dog treat in his jowls. The man took the aerosol and sprayed up and down and around Perkins, careful not to get any near his eyes or biscuit filled mouth. When he was done he reached again into the bag and withdrew a slip collar and a leash.

The dog remained still as the man slid the collar around the treat and over his head. When the collar was properly around the neck, the man snapped the clasp of the leash to the collar.

"Come along, Perkins. Let's go get a proper bath."

As they departed the park they walked past me. I could swear I heard the dog say proudly to himself as they passed, his words mumbled around his still uneaten treat, "Perkins. Sunt Perkins." I smiled for he said 'Perkins' with a Romanian accent.

Parcul Centru
III

THE PARK MAINTENANCE CREW was on duty today. Compared to many cities in Romania, Cluj does a good job with its parks and public spaces. There is little trash blowing about and the trash receptacles are emptied at regular intervals. Some of the benches are in disrepair or uncomfortably constructed and the grass grows longer than it should, but Parcul Centru is a pleasant place to observe the world.

There were a dozen members of the crew, nine men and three women. The job today was to rake up and dispose of leaves. While the nut trees had dropped many of their leaves, the rest of the trees were still green so the task would need to be repeated several times throughout the autumn.

The boss of the crew drove the dump truck. It was a big dump truck, construction site size. After the leaves and fallen nut husks had been raked into orderly piles, the crew teamed in pairs to gather the refuse in large woven baskets. They worked together to fill a basket, then took it to the truck where they had to lift it overhead for the guy in the bed of the truck to take and empty it. There were five pair of workers, plus the boss and the man in the dump. Two of the men appeared busy at their work, accomplishing a fair bit of raking. Two of the women, obviously put-off from some of the younger workers, were serious about the mission and raked more ground then all the rest put together.

The younger men were more interested in tossing chestnuts at each other than in clearing the park. It was a fine day and a few tossed nuts were harmless. An efficiency expert would have suggested that two men, or rather the working women, and a power leaf rake could have accomplished what it took twelve workers all day to complete, but then what would the other ten do? Sometimes the inefficiency of the system is not wholly wrong.

THE COWBOY
CONTINUED

12
Fallen and Found

BUDDY'S HOME, IF A homeless person can have a home, was beneath the Expressway Bridge in the southeastern section of the nation's capitol, Washington, D.C. There were few tourists here, fewer diplomats. He was left alone. Left alone to drink, and to die. He often wondered why he didn't die. His body had been abused, under nourished, exposed and neglected. People that took care of their bodies got sick and died. He, who wanted to die, couldn't.

Here, sleeping in the open, protected from the rain only by the bridge above, he scrounged enough money for an occasional bottle. Other days it seemed that simply the breath of his drunken companions could inebriate him. He was a bum.

On occasion he would hike to Lafayette Park, across from the White House. Many of the local panhandlers hung out in the park, sleeping on the benches. Buddy thought it was a nice place, conveniently close to the best soup kitchen in the city, but there the Capitol Police often hassled way too much, and the tourists walked by and sneered.

"Hey, Buddy." Howard's voice slurred. "I heard they got Polish sausage up at the Village Pantry. Let's walk up and get a good meal for once."

Buddy had forgotten what Polish sausage tasted like. He silently looked at Howard. It was a fine October morning, a good morning for a stroll. He had planned to walk down to the tidal Potomac for the afternoon, but maybe he should accompany his partner. That meant crossing the Washington Mall. Buddy hated to cross the green space that ran between the grand Monument and the Capitol.

Howard returned Buddy's vacant look, and finally asked, "You goin' or not?"

"What does Polish sausage taste like?" he answered.

"Damn if I know, but I aim to find out," Howard replied, starting off in the direction of the soup kitchen.

Buddy followed him, but somewhere in the expanse of greenery and museums that is the pride of the nation, he lost his friend. He was always losing people. He stopped to look in a window, and turned around again, only to find an entirely new set of characters surrounding him. When Howard disappeared, Buddy simply shrugged and ambled on.

Toward early afternoon he found the Village Pantry, and, as advertised, they were giving away platefuls of kielbasa and sauerkraut. Buddy listened to the obligatory harangue of the counselor, picked up his plate and found himself a seat. It had been a few days since his last meal, other than the morsels he found in the trashcans of city. Before starting he covered the cabbage with a layer of black pepper. He sat alone; he ate alone. When he was done, he still couldn't remember what Polish sausage tasted like. He thought that sad.

After lunch he figured he would stroll over to Lafayette Park to enjoy the sunshine and find someone that would share a bottle. On the way, he saw Paul, working the crowd of passers-by for a dollar.

"Paul, how you doin'," he called, thinking that perhaps Paul might have a drink on him.

"OK Buddy, but I can't talk to you now." Paul was his friend, why couldn't Paul talk to him, Buddy wondered.

"I'm panhandling man, you in my way. Hard enough to find a stiff to give to one bum, nobody gives to two." Paul answered the unspoken question.

Buddy stood by a minute, and then started walking away.

"Wait," Paul called. "Here, take my five bucks and get us a bottle. I'll meet you in the park in about half an hour. That's all I got all morning long. Don't lose it." Paul handed Buddy three wadded up dollar bills and eight quarters.

Five bucks won't buy quality, but quality and taste did not matter, alcohol was what mattered. Buddy found the liqueur store, made his purchase and carried the bottle out in the ubiquitous brown bag. He sauntered to his favorite park bench and sat to wait, showing extreme restraint by not unscrewing the bottle.

Lafayette Park, opposite the home of the President of the United States, was a most pleasant spot to spend a warm October afternoon. Derelicts and sleaze bums of all sorts and conditions congregated there. Tourists also made use of the park, and conflicts between the two classes were not uncommon. Orders to clean the park were issued about once every two months and the D.C. police would move in, making life so miserable that the vagabonds would move along, or be placed in shelters.

Buddy, like all the bums, hated the shelters. He wanted to die in the open. Nine months of the year jail was better than the shelters. Normally, he avoided Lafayette Park so as not to run into the occasional rehabilitation efforts. Buddy thought about this, how much he hated the shelters, as he sat patting the comforting shape of the full bottle while waiting for Paul. Postponed gratification, he thought, licking his festering lips with his swollen tongue. Behind him, from the direction of Pennsylvania Avenue, a commotion arose. He turned to see that indeed, his luck had placed him in the park on a sweep-out day. He hurried as best he could to the opposite side of the park to escape persecution, trying to hide his bottle under the remnants of his torn sweater.

He was much too slow, for as he neared the perimeter of the park a mounted cop blocked his way. The police found the mounted patrol to be an effective method of handling the homeless. Many of the panhandlers and drug abusers had no respect for the officers of the law, but they feared the four-legged beasts upon which the authorities rode. Secondly, on horseback, the officers' superior position gave them an advantage in angle and distance. The bums felt looked down upon literally as well as figuratively. A mounted patrol with the assistance of regular mobile units could clean the park in less than an hour with half the manpower of the foot patrol.

"Give me that bottle," the policeman demanded, leaning from the saddle and extending an arm.

"It ain't open, I haven't opened it yet. You can't take it from me," Buddy replied plaintively.

The officer inched his horse closer to Buddy. Usually that was enough to put fear into the derelicts, but Buddy's gaze went from patrolman to horse. He looked at the horse, looked into his eyes. The horse looked back.

"Blue," Buddy asked, refusing to give the policeman the respect of being called Officer, "you know the name of this horse?"

"Name? What's the name got to do with anything? Hand me the bottle."

Buddy continued to examine the horse, gathering the bridle in his hands, turning its head this way and that, stepping back and looking at its feet. The horse was a bay gelding, unremarkable, like a zillion other horses, like at least twenty in the mounted patrol stable. The horse leaned into Buddy. The horse sniffed, and through the stink of body odor, alcohol and general decay, the horse remembered.

Buddy handed the bottle to the patrolman. "Blue, it's unopened. It's my property and you've no right to take it."

As he handed the bottle up, Buddy stroked the flank of the animal. Buddy knew what the cop was going to do, open the bottle, and pour it out into the gutter. Buddy also knew the horse's name.

"Blue, I bet you call this horse Dummy."

"How did you know that?" the officer asked in a tone of amazement as he emptied the bottle, the liquid splashing on the curb below. The tone he normally used to handle these bums was gruff and laced with distaste, even disgust, but he had been caught off guard.

Buddy, weakened by the loss of the alcohol leaned against Dromedary's side, just as he had done that first night in the Lasix barn. "Don't call him Dummy," he said softly, stoking his old friend. "His name's Dromedary, call him Camel if you can't say or spell Dromedary. He ain't no dummy. He saved my life once."

The cop had often seen these old drunks fall into tears, play for sympathy and he was hardened against such tactics, but he had never seen one cuddle his horse. It took a moment before he regained his composure. "Go on! Get movin'. We're clearing this park today. I'll charge you with vagrancy, drunk in public."

"I ain't drunk Blue, you took my bottle before I even opened it," Buddy said, moving away from the Camel with a last pat on his shoulder.

"Stay away or I'll put you in the shelter," the officer threatened.

"I'm goin' Blue. Blue, his name's Camel," Buddy called as he backed away.

Buddy spent the night drinkless under the Expressway. The next day he ambled to the same soup kitchen by the park for chicken soup. Two decent meals in two days, he thought. After finishing his bowl, he asked the volunteer at the ladle if there wasn't an old apple lying around somewhere.

"We got good apples right there on the table," she replied.

"Don't need a good apple. Save them for those that want them. An old apple or maybe a carrot. Dromedary always liked carrots," he explained to the mystified lady. She retreated and returned with one of each. Buddy smiled his thanks and wondered why he didn't need a drink.

On the corner of F Street and 16th, straight across from the entrance to the park, Buddy saw Dromedary, the same policeman as yesterday sitting on his back. They were making sure the park stayed clean of debris. 'He looks good,' Buddy thought. 'He looks healthy.'

Buddy walked up to his friend and held out the apple.

"Hey, Buddy! What the hell are you doin'?" Buddy was not so amazed that the cop knew his name, as the cop had been that Buddy knew the horse's name.

"Just giving the Camel an Apple," Buddy answered.

"Don't give my horse nothin'!" the officer commanded. "You try to drug my animal and I'll blast your head off."

"What?" replied Buddy, incredulous. "I'm givin' my old friend an apple, and a carrot. Blue, I wouldn't do nothin' to your horse."

"You take a bite out of it first," the patrolman said, his tone a little softer.

Buddy bit into the apple, the juice of it running down his chin. Then he offered the rest to Dromedary, who had been waiting patiently. The horse munched it in three bites, shifting the apple pieces around the metal bit that rested in his mouth.

When Dromedary was done with the apple, Buddy snapped the carrot into three sections, and held one at a time for the horse to eat. With his free hand he reached up and scratched the old campaigner behind the ear. The policeman sat quietly watching from his perch on the saddle.

"We feed him carrots, you know; apples and carrots." The policeman spoke a little defensively. "We take good care of all our horses."

Buddy responded, "He is fit. Groomed almost as well as I used to do. He just needs a little respect is all. He don't like to be called Dummy."

The cop was having a hard time listening to himself have a normal conversation with a bum. "What the hell do you know about horses?"

"I don't know horses," Buddy responded, running his hand through Dromedary's mane, "I know this horse. I walked the hots at the track. I shoveled shit. Sometimes they'd let me brush and groom this one."

"Was that before or after you became a bum?"

"In between," Buddy returned.

The cop was silent. Buddy closed his eyes and communicated with Dromedary through his fingertips as they ran up and down the animal's coat.

The patrolman had been on this beat a long time. He had been spat upon, cursed, slandered and all the compassionate tendencies of his nature had disappeared. His job was to control the vermin, not to see the humanity in it, simply to control and master it. He realized that he had been still for longer than necessary.

"Alright, you fed the horse an apple, time to move on."

Buddy acknowledged the command with a nod and one last stroke of his palm against the Camel's side then began to move away. The horse turned its head, nickered and nodded toward the old drunk.

"Wait," said the cop.

Buddy stopped, not knowing what the policeman was intending.

The cop stopped, not sure what he was intending, either. Finally, he said, "You want to work with the horses?"

Buddy turned to look at him but did not reply.

"Work with the horses of the Mounted Unit. You said you'd shoveled shit before. You want a job?"

Buddy pondered, and then replied, "I don't need a job."

"Christ man! I didn't ask if you needed a job, you can fuckin' live and die out here in the gutter if you like. I asked if you wanted a job."

Buddy's eyes moved from the cop to the horse. Dromedary was still looking at Buddy. "Yes." Then he added with a little fear, "You ain't takin' me to no shelter?"

"They got bunks right above the stables. You'll like Jason. He's an old race-tracker himself." The policeman reached to his belt and pulled out his radio.

Within a minute a police cruiser coasted to a stop at the corner. The window rolled down and a voice called, "What's up, Dick?"

"Take this fellow over to the stables, give him to Jason. We'll dry him out and see if he really can shovel shit," the mounted officer answered, pointing to Buddy.

"Since when did you become a screamin' liberal?" asked the voice from the cruiser.

The cop on the horse hesitated, turned to look at his companion in the car, and made no reply other than a shrug of his shoulders.

The officer riding in front on the passenger side got out and opened the back door, pointing the way for Buddy to get in.

"You're not taking me to no shelter?" Buddy pleaded. "I won't stay in no shelter." He wanted to be reassured, but neither the police in the car, nor the patrolman on the horse would say anything.

After the cruiser began rolling down 16th street, the passenger side cop told the driver side cop, "Jason ain't goin' like this."

13
Jason

"I AIN'T IN REHAB work. Do I look like I'm in rehab work?"

"Look, Jason, we don't know anything about this, except Richard wanted us to bring this guy to you." The patrolmen slipped back into their car and disappeared while Jason sized up his potential new employee.

Jason was short. Where his left hand should have been was a metal clamp. He walked with a limp. He was in his fifties, though had not yet lost of all the vigor of his earlier life. He looked at Buddy.

"Man, you stink."

Buddy stood and did not say anything. No matter how mad Jason got, this was better than being in a shelter, and besides, he could see the horses in their stalls. After two years away from the creatures, it felt like home to be back among them.

Jason asked, "How long you been without a drink?"

Buddy replied, "Almost two days."

Jason asked, "What do you know about horses?"

Buddy replied, "How to muck out the stall, how to walk a hot, how to feed 'em hay and grain, how to brush 'em, how to keep from getting kicked."

Jason asked, "You want a drink now?"

Buddy replied, "Nah."

"This ain't no racetrack. No hots to walk here. We got good horses. We don't want no bums or drunks, no druggies. You do drugs?"

Buddy shook his head.

Jason asked, "How long were you at the track?"

"Little over a year, year and a half."

"How long were you dry?"

Buddy scratched the matted hair of his chin, trying to remember. "Almost that long."

"What made you start again?" Jason's voice had tempered itself.

"My trainer moved on, I wanted to stay and wait for my daughter to find me. I just needed a drink. Once I started, next thing I know I'm sleepin' under the bridge on 34th."

"What happens when you need a drink now?"

"You throw me out, I end up under the bridge on 34th."

Jason looked at Buddy. "Why do you want this job?"

Buddy answered. "Only job I can do."

Jason turned and started toward the dispatch area of the unit. "Follow me. We got to run a check."

Entering the office, they stood in front of a secretary. "What's your name?" Jason asked Buddy.

"Buddy."

"What's your full name?" the secretary asked, for Jason was too aggravated to clarify.

Buddy gave her his full name, surprised he could remember it all.

"Social Security number?"

Buddy was even more surprised when he could recall that too.

The secretary typed into the computer and waited a moment. "DUI, two DUIs back twenty and twenty-five years ago. Usual misdemeanors, vagrancy, drunk in public," she read. "Nothing violent. Wanted for back child support."

Buddy had been in a semi-attentive state during his interview with Jason and the background check, but suddenly a thought occurred to him as he heard the words child support.

"Does it have her address?" he asked.

"What?" said the surprised lady.

"Does it show how to get in touch with her, to give her child support?"

"The request is old. You don't have any money. You don't have any earnings, at least not yet. We'd have to check with the issuing agency."

A second thought hit Buddy. "I got money. She can have my money. Can you get her my money?"

Jason interrupted, "You ain't got no money. Probably lying about knowing about horses too."

Buddy turned toward the little man, "I got money. I remember. We put it in a bank account." He returned to the secretary again. "Look it up, see if you can't find my money."

"What was the account number? What bank?"

"I don't know any number. Bank was," Buddy hesitated, thinking. "Consolidated Edison."

"That's an electric company."

"First Consolidated."

The entry clerk typed on the keyboard and after a moment she said, "Yep, he's got money."

"Send it to her," he said. "Send it all to her. Tell her I'm dead if she wants me to be."

"Can't do it quite like that. Let me send an email to Connecticut to see if they still have her on record. I'll get back to you as soon as I hear anything, then we'll have to have you sign a wavier. Where can I find you?"

Buddy turned again to look at Jason.

Jason arched his eyebrows. "He'll be above the stables so long as he stays sober; otherwise you can find him under the overpass on 34th Street."

The secretary said to Jason, "If you intend to keep him, get his fingerprints to make sure he is who he says he is, then give him a shower. He stinks."

After Jason rolled Buddy's fingers in the ink, he showed him the way to the officers' wardroom and lockers. "This ain't no track. We got no track kitchen, but you'll always find hot coffee in here and most always donuts laying around so long as you don't show up during shift change." Jason pointed toward a corner, "Look through those Goodwill bags over there, I'm goin' burn the rags you have on while you're getting clean."

Buddy went through the paper bags of old clothes lying on the floor, searching for something his size. "You know, nobody gives away underwear," he observed. "Ties, Christ what do I need a tie for, plenty of ties, but no underwear."

Jason smiled; thinking that somewhere under that unkempt, smelly exterior there was intelligence. "Go without. Tomorrow you can go over to the dollar store and get some new."

"Got nothin' to pay for it with," Buddy replied.

"Man! You're part of the D.C. Mounted Police, the finest of the finest. We take care of our own. Your job is to muck out the stalls, shovel the horseshit. You do that good and you'll be taken care of. Screw up? You'll wish that you were back under some bridge somewhere."

Buddy stayed in the hot shower a long time. After he dried and dressed he went over to the stables to find Jason.

"Feel better?" Jason asked.

Buddy nodded.

Jason understood silence. He was not offended by it. "Your bunk's up the stairs there, above the stables. Six bunks, only one being used now, Sligo claims the one closest the stairs. You leave Sligo alone; he'll leave you alone. The other boys all go home when their work is done. Only had the one shift of horses on duty today, they'll be in soon. Need all hands to bed 'em down, then you'll be off 'til 6 a.m. Do you want to meet the horses, or the boys?"

Buddy wasn't much interested in meeting either. "How many horses are there?" he asked.

"Right now we got thirty-two," Jason answered with a bit of pride. "Couple of 'em are a little lame, but I'd put our Calvary up against any city in the country. We take care of our animals.

"There's a shift of eight out now, be back in a few minutes. We require the riders to do the initial unsaddling and brush-down, then we take over for the real grooming. Me and the boys, you too, we ain't nothing, ain't nobody, but we do the best by our animals, and they take care of us, understand?"

Jason looked at Buddy, knowing that if the old drunk had spent a year dry at the track, he understood the chemistry of horse and groom.

"Don't ask me no more questions right now, I'm tired of talking," Jason complained. "Walk down the stalls, talk to the horses, the boys are probably in that back tack room playing poker." Jason pointed down the barn with his good arm.

The barn was much different than those at a racetrack. Here there was a large center aisle with stalls on each side facing each other. The roof was peaked high above the floor and hay stored in the loft on one side. The other side above the stalls was the dormitory for the hands. The first room on the ground floor was Jason's office; opposite it was a tack room. Sixteen stalls a side ran down the length of the stable, broken halfway by a small aisle after the eighth stall. There was an inside wash area at the rear of the building on one side, a second tack room on the other. Halters and leads hung from hooks beside each stall entrance. The familiar double Dutch doors were gone, replaced by a sliding door, wooden on the bottom with metal grillwork on the top. Some horses had their doors open, the stall blocked only by a single chain snapped waist-high across the opening.

Wherever there are horses confined, there also is baled hay. Wherever there are 2' x 2' x 3' blocks of preserved summer sunshine, there also is a good place to sit. Buddy sat.

Presently a police pick-up truck towing a red slat-sided animal trailer pulled up in front of the barn. A van followed the trailer and from it eight uniformed officers appeared. Buddy recognized one of them. The rear trailer door was opened, and one by one cops and horses joined for the walk to the stable area. The horses still had their saddles tightened and it was the riders' job to remove bit, bridle and saddle, placing them in the appropriate positions in the first tack room. Each horse was given a perfunctory toweling and brush down, and then turned over to a groom

Richard led Dromedary from the trailer and spotted Buddy as he brought the horse to the tack room door for unsaddling.

"I see you made it," he said in a harsh tone. "Jason didn't throw you out?"

Buddy did not say anything, but assumed that he would be given his old friend to bathe, brush and bed down for the night.

The other grooms had quit their poker game to attend to their afternoon tasks. No one else spoke to Buddy; no one seemed surprised to find a new man in the outfit. Jason did not bother to make introductions.

"Sligo, Padre, Ray, you all double up." The little one-armed man barked orders. "Buddy, you take Dummy here behind Ray's first horse, that's Ray, the black dude in the wool cap. Give him a rinse, towel 'im, then back to his stall for a good brush down."

The stable captain then turned to the policeman known as Dick. "What the hell Dick? I ain't into rehab for drunks. Got enough trouble with the crazies I got, don't need more."

The cop answered defensively, "The horse knew him, liked him. If he starts drinking again, through him out."

"Not if, Dick," Jason answered, "when. Besides, out of character for you."

Richard turned back to look as Buddy walked the Camel toward the rear of the stable and the wash area. "It won't happen again."

As Buddy led Dromedary to the water spigot, he noticed that each horse had his name posted on his stall with a sliding plastic nameplate. Together they passed the empty stall marked Dummy.

The next morning before the other hands had checked into work, Jason was surprised to find Buddy sitting on a hay bale in front of the stall marked Dromedary.

"Who'd you work for at the track?" he asked.

"Mary Engler, mostly," Buddy replied.

"Engler? She's over at Pimlico. Doin' real good so I hear."

Buddy nodded, glad to know of the success of his former employer.

"You had anything to eat?"

Buddy shook his head, "Not yet."

"Not since yesterday?" Jason wondered.

Buddy said nothing, thinking nothing was answer enough.

"Go over to the office and get some doughnuts," Jason suggested.

"Don't like doughnuts."

"Well, after the morning shift goes out, we'll go over and see Dee and get you some petty cash to go buy yourself some underwear, some food and a haircut and shave."

Later that morning Dee gave him a paper to sign and three twenty-dollar bills. Buddy looked at the money, not expecting to be given so much.

Jason said, "The dollar store's across the street and up a block. The barber is another block up, same side the street, just beyond the liquor store. You go in the liquor store, don't bother comin' back."

Almost as an afterthought Jason added, "Tell the barber you're with us and he'll fix you up right."

Buddy looked down again at the three twenty-dollar bills in his hand. He turned to Dorothy, the same woman that had investigated his criminal history yesterday. "Any word about that child support?"

"Not yet," she responded. "I'll let you know."

Buddy nodded and then shambled off toward the dollar store.

When Jason returned after lunch to find his newest employee sitting in front of Dromedary's empty stall, he nearly did not recognize him, wouldn't have recognized him except for the way he sat on the hay bale.

14
Demons

BUDDY COULD NOT TELL why the devils under his skin left him alone. It was as if they had gone south, leaving his body here to suffer the winter as a bird might leave its house. He knew better than to hope for more than that. He accepted each day free from their scaly attacks, knowing that eventually they would be back, and when they returned, he would have no more defense than in all those previous times. He had no hope, but in the back of his mind, this time around, was a small something, which was different. He cherished each morning without the curse of the need for a drink.

Gradually he worked into a routine at the Mounted Police stable. He was a groom here, something he had refused at the track, but here the term held much less responsibility. These horses were not going to the races, not in competition. They were crowd control, symbols of authority. They needed to look good and Buddy had learned how to make a horse's coat shine. Dromedary was his normal assignment, although Jason was careful to rotate horses among the grooms so that no one horse and no one man became too dependent upon one another.

Buddy said little to the other fellows with whom he worked. They said little to him. He shared the upstairs dormitory with Sligo who said nothing at all. Sligo had the first bed, Buddy had the sixth. Each stayed out of the way of the other. Buddy never learned how Sligo had come to this place. The other grooms were all on some sort of work release from the city jail. Jason did not trust any of them, believing that they would steal a leather halter or lead as soon as his back was turned. The master gradually came to respect Buddy, knowing that so long as he stayed sober, the old man would neither steal nor leave. Jason felt a small camaraderie with Buddy because of the mutual background at the races and even began to enjoy his quiet, hidden sense of humor.

Towards the end of the first week of Buddy's stay, Jason came down to the stable headed for the poker game in the rear tack room. Buddy did not play, did not care to watch, and so was sitting on a hay bale beside the stall of the horse that he had curried earlier.

"Got the weekend work schedule up," Jason said as he walked down the barn. "You take two for the morning and evening shifts on Saturday, then you're off Sunday."

Buddy looked at him with a question in his eyes.

Jason responded, "You got a problem with that?"

"What the hell I need Sunday off for?"

"I got to give you days off," Jason replied. "Says right in the manual. Besides you can't be hoggin' all the overtime."

"If them fella's want overtime, let 'em have it. Don't pay me, but give me somethin' to do."

Jason looked at Buddy sitting on the hay bale. "Truth is, nobody likes shoveling horse shit on a Sunday. I'll change the schedule and give Pudge off."

Buddy never missed a day, never complained, kept to himself and did his job. A month after he'd arrived, had Jason been asked, he would have pointed to Buddy as his best employee. Jason knew, though, as Buddy did, that when the urge to drink came back, as it would, he would have to throw the bum out.

Dorothy had made contact with the authorities in Connecticut. It was determined that no state child support had been provided Buddy's daughter, so it was a civil matter between ex-wife and husband. Dorothy wrote the Family Services Unit,

Danbury, Connecticut informing them that a deadbeat dad had been found and asked advice. She found Buddy in an empty stall one morning, shaking out and restoring the layer of straw.

"You sure you want me to pursue this child support thing?" she asked.

Buddy remembered the last meeting with his daughter when she had warned him to stay away forever, but he also remembered the great debt, monetary and otherwise, that he owed his former wife. He answered the clerk, "Yes, Please."

She smiled and replied, "You don't have to give it all. I mean, it's not that much and you can save some for yourself." "Give it all to her," he answered. "Take most of my wages and give that to her, too. Does she have to know I'm alive?" "Never heard of garnishing wages from a dead man." Dorothy chuckled. "She'll figure it out. Seriously, though, you should leave some of that savings account for yourself. If nothing else, to bury you when you do die." Buddy shook his head, "Don't need no money when I'm living, won't need no money when I'm dead."

Dorothy assumed that everyone in the mounted unit, including herself, had become hardened. There was so much misery, deceit, and so little trust, so little to be trustworthy about, all these things hardened people. When she looked at Buddy, however, in his baggy good will outfit, his face and features sunken. She could feel a little softness, tenderness return to her personality. Again she smiled at him.

"I'll try to find her Buddy," she said. "When I find her, I will let her know that you are alive, but willing to be invisible except for what money you can send her."

Buddy looked at the clerk, aware that he now had a friend. "Dorothy, or do they call you Dot?"

"Some call me Dee," she answered, not sure she wanted to be as soft as she had appeared.

Buddy smiled back at her. "Thanks. I don't mean to sound sappy, but if I know that the money I am earning is going somewhere good, then maybe the damn devils will leave me be a little longer."

"Devils?" she asked, mistaking his meaning.

"Can't talk about 'em. You talk about 'em, they come back. They like to hear what you're saying about 'em." Buddy turned his back on Dee and returned to his work with the straw.

The Mounted Police were used less often in the cold weather, crowd control being less necessary. Normally a horse and rider were placed strategically along parade or motorcade routes, but for the last major event of the year, the Christmas parade and the lighting of the Nation's Christmas tree, the Mounted Unit took a special place at the head of the cavalcade. All thirty-two horses and riders were covered in full regalia and marched up Constitution Avenue and over to the White House. Extra effort was taken to make the horses look good. This was their day to be honored.

No thought was ever given to let Jason and his crew take part in the event, but they took as much pride in outfitting the Unit as if they were striding alongside. After the parade there was a natural let down. Sligo crashed into a funk, making him more standoffish than normal, and normally he was abnormally standoffish. The work release boys became more unruly. Jason reacted by become cranky. Buddy seemed to be the only one unaffected. The demons stayed south, leaving him alone.

Mid-morning a few days before Christmas Jason's mood changed. He came out of his office with a hurried step. "Buddy, you got your friend Dromedary looking good? He's not out on the road today, right?"

Buddy nodded and pointed to the third stall on the left hand side, where the Camel stood leaning over the chain.

Jason explained, "Andy Beyer's comin' to do an interview."

Buddy showed no emotion.

Jason caught the unenlightened look, "Andy Beyer. You been to the racetracks. Everybody knows Andy Beyer."

Buddy was not everybody.

"Andy Beyer is the columnist for the Washington Post. He does stories on racing. Everybody reads him because he writes well, and he knows what he's talking about. Hell, Buddy, the man wants to interview me. He wants a picture of an old racehorse. He's doing a feature story about how we take old, broken-down bag-a-bones and turn them back into useful horses again. He wants to take Dromedary's picture."

Buddy hesitated, "Hope he's bringing an apple. Dromedary don't give out pictures for free."

Jason looked at the horse. The horse looked good, would make a good picture. Jason looked at Buddy. If only Buddy looked as good as the horse.

Shortly afterwards a vehicle pulled into the lot out front and two men got out. One carried a small tape recorder and a pad; the other lugged around a heavy camera. Jason went out to greet them enthusiastically. For a while the three exchanged pleasantries in front of Jason's office.

"Each year around Christmas the paper wants me to do some enriching features," the tall man with the pad was saying. "Last year we ran a story about a horse retirement farm up in Maryland. They mentioned that sometimes they place horses with you."

Jason answered, "Yea, we like horses off the track. They're used to the crowd noise and excitement. Geldings, though, is all we take, no mares and no stallions. Geldings that I know are calm. We don't need hot-blooded horses here. No kickers and no biters."

"Can we go into your office and talk for a bit? Then John here can take a few pictures," Andy Beyer suggested.

Twenty minutes later the three re-emerged. Jason motioned for Buddy to bring out Dromedary.

"Buddy," Andy Beyer greeted him, "Jason tells me you are an old back stretch man."

Buddy neither affirmed nor denied it.

"We'd like to take your picture with the horse, what's his name?" "Dromedary. You don't want my picture. Take his picture," Buddy pointed to Jason.

"Oh, we'll get one or two of Jason, but we'd like one of you and your friend. You used to groom this horse at the track?"

Buddy thought as he snapped a lead onto Dromedary's halter, 'This horse saved my life once, maybe twice, but that ain't none of your business.' "His name's Dromedary. Can you spell it?"

Andy Beyer spelled out Dromedary.

Buddy continued, "He don't let his picture be took for free. You got to give the Camel an apple or carrot."

"Don't have an apple or carrot, but I've a pocketful of peppermints."

Buddy scratched his chin. "Bad for his teeth."

"It's Christmas," Andy said as he unwrapped a peppermint and held out his hand for the horse.

Dromedary liked the sweet. John began snapping away with the camera, the flash lighting the interior of the barn. When he was done, Andy Beyer pressed a rolled up bill into Buddy's unsuspecting hand.

"What are you doing?" Buddy asked as the money dropped to the stable floor.

"You said the horse doesn't give out his picture for free, that's for you letting us take your picture."

"Mister," Buddy answered sternly, "I ain't pretty enough for a picture. Don't ruin the horse by putting me in. And I don't need your money."

Buddy turned his back on the guests as he walked Dromedary back toward his stall. The five-dollar bill lay on the ground. Jason leaned down and picked it up.

"Strange fellow," the former jockey commented. "I'll use this to buy the next bushel of apples for the horses."

Winter in Washington is a damp, cold, and miserable time. February is particularly bad, as the Eastern humidity combines with the Northern freeze to turn the month to ice. Sleet and freezing rain pelt down more often than the sun shines. It affects the mood. It affected the mood of the stable hands at the Mounted Unit.

Three of the work release boys skipped town after stripping the tack room of whatever they thought was valuable or sales worthy. Sligo never awakened from his pre-Christmas funk, often refusing to budge from his bunk above the stalls. Jason had a good January, buoyed by the Beyer article and a subsequent visit by a local TV station to cover the same story. Buddy was as unaffected by February as he had been by January and by Christmas. The inner demons let him be.

Dorothy had found Buddy's ex-wife Melissa in New York State. She was remarried and not at all anxious to be reminded of a very difficult time in her life. Dee acted as Buddy's agent, patiently explaining the situation. She lied to Buddy that she had clues but had not located her yet; meanwhile she began to deduct a portion of his paycheck, placing it in his savings account at First Consolidated.

The policemen rarely took an interest in the grooms. The grooms rarely took an interest in the cops. Richard, though, feeling a little bit of proprietary responsibility for Buddy, kept his eyes open. One day, at the beginning of February, as the Mounties were responding to a request for a small contingent to be present at a Vice-Presidential appearance, Dick waited for Buddy to bring up Dromedary.

Normally they did not exchange words, but on this day the officer said as he cinched up the saddle, "You never thanked me."

Buddy looked at him, "You never gave my bottle back."

"You want it back now?"

"It wasn't mine. Belonged to a friend. I never paid him back."

The policemen took the reins of the horse and led him out into the horse trailer without saying more.

At the end of the day, as he finished up the last of the evening duties Buddy noticed a full liquor bottle placed at the entrance of

Dromedary's stall. Cockroaches began squirming on the insides of his cheeks. Wooly worms filled his mouth as he stood looking at the bottle. A voice called to him from the slightly open barn door. "Go ahead, Buddy. You know how much shit I've had to take 'cause I sent you here? Called me a Candy Ass, they did. A bleeding heart. Take a drink and get out of here or go give it to that friend of yours you owe a bottle."

Buddy knew who it was without looking. Buddy couldn't look, for he could not remove his eyes from the booze. Jason had left for the day; there was no one but Buddy and Richard. Really the only one there was Richard, for Buddy had lost his free will. The groom was consumed by his parasites.

Shakily, he wobbled over to the bottle and leaned down to pick it up. This was done without conscious thought. He had passed by the liquor store almost daily on his way to the diner where he had lunch without feeling the temptation, but this was different. He had no control over his actions, the addiction controlled him. The demons had not been south at all, merely hibernating for the winter in his shoes. Now they were awake and screaming for satisfaction. Buddy reached down for the liquor as Richard watched from the door. Almost four months since his last drink, the drunk could feel the liquid on his tongue as he twisted the top. This was not cheap stuff; this was name brand-whiskey. At least Richard had taste. Buddy fell to his knees on the soft stable floor as he brought the bottle to his lips. He closed his eyes so as not to see the Camel peering through the closed sliding door.

Before the rim of the bottle touched his lips however, another set of hands interrupted and took the pint from his grasp. Surprised, annoyed, Buddy opened his eyes to see Sligo standing over him. Sligo said nothing but hurled the bottle toward the crack of light coming through the barn door, whiskey pin-wheeling out as it flew. Richard had disappeared. Sligo said nothing as he marched himself up the stairs to his bunk. Buddy knelt a long time on the floor.

Jason arrived the next morning to see the empty bottle by the door and Buddy laid-out before Dromedary's stall. The former jockey walked over to where the man lay, and gave him a shove with his boot. Buddy awoke with a start, not quite remembering all that had happened the night before. He had been on the ground a long time and his face was pockmarked with the indentations of straw and dirt.

"Get your gear and get out," Jason said with a tone of authority.

There had been an unwritten rule that when Buddy began to drink he was to leave. Both employer and employee knew and understood the rule. Buddy stood up and silently walked over to the stairs leading to the upstairs dorm to gather those few belongings that he would need on the street. He did not object or proclaim his innocence. He knew the demons had awoken and would not leave him alone. He knew that he belonged under the Expressway on 34th Street.

Sligo stood at the base of the stairs blocking his way. Jason watched. In over four months Buddy had never spoken to Sligo. In four months Buddy had never heard Sligo speak to anybody. Buddy tried to squeeze by the man, but Sligo moved leg and arm against the door jam preventing the older, weaker groom for passing. Buddy gave up trying to get by and leaned passively, head down against Sligo.

The stronger man said, "Tell him."

Buddy could only shake his head.

Sligo grabbed Buddy by the shoulders, turned him around and pushed him toward Jason.

"Tell me what? What the hell is going on here?" Jason was baffled by this exchange.

"It wasn't my bottle. I didn't drink any."

Jason would not have believed him except that there was no stench of liquor on his breath, that and Sligo's strange behavior. Jason looked from Buddy to Sligo.

"Fuck it all," he said. "Get going. We got work to do." He turned and went into his office, slamming the door behind him.

Buddy, taking the words literally wasn't sure whether he was still fired or if he should start the morning rounds. Sligo was sure and handed him a pitchfork.

Later that morning Buddy sat upon a hay bale feeling the maggots in his mouth. He took his tongue, and with sucking sounds, tried to dislodge them from between his gum and cheek. He wanted to spit them out. He wanted to spit them out and smash them with the sole of his boot. He desired to be rid of the infernal creatures. The lunch diner was on the far side of the liquor store. He knew that today he could not walk by that liquor store. He had the choice of starving and staying sober, or arousing the cockroaches again, falling again to temptation and losing his place at the stable. He knew that the devils would prevail, but if he could only spit one out, expectorate it upon the ground and squeeze the puss out of it, there would be satisfaction in that. He broke a blade of straw and used it as a tooth pick hoping to break loose one of the bastards, but all he got was a pick full of saliva and crud.

Dorothy found him seated, working his straw.

"Got a toothache?" she asked.

"Maggots."

Dorothy looked at him strangely.

"I've got a letter for you," she said, holding out an envelope.

Buddy immediately brightened, forgetting the insects, "From Melissa?"

"No, from Baltimore." Dorothy turned the envelope so she could read the return address. "Mary Engler Racing Stable."

Buddy was disappointed. He took the offered letter but did not open it, folding it and sticking in his shirt pocket.

"Aren't you going to see what it says? I'm curious."

Buddy retrieved the letter from his pocket and handed back to Dorothy. "You read it."

The clerk took the envelope and started to rip a corner off, but stopped before completing the job.

"Buddy," she said, "you once asked if anyone called me Dot. I told you no, but some people do use Dee, remember?"

The man nodded in the affirmative.

"Why did you ask me that? You never call me Dee, you never call me Dot, you never call me Dorothy. You never ask me how my day is going. You never ask about my life, my family. Why should anyone care about you, if you don't care about anyone else?"

She was silent for a moment, looking at the man to see what effect her words might have. She did not wish to seem stern, but she spoke the truth.

He stood up agitated. "I don't want anyone to care about me. I ain't worth caring about. I got these fuckin' termites in my body, they're sucking me dry, killin' me. Everything I touch turns to shit. I don't want you to care about me."

"Buddy, you want Melissa to care."

"I want Melissa to forgive me. I love my wife. I love my daughter. I ruined their lives. God cannot forgive me. To punish me, he sends people like that prick cop Richard to torment me. He sends his maggots and cockroaches and termites and ants to torment me. He won't let me die. Why won't he let me die!?"

"God doesn't send the bugs, the Devil does. God sends you people like Jason and me. God sends you people like this that mail you letters," Dorothy said waving the envelope.

Buddy looked into Dorothy's eyes.

"Dot, I like the name Dot," he said after a pause. "I had a teacher named Dot."

Dee smiled and nodded toward Buddy's hay bale. "Sit down and let me read your letter to you."

Submissively Buddy sat.

Dorothy read the return address first. "Mary Engler Racing Stable, Pimlico, Baltimore, Md."

Then she torn away the corner and sliced the end of the envelope with her finger. "Cowboy," she read with a question in her voice. "I should have written sooner, but you know the pace of the race-track, even in winter. I saw your picture, yours and Dromedary's, in the Washington Post. It was a fine article about Jason and his work with old racehorses, but it was such a relief to see you safe and healthy.

"We were so worried about you after you dropped out of sight. The old gang is still together, John and Carol and Poncho. They all wish you well. I have never met Jason Crumly, but I know many that do know him. His reputation suggests that you are in good hands. Next time we have a horse racing at Laurel, some of us will try and find you. I still keep in touch with your lady friend from Kentucky. Shall I tell her to send socks?"

Dorothy folded the letter again and pushed it back into the envelope. "She signed it, 'Love, Mary'."

Buddy was smiling about the socks part. He couldn't remember exactly what the joke was about the socks, and he wasn't exactly sure what the friend in Kentucky looked like, but he knew it was nice that Mary remembered.

Dee sat down on the hay bale alongside Buddy. He moved over to one side to make room.

"See," she said. "People care."

After a moment of quiet, she asked, "Who calls you Cowboy?"

"It started as a joke at the track. Nobody calls me Cowboy anymore."

"Mary has an e-mail address on her letterhead. Do you want me to send a reply, let her know that you got the letter?"

Buddy thought a moment. "I don't remember what her name was, the lady in Kentucky. Would you ask Mary to tell her I need socks?"

"Sure," Dorothy said, putting a hand on the old man's knee as she rose. She walked toward the barn door, feeling that she had done all that she could do.

"Dee," Buddy called after her, hesitantly. "Dee, I hope that you have a good day."

The clerk turned to look at the man on the hay bale. Her smile was her answer.

15
Juan

"WE GOT A NEW boy comin' in today, another the judge sent us. I sure hope he works out better than the ones we been gettin' here lately." Jason was talking to himself. Both Sligo and Buddy were standing nearby brushing horses, but neither of them listened much to Jason.

"This guy's Mexican, from Honduras or Guatemala or some place like that. Juan. Sometimes they make good grooms. Christ, I remember riding against Pincay. He was from Panama. Pincay, in his prime was the best, that man could ride, but I beat him, that day at Saratoga, a stakes race."

Sligo and Buddy continued to brush their horses, although they had both gone over the same hide a few extra times.

"If you can keep 'em off drugs those little Mexicans can handle a horse. Most of 'em nowadays are full of drugs and crap. I hope this one speaks English. I get tired of pointing. Ought to make you teach this one Buddy." Jason was so taken by the idea he repeated it. "Yea, that would work. This boy's probably addicted to something. He needs rehab. Who better to give him rehab than a former drunk?"

Jason looked at Buddy for a reaction as he said this. It had been a week since the empty bottle incident. Jason had never figured out what had happened that night, but his groom had stayed clean, so perhaps it was best forgotten.

Buddy wondered how to tell Jason no. It was not that he didn't want to help some dude, he had nothing against Latinos, but this was much too much responsibility. He did not want to teach anyone anything. Before he could say the words that his eyes tried to convey, a car pulled up to the front of the barn.

A snappily dressed lady lawyer, complete with brief case, emerged from the passenger side door. "Mr. Crumley?" she called.

"Yes, Ma'am, do you have Juan?" Jason answered.

"Juan? I have Wan Leigh. Here to do six months work release and probation."

"He's to stay here overnight?" Jason asked. "We've a small dormitory upstairs. Six beds, only two are taken."

"She's to stay," the lawyer returned, with an emphasis on the word 'she'. "You'll have to make sleeping arrangements so she has privacy."

"What? She? No Way!" Jason was visibly upset. "This ain't co-ed here. Christ, I got nothin' against women, they make good horsemen, but we can't have a female around here."

"Mr. Crumley, it's the judge's orders. We saw the story on TV about your care for old race horses, and we think that you can do the same for Wan."

"Look, lady," Jason tried to reason, "we got nowhere for her to stay. We got nothing but hard-core men here. They see a skirt and they'll go crazy. I have a hard time getting 'em to do any work now. I'll spend all my time trying to keep them from fornicating in the hayloft. No, lady, it won't work."

The lawyer seemed unconvinced.

Jason turned to his second argument. "See these two?" He pointed with his metal hand, not an unconscious gesture. "These two, one's an old drunk, the other a psycho. You put a woman anywhere close and she'll be in danger. And they're my two best."

Again the women seemed unmoved. "Mr. Crumley, my client is a young lady of the world. She has been exposed to at least as rough as you could imagine. All she asks is a chance. Perhaps we can find her a space in the police barracks next door."

Jason saw that he had lost the argument. "Lady, I want you to write it down in your notebook, and I'll have Dorothy over in the office do the same, I want you to write down that I said this ain't goin' to work."

"Mr. Crumley, your objection will be noted. Would you like to meet your new employee now, or should we find a place for her to stay next door first?"

"Tell your client that Buddy here," again Jason pointed with his hook toward the old groom, "will be her mentor. She can get to know him while you and I go see about a bed."

The lawyer walked back to the car and opened the back door. A slight girl, a young lady in her early twenties, got out.

"Mr. Crumley, this is Wan Leigh."

Jason walked over to her, touched her on the elbow and said, "We ain't in the business of restoring human beings. What we do here is take care of horses. For some reason the judges think we can take care of people too. We've had a lot better success with the horses. See that old man in there brushing that gray horse? He don't care what you've done. He don't talk much, the other one, don't talk at all. You tell the old man you want to learn horses, he might teach you something."

Wan looked at Jason. They were both about the same weight and height. Wan had a wide face, dark hair and dark eyes. Her shirt was tucked into her jeans, a windbreaker open over her shoulders. Jason noted that it was a flannel shirt. He motioned with his hook that the introduction was over and she was to team up with Buddy.

Buddy looked for a place to hide. He noticed that Sligo had slipped over to the upstairs doorway, blocking it just as he had done a week before. The old man thought about sneaking into an empty stall, or better, an occupied one, but he thought too slowly, for Wan had approached him.

She looked at him, making eye contact, her face displaying no emotion. He patted the rump of the gray horse, and returned Wan's gaze. Neither said a word.

The horse had been standing getting curried for the longest time, and it finally decided it would rather be in its stall munching out of the hayrack. Buddy laughed at it, relieved that something had happened to break the silence. "You afraid of horses?" he asked.

Wan walked along as he headed the horse back to its stall. "Do I look like I am afraid?" she replied.

"You got something against horse shit?" he asked.

Wan shook her head negatively as Buddy put the horse into its stall, slid the door across the opening and latched it.

"End of today's lesson," Buddy said.

"You think I'm stupid?" she asked accusatorily.

He looked down at her. "I never said you were stupid."

"Don't treat me like I'm stupid. What do you mean 'end of lesson'? Like you taught me somethin'? You think just 'cause I ended up here, you tell me about horseshit, and that's it? Listen Cowboy, maybe this is better than jail by only a little, but I ain't but twenty-two. How old are you, sixty, sixty-five? And you're still in this place shoveling horse turds. Maybe you should wait 'til I'm old and wore out like you before you start lookin' down on me."

Buddy wondered how she knew his other name. "Fifty-three," he said.

After a short pause he asked, "You gonna' be mad at me all the time you're here?"

Wan looked at him, disarmed.

Cowboy continued, "I'm use to people bein' mad at me. Get mad at myself sometimes. It don't matter, just makes it a little easier if I know."

Wan answered truthfully, something that she was not used to doing, "I ain't mad at you Cowboy, sometimes I get mad at everything and everybody."

Buddy held out his hand. "My name's Cowboy, but around here they mostly call me Buddy."

Wan's face showed her disbelief. "You ain't no cowboy."

"Never said I was, but that's what some call me. That's what you called me."

"If you're not a cowboy what are you?" Wan had already more than doubled the normal length of her conversation; Buddy had tripled his.

"A drunk. Well, guess I was a drunk. Humph, once a drunk always a drunk. What are you?"

"Criminal," she said, "petty. Used to be incorrigible but you grow out of that."

They shook hands.

"Does that bother you," she asked, "that I lie and steal?"

"Hell, darlin', I'm a bum. I ain't got nothin' for you to steal. And everybody lies anyway, so why should it bother me?"

"Old man, so you're a bum they call Cowboy."

"They don't call me Bum, too many bums in D.C., more bums than Smiths. They'd get all us confused, so they call me Buddy or some call me Cowboy."

"Maybe I'll call you Chester."

"Chester? I guess you can call me Chester if you want, but I might not answer to it, besides you're too young to know Chester."

Wan's voiced rose in a hint of anger, "Don't say I'm too young for anything, Chester, but Cowboy does make more sense, you ain't got a limp."

"And what am I suppose to call you?" Buddy wondered, ignoring her defensiveness.

"Call me anything you like."

"Sunshine. I'll call you Sunshine," he said triumphantly.

"Sunshine? I ain't no Sunshine," she answered.

"I ain't no Cowboy," he replied.

Jason and the lawyer had managed, with Dee's help, to arrange accommodations in the police ward area. After examining the situation, Wan suggested that it would be better if she simply slept with the horses, being so close to the police made her uneasy. Jason indicated that such a plan was unacceptable, that this was the only place that she would have any privacy, and that he would not permit folks of either sex sleeping with the horses. He also took the opportunity to lecture the young lady, warning her that distracting the work release boys would not be tolerated.

The next day when the three other probationers came to work, it appeared as if all Jason's fears would be realized. The three had never been eager workers and now that they had an attractive girl to get to know, they were completely useless. Wan, however, was unimpressed. The boys averaged three years younger than she, and were much less worldly. Her attitude toward them was the same as it was toward Jason, belligerent. She hung close to the Cowboy for several days, figuring out the routine of work and food. She soon got the pace of the place. Within a week she had moved her bunk upstairs above the stalls sleeping halfway between Sligo and the Cowboy. Sligo did not object, he merely stared at her. Buddy did not object but tried to keep from staring.

He soon began to enjoy her companionship as they mucked out stalls, freshened hay racks, and washed and brushed the horses. He talked more to her in three days than he had all totaled in the five months he had been with the Mounted Unit. He took a strange pride in the vile and patronizing tone she took with everyone but himself and Sligo. Buddy could see her raw edge, her criminal tendencies, but they were never directed towards him. Perhaps because he accepted her, she accepted him.

He showed her the diner where he ate lunch, the fast food joint where he often ate dinner. Ten days after Wan arrived at the barn, she got her first paycheck.

"Cowboy, where can I cash this?" Wan waved her check in the air.

"I have Dorothy take care of mine, she gives me enough to get through the week and then sends the rest to my ex-wife," he replied.

Wan was surprised, for the old man had never mentioned a family before. "Well, I want to take you and Sligo to dinner tonight," she announced, "but I need to get this check cashed."

It was Buddy's turn to be astonished. "You don't need to do that Sunshine." He had gotten used to calling her that, although she had not yet gotten used to it.

"I don't need to do it, Asshole. I want to do it."

"Got to be a place that serves peanut butter and jelly," the Cowboy replied, ignoring her vulgarity.

She looked at him with a puzzled expression.

"Ain't you noticed? Sligo doesn't eat anything but peanut butter and jelly. Keeps it in a box by his bed. Morning, noon and night, peanut butter and jelly."

"Maybe all that peanut butter is what makes him crazy," she thought aloud.

Buddy did not answer. Ever since the bottle of booze incident he was not sure that Sligo was as crazy as he pretended.

"Go ask Jason. He knows where you can get the check cashed."

"I hate that little fucker. I don't want to ask him. I'll go find a bank."

Dorothy had just walked around the corner with a small box in her hand. "You'll need some ID," she stated.

Wan did not like anyone associated with authority, so she did not like Dorothy.

"You got any identification?" the clerk asked Wan directly. "You got a driver's license?"

"Suspended," was the answer.

"Anything else? The bank will want a picture ID."

Wan was silent, her eyes narrowing in distaste.

Dee turned to Buddy, "Here's a package for you, and your money."

Buddy was amazed to see a package. Who would send him a package? He took the box and slid the fifty bucks into his pocket. "Dee, she just wanted to get her check cashed. Can you help?"

"She's not asked me to help, Buddy."

"And I won't!" Wan shouted. "I don't need your help, you bitch!" Wan turned and marched to the foot of the stairway to the dorm. She would have slammed the door had there been one. Sligo had come down to witness the last half of this exchange, but even he of great doorway blocking ability knew to step aside.

Dee spoke to Buddy, "We don't need her here. Nothing but trouble. You watch your back with that one."

Buddy looked down at his package. It was from Ashland, Kentucky. "Dee, it ain't her. She's got demons. Sligo and me and her, we all got devils inside. One night they should take all the horses out and burn the barn down with us inside, get rid of the bastard creatures once and for all."

Dee looked at her friend. "Nobody's goin' burn the barn. Looks like maybe you got your socks," she said pointing at the package.

The Cowboy smiled. "She said she wanted to take Sligo and me out to dinner." He changed the subject; "You want to open the box for me?"

"You go ahead, but can I watch, I'm curious."

"Sure, but Dee, you know what I said is true."

"What?" she replied, not understanding.

"About the horned buggers. They get back in me, like I know they will, you'll hate me just like you hate her."

"That girl hate's me, Buddy. I don't hate her. I've never done anything to her. But enough; open your package."

Inside the box were four pair of white, heavy duty work socks and a plastic bag of half crushed chocolate chip cookies sandwiched in the middle. A note was at the bottom of the stash.

Cowboy,

You seem to have women friends all over the east coast. Tell Dorothy thanks for putting us back in touch. Wanted to let you know that my children are doing fine, growing everyday. We three are all quite computer literate now, thanks to you.

I've been promoted to asst. manager at the truck stop. Other than that, not much has changed. Mabel sends you the cookies. I send you the socks. Be sure and stop if you are ever through this way again.

Love,

Polly

The Cowboy handed the letter to Dorothy. His mind went back to the Easter Sunday at the truck stop. He remembered Polly as a nice person, a friendly person, but he could not recall her face. He wondered how old she was. Perhaps she had told him about her children, but now he could not remember anything about them.

"Dee," he asked after she had finished reading the brief note, "did you give all my money to my wife?"

Dee looked at him. He looked far older than fifty-three. "Buddy, your ex-wife doesn't want your money. She has started a new life and does not want to be reminded of the old one. I wrote her a lengthy letter telling the situation. She sent me one back saying that she hoped you would stay sober, and she was glad to hear that you were well, but that you and her were past history; history that she did not wish to go over again. She's remarried and I think she doesn't want to spoil that."

Buddy kicked the ground with his foot. "What about the money you've been taking out of my pay, I thought that you were sending it to her?"

"Buddy," Dee answered, feeling badly that she had deceived the old fellow. "Buddy, I've been putting that money into your savings account. You told me once you needed a reason to stay clean. Well, I figured that sending money to your wife might be the reason."

Buddy shook his head. "This money's a curse. I can't give it away. I started out by sending a weekly check to my old mother-in-law. She died. My daughter found me, only to throw the money back in my face. I tried to give it to the pony girl. She wouldn't take it. I bet it on a lark at the racetrack. Horse came in second, I had him to place, Smeltzer, dumb name for a horse. Only person got any of the money was Polly. She bought a computer for her kids."

Dee looked at him with gentle eyes, thinking that all the effort she was investing in him might be worth it. "How did you meet this Polly?"

"Waitress at a restaurant. Easter Sunday and I told her she should be home with her kids. She said she couldn't afford to be. I gave her a big enough tip so she could take the rest of the afternoon off. She bought a computer instead."

"Sounds like a pretty good trade, socks for a computer," the clerk reasoned.

Buddy smiled back at her, "Computer for chocolate chip cookies."

He opened the bag of cookies and offered Dee one. After she picked one out, he took a broken piece and tasted it.

"Dee, you got any children?"

"Grown and gone," she answered.

"I'd like to send some money to Polly."

"Oh, Buddy, I doubt that she'd take money. I bet she's got her pride. We all do. You got to trade her for something."

"Like what?"

"Oh, I don't know," Dee pondered. "You know, it's almost St. Valentine's Day. Send her roses. She'd like that."

"Roses? I don't know where to send 'em."

"Send them to the truck stop. Want me to call the florist for you?" Dee's voice had gotten excited with the thought of her idea.

"I've only got this fifty dollars, is that enough?" Buddy asked pulling the cash from his pocket.

Dorothy chuckled, "I got the rest of this week's paycheck locked up. Haven't sent it to the bank yet. I'll use that."

"Yellow roses. My father's favorite. He'd send my mother yellow roses. And Dee, is there enough money for two bunches?"

"Should be, who else do you want to send to?"

"You. And Dee, have them put in an extra rose to give to…" Buddy paused and indicated with his eyes toward the dormitory above the stalls.

16
Temptation

JASON HAD LOST CONTROL of the situation. He'd never really had control to begin with. His first great fear was that Wan would end up being screwed by all the work release boys, and that anarchy would spill over into the care of the horses. Jason was as hardened as the police. He did not care about the lives he was tending, only the horses. He loved the horses. They were his pride and his life. He had been crippled by a horse, but he still loved the creatures.

He was lonely. He had nobody to talk to about his horses. Nobody cared. The work release kids didn't care. The loony stuffing his face with peanut butter didn't care. The old drunk was hard to read, but most times he seemed not to care. He, Jason, was the one that held this stable together. He was the only one that made it work. Now this broad, this little chink of a broad with an attitude, a major attitude was ruining it all.

She had gotten the old drunk to talk. Jason had even seen him laugh. That wasn't so bad, but he was losing him, losing his allegiance. He knew it was out of his control when she'd moved up-stairs.

The Cowboy did not know any such thing. He did know that he half resented Wan taking up his time, shattering his quiet, disturbing his tranquility. He was used to being a loner. He had found that he was happier in a routine, seven days a week, each day the same, or nearly so. He was happier when he did not have to think.

She made him think. She made him respond. They both could spend hours in silence, but her hours were in thought, his were vacant. Eventually she would ask a question, engage him in conversation. He was polite, always turning on his brain to answer her, taking his mind away from whatever menial task he was about, taking his mind away from the horses.

Wan hid her belligerent tone from Buddy, but not from Jason. Jason tried to give as good as he got. He scolded her for not taking days off. "We work five days a week, eight-hour days. We start early, but we finish early. I assigned you Tuesday and Sunday off last week, and you were here working. Not allowed. I can't pay overtime, it ain't in the budget."

"Little Man," she called him, "Sligo and Cowboy, I ain't seen them take a day off."

"Juan, Sligo and Buddy are different," he replied, pronouncing her name as he had first heard it. "All the other work release boys, hell, I have trouble getting 'em to come to work. You take off two days a week. Sligo and Buddy don't get paid for the extra days anyway. They got nothin' better to do, so to keep 'em out of trouble I let them stay."

"I'm not asking to be paid. I got nothin' better to do myself. It's your job to keep me out of trouble."

Jason became more animated, "It ain't my job to do anything with you missy! I take care of horses. You can take your tight little ass, your fancy lawyer and leave anytime you want."

"Pee Wee, I got six months in this place. You're not gonna' get me to leave before my time is up."

"Christ," Jason replied, having nothing else to say as he walked away.

Wan tormented the younger boys, abused them. They would sit in the back tack room and joke to pass the time between the horses coming and going. There were only three of them now, so the poker games were lame. One afternoon she invaded their spot.

"You young fuckers play poker?" she asked, knowing the answer.

They looked at each other warily, believing that she was up to something. The boldest answered, "Yea, you play?"

"What you play for?" she asked.

"Quarters mostly," he said, "but if you've got dollars we'll use that as minimum."

"Strip," she stated. "Strip poker. You babies game?"

Again they looked at one another, the delightful prospect of seeing her tits outweighing any possibility that they might lose. They were professional gamblers.

Wan explained the rules, "Draw poker. One article of clothing to anti, one to draw. Loser is the one with the weakest hand. Any who fold before the draw automatically lose their anti. Losers throw their clothes out the open door. The deal rotates with each hand. No stopping 'til you're buck ass naked."

All three nodded, and two ball caps and a shoe were placed on the tack room table. Wan pulled up a chair and took one of her own shoes off. She lost the first hand, throwing her shoes out the door to the main stable aisle. She lost the second hand, playing stupidly, tossing her socks to follow her shoes. The boys were salivating. She pulled off an ankle bracelet and laid it on the table as anti for the next hand. "Does that count?" one of the boys asked. Wan just glared at him. It was her turn to shuffle and as she whipped through the deck, the wisest of the three grew uneasy. She handled the cards as if she'd learned in Vegas. An hour later all three lads were shivering and embarrassed as Wan wiped them out. She got up from the table in her bare feet; everything else still well covered, and walked out the door. As she went, she stooped and scooped up the clothes lying in a pile on the dirt. After putting on her shoes and socks, she walked them over through the cold to the police dispatcher next door, and dropped them by the Goodwill bags.

Even Jason smiled as he saw the three boys, wrapped in horse blankets, try to slip undetected out the side door.

One afternoon Buddy, Wan and one of the young men were busting open hale bales to spread out in the hay racks. Wan kept asking to borrow Buddy's knife to cut the twine holding the hay together.

"Don't you have a knife of your own, Juan," the dude asked, imitating Jason.

It'd violate probation if I carried a weapon," she said coldly, not liking the mispronunciation.

"Sunshine, you got to have a knife around here," he returned. "This is a horse barn. Just ask Jason, he'll tell you, carry a knife."

Wan ignored him and went about her business. The next bale that needed separating, she again asked for Buddy's knife.

The boy thought he saw a soft spot, a weakness. "You ever carried a knife?" he teased.

Without saying a word Wan slipped her hand into her front jeans pocket and pulled out a four-inch switchblade. She laid it upon the hay and went back to work. The blade had three notches in the handle.

The lad could not resist. "What are the notches for?" Wan turned coldly toward him, narrowing her eyes. "What are you in for? What'd you do?"

"Intent to distribute."

The woman looked from youth to blade and back again. "Assault with intent to dismember."

The boy was impressed.

"Piss ant," she spit, "room for another notch or two." Wan slipped her knife back into her pocket. When they came to the final bale that needed to be opened, Buddy handed her his knife before she could ask for it.

The morning of St. Valentine's Day, February 14th, the phone rang in Jason's office. "Buddy, when you get a chance, Dorothy would like to see you," Jason announced as he left the office to resume his chores. "Said it was no hurry."

Buddy had forgotten about Valentine's Day, had forgotten about the roses. When he entered the dispatch office he was surprised and pleased to see the bright splash of yellow and green standing in a vase on the counter.

Dee saw him coming and said, "Thank you for the flowers. Yellow roses like you said. They surely brighten the office, don't you think?"

"I didn't remember," he replied, "but they do look good."

"After a long winter you forget how dull and drab things are. How gray. But I like the bright yellow, and they even smell good.

"Buddy?" she asked, changing her tone of voice, "did you finish those cookies your friend from Kentucky sent?"

"Couple of days ago. I shared 'em around."

Dee reached below the counter and pulled out a round metal tin. "For you and the boys," she said. "Made 'em myself."

Buddy took the tin, "Thank you," he said and began to walk away.

"Happy Valentine's day, Buddy," Dorothy said.

He only smiled, not knowing what to say. He started again for the door.

"Wait, Buddy," she said. "Here's the single rose in a vase for your friend. Don't know that it will do any good."

Buddy reached for the vase with his free hand. "Dee, everybody needs a friend."

It was Dorothy's turn to only be able to smile.

Buddy managed to move undetected up the dormitory steps and placed the flower beside Wan's unmade bed. The single rose was not as dramatic as the dozen on the dispatch counter. It was almost swallowed up by the utilitarian grunge in which the three lived. He thought about leaving the cookies too, but Dee might hear about that, and she had made them for everybody. As he stood there thinking, Sligo quietly slipped into the room, desiring a spoonful of peanut butter as a mid-morning snack. Sligo never talked. He was so quiet that people often forgot about him. Buddy had not heard him come up the stairs, did not realize that he was there.

When Sligo spoke, Buddy jumped a foot off the floor, it was so unexpected. "Nice touch," is all that he said.

Buddy turned to be sure it was Sligo that had uttered the words.

"What did you say?' Buddy wanted to hear it again.

Sligo merely pointed to the flower. Buddy still holding the tin of cookies, opened the container.

"Dorothy made cookies, want one?"

Sligo shook his head and bent down to pull out the peanut butter jar.

"Damn!" Buddy exclaimed as he looked at the cookies. "I believe half of 'ems peanut butter cookies."

Sligo looked at Buddy curiously, unwilling to utter another word.

Buddy reached into the tin and removed a cookie, sniffed it. It seemed to be peanut butter. He left it on the nightstand by Sligo's bed and went downstairs to distribute the other cookies.

Within a half hour all the cookies were gobbled up. Jason remarked, "She never baked cookies before, not even for Christmas. Wonder why she made 'em now?"

The Cowboy thought it odd that Jason used his metal tongs to grab the cookie and put it in his mouth. He noticed that the sweet crumbled as he bit into it, losing large portions to the floor. Buddy wondered why Jason did not use his good hand.

After the cookies were gone, Jason made a general announcement. "Valentine's Day. Extra apple all around for the horses."

Buddy moved to pick up the bushel basket that contained the wizen old apples the stable used as treats for the livestock. He began going down the aisle holding a fruit out for each horse. It always amazed him that the horses could tell instinctively the difference between finger and apple. He had gotten to the third horse when Wan joined him.

"You hold the basket, I'll give 'em the apples," she said.

Buddy looked at her. She had pushed her black hair behind her ears and fastened it on each side with a beret. Above her ear on the right side was the yellow rose. The contrast of yellow on black was distinctive. Buddy smiled to see it there, but said nothing.

When they had worked their way down to Dromedary's stall, Buddy said, "Give the Camel two."

Wan looked at the horse and obliged.

"Why is this one your favorite?" she asked.

Buddy set the basket on the ground and reached up and scratched the old boy behind the ears. Dromedary always liked that. Buddy did not want to tell Wan while this horse was special.

"Why'd you give me the rose?" she asked.

Buddy did not want to tell her that either.

"Wasn't me," he lied.

"Dumb shit. I know it was you. What are you trying to prove?"

He picked up the apples and moved on to the next horse, refusing to say anything.

Wan wouldn't let it drop. "Are you trying to win me over? Hopin' that maybe I might like you? Hell, Cowboy, you think that 'cause I'm nice to you, and bitch at everybody else, you think I like you?"

Buddy hung his head. It was his natural reaction. He had been verbally abused so often, that most times he could grow deaf by simply bowing his head and closing his eyes.

"Cowboy, why would I like you? You are so fuckin' old and so fuckin' falling apart! Most times you stink. You got to be crazy or stupid; probably both to think that one lousy rose would make me like you."

Buddy was stung by the words. Seeing his reaction, seeing that she could reach into his skin and damage this silent man made her anxious to damage him more.

"You are a screwed up, fuckin' lonely old drunk," she continued. "Nobody cares a shit about you. Nobody gives a shit about me, either, but that don't mean I could ever like you, you sullen bastard. We might be the only two sane people in this barn, but damn if I ever like you."

While she was talking, she handed an apple to the next horse and together they moved on down the row.

"How long has it been since you left this place other than to eat and buy toothpaste?" her tirade had lessened in intensity slightly, but continued non-stop. "You are tied here. You're goin' die here. And when you do, I'll tell 'em to throw you into the stall with that Camel friend of yours."

Down the end of the aisle and up the other side she continued baiting him as they fed the animals their holiday treats. By the time they had come full circle, and offered the last horse an apple, she was nearly worn out from talking.

Buddy looked up at her. Somewhere around the halfway mark, her words quit hurting. He smiled at her and waved his free hand close by the rose. "Nice touch," he said and walked away leaving her speechless.

The living accommodations in the upstairs dorm were quite unusual. Sligo had the first bunk, a cot really, close by the stairs. Five other beds were lined up in the room. Wan had appropriated the middle two, while Buddy's was the final one against the far wall. Each had a small pile of goods and clothes under their respective beds, and each used the vacant adjacent bunk as a table. There was a small bathroom with a shower stall tucked under the sloping eaves off the main sleeping area, but there was no privacy. Wan had shown no hesitancy about stripping and bathing in front of the two older men. Sligo would lie on his side on his cot and watch her intently. Buddy made it a practice to turn his back towards her whenever she was changing clothes or heading to and from the bath.

The evening following the argument, St. Valentine's Day evening, he sat upon his bed and watched her. The room lights were off, but the bathroom bulb gave plenty of light through the open door. It was a naked, yellow light, and the angle of the illumination cast shadows through the dorm. Sligo was sitting on his own bed, spooning out Skippy directly from the jar. Buddy had gone to dinner at the fast food outlet and then returned to walk down the stalls, saying silent good nights to the horses, after which he had taken a long shower, lathering up an extra time.

Wan had disappeared after the argument. It was after nine when she returned, late for this crew, tromping up the stairs and past Sligo. She noticed Buddy looking at her, but neither of them said anything. Slowly she began to disrobe, first taking off the ever present windbreaker, then pulling a tattered sweat shirt over her head, messing up her hair, and dislodging the rose. Buddy watched as she pulled the flower from her locks and laid it back in its vase. She had cut the stem so that it would fit in her hair, and now it looked odd sitting so low in the little container. Wan returned Buddy's look, thinking that he would now turn 'round to offer her privacy as he had always done, but he did not.

She unbuttoned here flannel shirt, pulling it out of her jeans. She took it off and laid it on the open bed between herself and the Cowboy. She paid no mind to Sligo, but she was acutely aware of Buddy's gaze. She sat on her bed to untie her boots and pull off her socks. Buddy analyzed the way the light struck her skin along her side and belly. He was amazed at the tightness of it, the sleekness, the youth. Her white bra held smallish breasts, but that was not what caught his attention, it was the vitality of her body. He was used to seeing hags naked, with their drooping tits, and wrinkled flab surrounding their stomachs. Now, ten feet away, a young, vibrant, self-confident woman was displaying herself. He had avoided looking before, but now he was mesmerized.

She had become self-conscious. She stood again, in her bare feet. Normally she would have tossed off her jeans and underwear and given no thought to the mental state of the gentlemen she shared the room with, but tonight, with him watching so closely, she became bashful. She picked up a clean tee shirt and a towel and walked to the bathroom, closing the door behind her. When she had finished with her toiletries, she returned to the main room with the tee shirt as nightdress and her jeans and undergarments in her hand. Before she turned off the bathroom light she looked at Buddy. He was sitting exactly as he had been when she left. With the light turned off, the windowless dormitory was dark and quiet. The sweet smell of the hay and the horses seeped through the floor. It was a good place to sleep. It took a long time for Wan's eyes to adjust to the dim light that slithered through the cracks in outer wall and beneath the door, but when she did, she noticed the old man still sitting, watching.

17
Frostbite

THE NEXT MORNING AFTER the initial string of horses and police had been sent out on their winter rounds, Buddy walked the empty tin of cookies to the station house.

"Thank you," he said to Dorothy as he placed the tin upon her counter.

"Finished them already?"

"I shared them around. Everybody thought they were fine. Even Sligo," he commented.

"Sligo? You mean the psychopath liked my cookies?" she replied in mock amazement.

"The peanut butter ones. Did you make those special for him?"

"No, not really. Just using up some stuff left over from the holidays when the kids where home," she stated. "Nobody eats peanut butter at the house except the grandchildren."

Buddy looked at the roses, smelling their faint odor. They reminded him of his mother and father. He turned to head back toward the barn.

Dorothy interrupted his movement. "I got a note from your Kentucky girl friend."

Buddy looked at her suspiciously.

"The e-mail was to me, but I guess I can share it with you," she said, pulling a paper from the top of a pile on her counter.

Dee,

    Tell Cowboy thanks for the lovely roses. They've caused quite a stir at the truck stop. Everyone thinks I have a secret admirer. Quite a few of the truckers actually seemed jealous. Somehow I get the feeling that you had a hand in it. I really don't know anything about him, you know. Not sure that I should continue to accept his gifts. Assure me that he is not some lunatic.

                                Hugs,

                                Polly

Buddy listened as Dee read the message. He leaned again toward the roses and thought of his father, a genial and intelligent man, who, like his son drank too much. His mother was a candidate for sainthood, putting up with two such men.

"I heard the little bitch really laid into you yesterday." Dee changed the subject.

Buddy looked at her perplexed.

"Wan Leigh. I've asked Lt. Granger to sign a petition for her to be moved to a halfway house. She's done nothing but disrupt this place since she's been here."

"Dee," Buddy looked at his friend, not sure how to respond.

He tapped his fingers a few times on the empty cookie tin and left.

A few days later Wan got a visitor. He was a bright-faced young fellow dressed in shirt, tie and parka. He carried a satchel in his hand.

"Mr. Crumley?" he spoke to Jason. "My name is Wilson. I am a probation officer. I've been assigned Wan Leigh's case. There has been a petition signed by the police that requests that she be transferred to a halfway house and found other employment. I need to ask you a few questions, sir."

"Go ahead, ask," Jason said, not heeding the hint for privacy in the young man's suggestion. He was used to working with snot nosed probation officers but he had never seen this one before.

"May we use your office?"

Jason nodded and led the way, closing the door behind him. Buddy had been mucking out stall number one, and had heard the initial conversation. In his mind he still had not come up with a response to the possibility of Wan leaving. She had only been here a little over three weeks. They had not spoken since the argument on Valentine's Day. He had again taken up the habit of turning his back towards her when she needed privacy.

After a few minutes, Jason emerged from the office and hollered to Wan. She had been cleaning a stall about half way down the building.

"Juan, this fellow wants to see you in my office!"

Wan stuck her head out the stall opening, "What fellow?"

"Your probation officer, he says," Jason answered.

"Damn," she said, standing her pitchfork against the side of the stall.

It was a half-hour before she and the young man finished. Buddy had moved down several stalls and was about to start where Wan had left off. Wan snatched the fork from its resting place, giving the Cowboy a wicked glance as she slipped past him back into the stall.

"Mr. Crumley," Wilson began, "currently there are no beds in the half-way house on Maryland Avenue. As Wan has done nothing illegal, I think it safe to leave her here a few days until we can find a place for her. If you think it necessary, we can place her in jail, but as you have access to the police just across the yard, I should think she will be all right.

"I think she'll run," Jason mused. "I think she'll run and we'll never see her again."

"That solves your problem then, doesn't it," Wilson remarked.

Buddy looked at Jason and then Wilson. He turned and walked into the pen where Wan had disappeared. As he rounded the corner he noticed the tines of the pitchfork against his throat.

He thought that it would be a slow way to die, being pierced with a pitchfork. It would be quicker though, than the poison he had spent thirty-five years of his life imbibing. He was used to seeing disgust in people's eyes, but as he looked at Wan, he could see fear and hatred. He did what came naturally to him. He stood quietly, waiting to see what would happen.

He had no idea what Wan was thinking. He had never been any good at judging the thoughts of women. As he stood there, he realized one of two things was about to happen, either she would poke him, or she would lower her weapon. It was her choice; he would accept either.

Softly she whispered, the anger still in her eyes, "Why do you like Camel better than the other horses?"

He did not respond.

She hesitated, then lowered the fork.

As she did he said, "Dromedary saved my life once. Twice."

"How could a horse save your life?" she asked suspiciously.

"Not sure, but he did. Not sure I even wanted it saved."

The hatred had vanished from Wan's eyes as she looked at the old man. The hatred and fear had vanished, replaced by self-pity.

"Why are you making me go?"

Buddy looked at the wounded little girl. He wanted to offer her a shoulder to lean upon, as he had offered his shoulder to lame Sparky that night at the racetrack. He would have held Sparky up for as long as it would have taken to mend her broken leg. Wan was not a horse, though, so he did not offer the shoulder, she would not have accepted it had it been offered. Rather, she quietly laid the pitchfork against the back wall of the stall and walked out and through the doors of the barn.

Buddy picked up the tool and took it to the rack across from Jason's office where he replaced it in its proper space. He turned to see Jason watching him.

"She'll be back to pick up her gear," the old jockey told Buddy.

The Cowboy stroked his chin as if trying to coax the words out of his mouth. "What do you do with a horse that's hurt?" he managed to say.

"Depends how badly hurt, depends how good the horse. What's your point?"

"Put it out of its suffering," Buddy thought aloud. "That's it, isn't it?"

Jason looked at him waiting for the rest to come out.

Buddy turned to look at the doorway, partially opened to the cold February day. He wanted to follow her. He wanted to get his money out of the bank and follow her. He wanted to tell her that he wasn't as old as she thought he was. He wanted to touch her smooth skin. He wanted to go sit in the warm sun somewhere with her.

"She ain't done nothing wrong," he said softly. "Don't make her go."

"She's trouble, Buddy. Nothin' but trouble. Been a pain since the day she come here," Jason reasoned. "Her problems go well beyond what we can help her with."

Buddy silently looked at the little man. He recalled the words Mary's uncle had used, "No extraordinary measures."

The old man slowly moved toward the doorway, picking up speed as he did. Once outside the barn he walked next door to the clerk's counter. It was shortly before shift change and the next crew of the Mounted Unit were milling about. Dorothy was busy interacting with them and had only a smile of recognition for Buddy. Richard was there, awaiting his afternoon mount.

"Dee, how do I get my money?" Buddy interrupted.

"What's that, Honey?" Dorothy turned from her conversation with the policemen.

"My money. I want to get my money out."

The clerk was surprised. "What do you want your money for?"

"I want my money. I want to go to Florida and get warm. I want to go buy a bottle of expensive booze. I want to go lay on the beach. I want my money." Buddy thought a minute then asked Richard who was standing close enough to have overheard the request. "What was that stuff you got me? It smelled good, but people keep pouring the stuff on the ground before I can taste it. I want a fifth of that. What was it?"

Richard, with a look of great distaste said, "Once a bum, always a bum."

Buddy moved his attention back to the clerk. "I'm a grown man. You can't keep that money from me. I'm gonna' get a bottle of that good shit, and maybe a couple of gallons of the cheap. I'm gonna' get a bus ticket. If I can remember when I get to Florida, I'm gonna' find me a whore, then I'm gonna go lay on the sand and let the sun burn the pus right out of me, dry me out completely. What do you call that? Dehydrate. Suck me dry 'til there ain't nothin' left but bone and skin. Then maybe the wind will blow me away, or the garbage collectors with their pointy sticks will cram me into their gunny sacks."

"No," Dee said sternly.

"Dee, listen. You give me my money or I do the same thing, only here in Washington in the cold and without the good shit and without the whore. I got money enough in my pocket to buy me the liquor."

Dee shook her head. "I won't be a part of this."

Buddy grew heated. "Well, then send the money to my fuckin' ex-wife that don't want to hear from me ever again! Tell her I intentionally froze my ass in the nation's capitol," he shouted. "Tell her I'll never bother her anymore."

His voiced quieted. "Dee, tell her I'll never bother anybody again." He looked at the bouquet of roses still sitting on the counter. His father and mother lay buried together across the river in Arlington National Cemetery. A vision of his resting himself upon their grave came to his mind. If he could not get to a warm place, then he would chose to die there. He had not the credentials to be buried in that hallowed place, but he assured himself that he had the right to die there.

Saying nothing more, he left the station house.

The park police found him early the next morning, laying huddled against grave marker section 60 number 4862, two empty bottles of cheap whiskey at his feet. He was nearly dead, but not quite. Frostbite had begun to set in on his toes and fingers. He was taken unconscious to the hospital where a check on missing persons was run. They discovered that he belonged to the Mounted Unit.

The next day Dee sat along side his bed. "Seems to me I told you once," she began, not sure that he was listening, "In my job you get hardened. People like your friend Wan Leigh treat you like dirt. There's no end to the pain you see, you got to get tough. You can't let it get to you."

Buddy's eyes were open. He looked at his bandaged hands. He couldn't see his bandaged feet, couldn't examine his missing toes. He could tell that he was still alive.

"I thought that I had gotten strong enough. I thought that I didn't care anymore," she continued. "But you let your guard down for a minute. Let one person in, then what happens? They kick you in the teeth. They go out and try to die. Does anybody else care? Do you see any of the work release boys here? Hell, no. How about Jason or Sligo? Jason thought about coming, but he's too busy. Even your little friend Wan Leigh, is she here? No, just me. Just poor, dumb me."

As Dee mentioned Wan's name, Buddy turned is head towards her with a questioning look on his face.

"Oh, she came back." Dee picked up, sensing the question. "She came back for the night. Didn't say a word to anybody. Next morning she asked where you were. That was before they brought you in here. Couple hours later when we got word that you were still alive Jason goes to try and find her. She was hunched back in a horse's stall and wouldn't come out."

Buddy realized that his mouth still worked, and that his throat and larynx would still let him speak. "Which horse?"

"How do I know which horse?" There was an added tone of humiliation in her voice, thinking that he would ask about Wan. "What difference does it make?"

"Dromedary," Wan answered from the foot of his bed. She had slipped in unnoticed.

Dorothy turned to look at the young woman, and then turned back to Buddy. "I'm going. You're still an employee of the D.C. police department. You come back to work one day after they release you so that the insurance will pay for the hospital. I'll have your money so you can go to Florida." She rose from the chair and left the room without a further good-bye.

After a period of silence, Wan moved to the chair Dorothy had vacated. Buddy looked at her and commented, "We're a sad pair, Sunshine, you and me."

Wan looked at him, touched his forearm above the bandages, but said nothing.

"We got demons, can't get rid of our demons," he said, closing his eyes. It wasn't as if he was using that as an excuse, but only stating facts.

"I hate people." Wan stated. "I hate that bitch Dorothy. I hate Jason. I hate the work release boys. I hate you."

Buddy asked, "Do you hate the horses?"

"Horses aren't people," she replied. "I hate people."

"I don't hate," Buddy responded. "I hate myself, but that don't count."

In a few days Buddy was released to a physical rehabilitation clinic where he learned to balance himself without his toes, where he learned to work around the dead spots in his fingers. Wan did not come to visit. Dorothy did not come to visit. One afternoon, though, Jason showed up.

The former jock looked around the clinic with the eye of one who has been through a similar experience. He talked to one of the nurses, showing off his metal claw. Buddy sat on a bench in the workout room, warmed by the rays of the March sunshine bouncing through the window.

"Feels like spring out there today," Jason said to him.

Buddy only smiled.

"You comin' back to work?" Jason asked directly.

"You have me?"

"It'll be our busy time soon. Lost another of the work release boys. Seems like it's only me and Sligo."

Buddy assumed that because Wan Leigh was not mentioned that she had been moved. The quiet man could think of nothing to say.

Jason's patience had all been used. "The nurses said you were going to be let go tomorrow. You need to come back for a day at least, to be sure the insurance company doesn't pitch a fit. You got cab money?"

Buddy shook his head. He didn't have a dime in his pocket.

Jason pulled a bill out of his wallet. "Use this to get back to the stable." He turned and departed.

Buddy examined the money and thought of the bottle that he could buy.

When the Cowboy showed up at the barn the next afternoon the first shift of horses had just been exchanged for the afternoon patrol. Buddy slipped into his assignment without comment as he took a horse from the hands of a patrolman, led it down to the washstand and back to its stall. He limped as he walked, and his fingers still gave him pain. Dromedary had gone out on the second shift, so he had no one to share his thoughts with.

That evening, after his chicken sandwich, he slowly climbed the steps to the dorm. Wan's gear had been removed, the bunk stripped of bedding. Someone had taken the trouble of straightening his corner, putting out fresh linen. On his neatly made cot was an object wrapped tightly in a brown paper bag. Sligo watched him as he sat on the bed and picked up the package. He turned it over a couple of times before opening it. There was no writing or other marks on the bag. Curious, he opened the paper and pulled out Wan's switchblade. Around the closed blade a rubber band held a note.

> *Hold this for me. They'll strip search me at the halfway house. Careful, the blade is razor sharp. ---- Oh, and don't leave for Florida without me.*

The courts sent two new juveniles the next week. Jason figured that he had better not put one with Buddy. Because Sligo refused to communicate with anyone, the boss had to explain the basics of horse care and safety himself. Buddy still suffered occasional, excruciating pain, but he refused to take his medication. He had difficulty holding a brush in his right hand. Closing his fingers around the pitchforks took all his strength, but most annoying of all was that his missing toes kept itching.

Dorothy stopped processing his paychecks. She did set up a direct deposit account and pointed him in the direction of the nearest branch office. Every ten days or so he would shuffle through the neighborhood to the bank and retrieve enough cash to pay for his slim meals and necessary supplies. He found it difficult passing the homeless, the panhandlers. He imagined himself rumbling through the waste cans, or leaning on the corner lamppost with them. He was lonely, and wanted someone with whom to share his misery.

Dorothy wouldn't speak to him. Sligo didn't speak to anyone. Other than the day's assignments, Jason ignored him. In their arrogance, the young boys thought him useless. Buddy's only satisfaction came from grooming the horses. Using the curry brush in his left hand and the palm of his right, he went over each horse in his care until the beast was immaculate. He was slow and sometimes the animals became impatient with him, but for the most part, they all enjoyed his attentions. Dromedary, naturally, received his most intense affection and listened to all his sad stories.

Spring turned to summer; summer to fall, and fall back into winter. A cool civility came to exist between Jason and Buddy, between Buddy and Dorothy. Five new horses had come and replaced five aged ones. New patrolmen had replaced some of the old. The work release boys, the courts had sent no more women, had all recycled a time or two. Dorothy conveyed no message to or from Polly or Mary. Buddy's inner tide of devils remained dormant. It had been more than a year since his frostbite. Although his fingers often ached, the toes had stopped itching. He carried Wan's knife to remember her by. He wished that there were something of his wife's, so that he could run his hands over it and feel close to her. He deeply wished that that he had some trinket of his daughter's. Cowboy had become, without intention, a sad, sober, old man. The stable was a dispirited place inhabited by people and animals hardened to the circumstances of life. Buddy, Jason, Sligo, Dorothy, the work release boys, and the patrolmen had all succeeded in turning the Mounted Unit into a refuge from pain, but in doing so, they had abandoned any hint of pleasure.

18
Sunshine Returns

YEARS WENT BY, AS years do. Normalcy reigned. Routine was the rule. The work release boys changed at regular intervals yet stayed the same, while everyone else got gradually older, as people do, gradually, so that none of them noticed the aging except in odd times of recollection. The horses grew older too, the ones too infirm to work on a regular basis were sent to pasture. Dromedary had reached that stage, but Jason had reduced his workload and justified his stall space by saying that he was a calming influence upon the stable.

The judges again began sending young women, girls really, to the barn, but not one of them demanded to live on site. Each one, in their own way, caused ripples with the boys, but Buddy viewed their shenanigans and screwing in the tack room or on the hay bales as a natural part of life and paid no more than passing attention. Sligo would find cracks in the floorboards or peepholes in the walls to watch were he could. Jason, when he found out, would rant and rave to no effect.

The routine could have been maintained for years, but what story is there in routine?

"Christ, all we need around here is Quasimodo and we'll have the entire cast of Les Miserables assembled."

Buddy turned from wiping down a gelding at the bath. The voice was familiar, but as he turned the person was back lit by the open barn door and so he could not see her facial features.

Sligo must have recognized her though, for from a nearby stall he hollered, "Que Passa?"

"Sligo, you psycho, I ain't Spanish. Jason was the only one who thought I was Mexican," she said with a smile in her voice. "Hell, I didn't even know you knew Spanish."

Buddy still could not make out Wan's face, but he could see Sligo's smile. He hadn't seen it in a long, long time.

"Most people don't know that he speaks English," the Cowboy interjected with a warmth of recognition in his voice. "How long have you been standing there?"

"Long enough to watch you old bastards work." She opened her arms inviting a hug.

Buddy instinctively responded by opening his and stepping towards her. They shared a warm embrace. It had been a long time since anyone had seen Buddy smile; it had been a long time since he had felt a reason to smile.

"I thought maybe you would forget me," Wan said after she stepped back from the hug.

Buddy reached into his pocket, pulled out her knife, and handed it to her.

She took it in her hand and examined it. "Do you use it?" she asked.

Buddy nodded in the affirmative.

"I have no need for it anymore," she said, handing it back to him.

Jason limped out of his office. "Is he going?"

Wan turned to him and answered, "I ain't asked him yet."

Jason motioned to Buddy, "Put the horse away. Sligo, come over here, Juan's got a story to tell."

As Cowboy untied the horse to lead him to his stall, Wan interrupted in a quiet voice, "Is the Camel still here? I got carrots."

Buddy pointed down the aisle where the old boy had his head out of his stall, patiently waiting for some attention. In a minute the small band had all assembled before Dromedary to hear the story of Wan's travels. She seemed a little nervous to begin, stroking her four-legged friend, cooing to him while the three human geldings waited their turn.

Finally Jason could contain himself no longer. "Juan's a college graduate, can you believe it?"

Wan turned away from the horse to look at Buddy. "Wasn't it Mary Engler you said you worked for on the track? Wasn't that her name?"

"Mary?" Buddy's mind started rotating, trying to remember, searching for the right neuron path. At first the brain was dead, but then he looked over Wan's shoulder and saw the Camel looking back at him. "We both worked for Mary," he stated. "Both Dromedary and me. Mary Engler."

"She's got a horse in the Preakness on Saturday; didn't run in the Kentucky Derby, but looks like it might have a chance in the Preakness. Want to go?"

She was asking Buddy, "I got two box seat tickets."

Buddy could not say anything. He had awoken the recollections of his time with Mary and Poncho and John and Dromedary and with Sparky. His mind was back along the shed row. He was aware that Wan was speaking to him, but the vision before him was so vivid that he could not break away from it.

"I graduated from college last weekend, and as a reward to myself, I got these two tickets to the Preakness," she said a little louder, trying to draw him back to the present.

"I still can't believe you made it through college," Jason commented, shaking his head.

"What school? What major?" Sligo wondered, sounding intelligent.

"George Mason, degree in Marketing. Got three job offers."

"How the hell did you go from that brat with an attitude that we knew, to a college graduate with a real job making real money?" Jason wondered, still shaking his head.

"Never lost the attitude," Wan shot back, the hardness at the edge of her voice proving the statement.

"The Preakness is in Baltimore, at Pimlico, no more than an hour's drive." Wan returned to Buddy, trying to get through his fog. "I got a car, a little beat up, but I ain't started earning any of that job money yet. Jason says you got plenty of vacation time and he'll give you the weekend off. Listen, Cowboy, I'll be by Saturday morning at 9:30."

Buddy's countenance cleared and it was as if he had heard and understood it all. "I'll buy you a crab cake dinner. Not at 9:30, but after the race. I ain't been to the races in years." He looked at Jason and Sligo. "Jason, you goin'? Sligo?"

"Your party Cowboy, me and Jason, we'll watch it on TV," Sligo answered.

Buddy looked at his dorm mate quizzically. Why was he sounding human? He never watched television. This was all too much for a frostbite old drunk with half a brain. Crab cakes, though, that sounded good. Buddy hadn't eaten crab cakes in twenty years. What made his mind remember that crab cakes and Baltimore went together? To gather himself he looked at Wan. She had matured. She was not feminine, not even pretty, but she had filled into a woman.

"Cowboy," she said, looking at him with a slim smile.

"Sunshine," he replied.

"See you Saturday." Turning to Jason and Sligo, she added, "Have him ready."

19
To the Track

BUDDY WAS CURIOUS AND thoughtful as he waited for the week to pass. He hadn't been either for a long time. His brain was unaccustomed to the electron stimulation in the region where curiosity resides. It gave him a headache and it caused him worry. He wondered, if his curiosity were awakened, mightn't the demons also awake? They had left him alone these past years, as if they were content to have sucked him dry, but he knew that they were there somewhere, waiting.

How does a conscious mind intentionally cease to question? An unconscious mind can function by rote, ignoring outside stimulus. When that stimulus is so great as to scale the wall of the coma, well then, the man awakes and wonders and suffers a headache. Of all the things Buddy could have thought about, questioned, his mind chose an odd one, 'Why didn't Wan want her knife back?' He flipped it over and over in his fingers as he wondered. He had gotten used to using it, cutting the string on the hay bales mostly, but for all sorts of odd jobs, whenever a sharp blade came in handy. He had taken care of it, attending to it so as not to misplace it, assuming that one day she would come asking for it. He had never taken it for granted, but always thought of its owner each time he sliced the binding of the hay. It was his connection to her.

Wan had come back, as he had imagined, but she was not interested in the knife. It had lost its importance to her. It was no longer a symbol, a connection. It was now only a utensil; his tool, its value much diminished. He pondered from every angle, turning the knife over and over in his hands.

The week wound its way toward Saturday. Jason became more animated then anyone had seen him in years. He talked of Mary Engler's horse's chances in the upcoming race. On Friday he even went so far as to buy a Daily Racing Form to analyze its prospects. Sligo took some mild amusement in watching the change in the boss' behavior. Except for fidgeting with the knife, Buddy's routine did not alter until Friday afternoon.

Dromedary had been out for the morning shift, ridden comfortably by one of the more horse-knowledgeable officers. Jason took pains to schedule the old campaigner with a rider that would respect him. It was a brilliant day in May, and the Camel had enjoyed his stroll amongst the last tulips and the spent cherry blossoms around the Jefferson Memorial. That was his favorite duty post, Buddy concluded, imaging the steed peering over the shoulders of the tourists by the lake and the Roosevelt gardens, walking his rider past the statue of the Virginia gentleman, feeding off the attention when the young girls would oo and aw over his burnished coat and strong muscular body.

"Remember Poncho?" The Cowboy whispered as he began to groom his companion that Friday afternoon. "Remember that black horse, you whipped his ass, busted his balls, but he didn't have none?" Buddy hobbled about, leaning against the Camel as he brushed with his good hand. "Remember Mary? They used to call you a terrible name, but I made 'em stop. Remember?

"Remember how bad I wanted a drink? I don't want no drink, no more. But I did then, needed one, remember?"

The horses nickered and shook his head, but it was impossible to tell if it was in agreement or disagreement. Buddy worked over every inch of the animal, first with the hard brush then with the soft. He picked up the feet, cleaned out the hoof cavity. He patted and snuggled and spent more time in Dromedary's stall than usual. Dorothy came to stand by the stall opening.

"Will you place a bet for me?" she asked.

The years had softened the anger in her, but there had been no cookies or flowers exchanged since Buddy's night spent in the graveyard.

He finished with the horse and stepped out of the stall, sliding the metal mesh shut behind him.

"She turned out alright," he said, not directly answering the question.

"That remains to be seen," the clerk replied.

"How much you want to bet?"

"I'm cheap. Two dollars to win, place and show."

"What's the horse's name?" Buddy responded.

"Llewellyn. Mary Engler's horse."

"Not sure that I should go," the old man shook his head.

Dorothy handed him a five and a one-dollar bill. "Go. Have a good time."

She turned and began walking toward the barn door.

"Dee," he called after her, using a name he had not used in years. "Dee? Can you write it down? The bet I mean. You know how I forget things."

"Buddy, you're not that old," she said turning back to him with a smile. But she found a scrap of paper and a pen. and wrote done her wager. She handed it to him and turned and walked through the door.

Just as she left, Sligo appeared from the shadows. He had some dollar bills in his hand that he gave to Buddy. "Same bet," he said and disappeared again.

"Write it down," he called to Sligo. "I can't remember this crap. Don't even remember how to bet. Horse don't care if you bet on him or not."

"That's true, but the people do." It was Jason. "They'll be tens of millions of dollars bet tomorrow. Horses don't give a damn. Our few dollars won't make a difference, but still it's kinda' important."

Buddy looked at him. "Sligo don't know Engler, Dorothy don't know her either. They don't know the owner of the horse. They don't know nothin'. Why are they bettin' on him?"

"Everybody likes a connection," Jason responded. "They're betting on Llewellyn 'cause they think they have a connection to the horse through you. Sort of like if the Camel wasn't a gelding and he had babies at the track. You show support by backing his offspring."

Buddy thought a minute, still not getting it straight.

"I know Dromedary ain't a stud," Jason continued. "I know he ain't got babies, but you back your friends, is what I'm trying to say. Sligo and Dorothy didn't bet 'cause of the horse, asshole. They bet 'cause of you."

The former jock reached into his pocket and pulled out a twenty-dollar bill. "I ain't bettin' 'cause of you. I'm bettin' 'cause I think the horse is going to do well. Put twenty on him to show."

"Show?"

"Yea, doesn't have to win, just needs to be respectable."

"Write it down," Buddy said accepting the cash.

The first Saturday in May is the Kentucky Derby. Two weeks later comes the Preakness stakes, followed in another three weeks by the Belmont. The combination of the three races is known as the Triple Crown. To win all three is to become enshrined, bronzed and immortalized all at once. Three-year-old horses, animals not yet into their prime, vie for the glory of it all. It takes skill, stamina, speed, good health and good luck to win even one of the three. It takes a miracle to win all three.

Mary Engler trained a good horse. Llewellyn wasn't quite ready for the Derby, so she passed on that entry, and worked toward the Preakness. The horse had an advantage beyond being more rested than the Derby combatants. Baltimore was his home track, his normal training ground.

The Derby winner, a California horse, had been racing out west all late winter and spring, and had come to Kentucky to take the roses. The pressure on the horse and his connections was now immense, for there could be only one Triple Crown winner and he was it. Horses might not know anything about triple crowns, but they can sense the tension of the humans around them. One reason why it is so tough to win all three of the races is the build up in hype. There is even a special stall at the Pimlico track for the Derby winner.

Llewellyn avoided most of that commotion, residing in his own quiet stall. This was Mary Engler's biggest race to date, and she and her staff were on edge with excitement, but they tried to shield their charge from nearly all the tension, bringing him to the perfect level of anticipation on race day. Too much pressure and the horse frets and leaves its best race in the stall. Just the right amount of pressure and the horse is on its toes, prancing, ready to show the world what it can do. Over a hundred thousand people would be crammed into the old horse track, most in the infield, most intoxicated, all yelling through the preliminary races for four hours before the Preakness horses even walked on to the track. A fresh horse, an even-tempered horse has a small advantage. Mary hoped that was enough of an edge, as she was about to send out her uncle's horse against the best animals, and the best trainers in the country. She hoped that she could win. She prayed that she would not be embarrassed.

When Wan had purchased the two reserved seats, she had not anticipated the problem of parking. Had she thought of it, she could have somehow procured a handicapped pass. The Cowboy used a cane to walk any distance, and to get to Pimlico on Preakness day requires walking some distance.

She thought about it as they drove up Route 95 between Washington and Baltimore.

"I'm not sure where to park. You ever been to Pimlico?" she asked.

"No."

"Not much help."

She glanced down at his cane resting beside him. "Hate to make you walk."

"Don't mind walking, but I don't want to hold you up."

They were silent for a while. They'd been silent most of the trip so far.

"'Member? You were goin' call me Chester once," Cowboy said marveling to himself that he himself could remember. "You got a right to call me Chester now."

Wan paused before answering, "Who the hell was Chester anyway?"

For some reason Buddy could see it all clearly. "Gunsmoke. James Arness. Had a girl friend, Kitty. Chester was the sidekick. I always liked Doc the best."

"Chester was the cripple?"

"Walked with a limp. Gunsmoke, a western. You ever see it?"

Wan shook her head, "Just heard about Chester is all."

Buddy felt in his pockets. In one pocket was everyone's cash and the directions for betting. In the other pocket was Wan's knife with two hundred-dollar bills wrapped around it. That money was for crab cakes. He had no idea how much crab cakes would cost, but he felt that a hundred should cover it. They had called ahead from the barn before departing this morning to make reservations at a restaurant that Jason recommended, to be sure that they would be seated.

As they drove along the crowded highway, Wan thought of another worry.

"Cowboy, maybe this wasn't such a great idea. The place will be packed." She didn't know how to explain her new fear to Buddy without potentially hurting his feelings.

He, at first, did not understand what she was saying, but he could feel the unease in her tone. Then a picture of the swarming crowd came to his mind. He could tell that she was worried about him and his reaction to the mass of bodies.

"I lived in the city forever, people don't bother me," he said, trying to reassure her. "I can shut 'em out, close down. You stick with me and I'll be fine. The crowd doesn't sweat me, I'm just worried I'll forget something."

He reached into his pocket and pulled out the knife with the cash held around it by a rubber band. "Hold this for me," he said handing it over to her. "I'm afraid I'll lose it. It's our crab cake money."

She took the bundle not realizing at first that the bills concealed her blade. "Hey, this is your knife now. I gave it to you."

"Nah, you had me hold it for safe keeping. I kept it safe, now you got it back."

"Cowboy, I got no need for it anymore. You can use it everyday. I gave it to you."

Buddy, remarkably remembering a conversation years ago, replied, "You might need it to dismember somebody at that new place you're goin' work."

Wan glanced from the traffic to her companion and said with a smile, "I ain't goin' dismember no body, no more. I went to college. I completed what normally takes four years in only three. I didn't take no lip but I tried not to give no lip either. My dismemberin' days are over."

Buddy thought for a minute.

"Put it in a little case and hang it over the fireplace. Tell you husband what the notches stand for. It'll help keep 'im in line."

"Hah," she exclaimed. "I ain't got no husband, and I ain't got no fireplace."

She paused a moment and added, "And I don't want either."

"What was it, three years ago, four years ago? You didn't have no education or no job and you didn't want 'em, either."

They fell silent for some minutes as the car motored north.

Approaching the Baltimore congestion Wan said, "Directions say 695 Beltway North. Help me watch for it."

But Buddy was still thinking about the knife in a case over the mantle.

"Why'd you come back? And why'd it take you so long?"

"Once I started in school I didn't want to come back before I'd finished. I wanted to show you I could accomplish something. No, that ain't right. I wanted to show them I could accomplish something. I had nothing to prove to you."

Buddy rubbed his chin as Wan located the exit for the Beltway, and slowed to make the turn.

"But why'd you come back in the first place?"

The young lady was concentrating on merging into the speeding traffic and didn't answer immediately. Once up to speed, she half turned her head and said with a combination of affection and consternation, "Cowboy, you got to figure that one out for yourself."

20
A Day at the Races

"**H**OW DO YOU KNOW which horse to bet on?" Wan asked looking at the first race in her program.

They had found their seats after a slow walk from a far parking lot. Buddy had never been to Pimlico, but he recognized the run down neighborhood, the crumbling facilities, the dirt and grime. It was similar to his old track, but bigger. It was Pimlico's special day, and management had tried to do all it could, but when the grandstand is as old as this, and the environs are as poor as they are, there is not a lot that can be done. For the Cowboy, though, it all felt comfortable. He ignored the steadily building crowd and was glad to have a seat next to Wan. It was a pleasure to have somebody ask his advice. It was nice to have a friend.

"Bet on the names, bet on the color," he replied. "I never was much into betting. I only really bet once and got lucky. I liked the horses and I keep telling everyone that the animals don't care whether you bet on 'em."

The horses had come to the post parade for the first race and as they slowly walked by the grandstand, a pretty dark gray caught Wan's eye.

"I'm going to bet on that one," she said. "Number ten, what its name?"

She looked in the program and number ten in the first race was Shenandoah Grey.

"Shenandoah Grey, what a fine name. Two dollars is the least I can bet, right?"

Buddy nodded, as that seemed right to him. "You choose first, second or third; win, place or show. You get in that line at the ticket windows behind us."

"Do you want a bet?" she asked him, standing to begin making her way to the tellers.

"I'll root for Shenandoah Grey with you," he said.

As the horses were turning for home in that first race, Buddy began to understand why people would throw money away gambling. He caught the excitement. These particular horses didn't mean anything to him, but as the gray horse moved into contention he and Wan rose to their feet, shouting home her two-dollar wager. Together they shared a common interest and goal. Even as they were cheering for this horse though, he recalled a night at a smaller race rack with far fewer people, where he had watched a chestnut horse so very dear to him run her last race.

The race ran to its conclusion and the old man became sad with his memories. Wan, though, was still excited and joyous. Shenandoah Grey finished second, about a length from the front. Wan gave Buddy a hug. He was a little perplexed, being drawn out of the past.

"She didn't win?" he questioned, wondering why she was still so exuberant.

"Ticket was to place," she smiled at him and turned and gave him a second hug. "How much do I win?"

"Wait a minute and they'll post it on the tote board there," he pointed to a portion of the infield sign. "When they change the wording from unofficial to official, then they'll also post your winnings."

Shortly thereafter the payouts were posted and Wan discovered that her two dollars and become four dollars and sixty cents.

"Maybe we should take this up as a living," she teased.

"Maybe you should find a rich man to marry," he teased back.

The man in the seat next to Buddy returned from placing a bet on the second race. The assigned seats were narrow but Buddy hadn't minded for he was a slim man. The gentleman next to him had been courteous, but when he returned to watch the second race, he had a full cup of beer in his hand.

Buddy could smell the alcohol. It made him ill. He needed to spit, but his mouth was full of cotton and no moisture would come out. He couldn't take his eyes away from the fellow's hand holding the beer. The moisture that had departed his mouth went to the pores of his face and he began to sweat. His body was cold and hot at the same time.

Wan noticed her companion's discomfort and leaned to whisper in his ear.

"How can I help you?"

At first Buddy thought it was the demons talking to him, but then he realized who it was.

"I need to pee," he said. "Walk with me to the restrooms."

Together they edged to the aisle and worked their way through the crowd to the toilet facilities. Buddy went in and leaned for a long time in front of a sink. He rinsed his face off. The water felt faintly refreshing. He held his cane in one hand and the edge of the sink in the other as waves of trembling past through him. Gradually he gained control and a thought went sailing past his brain. He gripped the sink harder and the thought came by again, staying long enough for him to turn it over and examine it. The thought was this: *Today was going to be either the best day of the rest of his life or the worst.*

He looked at himself in the mirror. A sad sight. He had tried so many times in the past to fight the devils inside him, fought alone, and fought with friends by his side. Every time he had lost and the demons had ruled. There was nothing about today that told him the outcome would be different. It had been years since his last drink, but the maggots were awake now. They were crawling under his skin. He felt them climbing from his shoes, up his legs headed for his groin and his gut. He could feel tiny cockroaches swimming in his blood, circulating to every pore of his body. His mouth was sticky with the cotton that clung there, impeding his voice and swelling up into his nasal passages, making it hard to breathe.

There was nothing about today that gave him any optimism that this time would be different. The reflection in the mirror showed him to be a decrepit man, old beyond his years. His best shirt could hide nothing of the feebleness that he felt, but then the thought came sailing by again. His mind caught it and turned it over again. The word he focused upon was *either*. Either, as if there were a choice. For the past thirty years, he had had no choice. He was destined to answer the calling of the buggars that had control of his body, but if it was truly destiny that ruled him, then he was absolved of fault. If it was fate and destiny that directed him, then he was not responsible and if he was not responsible then he was not guilty. But Buddy knew he was guilty. He himself had taken the course into drunkenness. It was his fault. It had been his choice. And if it was his choice, then, now certainly for this last time, he could participate in the choice, in the *either*.

He leaned his cane against the sink, leaned over and with both hands splashed his face with cold water. He splashed it again and again.

"God Damn," he said barely audibly as he doused himself.

"God Damn, God Damn, GOD DAMN, **GOD DAMN**." Getting louder with each repetition.

The men in the rest room had until now ignored the frail man standing at one of the sinks. Some now looked his way in apprehension, others tried to pretend he wasn't there. Many wondered if they should call a security guard. Buddy finished his damning and his splashing, grabbed his cane, turned and walked out of the toilet in the most confident manor he could muster.

Wan was waiting for him as he exited the bathroom doors.

"You alright? I was worried. Look you're all wet. What the hell you do in there, take a shower?"

She began to straighten his shirt and brush back his hair.

"Wan," he began smiling, "anybody ever told you that you are a beautiful lady, inside and out?"

She seized on his bright tone. "Nobody's lied like that," she smiled back at him.

"Not even your mother?"

That was the wrong thing to say, and her eyes told him so, but the hardness of her look quickly softened as she realized that he had meant no harm.

He took her arm in his free hand and motioned that they should go back to their seats.

"I had a daughter. I should have told her more often," he said.

He paused in his thought but kept walking, then offered, "I probably told her too often, but she wouldn't believe an old drunk."

"Doubt that you were old back then, just a drunk." Wan said this knowing that she was taking a chance. It would have been safer to simply inquire about the daughter. Wan remembered that she knew nothing about the history of this man. She was curious about his past life and family, but she had been trying to be safe for the last three years. Only with Cowboy did she feel comfortable enough to exchange truths.

"Once a drunk, always a drunk, but today, I got an either."

She looked at him, wondering about that strange remark.

They found their seats in the excited throng. Wan moved to the chair next to the beer drinking gentleman, although his beverage had long ago been finished.

"Let's pick a winner for this race," she urged, opening her program so they both could see.

Buddy stared at the program. "What race is this?"

"Sixth race."

"I was gone a long time, wasn't I," he said.

"You old bastard, I was getting ready to come in there after you, but don't worry about it now. Help me find a horse."

Buddy glanced again at the program and immediately a name caught his eye.

"Number five," he pointed to the number beside the name.

Wan looked at the name printed in large black type by the number. **My Melissa**. "Why that horse, Cowboy?"

"Reminds me of some one."

"Who?"

Buddy turned in his seat to face Wan. "Didn't your mother ever tell you, you were pretty?"

His tone was compassionate, but not with false sympathy, more of an understanding compassion. Wan did not let the bitterness show in her eyes this time. "Cowboy, you and me, we are two fucked up people, aren't we?" she said with an understanding smile. "Now, let me by and I'll go wager that four bucks we won earlier on Melissa."

She stood and began to squeeze by him to the aisle. As she passed in front of him, she asked quietly again, "Who's Melissa?"

The Cowboy shook his head in reply.

My Melissa won going away. The two dollars that had turned to four had now turned to twelve.

"God, Cowboy, maybe we should take up this gambling," Wan laughed.

"No chance," Buddy replied. "I got one too many vices already. I think that maybe we shouldn't do anymore until the Preakness. Did I give you the money for everybody's bet?"

"It should be still in your pocket. Want me to go ahead and put down the bets now?" she asked. "I can do that."

Buddy fished into his pocket and pulled out the small wad of cash and the betting instructions.

Wan looked over the paper. "Everyone's bet is here but yours. What do you want to do?"

Buddy shook his head. "No bet."

"Don't you want to support your old trainer's horse?"

"Horse don't know if you bet on him. People won't know either."

Wan stood up. "But how about putting down money so you have a reason to root the horse on?"

"Got plenty of reason to pull for the horse. Two dollars more, two hundred dollars more won't make a difference."

Wan shrugged her shoulders and began to squeeze past the crowd to get in line to lay all the different wagers. Just for luck she put two more dollars across the board for the Cowboy.

Finale
Crab Cakes

THE RESTAURANT WAS PACKED. It seemed like half the crowd from the racetrack had made reservations at this spot for dinner. Buddy and Wan were squeezed into a tiny table near the back. They felt as if they were part of the excitement of the crowd, but also distanced from it. The noise level was high which made conversation difficult, and as both had used much more than their normal quota of daily words, they didn't talk much.

They both ordered the traditional Chesapeake Bay crab cakes, branding themselves as out-of-towners or worse. Everyone who knows, knows that the Chesapeake Bay doesn't produce crabs in May. Just as the blanket of black-eyed susans spread on the winner were painted daisies, because Maryland can't produce that breed of flower until later in the summer. Reality however, is not romance, and everything to do with horseracing is romance. Thus, Wan and Buddy were enjoying their cakes. He had dumped a blanket of pepper on his cole slaw but had wisely left his crab unseasoned.

It had been a long day and both were tired. Cowboy was nearly exhausted, but he was happy. The day was almost over and he understood that it had been the best day of the last two thirds of his life. He knew it wouldn't happen again, but he was content. For Buddy, being content was a big deal.

As they were enjoying the dinner – Wan finding the hush puppies curiously tasty – there was a commotion at the entrance. The decibel level of the place increased and some of the diners got to their feet and began applauding. A contingent of folks, an entourage, led by the chef/proprietor himself, made their way toward a closed room, apparently for a private party. Buddy watched; Wan turned in her chair to see.

"Wasn't that your trainer? Wasn't that Mary Engler?" she shouted after the gang had been admitted into their room.

Buddy nodded.

"Go over to them. Say hello. Congratulate them."

Buddy shook his head.

"You know them, don't you?"

"I knew some. I missed Granny, but she must be dead by now."

"Buddy, listen to me," Wan leaned over the table shouting to make herself heard. "These are you friends. Go say 'Hello'."

"They don't need me. They don't care about me. They probably don't even remember me."

"You Bastard!"

"Look, Wan. It's enough to know that I know that they've made a success for themselves. I don't need to see them, to talk to them. They've lots of people to cheer for them now."

"Now, you listen to me, you old bastard. Did I come back for you? I could have just sent a graduation announcement so you'd know I 'made a success'. You get off your ass and go say 'Hello'."

Buddy didn't move.

Wan came up with one more argument.

"Cowboy," she said softer, "go tell them that Dromedary congratulates his former trainer."

The set of his jaw, the light in his eyes changed as she said that. She could tell that he was considering it.

After a long pause he said, "Write it down."

The only thing to write upon was a table napkin. "I can't write on this?"

"Sure you can," he replied. "Hand the note to the waiter. Tell him we're friends."

Wan motioned to the over tasked waiter. "Could you please deliver this note to Mary Engler. We're friends."

"Lady, today, everybody's friends with Mary. See that dude just now leaving the room? That fool's the Governor of Maryland."

"We're old friends. My partner here used to work for her."

The waiter eyed them both for a moment then took the napkin, reading it as he went. A few moments later the napkin was delivered to the private party. The Cowboy got up from his seat and said, "Let's go. It's been a long day and I need to get home."

Mary got the message, but only after it had been passed between several intermediaries. She read the note: *Cowboy and Dromedary both send you and your crew congratulations.* She jumped out of her chair and dashed into the main dinning room, but by then Wan and Buddy were traveling down the interstate back to Washington. She asked the maitre d' who had sent the napkin. After some discussion they found the appropriate waiter.

"Some old guy and a young, oriental lookin' lady. They said the old man used to work for you. Never saw a man use that much pepper on slaw before. Got up and left right after I'd passed on the note. Left a pretty good tip." With that the waiter brought out an uncashed mutual ticket from the track. "Two dollars 'cross the board on your horse."

BANSEE BREEZE

OUR MAN WAS FLABBERGASTED. He rested on the bench at the foot of the stone turret in the expansive gardens of Powerscourt. He sat there on the bench calculating, for that was what he did to ease his mind whenever it was troubled. He should have been an accountant or a statistician, for he so loved figuring. This is what he was calculating: on average he would encounter perhaps five women a day. Five women, unknown women, he would pass by, run into, see for the first time. Sure, some days there would be none, but other days, in an airport or a shopping mall there might be hundreds, so it seemed five a day would be a good average. Five women a day for three hundred and sixty-five days a year. Considering that he should start counting from his sixteenth birthday that would be 32 plus years. So, in sum, there would be close to 60,000 women.

Our man sat pondering this. He sat upon the bench outside the tower that overlooked the east and south gardens and grounds of the Powerscourt estate. These gardens are the legacy of a rather bizarre aristocrat, Daniel Robertson. He found this harmonious site, on a south-facing slope in the gentle rolling hills of county Wicklow, south of Dublin in the mid-nineteenth century. His dream of a botanical potpourri cost him millions, and the better part of his life. Robertson was not an Irishman, or English noble, but a self-made Scot, which excused his eccentricity, though not his extravagance. In the intervening century and a half since the founder's death the mansion had fallen in to some disrepair and is currently being rehabilitated, but the gardens, the joy and pride of the place, were always maintained even while the rest decayed.

What gardens they are. Where the turret stands, large pine and cedar from every continent have grown supple and full in the accepting Wicklow climate. The trunks of the trees are several meters round; the branches either swoop close to the ground, or are clear for some distance overhead, depending upon the nature of the tree.

The flabbergasted chap was looking at the trees but not seeing them. He was still figuring, his mind whirling through the percentages and possibilities. Of, say 60,000 women; maybe one in ten would acknowledge his presence, 6,000 women. Of those 6,000, ten per cent would take the time to exchange a nod, a smile, a spoken word of greeting, 600 women. Many of those were in the service trade, whose job it was to represent some business enterprise and thus were paid to be friendly. Ten per-cent of the 600, 60 women in over thirty years, about one every six months had been welcoming enough at first greeting to extend the conversation to something other than mere pleasantries. Of the 60, ten per-cent had touched him deeply enough to cause him a turmoil in his soul. Six women had touched him at first sight. He tried to remember the six. Surely his wife was one. On the fingers of his hand he counted four others, mostly from his youth. The sixth woman, the lady that made all the per-cent ages work, he had just met, had just exchanged glances, had just fallen in love with, if that is what love is, at the top of the tower.

His wife had recently passed away. She had not died, but to him, she had passed away. She had concluded that twenty years of shared memories were not enough, and the excitement of their courting had faded beyond those memories. The parting had been amicable on the outside, but he was wounded on the inside.

That was why he was here, in Ireland, on this tour of famous gardens with thirty-two mostly female, mostly unattached, tourists. He was lonely, and he was looking for the sixth woman. The ladies on this tour of the gardens of Ireland were all chatterers. The dearest ones were much too old for him, the ones nearer his own age where either too talkative or too stiff. He had given up trying to make a connection with any of them; he had given up trying to flirt. Instead he had become immersed in the beauty of the Irish countryside.

It was a beautiful country with rolling hills and lakes and green and more green and horrendous roads, which he was glad that he did not have to negotiate himself. He was enjoying his tour, even if he had given up trying to ease his sorrows by finding a replacement for his wife. It seems that in giving up his quest for the sixth woman, the lady that could touch him with a glance, at least temporarily, he had found a small measure of peace. In giving up the quest, he had apparently made himself available to that woman, for in the tower, a moment ago, he had looked into her pale gray eyes and been devoured.

The woman of whom we write was not a member of the tour group, but seemed to be traveling independently. He had encountered her romping through Powerscourt with her two children, a boy in his teens and a younger girl. He had been standing alone at the top of the tower, looking over and through the great pines that surrounded it, when he had heard the three laughing and bellowing as they climbed the stone stair-way. Not knowing the manor of company that was coming his way, he was a little perturbed at being disrupted, but the family's obvious good nature and high spirits made him remember some of his own happy times with his stepsons.

As the threesome emerged from the core of the turret to the outer overlook, the boy, the girl and finally the mother, it was then that he felt the touch. She and he exchanged glances, and seeing that her family had disrupted his quiet time, she made apologies. "Oh, sir, sorry for the commotion." He could tell from her accent that she, like him, was American.

"Not in the least," he said. "It is good to see so much joy in a family. The manor lord built this tower for his young nieces, as their playhouse, so it is appropriate that there be noise and laughter." He hoped that he did not sound overly pompous.

As he spoke, he maintained eye contact. He felt the woman reach through his open mouth with her hand and slide down his throat to grab all those vital organs known collectively as his guts, and turn them inside out. Strange as it sounds it was not an altogether unpleasant feeling. "Excuse me, though, I leave this fortress for you to enjoy with your children, for I have a tour group to catch up with."

He tipped his cap and walked down the circular stairs of the tower. Once clear of the structure, he felt the need to sit and reflect, and this is where we found our man, flabbergasted. Twenty-five meters above him the family was in animated conversation, pointing and shouting, paying him no mind at all. He wondered what he was supposed to do next. Should he pursue this woman that had been so forward as to massage his innards, and risk being jailed as a stalker or beaten to a pulp by her husband who was probably waiting beyond that last cedar tree, or should he let her disappear from his life as he had three of the earlier women, touched for an instant and then relegated to a dim spot in his memory?

He sat on the bench and tried to think this through. What conversation would he use to re-introduce himself? Perhaps, he thought, he could point out the magnificent specimen of *Picea mariana* growing at the foot of the tower. Or perhaps, he imagined, he could simply trail behind the family, and thus overhear some point of discussion that would be helpful later. He, being confused, of course would do neither; if left to himself, he would do nothing.

Presently the threesome descended the stairway and bumped out into the grounds. The two youngsters rushed out laughing, and began chasing and hollering down one of the paths leading away from the tower. The lady was the last to leave, a little less in a hurry, and as she left the building she noticed our man sitting on the bench. In the same instant, she noticed the tree that he had proposed to himself as a means of entering conversation.

"What a magnificent Picea mariana," she exclaimed.

He looked at her, looked at her right hand and arm and he wondered why she did not have blood or spit covering it, for she had thrust it down his throat and turned his insides out with it, but the arm was dry. "Are you a witch," he asked?

"Ha," she exclaimed. "Slim, I have never been called a witch before. My former husband used to call me 'the bitch' but no one has ever called me a witch."

As she said this, the man was shocked by the fact that she knew his name. Seeing his surprise, she nodded toward his obligatory tour nametag and so relieved some but not all of his amazement.

Unlike many gardens, Powerscourt did not identify their specimens with nameplates and the garden maps that are handed out for the eight Euro entrance fee do not label the varieties either. Slim figured it more likely that this woman had some supernatural power and could read his mind, than that she knew the Latin name of the tree, native to Norway, that rose high and full before them.

Suddenly he realized that he had better stop acting like a fool and an idiot or this charming woman would find better things to do with her time. Strange choice of words he thought, charming woman, as in magic charms or in mesmerizing. He got to his feet with some energy and said, "We should go find your children before they escape this garden completely."

Down the garden path they walked quietly together. Through the section planted with evergreens, and out into a more open portion known as the Japanese gardens, with small brooklets, half-moon bridges and sculpted dwarf shrubs and trees. The children spied Slim and their mother and ran over to them.

"Children," spoke the mother. "This is Mr. Slim Audredge. Mr. Audredge, these are my children, Drew and Lauren."

"Hello Drew, enjoying the unusualness of a cloudless day in Ireland?" Slim asked offering a handshake. He sensed that the boy, as a teenager, would appreciate being treated with respect. He remembered making the mistake of condescension with his own children, calling his oldest stepson Stephen too long while everyone else knew him as Steve.

"The day is fine," the boy replied.

"I never knew anyone named Slim before," Lauren said. "I thought that was only a movie name or something."

"Well, Lauren, now you know a Slim, a real, live one, and it seems to me that Lauren is a movie name too," Slim responded to her good natured comments with equal good nature.

"Have you found the caves and canyons yet?" he asked the children. "According to my information they are great places to hide out. They are over somewhere against that hillside, you run and your mother and I will see if we can find you."

The children ran off to explore for the caves. The lady said to Slim, "You have a way with children it seems, you go find them, I shall be along shortly."

Slim, as always, obeyed the female command dutifully, as he had been taught, and wondered again why his wife would have ever left him.

He found the children, each in a canyon cut out by a small watercourse hidden by shrubs and bushes of an oriental nature. Coming along the path, enjoying the gardens from the opposite, direction was the sweetest of the older ladies on his tour, Mrs. Carlisle, and the tour director, Ms. Cuthperson.

Mrs. Carlisle carried a slender cane, which she used as much for demonstrative purposes as extra support. "Mr. Audridge," she said with lingering gracefulness to her speech, stopping him with a wave of the cane. "Mr. Audridge, who are your young friends?"

"Ah, Mrs. Carlisle. Before you is Drew, and that young hellion, if I may use the term in an affectionate manor, is Lauren," he said, pointing to the young girl as she splashed in a nearby stream. "Their mother is a witch."

"Oh, I doubt that," replied Mrs. Carlisle, "not in Ireland. A gypsy perhaps, or a fairy or more likely a leprechaun, Mr. Audredge."

"Too tall for a leprechaun, Mrs. Carlisle," Slim suggested.

"Perhaps a banshee then," Mrs. Carlisle said thoughtfully.

"Indeed, yes!" exclaimed Slim. "A banshee."

"Oh, and Mrs. Carlisle, as you make your way through the evergreens along the path, notice a splendid specimen of Picea mariana growing by the tower," he added.

"Picea mariana, yes the sorcerer's apprentice tree," commented Mrs. Carlisle.

Slim looked dazed a second, never before having heard this common term used for that variety.

"Surely, Mr. Audredge, you remember the story of the sorcerer's apprentice, Mickey Mouse and Fantasia?" Mrs. Carlisle responded to his questioning look.

"I remember the story, but did not know the tree had anything to do with it," he answered.

"Not sure how the tree and the story are linked Mr. Audredge, perhaps the wood of the bucket used to carry the water, but anyway, that is how they refer to it in Norway."

"Thank you for that information, Mrs. Carlisle. I had not known of the connection."

Mrs. Carlisle starting walking down the path still accompanied by the tour director. She turned as she went and said over her shoulder, "Mr. Audredge, do be careful of banshees."

The tour director added, "Mr. Audredge, the bus is to leave in forty-five minutes, please don't be late."

"I have not been late all week, Ms. Cuthperson," he answered. "And Mrs. Carlisle, I appreciate your concern, and your warning, but I fear that destiny will lead me where it will."

Slim found the family re-grouped and preparing to follow the main path to the next garden area.

"May I rejoin you," he asked.

"We've been waiting for you," the banshee replied.

Slim caught her eye, and was again dazzled. He realized that back at the tower, when she had her hand down his throat jostling his innards, she did more than tickle; she had attached a fishing line, a monofilament of great strength, which she used to adjust his emotions. A pull of the line and he was in admiration, another pull and trepidation showed up. There was fear and friendliness; seriousness and humor, all exposed when she pulled. Mrs. Carlisle must surely have noticed the end of the line dangling from his mouth.

He concluded, quite rightly, that this destiny of his was beyond his control. Perhaps some action of his own could serve to screw things up, but if anything good were to come of this encounter, then it would be the banshee's doing. He was too awed by it all, by her, to even ask her name.

The one thing he did manage to do, standing by the great pond with its water lilies, its Neptune spouting water, and its view up the hill to the mansion; he managed to ask if the three of them would be interested in attending the theatre that night.

"It is the Gate Theatre, famous and old. The play is Uncle Vanya by Chekov. This is National Theatre week but some of the ladies on the tour are uninterested. I am sure that I can obtain three extra tickets if you would like to go?"

"Chekov done by the Irish?" the banshee asked. "Sounds an odd combination, do you think it suitable for the children?"

"I suspect that there is lust and greed and avarice and sloth, but probably no violence and certainly no nudity, so it should be fine for the children, and the experience of being in such an historic place, creating memories, is reason to go by itself," Slim answered.

"The tour is staying at the Jury's hotel in Dublin. Think it over and give me a telephone call prior to six if you would like to go." He pulled out a tour itinerary from his pocket, examined it and said, "Yes, the play starts at eight, Gate Theatre, Cavendish Row, Parnell Square." He wrote down the telephone number of the hotel and his room number on a scrap of paper and handed it to her.

The banshee was non-committal, but Slim could see that Drew was interested in the lust part and Lauren was interested in the memory part.

"I have to run now," he said as a good-bye. "The bus will be leaving soon, and I haven't been late all week. It was a great pleasure to meet you, and do call if you are interested in the play." As he said these farewells, he wondered what emotion the Banshee would pull from his guts next. The current emotion was curiosity.

On the bus ride from Powerscourt to Dublin, Slim cajoled three additional tickets to that night's performance. The tourists were all tired after a week of viewing the gardens, and it was not difficult to find three souls that preferred to be in bed on the night before the flight back across the ocean. What was difficult, though, was arranging four seats in a row.

Slim looked at the clock in the hotel room. It read six-fifteen. The emotion that he experienced now was embarrassment. After all the weaseling and explaining to get the ladies to adjust their seats, what was he to say when no one sat in those seats? The only member of the tour whose opinion really mattered to him was Mrs. Carlisle. She had replied with a tap of her cane upon the bus floor, when he asked about her intentions for the evening, "Highlight of the tour, Mr. Audridge."

"Yes, ma'am. That is what I think too, Mrs. Carlisle," he answered.

Slim looked at the clock again. He was about to give up on both his banshee and the play and go out for a pint of Guinness and fish and chips at the nearest pub, when the phone rang.

"Yes, Slim, we would be delighted to go to the play with you," she said. "You have the tickets? We are running late, though, so how about we meet you at the entrance to the theatre about quarter to eight? Is that a problem?"

His emotion after the call was anxiety. Were they really going to show? Would they be disappointed in the play? Would they be disappointed in him? Would they find the Gate Theatre? It was hard going on a first date, he thought, tougher still going with a banshee and her family!

He was at the theatre in plenty of time, forgoing the Guinness and the fish. The lobby was beginning to fill with excited chatter; for this new version of the old play had been well received at its opening the evening before. The house was sold out, and all attending were with high expectation - none, however, with higher expectation and apprehension than those of our man Slim.

At quarter to eight the family came walking up the sidewalk. He greeted them at the door. The banshee was dressed in simple elegance. She wore a black dress cut modestly to the base of the neck and half sleeves. A red sash was tied around her waist as a belt. On her shoulders she wore a white summer shawl to protect against the chill of the Irish evening. She had no jewelry for she needed none. She was stunning, and Slim was stunned.

When he noticed the children, he could tell that Drew was a little uneasy in his necktie, but Lauren carried her beauty as easily and naturally as her mother. Slim was dressed as dapperly as he could manage, in his old Harris Tweed coat with a hurriedly pressed shirt. Altogether they made an attractive crew. When they entered the theatre to find their seats, heads turned.

The four seats were at the end of a row. The woman went in first, and sat next to Mrs. Carlisle, who greeted her with courtesy. Lauren went next and sat beside her mother, then Drew and finally Slim. As he sat down to wait for the curtain he thought to himself, *there is no way that I will have an intimate word with that woman all night.* And so it was. The play was splendid; the cast well versed; the intermission noisy. Slim spent the evening in conversation with Drew on all manners of things, from baseball to fishing to women. Neither was an expert on any of those subjects, but each had his own opinions.

At the end of the play, after the glow of the performance had subsided, Slim led the way out to the street and found a waiting cab. As he held the door for his guests, the woman got in and slid all the way to the other side, followed by Lauren and then Drew. Slim closed the door and let himself into the front passenger's seat.

"Where too, sir?" Patrick, the cabby asked.

"Number 31 Leeson Close," the woman said.

Both the driver and Slim were impressed. Number 31 is a particularly fine and expensive bed and breakfast just off St. Stephen's Green.

"Yes, Ma'am. Won't take us long at all."

As the car drove through downtown Dublin Slim noted that this was perhaps the oddest day of his life. Not the best day, but certainly the most unusual.

At the entrance to Number 31 the car stopped so its passengers could disembark. Slim again held the door as first Drew, then Lauren and finally the woman exited. The children, still full of energy, dashed for the lodging door, but as the banshee stepped out of the car, Slim touched her on the forearm as a sign for her to hesitate. At that instant, she must have pulled on the string again, that fishing line, for his emotion changed immediately from resolve to lust.

"Lois," he said (he had been talking to Drew about more than just baseball). "Do banshees have sex?"

She was taken aback for just a second by his remark. This was the first time all day that he noticed that she was not in complete control. "Mr. Audredge," she spoke in a perfect impersonation of

Mrs. Carlisle, so perfect that Slim dropped his jaw in amazement. "We banshees have sex on a higher level, out of this world." There was no indication of invitation in her tone.

"Heavenly sex? Sex to the seventh heaven?"

"Seventh?" she smiled resuming her normal tone. "I believe I am the sixth, Slim, for the seventh you need to keep looking." With that, she walked up to the entrance and into the building.

Just before the door shut, Slim shouted plaintively after her, "You mean I have to go through another ten thousand women?"

The door was not shut completely, but hesitated on its hinges. Lois opened it halfway again so she could see the befuddled man standing by the taxi. She smiled at him and blew him a kiss and was gone.